THE WORLD
BEYOND
THE WOODS

Written by Philip O'Reilly,
who identifies as the author of this work,
with additional poetical contributions
from Snap Roundtop

Illustrations produced in Midjourney,
depicting scenes on page 363 (front)
& page 415 (back)

Published in the United Kingdom under the auspices
of the Wellington Ladies Welfare League Ltd

Enquiries welcome at info@wlwl.uk

THE WORLD
BEYOND
THE WOODS

CHAPTER 1

Considering the great variety of events that would affect
the subject of this tale, and the heights to which he would
rise, the birth of one Gurgle Roundtop was a very humble
affair. At that particular time the society of goblins was
comparable in scale to the neighbouring communities of
humans and hobgoblins, though it was the humans who
held sway and did the most to determine the fate of all
three groups. The landscape which they all inhabited was
generally a mixture of forests and farmland, the distant
boundaries of which were greatly feared and as such little
visited. The men were most likely to be found on the
farmland and the goblins of whatever flavour were
invariably to be found in the forests. From this all the
individuals comfortably held their level and co-existed
peacefully.

Goblins and hobgoblins tended to be tree dwellers. Great
elevated communities could stretch through the gloom of
an entire forest. They had a loose and disorganised way of
living and as such had little impact beyond their own
borders. They usually lived separately however, as long
standing historical prejudice meant they were hostile
towards each other and suspicious of the other's motives.
Natural cousins they may have been but friendly they
were not. From whatever walk of life you came though
there was enough of a culture of freedom to allow anyone
to go where their instincts pushed them. Some individuals
found the company of foreigners enjoyable and small

mixed communities were not uncommon.

The men preferred to live in farm cottages or castles depending on their means. Those with status might carry a silver bowl from which to eat and those without status might carry a begging bowl from which to eat very little. A clear hierarchy existed amongst the men as that is how men understand their place in the world. Kings and Queens and pretenders to such titles were well established, as were the inevitable intrigues that came with them. Below them came the soldiers, whom, with sufficient pay, were persuaded to enable the royals to live in their well-appointed condition. Below them came the professional tradesmen, craftsmen, farmers, and the like. They were the people that actually created things and got things done. At the bottom of the hierarchy came those without the support or respect of anyone, those that could rely only on themselves to survive. It was to this group that the charms of an association within the forest most appealed.

The men tended to regard the goblins and hobgoblins in the forests as inferior and as a homogeneous group best suited to whatever form of exploitation was felt necessary. The goblins and hobgoblins had each developed a different approach to this treatment and it became a useful way for the men to distinguish between them. The goblins, being good natured and honourable, would most often accept bad treatment without too much complaint. Only after prolonged provocation would they refuse to cooperate. The hobgoblins, being generally bad natured and much less honourable, tried to make practical arrangements with men to best suit themselves, often at the expense of their goblin neighbours.

Those individuals that stayed within their own kind found little difficulty or prejudice in life. Latent fear and suspicion of outsiders was natural to some. For others, the lure of adventure and excitement was as irresistible as the air and a life of great risk and reward lay open to them. A wandering nature led many members of the three groups to live and work closer together than some would think appropriate. Conflicting opinions could be found everywhere about the nature of living things and how best they should interrelate. What written histories existed could only look back so far, and there were several very obvious and undeniable things that spoke of the combined origin of goblins, hobgoblins and men.

For the majority of the time the three communities lived largely independent lives, with separate identities and activities. From time to time however, there would be the need for the cooperation of one or both of the other groups to help with an internal dispute that had spilled out into open warfare. A private dispute between a powerful few so often became a dispute between the many. For some though, whether man, goblin or hobgoblin, warfare was a profession and its frenzied application was like mother's milk to them.

It is a rule of nature that there will be times of great desperation during which people will be forced to disrupt whatever harmony may exist. Roughly halfway between two such tumultuous periods the youngest and last child of the prodigious Roundtop family was born. In keeping with the traditions of the time the mother and father were the only ones present at the birth. It was not a thing considered secret or unpleasant, merely that the hollowed out tree trunk in which it occurred could not hold more than a few bulky goblins at one time. To give you an idea of scale, the trunk of a mighty oak tree would provide a fine and spacious home for a family of goblins. Thump Roundtop, the patriarch of the Roundtops, had created a large family but had not managed at the same time to create the wealth to provide a large family home. This was not a concern which greatly troubled himself, his wife or his children however. Thump was a well-liked and widely respected member of the goblin community in this part of the forest and wealth in general was not something that troubled a goblin in the same way as it might trouble a hobgoblin and would definitely trouble a man.

Thump provided for his family as a practitioner of the fine art of mulching and was a distinguished member of that hard working guild of goblins known as the 'Mulchers'. This job involved collecting rotting leaf matter, typically to be found in the soggier sections of the forest. After the necessary drying and packaging stage the mulch would then be sold as a powerful fertiliser to the human men for their farmland, and occasionally, after much refinement, as a dubious anti-aging remedy for the human ladies. What distinguished a good mulcher from another was their knowledge of and skill in finding the richest, darkest and most jelly-like mulch. Thump and his wife, Screech

Roundtop, were considered experts.

Hidden inside the gnarled and blackened walls of their tree trunk Thump and Screech were first introduced to their eighth child Gurgle Sycamore Roundtop. Outside, their first seven children, supervised by elderly relations, watched and waited. To the onlookers the only indications of activity inside the tree were the intermittent groans and the soft thuds of Screech pounding her fists against the insides of the tree and against the insides of Thump. For Gurgle's eldest siblings the process was becoming a familiar exercise and they wore expressions of profound boredom on their faces. In contrast the excitement of the younger ones could hardly be contained. Standing protectively around them was the extended Roundtop family and a scattering of friends and neighbours. They all stood in a misty glade close to the heart of Milton Greens, which is the name of the forest where they live. During moments of quiet the sound of restless horses straining at their harnesses could be heard. A light rain also fell, which encouraged them to check regularly on their mother's progress. Following the loudest and longest groan and a further sound which the assembled throng fortunately could not quite identify, an exhausted but very proud father staggered, after some difficulty with the door, into the early morning air. He triumphantly held up his son for all to see. Gurgle quickly caught everyone's eye with only the odd glance behind father and son to the figure of Screech within the gloom of the tree. Noisy gusts of her steamy white breath emerged from the shadows.

*

You might have heard of the Native American tradition of naming a child after the first thing that the father sees after emerging from the tee pee as soon as a baby is born, for example 'Crazy Horse', 'Sitting Bull', 'Squawking Bird', 'Rubbish Dump', 'Awkward Flap', 'Mother In Law', to name but a few. Well, goblins are similar in that a child is named after the first *sound* that a father hears after emerging from the tree trunk. In Gurgle's case he named himself, as that was the sound he made just as Thump opened the door. It follows then that the first name of each goblin is also a sound.

Goblins generally have very sensitive hearing. In fact they are a race renowned and recruited for this attribute alone. Goblins have deep and rounded green ears which taper to a point at the tip. These will sit on either side of an often lumpy and unnecessarily large green head. This head will then be perched on a short stocky body covered in a mist of fine pale hair. Surrounding this body will be clothing suitable to that of a goblin, namely, tight fitting, earth-tone rich, water proof, hard wearing, peasant style fare. Their fashions could never be described as chic or stylish as such concepts are regrettably alien to them. For instance, if you were to stress the need to accessorize a plain garment with brightly coloured stones or exotic feathers and furs (vulture and badger being particularly highly prized amongst the hobgoblins) you would most likely be wasting your time. Only if you thought yourself the King of the Goblins (there was in fact no such position at that time) and had delusions of grandeur might you try to get away with wearing bright colours and snazzy accompaniments. Few goblins have tried such a feat and ever fewer have escaped with even a shred of their dignity left intact.

Might I suggest, that as part of the great designer's plan for life it was decided that no creature should have too much of one thing without there being a natural limit on another of their qualities to make up for it. Some would say there is no such honourable balance to nature. For the goblins however their great capacity for hearing was not matched by their capacity for seeing. Perhaps it was the very shape of their heads that benefited them so when it came to hearing that simultaneously caused them such problems with their long vision. Needless to say, this characteristic does not harm forest dwellers very much as so often the mist falls there and one cannot see far beyond one's nose anyway.

Goblins are also interested in the culture of words and their public expression. They are gregarious, social and full of enthusiasm for each other. One well established pastime which expresses all these qualities is the poetry competition, a common climax to many a carnival.

Very shortly after Gurgle came into the world there was arranged just such a public event. Though goblins require very little incentive to celebrate, and have celebrated births in the past in this way, this was nothing to do with Gurgle. This event had been in preparation for some months and was a regular affair. The main thoroughfares and public spaces would soon be devoted to all manner of stalls and exhibits and you could be sure of finding the most curious types of things for sale that you would never find under normal circumstances. If you were a person in any way inclined to selling specialist produce or pickpocketing or political canvassing or even just making a fool of yourself in public this was the time to indulge in such tendencies.

Numerous activities would take place. The poetry competition would be the highlight of course and would signify the end of the festivities. Other lesser but no less well attended events would include snail racing, a beauty competition, mud wrestling, conjuring and magic shows and perhaps even a marriage or two.

The two days over which it occurred were very much favoured by the weather and this ensured that all those minded to make an extra special effort in what they were planning had no excuse to change their minds. One such individual was Gurgle's great uncle. He was the person in the Roundtop family most able to write and express poetry and had much recognition for this fact amongst local people. Such events gave an important opportunity to perform in front of an audience beyond one's own circle and he never missed the opportunity when it was offered. His particular style was informal and crowd pleasing. He had performed well in the past; winning on two occasions, but that was when the number and quality of the entrants was lower. These days the event was hard fought and he had not been in a winning way for many years.

Whilst Gurgle was wrapped in warm swaddling clothes, and carried by his mother, the Roundtops assembled together to make a group. This group then mixed with other groups nearby as they left their homes and formed a crowd and then they all made their way down past the marker trees showing the route to the main gathering. Marker trees were hardly necessary as so many people filled the pathways going toward the heart of the celebrations that the route was illuminated by them. A warm rumbling sound shook their bodies as they neared the centre. Only the more delicate frequencies of laughter and shrieking could be heard clearly. Alongside the road, displays of goods and handicrafts started to appear hoping as the proprietors were to capitalise on the first visitors at the highest of their hopes for the day and in their wealthiest condition. They had miscalculated sadly as they were mostly ignored. There was little time or space in which to stop and look at the offerings without being jostled by others as everyone streamed past.

Gurgle's great uncle hurried amongst them and was the only one who seemed not to share in the general excitement. He was deeply nervous and thumbed repeatedly at the poetry notes in his pockets. The previous week he had spent many a furious hour trying to outdo and amaze himself with his poetry in hopes of walking away with the contest. He felt he had done well but had many lingering doubts about how his efforts would be received. His confidence had suffered greatly since the previous year. He had come close to winning but had lost his composure during the final stages when his rival at the time (and some would say his nemesis) made a spectacular effort which clearly put the others in a lower category altogether and led Gurgle's great uncle to suffer thence forth from the inferiority complex which he now felt growing and strengthening inside him as the moments passed. There were many festivities that would occur before he would be called upon to perform and he could be sure that the nerves gripping him would sap any enjoyment there might be in them.

Once they had arrived near to the thick of it Thump did his best to separate and gather his clan from the crowds. He asked them what they all might like to see. With a simultaneous yell the young ones charged at their father and a different thing was demanded by each and so to each he gave a few chestnut quarters and bid them on their way but not out of sight. By the way, the common currency in the forest is the chestnut, such as you find on the horse chestnut tree. Naturally, you might think that something which grows on trees couldn't possibly work as a currency. You might think that the tallest goblins or the best at throwing rocks would be the richest. Well, you would be right, at least in the early years before the chestnut stabilised. Initially, the humble leaf was used but then abandoned after the reserves of the Milton Greens Central Bank were lost to a very windy spring.

Toadstools were tried but were too easily counterfeited by mushrooms. Even snails were tried, but that was stopped soon after as a lot of the money tended to escape. In the end the solid and reliable chestnut became the recognised choice, being as they were hard, easy to handle, regular in size and shape, and didn't hide upside down under the furniture when you needed to pay the rent.

*

In one of the large open sections of the forest, Thump and his children were part of a crowd gathered around one of many flat and perfectly circular tree stumps. Upon them were painted a series of white lines, the edges of which were slightly raised. Moving upon this particular stump and looking out, each through two great slimy stalks slid several numbered racing snails. Following the lanes over the stump they competed with each other for the benefit of the gamblers and gawkers that yelled all about them. It is hard to say how much awareness they might have had of their situation. Considering the rather random paths they sometimes took and frequent periods of inactivity I would say that they had very little sense of their purpose and status in the universe. Though perhaps they had more wisdom than one might imagine, as whether by accident or design they caused great misfortune to many of those that sought to exploit them for financial gain. This is naïve perhaps, as a snail that could reliably move in a straight line was worth more than its weight in gold and would be treated like a little snail god and would be given all the lettuce it could possibly want to excrete onto. Who knows what may pass through their little minds?

Thump had something of a weakness for the snail races and this was his only real interest of all the attractions on offer. In this particular race he'd placed an impressive sum on number six, racing under the epithet 'Greased Lightning'. His number had been rather crudely daubed on his shell, like all the others. The contest had been underway for some ten minutes and the leader 'Prime Slime' had only just passed the halfway mark. Naturally there was plenty of the race still to go, and one thing you must always remember in snail racing is that there is no such thing as a dead cert! It was developing into a two shell race though as the four others bringing up the rear (or more accurately, sliming around in circles or sitting perfectly still) and racing under the names 'Unlucky Jim', 'Don't Tread on Me', 'The Destroyer of Worlds' and 'A Slug of the Hard Stuff' were not in the contest at all.

With admirable enthusiasm Thump's children stood around him and did their best to mimic his maniacal screams of encouragement towards Greased Lightning. The only ones that were quiet were the money men who took the bets and would most likely make money whatever the outcome of the race. As their hearts pumped and pounded furiously inside their chests the crowd willed that whatever force motivated a snail to move from point A to point B should take effect in their particular slimy hero.

With a great moan from their respective supporters upon the realization of what was about to happen Unlucky Jim lived up to his name as A Slug of the Hard Stuff moved up behind him and mounted him with slimy inevitability. Within a few moments there were no longer six competitors. This was one of the very rare occasions when adding three to one makes thirty one. This event thinned the crowd somewhat. Any seasoned fancier will tell you that when snails mount each other they can be relied upon to take no further part in the race, no matter how enthusiastic the load bearer might be. They were picked up together from the course. Shortly after this unfortunate coupling Don't Tread on Me was withdrawn from the race by his trainer as was required by the rules after a period of five minutes with no movement. Wisely, he quickly bundled him to safety to prevent those that had foolishly backed him from inflicting some poetic justice upon him with their feet.

Thump was understandably pleased by these developments. Now there were just three left in the race. The Destroyer of Worlds was a distant third, and tiring, and unless he also existed in a parallel dimension and was possessed of great power there and was able to cast fire and brimstone on the ignorant and cowering masses at his whim bellowing with cruel laughter all the while, then his choice of name had been a sad overestimation. Those left with an interest in the race closed in around the trunk and their intensity increased with their proximity to the action. Race stewards intervened and pushed some people back to make sure that there was no direct interference with the competitors. The final stretch beckoned for Prime Slime and with his customary clinical instincts he finished the race in clear first place. With a little gesture aimed at his supporters, as they saw it, he slowly blinked. He was the favourite after all. Greased Lightning was the only other one to finish the race some two minutes later. The Destroyer of Worlds was carefully retrieved for battle on another day.

With a gradual diminution in excitement the crowds quietened and withdrew. Those that'd had the sense to bet on the favourite queued up to make their meagre profits on the short odds for the winner. Thump's children were despondent that their efforts had failed to produce the desired result. They hung unhappily around their father. Some dried their eyes. Thump however joined the queue with a warm satisfied smile upon his face. He had wagered that Greased Lightning would come in second and that he had. Soon, Thump collected his purse full to the brim with winnings and the mood of his children warmed instantly at the sight of the bulging bag. This amount would not change their lives but it would make them much happier for the day. Thump quietly decided that with his winnings he would arrange lodgings for them all tonight in the heart of the events and they would therefore be fresh and well located for the poetry competition the following day. Shortly after the race Screech and her uncle arrived to find their family in a wild eyed and wealthy state. They combined and began to wander gently through the rest of the attractions and through the rest of the day. In his mother's arms Gurgle gurgled happily through all things. After some relaxing pursuits, and some sadly inferior meat pies, the whole family gathered together and decided to find rooms for the night. They all had high hopes for Gurgle's great uncle and Thump could fondly remember the times when he had been the first to hear his uncle's poems. He had always been a good guide to the quality of a poem. If he had laughed and admired then his uncle could be confident that others would also. This time Thump was saddened not to have been consulted. Perhaps he was too old now. Perhaps his uncle felt his attitudes would be coloured by his maturity. One look at his uncle suggested that he was too preoccupied by his own anxiety to take the time to share his work.

With the chestnuts rubbing a serious hole in his pockets Thump decided that they would go out on a limb (quite literally!) and stay at 'The Green Tree'. Inside an ancient and colossal tree was where they would spend the night. Up the dozens of circular steps around the trunk they went, passing the influential, wealthy and well-to-do of the forest all the while. The family followed Thump walking neatly in a line behind him as he stepped proudly into the lobby of the hotel.

"Good evening Sir. Can I help you?" said the employee politely.

"Yes, indeed you can my dear fellow," replied Thump, in a manner that sounded much more sophisticated than usual.

One or two of his children sniggered a little at the silliness of their father and Screech tried hard to control a creeping smile breaking out upon her face.

"I would like a suite for my family for tonight if you please."

"Certainly Sir, I believe the Acorn suite is available. If I could take payment from you I will escort you to your rooms."

"Ah, yes of course," said Thump quietly. He leaned over the desk trying in vain to stay out of earshot of everyone about and whispered, "Could you just write the price down here for me?"

The employee understood and laid out brochures about their mud spa and general activities in the area in an attempt to deceive any onlookers as he jotted down on a notepad (for Thump's eyes only) the substantial cost of a night in the Acorn suite. After a moment of reflection and a moment of quick calculation Thump decided that he had enough to spare and nodded to the Goblin opposite, who smiled sympathetically.

"There you are," said Thump, as he handed over the greater proportion of the chestnuts he had with him.

"Now, if you would like to follow me?" said the employee, after a few moments of some inevitable paperwork which Thump was asked to fill out and sign.

With that they all lined up once again and made their way up to the Acorn suite behind this smartly dressed young chap. Once past the thick door to the suite, which seemed older than all of them combined, they fanned out to examine all the comfort and finery on show, a proud and satisfying moment for Thump. With yet another chestnut or two handed to the employee to get him to leave they enjoyed some valuable moments alone. The young ones charged about going from room to room and bouncing on each and every bed. Screech and Gurgle settled down in one of the many soft chairs to suckle some of mother's milk. Thump and his uncle stepped onto the balcony and looked out at the warm and noisy evening below.

"How do you like it?" said Thump to his uncle.

"It's marvellous, thank you, and your family seem to love it."

"They're your family too you know," said Thump with a smile.

"Yes, I know. I'm sorry. I'm in my own world at the moment."

"I know, but don't worry I think you're the best poet there is. I look forward to a fine victory tomorrow. I hope that some of my children have inherited even a little of your talent," said Thump warmly, as he placed his hand on his uncle's back.

"Kind words, kind words. I'll do my best and while I'm alive I'll keep doing so."

"I haven't seen you so worried and distant from us like you've been today. Is it your poetry that worries you?"

"No, not really, I'm still writing some good poems. It's him, Woodstack. You saw him last year."

"Yes, I remember, he was pretty good."

"Pretty good? He walked all over us!"

"I wouldn't say that, I think you're underestimating yourself. Is he back this year?"

"Yes he is...and I'm not sure if I can beat him."

Thump looked up at the stars as they began to twinkle through the dark blue of early evening. His uncle, standing beside him, seemed to be looking only at the ground. Someway below them the torch lights around the hotel flickered and fizzed, revealing figures shifting through the shade.

"I know you'll do the Roundtops proud," said Thump after a while.

His uncle turned and smiled, opening his mouth slightly for a moment but saying nothing.

*

As is often the case a new day brings with it a new perspective. Gurgle's great uncle was the first to rise, partly from anxiety over the day ahead and partly from a full bladder. He stepped to the window and looked down below. Already people had begun to prepare for the events planned for later in the day. Many cooks were at work in the open air on the festival's most special tradition. The meat pie. Great piles of pastry and ingredients had been assembled. Carrots by the cartload, worms by the bucket load. He could not think of food however, despite his stomach willing him to think otherwise. The day was bright and not too breezy. Good for open air speaking he had to admit.

As the morning drifted on the others slowly emerged one by one from their happy slumbers. They savaged the breakfasts laid on for them. They had all enjoyed their time there very much and were looking forward to even more excitement from the competition that afternoon. From the balcony they could just about see the stage some three hundred metres away and many were working to make it ready. Behind the stage were a row of great gloomy trees packed closely together and which would provide an imposing backdrop for the performances. In front of the stage many tables and chairs were stuck in the dry mud. Soon great screaming crowds would occupy them. That stage had seen many triumphs and failures, much that was ridiculous and funny, and much that would make you cringe with embarrassment.

Being associated with a competitor meant that the Roundtops would have a table reserved for them within easy shouting distance of the stage. There were about a dozen entrants to the competition, most of whom would not last till the end. A few eccentric individuals could be relied upon to take part each year, usually with disastrous results. Good natured heckling would force them to withdraw. Only a few of them would be seriously going for the win, amongst them Mr Roundtop and Mr Woodstack. The competition would nevertheless be a well organised affair. A master of ceremonies would announce and then often denounce each participant. An odd number of judges would sit to the side of the stage. The odd number to make sure that a clear decision would always be given. The judges would include local dignitaries, seasoned ex-competitors and the winner of the previous day's beauty contest. This year that honour fell to Miss Sigh Blackberry, a deserved winner in the eyes of the other, exclusively male, judges.

The sun in the sky followed its perfect arc as the great pie bubbled beneath it. Only once it was declared cooked by the chef in charge could the poetry competition be allowed to start. In any case no goblin would take his seat without a slice of pie in front of him.

The ingredients of a 'Goblin-Style' meat pie are as follows, but may include other ingredients for special occasions:

- Nice thick pastry
- Meat (usually rabbit and worm; occasionally frog)
- Carrots (left whole)
- Onions (finely chopped)
- Rotting leaves (sycamore are considered the best)
- Boiled snails (most goblins will say the bigger the better)
- Gravy (made in advance from the choicest pond waters)
- Finely grated tree bark as a garnish.

Thump and his family left the hotel and strolled towards the festivities. The warm nutty scent of the pie drew them to where most now stood. All eyes were fixed on the head chef as he hung suspended over the centre of the huge pie, which was reported to measure some five metres in length, two metres in width and a few inches in depth. The pie was held in a flat metal dish several feet off the ground.

Beneath it glowing red coals gave plenty of heat. In the centre of the pie the gravy had burst through the pastry and coalesced into a little sea. Dozens of long boiled worms bobbed and span about in the swirling brown vortex. Some, marooned on top of the pastry, dried in the midday sun. Here, the daredevil chef, held up by several sturdy ropes, dipped in his ladle and took a sip to taste. After some unexpected tipping towards the sea of gravy he shouted at his handlers to take more care. The laughs of the spectators morphed into cheers as a few moments later he declared that the pie was ready. He was lifted out of danger and given a knife with which, by convention. it was his duty to cut the first slice. First in the queue with a bowl and spoon was once again Miss Sigh Blackberry, who declared prettily that all was well and that the pie tasted as nicely as she looked. Many quickly suggested under their breaths that that was indeed the case, although not in the way she meant.

The army of chefs did their best to distribute the pie quickly and evenly to all those waiting. Since each slice was free they had quite a job on their hands. Steadily people took their pie and then their seats in front of the stage. For many the combination of pie and poetry could not be beaten and the atmosphere was therefore happy and energetic.

Whilst Thump and family waited patiently for their pie Gurgle's great uncle had quietly withdrawn to join the other competitors who were backstage preparing for the contest. There he took his seat alongside them. Once again he felt his nervousness surge inside him. Glancing to one side he caught sight of his nemesis that had been waiting patiently for him to look in his direction.

"Hello again," said Crunch Woodstack calmly.

Onstage the master of ceremonies stepped out to a smattering of applause and the odd frenzied shout of disapproval. The seats were nearly all full and the Roundtops were just making their way to their table with their bowls of pie cradled in their arms. They quickly sat down and fixed their attention on the stage just in time.

"Goblins!" the master of ceremonies yelled. "What do you want?" yelling even louder, waving his hands at them.

After a moment or two of noisy confusion and the not so witty shouts of "more pie" and "for you to twizzle off" he answered his own question with a cry of "Poetry!"

"Welcome to the 45th Annual Milton Greens Poetry Competition! How's the pie you guys?"

After another moment or two of noisy confusion, this time with no coherent answer from the crowd, he chose to answer his own question again.

"Great! Let me introduce you to the judges. With us today we're privileged to have the Honourable Groan Twigtidy, deputy leader of Milton Green's Council. Say 'Hi' to the people your honour!"

He looked out at the crowd, waved and mouthed a rather weak little hello. The crowd responded in a similarly quiet way.

"Also with us, we have two elder statesmen of the poetic world, the siblings of the spoken word, Bang and Crack

Oakleaf. Take a bow Gents!"

This they did, though with some difficulty in standing on their creaking legs.

"Anybody catch the beauty contest yesterday? I sure did! And I caught the winner right here. Miss Sigh Blackberry. Let's take a look at you!"

With clearly no affection for him at all, she stood, took his hand and moved to the centre of the stage giving a smile to all who could see her. Cheers and laughter rang out at the sight.

"Right, lastly but not leastly, the fifth judge for today, a special guest, the travelling sorcerer, the fire for hire, Zebulan McCranahan! Give us some magic Zeb!"

With thunderous eyes Zebulan stared at him and then raised his hands. Blue fire then began to swirl between them. In a flash, a bolt of blue flame shot out and flew into the sky. Groan Twigtidy disappeared under the table. This was simple chemistry on his part and not magic, but he didn't trouble to reveal this to his hosts.

"Nice!" said the master of ceremonies. "Anyone would think you were aiming at me!"

A great cheer erupted and Zebulan smiled a sly little smile. Unconcerned, he continued.

"OK, let's get on with the contest shall we. As you all know everyone gets to give a poem in the first round and those that don't make the grade get eliminated! Then we have those left over battling it out in round two, until just the final pair remain. Can we have the contestants please?"

From behind the stage the poets stepped one after another

into the afternoon sunshine and took their seats opposite the judges on the far side of the stage. Neither Crunch nor Gurgle's great uncle were in the first few to perform and as such avoided most of the yelling and flying pie.

Few of the early poems were worthy of note and most of the poets escaped with light applause. One notable exception was poor Thud Longway. He foolishly tried to rhyme 'Onion' with 'Nibble on', much to the disgust of the crowd, and with several well placed onions dripping with gravy he was quickly persuaded to take no further part in the competition. Crunch Woodstack was to follow young Longway and much expectation surrounded him. He was introduced by the master of ceremonies and there followed the first period of real silence from the audience. He moved graciously to the centre of the stage and looked skyward.

"People!" he began, "Here is my first offering and I have entitled it...'The World Keeps Turning.'"

A moment of nothing then came, in which he stood perfectly still. A moment later and with a sudden shift in the direction of his head he began to speak.

"If a leaf should fall upon the forest floor,
and settle there to move no more,
does the world stop turning?

It does not.

If a tree should fall upon the forest floor,

and settle there to move no more,
does the world stop turning?

It does not.

If two castles crumble and trap those within,
wailing with sadness and a scraping din,
does the world stop turning?

It does not.

If a saviour is born, light of our lives,
and around him the weak start to thrive,
does the world stop turning?

It does not."

At this stage people had gathered the pattern of it, and
murmurs of "It does not" could be heard at the
appropriate moments, from such as were his supporters.

"When subtle plans are laid,
and fantastic inventions made,
does the world stop turning?

It does not.

When the righteous triumph over the wicked,
and the wicked triumph over the righteous,

does the world stop turning?

It does not.

So when does the world stop turning?
When it is good and ready,
for now it is not."

This was an assured performance and because of the involvement of the crowd sure to score bonus points with the judges. Crunch knew he was easily through to the next round. He calmly drifted back to his seat, satisfied at a job well done. The master of ceremonies stepped forward to address the crowd.

"I think this competition is about to get even more exciting! Reading the next poem, let me introduce to you, Snap Roundtop!"

He beckoned the next competitor to stand up. Tentatively, Snap made his way to the front of the stage. He looked nervous but had vocal support from the other Roundtops, not ten metres away.

"Hello everyone," he said, "This poem is called 'Mother Nature'. I hope you like it.

When the turtle with a butterfly's wing,
summons her energy with which to sing,
to the audience of animals laid out below,
nothing to remember and nothing to know,
just open your eyes and go with the flow.

Nature is wild, and wildness it adores,
complication feeds it, uniformity it abhors.
From the otter with a thousand faces,
to the snake with many paws,
find in mother nature,
the truth, light, and magic,
flowing from her laws.

As she swims inside all our zones,
giving us the life force we crave,
she boils the bare matter of our bones,
until we fall into the grave."

Quietly he stopped and went to sit back down. Again
there was light applause and nothing more, though the
Roundtops cheered him on. Snap was worried that it was
a little too short. He could not know this of course but
Zebulan liked the poem very much and he would ensure
Snap a place in the next round. With his pencil Zebulan
scrawled a high mark against Snap's name on his score
sheet, though, as he led Miss Sigh Blackberry to believe,
he could have used beams of fire from his eyes to achieve
the same result.

Gradually the other competitors were gone through and
their offerings heard. The standard was pretty good
judging by the general good humour and high spirits of
the crowd. The first round had gone largely to form. Most
of the competitors that were considered not to have
performed well enough were asked to sit in the audience to

watch the remainder of the performance. Snap and Crunch were happily still on the stage with three others.

There then followed the second and penultimate phase of the competition, in which the remaining poets would be expected to speak in sequence, be judged and then two would be chosen for the final. It was important to be able to pace yourself and to save your best till last, but not so much as to be left behind with an inferior poem. Snap had decided on animal poems this year; the one just gone, one to perform now and the other to be saved for the final should he get there. Crunch had also thought about his poems and had planned a spectacular for the final, designed to appeal to each goblin's patriotic spirit.

The master of ceremonies stood and moved to the centre of the stage. He seemed to have a more serious tone now that the competition had been reduced to the more serious players. He beckoned Crunch Woodstack to step forward and be the first in this round to speak. This he then did.

"Friends, here is a little poem for all our smaller friends, upon whom we rely. 'The Little Ones.'

In each of us there is a clear instruction,
from which the little ones make our construction.
Block by block they put us together,
and block by block they make our destruction.

Whether it is small or large, it goes,
with the passing of each moment, row upon row,
with such intricacy we can only suppose.

A slice of light passes them by,
only scale separates us;
a drop in my ocean as they say goodbye.

The little ones man the barricade, invaders to foil,
Doing as they were bade, keeping us above the soil.

Their battles are fought in an instant by an atom's side,
a myriad of efforts to give us just one moment of pride,
each second of pleasure because a million laid down and
died.

I love thee, my little ones, for you sustain me.
Your duty gives me life, and your efforts built this tree.
I love thee, for each moment you give is just to me."

From the great hush that shadowed his speech warm
applause emerged. This was a fine and well received effort
and he felt satisfied that this would see him into the final.
The judges looked pleased and scribbled furiously.
Between Crunch and Snap the other three competitors
spoke. The second of these went by the name of Trundle
Firestoke. He stepped forward and gave the following
rather curious entry.
"My poem everyone, is dedicated to my vegetable patch.
It is called my vegetable patch...and so is the poem.

At the bottom of my garden, sits my vegetable patch.
There I sit with my seeds, ready to sow the next batch.

I like carrots, beans, and potatoes especially,
but I don't like sprouts, courgettes or celery.

Sometimes my wife gives me advice about the best types
to cook.
All I say to her is, leave me be woman, don't even take a
look!
These veg are mine see,
if you want some veg off me,
all you have to do is say po...lite...lee...
gimme some veg, or I won't be friends no more with thee."

This felt less like a serious poem and more like a message
to his wife who was sat in the front row. He had stared at
her throughout. He seemed to be concentrating more on
his marriage than the competition and this was not missed
by the judges.
Snap came last in the sequence. The master of ceremonies
announced him once again and the Roundtops cheered
him once again. He stepped to the front of the stage and
steadied himself for the important moments that were to
follow.
"This poem is about my little ox, who sadly could not be
with us today. I hope you like it.

My little Ox is a fiendish fella,
for he likes too much the taste of shoe leather.
Whenever my back is turned it becomes his goal,
to nibble away right through to the sole.

So many pairs have I had to buy,
that I just want to sit down and cry.
Oh, how to say to him in the Ox dialect,
stop it you mad thing, you bovine reject!

I wish I could make him understand,
that if he keeps this up he will force my hand.
His actions put me at the end of my tether,
and soon I may make *him* into leather!

I don't want to do it of course,
because of my joy he is the source.
Plus, I made a promise to his mother,
to look after him like no other.

I went about approaching a specialist,
to help me clear away this problem's mist.
This gentleman came by to have his say,
take two of these, three times a day.

This the ox and I did for each and every pill,
though nothing happened, my shoes suffered still!
I called him back to say he had failed,
yet with tales of his successes he regaled.

I spoke with my neighbour about the problem.
At first she said potions of root or stem.
I want a tried and tested technique said I,
not some foul brew that may make him die.

Perhaps your ox is lonely, she thought out loud,
lonely for the company of more of his crowd.
Why don't you find him a friend, she suggested?
A horse, a sheep or a *lady* ox might be tested!

Straight away I saw the value in the idea,
and went to the market with my mind much freer.
I came back with a beautiful four legged companion,
as a gift for my hairy shoe eating champion.

I can honestly say that from that day till this,
all they ever seem to do is kiss.
And the lust for shoes that filled my little ox,
is now just a lust for her shiny brown locks."

This poem was met with very warm applause and many
smiles of pleasure at the ideas inside it. Snap was instantly
relieved and staggered back to his seat to take it all in. A
minute in the spotlight can sap the strength of even the
toughest of people. A break of ten minutes or so then
occurred to allow the judges to decide on the two finalists
and to allow the spectators more pie if they wanted it.
The five poets sat side by side and looked over towards the
judging table to try to discover the general feeling towards
their poems. They could tell no more than the obvious fact
that there was considerable discussion amongst them. The
Roundtop family was quiet and paying equal attention to
the judges. Gurgle snoozed oblivious to everything except
his nascent senses. Some of his siblings had disappeared for

more pie. On stage Snap had relaxed a little and felt in his proper sphere once again. It was a very welcome feeling and one he had not experienced for a long time.

After the ten minutes seemed to have gone by the judges calmed their discussions and looked away from each other. The master of ceremonies collected a piece of paper from them, which he studied in some detail. He moved forward to speak whilst still reading.

"Well, the results are in...and we have two finalists," he said eventually. "Will the following two competitors please stand up and join me to take part in the final?"

After a few deliberately prolonged moments he spoke again with his arm raised and pointed at them.

"Crunch Woodstack and Snap Roundtop!"

Amidst great squeals and shouts from the crowd they both stood and moved over to shake hands with him and then each other. The Roundtop family was clapping furiously except those members that were absent and still queuing for a second slice of pie. The other three competitors hung their heads and quietly withdrew. The general consensus was that the judges had picked the best two from the five and the spectators were therefore very happy with the decision.

For a minute or two whilst the noise swirled around them Crunch and Snap stood waiting rather awkwardly for the next phase to begin. Both goblins squeezed and played with the papers in their hands as they waited. The master of ceremonies shushed the crowd and announced that each poet would give one further poem and that the winner would then be chosen. He took a pointed stone and placed it on the floor of the stage. He would use it to determine who would go first. He asked Crunch and Snap to step some distance apart so that they were facing each other. He then spun the stone. It turned rapidly and its shape blurred into a circle. Air and friction played their part and it slowed and resolved itself back into shape. It groaned slowly towards Crunch as its energy died away to nothing. Crunch would go first. This was generally considered to be a slight disadvantage as going last meant that your poem would be fresher in the minds of those listening. This did not concern Crunch too much as he was nothing if not confident in his own ability.

Crunch stepped forward to give the poem that he felt sure would make him the winner of this, the 45th Annual Milton Green's Poetry Competition. This would be his third victory in a row.

"Hello to you all again. I hope you have enjoyed my poems...and the others perhaps. This last one I want to say to you to make you think back to when you were young and brave, and if you are young and brave now then just listen."

He coughed quickly and continued.

"To all you outsiders I have something to announce,
there's only one place in this world that's worth an ounce.
Only one place where the trees are their tallest,
and where the crops and people are their greenest.

I am talking about a place full of bravery,
of struggle, of fine goblins, and of adversity,
where in the very leaves is written our history.

What a privilege it is to be a part of this race,
with our qualities written on each babies face.
I wonder about our great designer,
and the genius he blew into our hearts.

Ever since I was young I have felt like this,
my grandmother would tell me of events past,
things that her grandmother had said to her,
and I would sit by her side and look into her eyes of flame,
imagining our triumphs past over enemies of old.

Can I take you back and forward to see our proud nation,
laid out in her finery on the road from beginning to end,
as the other nations in rags pass by?

From the first struggles of independence,
came our dignity and pride,
hard fought and hard earned side by side,
and so to this land of freedom.

Take a look around and breathe it all in,
a wonderful place surrounds you.
It is our home, and it is called...Milton Greens."

He stopped abruptly and moved back to his seat. Some

members of the crowd were quite excited by what they had heard but it could not be said to be the reaction of more than a minority. It was a less than enthusiastic response and beneath his confident demeanour people could tell Crunch was surprised by the lack of reaction from those laid out below him.

Snap was then called up and he felt suddenly to be in just the right place at the right time. He knew his poem was of an entirely different and more relaxed flavour to the one just gone by and that they would receive it well because of that fact. His inferiority complex was gone.

"My fellows, here is a poem I hope you will like. I stayed up one night to write it, and I call it 'Ode to a Bumblebee.'

There once was a Bumblebee christened Woolly.
He had trouble in life for he wasn't formed fully.
Wanting of black and yellow stripes he was not.
It was a lack of wings that summed up his lot.

He had a disposition that was rarely sunny,
though using hard work he still made his honey.
The Queen liked his honey best though,
as the slow formation gave the best flow.

The other drones gave him such a hard time,
he pleaded for sympathy for he'd done no crime.
When it came to tasting the Queen would opine,
look after Woolly, his honey keeps me in my prime.

At night, when the rest were all snoozing on,
Woolly would be still at work in his hexagon.
For with no wings it took him longer to collect the nectar,
he had to walk...and had a smaller sector.

As the others buzzed and fuzzed around,
poor Woolly could only look up, rooted to the ground!
Oh, how he longed to feel not so sullen,
and to be able to fly all covered in pollen!

The reds and greens and blues of the flowers,
were to him like cruel unassailable towers.
With the assistance of others, a sting high in the base,
down came the nectar with a great splash in his face.

One day little Woolly, whilst walking about the hive,
happened to overhear the Queen injured but alive.
A wall fell in on me, help me before it's too late!
Pull away this rubble, quickly, I'm in a terrible state!

As Woolly instantly readied his claws,
a thought occurred to him that gave him some pause.
Will you give me a pair of wings he said,
in exchange for you not ending up dead?

In a moment she agreed, with no time to consider faking,
she was a bee of her word and would honour her
undertaking.
In short while, Woolly set her free,

and soon she was safe in the infirmary.

With royal jelly on tap, and a good book in her lap,
the Queen received a visitor from amongst her ranks.
Little Woolly came first to receive her thanks.
Quietly she whispered, and laid it all out.
If you want a pair of wings, just give me a shout.
Woolly said how long would it take and from where
would they be shipped?
Ha! Just pick any of my drones and their wings shall be
stripped!
Woolly stood back, unable to accept, that his wings
would be stolen on a false precept.

No my Queen, like that I cannot behave,
for where would they then go except to their grave?
It makes no difference to me my sweet,
you are all destined to live beneath my feet.

With feelings the likes of which he had never felt before,
Woolly stung his queen and her book fell to the floor.
He turned her over and pulled out her wings,
two painful jabs - he leapt from the window - the alarm
bell sings!

Within moments he is flying with no more thoughts of
the hive,
now he must flee just to stay alive!
Instinctively, he buzzed and flew to safety,

far from his home, soon a hive of activity.

His maiden flight led him to my doorway.
He crashed there, a wild eyed yellow black sleigh.
I hid and protected him from those buzzing police,
and nursed him back to health by stroking his golden
fleece.

In the dark of my tree he told me his tale,
and I tell it to you now, free, never for sale.
Do you know what he said to me?
'I have nothing to give you for your kindness, I have no
money.
Will you take something else instead, do you like honey?'"

With a justified roar the Roundtops stood together and
shouted their approval. To their delight the rest of the
crowd followed them. The decision was down to the
judges of course but the spectators knew who the winner
should be. In truth, it was indeed a formality for the
judges. In short order Snap Roundtop was announced as
the winner and his name was then expertly scratched into
the ceremonial tree trunk which recorded the history of
this fine competition. Snap stood on the stage in a state of
pure delight. If you are wondering what was the prize for
the winner, beyond the admiration of one's peers of course,
then let me tell you. It was a small wooden trophy and a
significant cash prize of one hundred chestnuts.

CHAPTER 2

Gurgle's early years were largely uneventful. The mulch was plentiful and his parents found no difficulty in supporting their family. Though he had little awareness of it his existence was a happy one during the first few seasons of his life. From a crawling creature he bravely took his first steps as his legs straightened and lengthened. He strained to make sounds which after a while became intelligible instead of merely gurgles. So it was that a baby became a youngster who could walk and talk.

The other members of the Roundtop family quickly grew to appreciate their youngest partner. Gurgle developed a warm and sincere nature, though he could sometimes be shy, a little frightened as he was by the world. He found most comfort by the side of his mother and the most excitement alongside his brothers and sisters. He found that playing in the branches of trees and making nests amid great piles of leaves were about the best things in the world to do. He could see all manner of things from both positions. Sat on a branch and held in the arms of another he could see the carts in the distance carrying their cargoes. Peeking out from a pile of leaves he could secretly watch his neighbours going about their business. As a gang Gurgle and his siblings would roam the nearby forest looking for fun and adventure, though at this stage he was a little too young to play any significant part.

Gurgle enjoyed the safety and warmth of his family home. It was not in one of the prettier stretches of the forest, but it was part of a neighbourhood of great variety and friendliness. The Roundtop home consisted of the insides of a tree, like virtually all other goblin's homes. Theirs was a large but decrepit looking oak tree. The entrance was a small door in the base of the trunk. Behind this was the dusty floor of the main room where they cooked, ate and relaxed together. Opposite the door at the back of this room was a ladder cut into the wall of the tree. This led up into two bedrooms. The largest of which was where Gurgle's brothers and sisters slept. This room had originally been occupied by Thump and Screech but they'd had to move out once the family reached a certain size. The smallest room was occupied by Thump and Screech and any infants they had to care for. Currently, this warm and protected cocoon next to the parents was taken by Gurgle, though he was quickly getting too big for it and might soon make his way alongside his siblings in the room below. For the moment at least, this bed of leaves and soft furs Gurgle could call his own.

This period in Gurgle's life, when his freedom was fiercely protected, would prove to be the happiest in his life. He was free to spend his days in the relaxed company of his brothers and sisters and to explore the nearby forest to his heart's content, though never unsupervised of course. Strangely, he noticed that when his elder siblings reached a certain age they seemed to disappear each morning only to return a few hours later in the day. They often carried with them a little bag of things and seemed unhappy to be going but happy upon their return. Steadily, this curious duty fell upon his elder siblings one by one until it was almost upon Gurgle himself. Realising this inevitable pattern might one day apply to him he asked his mother if he would soon be disappearing too. This she confirmed by telling Gurgle about school and what was in store for him. It was all explained in as much detail as he could take in. He seemed to take it well.

When the sad day arrived Gurgle was escorted to school by his mother and chaperoned by his brothers and sisters throughout those first frightening and overwhelming hours. Soon he realised that it was nothing to be afraid of and he began to settle into the routine of activities laid out for him and the others of his age. Here he was exposed to a wide variety of people. Youngsters came from quite far away to attend. However, schooling was less formal than you might imagine. They came to learn about life and living. There was no requirement to attend and no examination would ever be given to a goblin. There were also some curious adults that taught and supervised them. Chief among them was Gurgle's first teacher, Miss Scrape Oliphant. A slim and slightly deranged goblin lady, but a lady nevertheless possessed with a great affection for her students. From her Gurgle learned the basics of proper speaking and writing and painting. She taught him and his companions about the arrangement of animals in the world and about the world itself and the sad but inevitable dangers in it. She taught them to appreciate the value of their food, their families and their health.

Gurgle did his best to find enjoyment in other things in life besides school. He would often read some of his great uncle's books when he had the chance. This encouraged his mind to grow and his imagination to go places where he felt he could not. His childish enthusiasm for play and excitement was gradually replaced by an interest in the more serious concerns of life. He would also sneak out at night when he would not attract attention and go for small exploratory walks in the forest. He was growing up quickly and developing a cautious and observant nature. He was wiser than his years might have suggested to strangers. He was however forced to cope with great loneliness in his new position. His most cherished wish was for the companionship of someone similar to him, someone who would be able to understand him. Sadly, this wish would not be fulfilled by the fates for quite some time.

*

On a small farmstead by a babbling river with trees and hills surrounding it, there lived a family of men, or more precisely, I should say a human man, a human woman and several human children. For survival they depended on the fish in the river, the crops in the soil and the continued favour of the local Lord that held power over them. Their farmstead was one of some fifty or sixty similar dwellings in the area and the people inside them also had the same predicament. Despite their most earnest wish to live quiet and self-contained lives their Lord had other priorities for them that were also equally earnestly held. These people were considered a part of this particular Kingdom and as such had a responsibility to help their Lord to protect it from outsiders. However, due to the fearsomeness of their Lord they were more often called upon to assist him in attacking other communities.

Further down this babbling river there sat an imposing castle. At its back there was a ring of low and craggy hills which provided some natural protection from the elements and from invaders. This castle was occupied by Lord Spikepoint, the Lord in question, and unsurprisingly the castle was called Spikepoint Castle. He was the most powerful man in the region but within his own sphere he felt that he was lacking power in comparison to his master, the King. Lord Spikepoint had ambitions to be the King one day and was quietly spending each spare moment either planning for or fantasising about just that. No objection or complaint would be tolerated by him if it interfered with his grand, though confidential, ambitions. Lord Spikepoint was keen on many things beyond the exploitation of others. He was a famous rider and warrior and was much feared in battle. He had a fascination for strange animals and kept owls, weasels and a bear. To this list he would also have added his retinue of goblins and hobgoblins, for he felt they had little status above that of useful animals. Within his household he found uses for many of them. They fulfilled various roles, such as grooms for his horses and as makers of unusual weapons. He had one goblin and one hobgoblin to whom he gave a special role as spies within their communities. They were both deeply unsavoury characters and were long past the point of caring about the interests of anyone but themselves and their paymaster. They were both seasoned and savage fighters but you wouldn't think so looking at them. This was perhaps what made them so dangerous.

On this small farmstead one member of the family that occupied it was about to leave. He was the eldest male child and a fine specimen of a young man. Waiting patiently for him were several of the Lord's men. They sat on their horses in the early morning haze with their eyes and those of their horses quietly fixed upon the scene in front of them. They had come to claim what their Lord saw as his right, the right to call upon the arms of the able bodied men under his influence to make up part of his army. The young man calmly tied and packed up his necessary possessions and made ready to leave. He had obeyed the call with solemn frustration. It was expected, and he had decided to submit to the inevitable flow of events rather than put his family under greater pressure by escaping. This was a sad but unavoidable day for his family. They were praying for their son's safety and barely managed to suppress their anger and sadness at what was happening. Behind the horses stood a couple of other young men caught up in the same duty. One was perhaps a little too young for such a dangerous and unpleasant adventure. Neither of them knew this family nor the names of the men wrapped tightly in armour above them. The young man said a tender goodbye to each member of his family. He moved off with the others and regularly looked back, only to see them becoming smaller and smaller with each glance. Soon his attentions turned to the group of men of whom he was now a part. Spikepoint's men were silent as mountains and gently instructed their horses to keep to a walking pace as they mounted the slopes of the nearby hill. The three youngsters did their best to keep up close behind them on the rough terrain. It was windy and cold and the best place to keep warm was huddled tightly behind the horses. The young man did not know their destination. He quietly asked his two companions if they knew but they did not. One suggested that they would be heading for the garrison some five miles distant. He would prove to be correct.

The group made their way around the brow of the hill and after a while diverted down into the valley beyond. A little sunshine found them and they were relieved to be warmed up. They found a path through the heart of the valley. The journey was dull and uneventful, and all the while the three youngsters heard no words from the men. They had just a sense of sickness and fear in their stomachs about what would happen to them. As more of the valley came into view, one of the men suddenly halted and turned to those on foot behind him. He looked at them all in turn for a moment then looked ahead and pointed.

"That's where we're heading."

His tone of voice and the look in his eye were such that he gave the clear impression that he did not wish to start a conversation. The two other men looked at him as he spoke then beckoned their horses forward once again. On they all went, towards this distant hazy speck.

*

Gurgle decided that this particular evening he would take a walk down by the river at the edge of the forest. He was now a fully-fledged youngster and nurtured a wilful streak. The prospect of taking on the family trade of mulching did not appeal to his imaginative and curious nature. As it would prove, Gurgle would never be associated with the mulch on the forest floor except where it clung to his feet as he walked through it.

He stepped out when it was very dark and decided to follow one of his regular routes. He enjoyed his solitary night time expeditions and always found something of interest. He managed to leave without disturbing anyone, though he chose to softly kiss his mother goodnight as she lay asleep. If she knew that Gurgle so often sneaked away during the night she would be most worried and angry with him, as would the rest of his family. He hoped to return before they all rose the next day. He had with him a little knapsack with a blanket and some cheese. He might like to find a quiet spot and observe the comings and goings of others in some warmth and comfort.

A soft crunch emerged from under each foot as he started to step through the forest. In the distance he could see and hear many things. Some people were calmly chatting with each other by a tree. In another direction there was a couple strolling gently together. Beyond them were the torch lights of the main path leading towards the heart of the forest. Behind him he could see someone leading a horse. Ahead of him he could see very little but he could smell the moisture in the air. This was the way to the river. Gurgle strode confidently with his young and powerful legs through the light brush on the forest floor. After a while the people about him thinned in number and soon he was fully alone. As he neared the river the vegetation grew lush and more closely packed, though the density of the trees had not changed much on his journey through the forest. They were on average about five metres apart and nearly all of them disappeared beyond his resolution up into the blackness. Gently, imperceptibly at first, the soft trickle of watery noise found out his ear. The ground started to slope downward. Gurgle followed it till the dirt stopped and the mud began.

This river was without a proper name. It was known simply as the river, for it was the only one in the entire forest and had the characteristics of being similar throughout its length and, though irregular, of travelling completely through the forest almost without diversion. Gurgle had encountered it many times before but had never travelled upon it, though he had seen many others do so. Tonight he hoped to find a secluded little spot from which to quietly observe any boats and passengers that might float by, or if they be scarce, to wait for the gentle footsteps of the forest deer that would only emerge if confident no other creatures were about.

He looked both up and downstream but could see no bridge nearby over which to cross. He decided then to settle in some place on this bank of the river. Gurgle placed his blanket in a spot where the edge of the bank was set back one or two metres from the water and where some natural shadow was thus formed. He pushed at the folds of it to match the shape of the ground and did his best to make himself comfortable and concealed. Now that he was free from the water and the mud Gurgle opened his pouch and pulled from within an impressive chunk of cheese. For the next thirty minutes or so he proceeded to nibble on this crumbling yellow monolith till it dwindled to nothing, all the while staring vacantly here and there into the distance. He brushed away those bits of cheese that had escaped his mouth and watched them fall into the water. After a few moments and some careful staring he saw them disappear one by one as the fish underneath grabbed and snapped at them, with their mouths agape.

The ebb and flow of the river and the pattern of the ripples were communicated to Gurgle by the moonlight reflecting off the surface of the water. The patterns were hypnotic. After a little while, once the cheese was all gone, and at which point Gurgle was playfully chewing on a twig, these patterns began suddenly to alter. He noticed instantly and supposed that a boat was disturbing the water and making these changes. He was correct. Coming from upstream around a bend, which was beyond his sight, he began to resolve the leading edge of a wooden boat. At first it seemed small and empty but as the moments passed and the boat came further into view Gurgle could see there were people on board.

A small orange light flickered on the boat but it seemed to illuminate very little. This was odd, since he could not believe there was enough light for them to navigate by. Several people seemed to be moving about on the boat, which Gurgle also saw had a cabin in the centre of it. Those on board seemed to be working together on some activity which he could not quite make out, but he obviously had no desire to stand up to take a closer look or to shout at them to see what they were doing. He preferred to stay in his protected spot. He could not say why just yet but something about the figures on the boat struck him as unusual. He sank into his shadow as the boat grew nearer. To his alarm he saw one or two of the figures on board suddenly leap from the boat to each shore as though it were a mere skip from one to the other and this just fifty metres distant from him. They quickly disappeared in the darkness. Minutes later these figures returned from the shadows with large bundles over their shoulders. They passed them over the water and into the boat and they wasted no time in doing it. Gurgle could make out soft conversation. Such things were said as "how many did you get?", "quieten down!", "keep a look out!", and most ominously of all "this one looks dead, what d'you do to him?" followed immediately by "just leave him here".

Gurgle instantly recognised the danger he was in but had no place to flee to. He was concealed and would surely be seen within moments of raising himself from the shadows. His stomach bubbled and tightened as he sank into the shadows as far he could go. He tried to remain silent like the tree roots around him. He wished his heart would slow for the blood to quieten in his veins. His eyes grew wide as he followed every movement of these figures ahead of him. The natural currents of the river drew the boat nearer and nearer to his position and it seemed these dreadful activities on shore would continue directly to him, and perhaps even over him. The noise of them grew louder as they approached though they still made every effort to remain quiet, lest they be discovered. Gurgle held his breath as one of them walked slowly along the opposite bank to him. He seemed to stop for a moment to regain his breath. He was but ten steps away. He turned and looked in Gurgle's direction, almost at him....but he was not seen. It was a human man!

The boat came ever closer and he suddenly realised the light on board might illuminate him. The bump and sway of the boat itself could now be heard as it settled close by on the bank opposite. More men approached the boat and put in their cargoes, one from almost above Gurgle himself!

"Have we got enough?" whispered one to the others in the boat.

"I think we have. Call them in," said another, who seemed to be directing things.

One of those on the boat stepped onto the opposite bank and motioned for those around and about to return. This they did. As he directed them back onto the boat he suddenly froze and snapped his head in Gurgle's direction. "Fetch the light! One's escaped!" he shouted.

With this the man bounded into the water and rushed at Gurgle's hiding place. Gurgle yelped, jumped from the shadows and began to scramble back up the bank.

"Grab him for God's sake!" said another, poking his head from the cabin on the boat.

Gurgle had no ally in good fortune for as he scrambled back up the bank he was met by the ugliest creature he had ever seen who grabbed him securely around his waist and pulled him back towards the boat despite kicking frantically for freedom. He was held neither by a human man nor a goblin.

"Get off me! Let me go!" he managed to scream before having a hand placed firmly over his mouth.

"Settle yourselves, and make the boat ready," said one of them on the other bank.

Once they had safely placed all back into the boat and were on their way they looked more closely at what they had found. A short discussion was started up.

"Tirgu, he's too young I think, let's leave him," said one of the human men.

"He's a boy, not a baby, let's have him," said another.

"He's a little young Tirgu, shall we take him or not?"

After a moment's thought, and some very close and frightening observation of Gurgle, and only after he allowed time for a huge and devilish smile to spread fully across his face did there come a reply from this Tirgu.

"We shall."

*

The three riders and the three young men in their charge continued their early morning trek through the low valley to their Lord's garrison. As they drew closer more of its shape could be made out. It was made entirely from wooden poles tied upright together. One corner had an extra level upon which a man could be seen looking out on to the flat terrain all around. Wandering below they could see several horses being led about by their attendants. The place looked filthy.

The three riders appeared to be in no hurry to arrive and those in the garrison seemed in no hurry to receive them. The three young men trailing behind were indeed anxious to arrive and find shelter from the bitter wind which had been pushing them for much of their journey. They had introduced themselves to each other along the route. Samuel, John and Joseph. They knew nothing of each other previously except the names of the small communities from which they had come, or rather, from which they had been taken. All had at one time or another anticipated this day and were not surprised when notice of it had come to them in the previous month. Joseph had had an elder brother to whom this painful honour had been given. He had never received all the facts of what befell him but he was informed that his life had been taken in a small dispute between the Lord's men, of whom he was only a junior player, and some unexpectedly well-armed farmers in the matter of some tax collection. Thus it was that Joseph had more reason to fear and resent the call to arms than the other two. John was the smallest and perhaps the weakest of the three, though not so weak as to excuse him from this duty. Samuel seemed the fittest of the three and the most likely to be able to accommodate himself to the hardships that would shortly face them.

It seemed the men behind the wooden walls went about their business quietly, as little sound seemed to find its way over the tops of the battered trunks that enclosed them. Wet dirt went all around the base of the garrison and some way distant from it. The men's and the horse's churning up of the ground as they were led in and out was no doubt responsible. Samuel, John and Joseph were expecting the main gates to open for their party but instead they followed around to the rear of the structure and found several ramshackle huts and lean-to's. Various activities seemed to be going on in them, chiefly the smelting of minerals to make molten metal and other matching labours needed for it. The three of them were directed to lay down their small packs together. The three horsemen that had led them then withdrew by unseen passage into the garrison. For a few moments the three young men simply looked at all that was going on about them and were waiting for someone to direct them further. This came instantly when a sudden bellow from behind them startled them from their fascinated observations.

"Move!"

They jumped and turned to see a figure clad in leather and scorched cloths of all sorts hurry them out of his way. With thick gloves he carried the heavy burden of a hot orange axe head. He plunged it straight into a trough of water from which sizzling white gas rapidly emerged. He then stood up straight and arched his back, which gave him great relief after a moment's pain. He groaned and then caught his breath ready to speak.

"There's not much for you to do right now. Just sit on the hay bundles there and watch what we're doing as you might be doing it yourself. That and many other things."

This Samuel, John and Joseph immediately did. The various fires and cauldrons about them were a welcome source of warmth as they sat with their backs to the wooden poles of the garrison wall and observed all as they had been instructed. They were most surprised by one sight in particular. The person that had carried the axe head and had ordered them about was a goblin. Only John had seen such creatures before. John's village was near to the large forest in which these curious creatures lived and it seemed from where some had obviously emigrated. John was not alarmed at the sight and had even (as he later told his fellows) struck up conversation once or twice with a goblin, without any harm coming to him. This goblin struggled at his work with yet more heavy irons to move to the trough to be cooled. The other men working about the place called him Grumble, which made no sense at all as a name to Samuel's and Joseph's ears.

There the three of them sat for more than an hour without

a single word being said to them. Soon they began to feel hunger after such a long journey and thirst for being in the midst of such heat and flying sparks. Something suggested to them that a polite enquiry as to when food might be served would be met either with laughter or a painful thump to the head. Samuel stood and decided to have a look around, against the advice of his companions. He was fixed by various glances from the metalworkers but since no objection came from them he continued to move. He went around the side of the huts in which they worked and noted as discreetly as he could the lay of the land and the positions of those that watched over him. He approached the nearest corner of the garrison to see what lay around it. A sudden rumbling stopped him and he froze back against the wall. A snorting, sweaty and heavily armoured horse with an equally armoured rider surged around the corner past Samuel and straight towards the men at work beyond him. The rider yelled at the first man that emerged from the shade of the huts.

"You there! When will you finish the armour?" he said, with unpleasant impatience in his voice.

"Two more weeks Sir, for the fifty pieces you requested," came the cautious reply.

"Two weeks? Have you everything you need?"

"I think so Sir. We'll try to make things go faster if it pleases."

"Oh it pleases me, it pleases me." At that moment the rider caught sight of Samuel standing to the side of him and of the two others sitting idle beyond. He turned his huge horse to face them.

"Stand up! Come here!" he shouted. "Who are you and what business have you at my camp?"

"We were brought here today by three riders, to be in our Lord's service Sir," replied Samuel confidently.

The rider looked at them for a moment and his anger and alarm seemed to subside. He turned back to the metalworkers.

"And the weaponry, what of that?" he said, flatly this time.

"That'll all be ready by tomorrow evening Sir."

The rider gave no response but simply signalled his approval.

"You three follow me."

With this command they moved towards him and followed as he turned and made for the main entrance to the garrison. Just before they all were to enter the rider looked slowly at each one of them and said the following.

"I am the commander of this garrison. All here call me Sir. You included. Do your duty. Follow the orders given to you and carry them out completely. Do these simple things and you'll be well fed, well watered, well protected, and you'll soon become fighting men. You, what's your name?"

"John...John Page, Sir."

"Is it two John's or one young man?"

"Just one Sir," he said smiling.

"Do you have any skill with horses?"

"Some Sir, we had two on our farm at home."

"Excellent. Help me with mine. Take it to the groom who'll approach us as we enter. He's like no creature you'll have seen before but don't be alarmed by him young John for he'll do you no harm."

John nodded and stepped a little closer to the horse as the rider yelled up at the gates for them to open. This they immediately did but with some scraping through the mud at the base of each door. Inside they could see men wandering from one place to another, whilst others stayed perfectly still at their posts. There seemed as little furniture on the inside as on the outside.

The rider got down from his horse and walked slowly around it then handed the reins to John. They both looked inside to see someone approaching them just as predicted. With a curious limp and an even more curious appearance the groom met them and took the horse from John. A subtle signal from the garrison commander caught the groom's eye and he was thus instructed to take John with him.

"You two!" the commander's attention moved back to Samuel and Joseph with startling speed. "Stop enjoying the sunshine and get to work. Report to that man yonder and help him prepare the food. Meat doesn't chop itself."

With this they both moved swiftly to one corner of the garrison as directed. There they found a man with a wooden spoon that he swirled about in a large iron pot. At first this man did not react to them despite the fact that they were standing directly in front of him.

"We were..." Samuel began.

"I heard!" came the instant retort. "See that pile of potatoes behind me?"

They both acknowledged that they did.

"Hands off! If either of you touch them you'll end up in here," he said, motioning frantically with his finger inches above the boiling gloop. "Peeling potatoes is too good for the likes o' you. Grab knives the both of you and start slicing up that flesh on the table there. Put the off cuts, gristle and bone in the basket below...and don't wash your hands! It'll spoil the flavour of the meat!"

Samuel and Joseph did as they were told and started work on slicing the meat. They placed each decent piece into the cauldron as they went, though for each decent piece they had to cut through several that were not. Joseph's attention was quickly directed elsewhere in an attempt to study the place around him. His period of service like the others would be required to last for at least a year, though if a suitable opportunity arose to shorten his stay he would eagerly take it. Samuel also looked at what could be seen beyond the table in front of him. He saw there were no fewer than ten men guarding the garrison and that they walked around the elevated inner perimeter. He also saw that there were a further fifty or so men that appeared to be troops engaged in other matters or duties and a further seven others that were workmen of one kind or another and were perhaps free to come and go.

The commander was at the other end of the garrison removing his armour and washing the sweat from his body. Two men were standing nearby talking to him in a most agitated way. They seemed like his attendants but they were well armed. He did not seem too concerned by what they were saying to him. He responded patiently but this did not calm them down at all. He simply waived them away. They then withdrew speaking angrily as they went. It seemed to Samuel that all was not well here.

Meanwhile, young John was slowly adapting to his new situation. He had found a sympathetic companion in the form of this strange groom. Muresh, for it was his name, spoke gently and calmly to him when giving instructions. This was a blessed relief as his appearance was so startling that to have added ferociousness to it would have been overwhelming for John. Muresh reminded him of the goblins that he had seen and once or twice met when he was younger. Something about him was different though. He was narrower, taller, though not as tall as he, more brown skinned than green and with more prominent and sharp features within his face. He was similar to but distinct from that Grumble creature on the other side of the wall.

John decided to do all that he would be asked to do and to find a niche for himself that would keep him out of trouble and more importantly out of harm's way. Watering and brushing horses was not a bad way to spend a year in the Lord's service. Samuel and Joseph were instead determined at the first opportunity to get out of the foul duty to which they had been allocated. They admired the commander and his easy strength and dignity. They were eager to learn the necessary skills for the proper use of the blades they held in their hands. Despite the enforced departure from their homes, which they naturally still resented, these feelings would soon fade when faced with the necessities and opportunities that would meet them. Much like their elders all about, seasoned and scarred by age and use, they would prove to be ideal recruits to this body of men.

*

Gurgle fainted. For a while there was blackness known only to him. He awoke in a strange place and in a strange position. He felt his arms suddenly constricted and his vision blocked by a cover over his head. He was completely tied with his arms behind his back. He gasped and let out a moan. This was met with similar sounds from others about him. They wriggled and responded to his movements and were worked up by it.

It seemed to him that he was in amongst a pile of people. That sensation, of waking up tied and not knowing where he was or what danger he might be in and with the full remembrance of what had happened to him flooding his brain led to poor Gurgle feeling the most frightened that he had ever felt in his life.

"Quiet you lot!" rasped a voice low above them.

They all stirred and shook together once again but the sounds they made quickly diminished. Gurgle listened instead and heard the soft slaps of the water below him. He was still on the boat. He listened further.

"Can you see them yet?" said one voice, further away than

the last.

"It's too dark," said another.

"Wait, there they are...shine the light there!" said the first voice.

"Pass me the line!"

"No, just run her aground on the bank. Do as you're told!"

After a few moments a heavy bump shook all on board and caused more noises of discomfort and distress to come from those unknown people lying with Gurgle. A more distant voice drifted into his attention.

"Two hours I've been waiting for you! I almost went home."

"If you had gone home I would've followed you there and sliced you up in your bed!" came a sudden snarling voice from what seemed just inches from Gurgle's ear.

"Tirgu, my old friend. I see you've lost none of your viciousness. How many did you get?"

"Eleven. One I'll keep, the rest are yours."

"Fine, bring them on shore and let's take a look at them."

With this Gurgle felt the weight about him reduce and the noises increase as those nearby were lifted from the boat. They complained bitterly and he could hear them being thumped bitterly for each complaint. He fully expected that he himself would be lifted clear but that unpleasant moment never came. Instead a firm hand settled itself upon him to keep him in his place. It seemed that he would be the one to be kept by Tirgu. He was not sure whether this was the better option. He managed to control a powerful urge to bite viciously at the fingers that were placed upon his chest to hold him down.

"That's all of them. Got the money?" said one of the men, groaning for breath after lifting the last one off the boat.

"They look a little weak, not ready for much hard work any time soon," replied the man on shore.

"They're as good as you'll get! Stop wasting my time and pay what you agreed!" snapped Tirgu from inside the boat, still with his hand held tightly to Gurgles body.

"Fine. Fine. I'm sure you'll replace them if they aren't any good," he said, laughing softly to himself.

Moments later the boat rocked violently as the men jumped back on board. Tirgu coughed.

"Let's go. I'm tired and haven't eaten for hours. I have some dreams to dream too."

A kick and a grunt followed as the boat lurched away from the bank and back into the water. Amidst such complex and powerful emotions Gurgle wasn't quite sure how to react. He could see nothing except the dark blur of fibre in front his eyes. He could not move in any meaningful way and any sound he could make would most likely lead only to a painful response. He could only listen.

The soft sway of the waters moved him now. He tried to pay attention to all that went on around him. But soon, to his great frustration and anger he could not control sudden feelings of tiredness. How could he protect himself if he did not stay awake and alert? This inner conflict pounded away within his brain until, unnoticed to Gurgle, he fell unconscious.

He awoke again with a gasp after God knows how long and reproached himself for his failure to stay awake. The noise caught the attention of those about him.

"Your little friend is awake Tirgu. When we get back will you give him a sweet kiss goodnight, so he'll sleep all the better?" said one of the men, and the others chuckled in response.

Gurgle felt a rush of air beside him. The boat lurched suddenly. Subtle noises occurred that he couldn't make out - a soft crunch, a moan of pain and a great splash in the river. Gurgle felt Tirgu's presence return to his side. The others seemed shocked and surprised but had nothing to say as their colleague floundered in the water semi-conscious.

"Spikepoint gave me power over you. Unless you wish to join your stupid friend in the river keep your mouths closed and don't forget who's in charge here. Now watch the way ahead."

This unpleasantness seemed to calm everyone down, or at least it kept everyone quiet. Gurgle heard no more talking after that. An unknown period of time elapsed. He couldn't be sure how long but not more than an hour he felt. After a while the boat seemed to slow in the water and begin a gentle diversion to the left.

"I can see the torch lights now. We're back in camp," said one of the men. "Carry your own baggage," commanded Tirgu, "and be ready early tomorrow morning. There's much to be done and you're going to do it."

The boat bumped against soft mud and sludged to a halt. Suddenly there was air between Gurgle and the wood of the boat deck. He was picked up and being moved with a frightening swiftness though he did not cry out. A cold wind penetrated through his clothes to his skin. It really was the dead of night and he felt completely exposed. The grunts and groans of men laden with equipment and supplies followed beside him. He could still see nothing. They all moved some distance on foot together and uphill. Soft conversation greeted them as they entered their camp. Though he could not see them some half a dozen tents formed it. There was pure dark forest beyond and the camp was kept lit by only three weak orange torches.

Tirgu left the others and approached his own private tent. Once inside he threw Gurgle down in a heap upon a pile of straw at one end. After putting down his own pack he unwrapped his live struggling bundle and pulled away the hood, though he did not untie Gurgle's hands. He found two blinking and fearful eyes staring back at him. Tirgu smiled that large frightening smile once again. He sat down on his bed behind him, which consisted of tightly packed straw with furs draped over it. He searched around behind it and produced some dried meat and a few pieces of fruit, which seemed very fine to Gurgle's eyes. He kept most for himself but tossed a little of it to Gurgle. It landed in the folds of the sack in which he still was sat. He did his best to dip his head down and grab at the loose pieces of food. He snatched one or two with his tongue before they could fall on the ground.

"Well well. How are you doing my little friend? I'm glad to see you're alright."

Tirgu considered things for a few more moments. Before he spoke again he pulled out his knife and gently wiped it clean. In the flickering candle light Gurgle could not quite tell what it was that he washed away from the blade.

"You're going to be very useful to me. Do you know that? My last goblin scout was very useful, but he foolishly went and got himself killed didn't he? But you I think will fill his shoes very nicely, very nicely indeed. Now behave yourself and get some sleep or I'll tie you up outside."

With those words Tirgu then blew out the candle.

Gurgle was at a loss what to do. He was far too frightened to sleep. He leaned over and turned his back to Tirgu and curled into a ball. He did his best to pull the edges of the sack up above his shoulders with his teeth. What a deeply unpleasant taste! The temperature inside the tent was warmer than outside, but not by much. Tirgu had furs to warm him. Gurgle had no such comfort. He wished that he could somehow have kept his blanket with him. He wondered where it was and whether anyone would come for him. He indulged in a moment of self pity, thinking of his poor parents and what they would think when they discovered he was gone and with no sign or clue as to where he went! They would have no idea where to look. One or two tears fell.

He didn't have any idea where he was, though it occurred to him that after such a long journey he would be farther away from home than he had ever been before. His feelings of self pity migrated into something else. He fantasised about rescue and other things, such as grabbing that knife wherever it was and plunging it into his stinking heart.

It was completely dark.

CHAPTER 3

Thump Roundtop awoke with a start and looked about himself for a few moments, being not quite sure where he was. The machinery of his mind was still engaging. He felt a certain prodding in his left arm and reacted to it in the following way.

"Stop it! What're you doing to me?" he said.

"Wake up! Gurgle's gone! Our youngest is gone!" yelled Screech to her husband.

"Gone? Gone where?" he replied after a blink or two.

"I don't know. His beds empty, his bag and blanket are gone. Don't you know? Didn't he say nothing to you?"

"No, he said nothing to me. Ask the rest of them where he is. They'll know most probably."

"They don't. They heard nothing. Get up for God's sake and help us search for him!"

She pushed at him once again, and he groaned and coughed.

"Lord, give me a couple of minutes to get myself ready."

"Don't be long! We're waiting for you downstairs, and we're going straight out."

"I'll be there," he replied and coughed once more.

Shortly he arrived below to find all his family dressed and anxious to leave. They looked alarmed and impatient. Screech took the lead and organised her brood.

"You lot with me, the rest of you with your father. Thump, I'll ask the neighbours around here if they've seen anything or know anything. You go down the pathway there and look for any tracks to see if he went that way. We'll catch you up once were finished."

They all went through the door into the cool morning air and separated as she had instructed. Screech strode confidently into an open stretch of ground in front of some five or six other trees that were nearest to their own tree. She told her children with her to knock on all the doors, which they did in a flash. Steadily, one after another, doors began to creak open and several sleepy heads emerged from behind them to see a little face looking up. Screech shouted to all of them together.

"My youngest, Gurgle, is gone! He was with us last night but now he is gone! Did any of you see or hear anything?" Silence followed for a good while until negative murmured replies came from all the neighbours. Screech was disappointed and felt like questioning them some more but decided instead to beckon her children back to her and to move onto the next little glade of homes.

"If you see or hear anything you must let us know!" she said forlornly as they withdrew behind their doors.

Meanwhile, Thump had set off in the other direction with the other half of the family down to the main pathway which led to most of the other places in the forest. This was where Gurgle was most likely to have travelled. They began to fan out to look for his tracks in the dirt or to see if any property or trinket of his might be found. It had rained earlier that morning so it wouldn't be easy to find such things.

"Keep a sharp eye out all of you and don't get too far away

from me. I don't want to have to search for you too," said Thump.

His children did as requested and searched through the undergrowth at the side of the pathway, but still keeping an eye on their father. They found footsteps and horse steps in the mud but they were usually on their own or seemed too old to have been made just last night. Little pieces of paper, old nails, bottles, even odd bits of shoe leather were all on show to them. Thump also looked but tended to spend most of the time glancing around to see that all his children remained in sight. They continued at this for quite some time, finding nothing of value or interest. Steadily they approached the main intersection where a much greater amount of traffic, both goblin and horse, tended to flow. There, Thump could be sure they would find nothing on the ground to guide them considering the number of feet and hooves passing through that stretch of mud every day. Soon enough they reached the road, yet were satisfied that they had scoured the ground between it and their house. They had found nothing.

Thump and the others looked around at the junction. They seemed at a loss as to where to go next. One or two goblins passed this way and that up the road, going about their business. Thump spoke quietly to each and told them of his problem. They were deeply sympathetic but could say or do very little for him. Each went on their way. Thump looked back up the pathway to see where his wife might have got to. She would be frantic with worry when she discovered they he had found nothing. He considered a little more about where to go or who else might be able to help them. He bit his lip as the seriousness of it began to dawn upon him. He sighed deeply and gathered his children about him. He turned to walk back up the path. Before he could do so, his attention, in its heightened state, was caught by a gathering sound at one end of the road behind him. He strained to see many goblins in the distance moving swiftly down towards them.

"What are they doing?" enquired one of Thump's elder sons.

"I don't know. Just wait with me a moment. Let's see shall we," said Thump, without taking his eyes away from the gathering storm in the distance.

As they drew nearer the sounds resolved themselves into the clatter of metal against metal and the thud and splatter of feet surging through mud. Thump recognised them as army irregulars, forest security of sorts. Thump wondered why they'd been called out in such a hurry. He and his children were observed by the approaching group. Thump motioned for them to stop and one of them did so. Before Thump could open his mouth this one began.

"A Raid! They've raided us," he said, alarmed. "Down by the river. Not far from here. That's where we're going now. I think you should stay indoors for the moment."

He set off to run once again but Thump grabbed his arm and stopped him.

"A Raid? By who? My son is missing, it happened last night," shouted Thump over the din of clanking armour.

This goblin stared at Thump for several seconds putting it all together in his mind.

"Did he go anywhere near the river?"

"I don't know, he might have, though he had no permission to be out," Thump replied.

"Take your children back home then follow me to the river. I have to catch the others."

With this he turned and chased after his fellows. Thump beckoned his children to return home with him. They all ran as quickly as they could and he told them to stay at home, but also to keep an eye out for their mother, and if seeing her to tell her to follow him to the river. This they promised to do and once within sight of home he turned and left them to find their own way back.

He charged away as fast as he could, with his mind racing as much as his legs. He avoided the road and took the direct path through the trees. It suddenly occurred to him that Gurgle would most probably have taken a quiet route such as this and he slapped his head metaphorically for not trying to think of the matter as his son would have thought. Along the way he did indeed see the odd footprint and signs of recent travel but he didn't waste time to inspect them. He felt a sudden sinking in his stomach. Abducted! Oh no! Terrible! The worst thing that could have happened!

He made very quick progress, soon finding the slope of the land beginning to aim downwards towards the river. He swerved around tree after tree. He began to hear the moving of the water and soon saw it flowing beneath him.

He looked over the bank and could see one or two of those that he had glanced at in the group on the road. They were milling about and talking to people that seemed as distressed as he was. He looked about for a bridge but could not see one. Bravely, but perhaps foolishly, he bounded into the water. He hurt his ankle as he landed but with only a short moment of pain. He soldiered on through the deep and chilly murk. With soaked trousers, yet with his determination undiminished, he emerged from the waist deep waters and scrambled up the other bank. He ran towards the first of these military types and begged to be told all that was known. This one seemed the wrong goblin to approach as he was reluctant to speak and knew nothing of Thump's earlier enquiry. He looked at him blankly. He was instead beckoned over to the one with whom he had spoken on the road not twenty minutes before. Thump immediately went to him only to find him engaged in heated conversation with another.

"Now tell me what happened," he said as calmly as he could to an elderly goblin who seemed deeply agitated.

"My husband, he's gone! He went out last night and didn't come back!" she said, whilst waving her arms and clawing at her clothes.

There were others about her who seemed to also have a direct interest in all this. They all pointed their noses at him and were giving their earnest support to anything that the others happened to say. Around them and up to the edge of the river the remainder of his troop wandered here and there. One bold soul poked a stick into the water a little.

"Where was he going? What did he tell you?" he said again.

"He was just putting the cat out to do its business, like he does every night. Sometimes he stays out to do his own, sometimes not. He said he'd be just a couple of minutes, like always. The cat came back but he didn't!"

"When was this?"

"I don't know, a little after midnight I think," she replied.

"What about the rest of you? Did your folk disappear at midnight...or thereabouts?"

Most nodded, some pushed and shoved to get closer to him so they could speak. He backed away.

"Who raised the alarm?" he suddenly demanded.

"He did!" came a voice from the back.

All the eyes and bodies turned towards the voice.

"Who did? Where is he?" he demanded again.

"Sitting on that rock over there. That's my uncle," came the voice again.

Immediately, the whole group moved en masse towards this tired and dirty figure. He was lying on the rock rather than sitting and he was clearly exhausted. Thump followed them then barged to the front, all ears.

"You Sir! What happened to you?"

"Who're you?" came the meek reply from the uncle on the rock.

"I'm Lieutenant Chirp Tilestain, of the 11ᵗʰ Milton Greens Militia."

"Are you indeed?"

"I am Sir, I am."

"Where were you last night, that's what I want to know?" he retorted.

"On other duties," he replied, after a moment in which to consider a respectable response.

The man on the rock sat up and looked at the Lieutenant directly.

"My wife was kidnapped. I chased them and tried to stop them but they walloped me."

He turned his head slightly so that all could see a large and painful looking swelling behind his left ear. They could also see a dried and bloody stream below it.

"They took her away. When I came to I searched around all night but couldn't find her."

"Who took her?" asked the Lieutenant.

"Men! And one stinking great hobgoblin amongst them!" he shouted angrily.

All within earshot let out a collective gasp, which soon transformed into an ugly murmur.

"Did you see a boy amongst them?" asked Thump suddenly.

"No."

"You sure?" Thump urged.

"I'm sure damn you!" he snapped back.

He stood up from his rock and said that he was off again to look for his wife. He drifted away until his nephew came over and guided him back with his arm and soft words. The Lieutenant decided to let this man go and gathered the group of people about him.

"Now, can you tell me who is missing?" he asked all of them.

Mumbles of "my husband" and "his brother" and the like came out of them.

"I'll start again," he said after a sigh. "Give me their names."

He listened as one after another of these anxious and teary eyed loved ones gave the descriptions and particulars of those goblins that had been taken from them. He wrote it all down diligently. He ordered one of his men to go after the man and his nephew and to find the name of his wife. The Lieutenant turned to look through the people about him once more until his eyes met those of Thump. He moved towards him and began to speak discreetly so as not to announce this most sensitive loss to all who were listening.

"Can I have your name and the name of your son please, Sir?" said most sympathetically.

Thump's head dropped as he answered. He stared blankly at the front of the Lieutenant's armoured body. He noticed that the armour was old and cracked and the pieces did not match one another. He also could have sworn that the plate which sat over the Lieutenant's abdomen was knocked up and fashioned from an old shovel blade. He gave all the information that he could. He glanced back up at the Lieutenant.

"What will happen now?" said Thump.

"Ah, I think you'll agree, this matter is somewhat beyond a troop of militia men like us. I suspect they'll all be outside the forest...and for some hours. This is a Council matter now. If they choose to pursue them, which I hope they will..."

"If!?"

"*If*...they choose to pursue them we'll have to raise an army. You do understand this could all take weeks to organise? If we go abroad we're sure to meet hostility. I suspect I know the types who've taken your son and the others. They won't take too kindly to us challenging them. We're more likely to have success by quietly searching and freeing our people where we find them. But we'll need the safety of numbers for that. Don't be afraid Mr Roundtop, we'll find them again I'm sure. Though...you're welcome to join up and help in the attempt if you feel up to it?"

Thump was startled by this as he hadn't considered that thought until it was suggested to him. The Lieutenant continued.

"Have you served before?"

"No," replied Thump.

"Well, that shouldn't stop you. Don't think about it seriously for the moment. You'll know where to go if you're interested. There'll be announcements and notices put up on this matter I can promise you. Just follow one of them when they call for the able bodied to attend."

"Lieutenant, Lieutenant!" came a sudden shout from the water's edge.

They both turned and jogged down to the river from where the shouts originated, the Lieutenant being the noisier of the two as they moved. They stood on the edge to see two of the Lieutenant's troop up to their knees in the water. They were crossing from the far side to this. One of them carried a blanket, one edge of which was scrunched in his hand.

"I found this Sir. It was dirty underneath but clean on top. It can't have been out very long," he said.

"That's his! That's Gurgle's blanket!" yelled Thump, almost falling into the water in an attempt to reach for it.

The Lieutenant steadied him and held onto him until the others were up and free of the water. They were then in a group of four. They all pawed at the blanket to see the size and condition of it. It was a sorry sight.

"There were many footprints around where we found it Sir. Big ones, like men's. And all along the bank here Sir," the youngster continued.

"Give me the blanket!" demanded Thump, almost snatching at it.

The youngster resisted giving it to Thump until a nod from the Lieutenant caused him to let go. Dust flew up amongst them. At that moment a high pitched noise became evident from some distance away. Thump recognised it first of course. He looked beyond the three others with him and back across the river. He saw his wife approaching in a dreadful condition. She recognised him too when he separated himself from the group. Her eyes then drifted down to his arm where the blanket hung. She knew it instantly, she had made it herself. She reeled and slipped to her knees, and leaned over sobbing at the foot of a tree.

*

The heavy chink of hammer blow against sword greeted Samuel and Joseph as they were roughly booted from their exhausted slumbers. It was the cook who had so warmly integrated them into the camp the previous day. They shook, startled, and fell from the narrow bales of straw on which they had slept.

"Come on, wake up! Work to do!" he growled.

The cook was dressed in his apron and moved back to where he'd been working. He slid and slapped his knife against a sharpening tool, no doubt readying himself for another day of award winning food preparation. Samuel and Joseph, now known to each other in a more friendly fashion as Sam and Joe, controlled their anger at such a malicious awakening and rose wearily to their feet and to his attention. The same sentry posts all about the interior walls were occupied as they were the day before, though not by the same men. There was no sign of John the third member of their group. Presumably, this was because there were no horses around either.

"We need water," began the cook, "and lots of it. As many bucketful's as you can carry. You'll find the buckets outside. Go to the river, take the water from the middle where it runs fastest and make sure you take it upstream of those dirty devils washing their stinking bits in it!"

He stared at them both in turn for a moment or two.

"I'm sorry, did I forget to say *now!?*" he bellowed, and then turned his back to them.

They quickly grabbed their necessaries and struggled towards the main gate. Once ready they moved in behind a group of soldiers that were already assembled and walking through two by two. They kept their heads down and smiled at each other as they momentarily mimicked the strict formation which led them out. The heavy clod of boots masked their laughter. The men in front moved in a graceful curve which led them towards a dirty road leading to parts unknown to Sam and Joe. They were being led away from the river so the two of them separated and looked around for some of the buckets. They found several in a careless pile at a nearby corner of the garrison. They grabbed one bucket in each hand, four in total, and reckoned they could carry forty litres between them in a single trip.

They walked to the river and found that there were indeed some dirty devils languishing in it. Several of their horses were drinking from it too. Sam and Joe did not fancy the prospect of talking to them lest they should be encouraged to join them, or worse, be made fools of with water by those already wet. They stayed well clear and went upstream. This was one order with which they fully agreed. Sam stepped first onto one stone and then another at a convenient place in the river so as to move to the middle where the water moved fastest and where there was none of that suspicious looking brown foam cuddling the edges of each bank. Joe followed him halfway and passed over the first bucket when he was in position. Sam lowered the bucket into the water only to find it colder and faster flowing than expected. He found it more difficult to hold the bucket in position and he decided to draw back on his extravagant estimates, filling it only half full. He passed it at arm's length to Joe who was surprised that the bucket was not full to the brim. He understood why when the full weight of it was passed to him and it was all he could do not to be taken into the river by the unexpected strain it placed upon him. He wobbled back to the shore taking the utmost care not to slip on the wet stones.

Once four buckets were half filled, the two of them staggered back to the garrison. Their arms were stretched and their necks were strained and their heads were held far back behind their strides. They landed back at the cook's side gasping for breath and nursing their sore and swollen arms.

"That'll do nicely. Pour them into the pot," he said.

Slowly, uncomfortably, with four sloshes, they complied. Once it was all in the pot it did not seem much.

"Just three more journeys and it should be full. Then you can fill up the wash troughs on the other side there. Not to mention the commander's bath tub. If you're lucky he'll invite you in for a soak!"

He laughed at them as he sauntered away. He turned back towards them and then laughed again, the second time with more feeling.

Onward they struggled with fetching the water for more than two hours, throughout which they felt exhausted.

They had no chance to become sweaty however as they were soaked through from each falling into the water at least once. During this period they were left largely alone to their task. As the morning wore on people came and went but there was no sign of an excuse or an opportunity to have their labours ended prematurely. In an unexpected moment of charity the cook gave them a chunk of decent looking bread, a hefty slice of ham and ten minutes of solitude in which to eat them.

Once they had finished the meal they began again to carry their buckets to the river in the hope of completing their arduous task sooner rather than later. They continued in a daze for a little while, oblivious to a steady build-up of activity in and around the garrison. On one return leg of their journey they were met by the cook at the gates, who seemed preoccupied with something of much more consequence than they. Barely looking at them he motioned them inside and told them to lay down their buckets in one corner.

"Stay here," he said softly.

He moved carefully away from them and peered back out of the gate. He wiped his hands on his apron and looked all about. He turned suddenly and shouted up to one of the men above him looking out over the walls.

"What's happening?" he said.

After a moment or two of silence there came a response which was muffled to Sam and Joe, since they were separated from the voice by many layers of wood and straw. Fortunately, the cook repeated the words in alarm.

"They're coming back? So soon?"

A moment later.

"With wounded? Oh Lord..." he withdrew from the gate and looked around frantically. "You two, help me clear these tables."

They did so, quickly bundling away food and kitchen tools into sacks and placing them well out of the way. Together they swiftly and silently assisted the cook in moving two large wooden tables into the centre of the inner courtyard. It was at this time that he chose to show that he knew the names of his two assistants very well. Sam was told to pour clean water over the tables to wash away any bits of food and dirt, of which he found there was plenty. He then dried them down as best he could. Joe was directed outside to fetch some large clean cloths that had been washed and were drying in the wind. Between them they laid out two large tables, big enough to hold at least one man lying down. Each was then covered by several sheets of dry white linen. The cook delved about in one corner as they were finishing. He brought out a large rolled up leather pouch and unrolled it on the edge of the table in front of him. Glint after glint of sunlight reflecting from polished metal demonstrated to the two boys that the garrison cook was also the garrison surgeon.

"Sam, put a pot of water on the fire. When it's boiled I'll tell you to pass it when I need it. Got that?"

"Yeah," he replied.

"Get a few jugs for it."

Sam picked up one of the buckets and filled a small metal

cauldron with water, which was resting gently on some flaming coals. He searched around quickly and found some wooden jugs. Joe meanwhile had been told to collect some blankets and bandages from elsewhere. No sooner had they all finished and were standing about the tables when there came a steady rumbling towards the main gates. They were flung open in advance of several men on horseback. Many more riders could be seen some way behind them but since they had no room or business inside they simply held their ground. The men that came inside leapt down from their horses which were then led back out. One horse remained however. It had upon it a man with his head dangling down one side and his feet dangling down the other. He was quickly pulled down and placed on the table nearest the surgeon.

"Alright, I've got him," he said, helping the men to place him there.

One of the men spoke after removing his helmet.

"He was hit with an axe whilst on his horse, pretty deep gash. He's been quiet for a good while."

The surgeon sliced away at the man's clothing around the very obvious wound in the side of his body.

"Was he injured anywhere else?" he enquired calmly without looking up.

"Not that we saw," replied another of the men.

"How long ago did it happen?"

"No more than thirty minutes," answered the first, and the others agreed.

The surgeon looked up at both of the boys and nodded to

them. Sam was nearest the cauldron and filled a jug with some of the now warm water. He brought it around the table. The jug was taken neatly from his grasp and quickly poured over the wound. The man on the table did not react but those with a good view of events certainly did. The water cleaned away dirt and dried blood to reveal a horrifying slice through the man's middle, just above his left hip. The layers of fat and muscle beneath his skin at both edges of the wound clearly curled out, in waves of plum red gristle. The skin itself was deeply pale and there seemed little sign of life in the man. The surgeon examined him for only a few more moments before announcing what most others had already deduced.

"He's dead," he said soberly. "He's lost too much blood." To Sam's surprise there wasn't much of a reaction from the men that had brought him in. Some lazily wandered outside once again or went to wash off the blood on them with some of the water he had carried in earlier. He rightly suspected that it wasn't just their own blood or that of the dead man that they cleaned from their hands and faces. The gates were still half open. In came several more men that appeared to be wounded but only in a minor way. One of them hobbled in with his foot clearly bandaged whilst another approached nursing a painful looking shoulder wound.

Behind these men there appeared the commander, striding purposefully towards those still standing around the tables. He pushed the gates open fully and called all those within earshot to come. Those at the tables made way for him. He stood next to the surgeon and looked at the corpse on the table. He suddenly began to berate those around him.

"This is what happens when you think yourselves indestructible! This damn fool deserves what he got! Are you listening to me?" he said, addressing himself directly to the dead man.

He viciously slapped the dead man's face with the back of his hand. He looked at the faces around him to see if any disapproved of this burst of feeling. None did, or if they did they did not reveal it. He continued.

"If I catch any of you doing what he did I'll kill you before the King's men get the chance. Do you understand?" murmurs of approval came instantly. "I'm responsible for you all, we work together and you follow my lead or else we'll all be killed like this fool."

He glanced around, allowing himself a moment to think of more insults. His eye caught Sam and Joe standing nearby though they were clearly trying not to be seen.

"Come here you two. Take a good look."

They approached reluctantly when they saw he was serious. They moved alongside him and within touching distance of the body. He spoke quietly to them.

"Look into his eyes," he said softly. "An hour ago there was a person behind those eyes. With thoughts and ideas, and no doubt many memories and maybe a funny story or two that he could tell you. He'll have a mother worrying about him, maybe even a wife and a family some place, probably not too far from here. What's in there now?" he said pointing. "Nothing. Meat. No better than that which you were cutting up yesterday...and why? Because he didn't do what I told him to do."

With a gentle pat on Sam's back who was closest to him, he ended his little speech. Sam and Joe had indeed not seen such a sight before. They were not as frightened as the commander had hoped however. Nevertheless his message was undeniably clear to them. He turned back towards the pile of people crowding around. He suddenly shouted once more.

"Somebody bury him before he starts to smell!"

This command encouraged everyone to stream out in hopes of avoiding that particular task. It was a sad testament to the man that no friend of his stepped forward to perform it. The surgeon wrapped the uppermost sheet around the man and tied it in several places as the commander withdrew. He beckoned for Joe to help him with the feet as he held the man under his arms. Together they carried the man some ten feet and out of the way. Quickly, those men injured by the day's action jumped one after another onto the tables for the attention of the surgeon. They sat side by side, some leaning on each other for support.

The surgeon held onto Joe's arm as he moved back towards the table and told him he would need his help with cleaning and dressing all the wounds. He looked towards Sam and called him over.

"I have a job for you young man. How are you at peeling potatoes?" he said.

Sam smiled and so did the surgeon.

"You won't be smiling in a minute. There are two sacks over in the corner. Should take you a couple of hours at least. Off you go."

He felt that he had been given the preferable task of the two and set to his duty. He laboured without complaint, despite the pains and strains the peeling action soon began to cause in his hands. After a while he noticed a figure standing over him. It was John.

"Hey, how are you?" he said to Samuel quietly.

"I'm fine, come and sit with me. They won't notice you gone for a few minutes. Here, peel a few of these for me," he replied.

"Alright."

John put down his belongings and settled into a comfortable position next to his companion. He sighed with relief after being hard at work on his feet all day. He grabbed a potato and started to peel. One or two were done before a conversation was started up.

"Did you see all that just now?" asked Sam.

"Not much of it. I've been out and about today. Not up to much," replied John.

"Who were they fighting, do you know?"

"I heard some of what happened from my friend Muresh. He was there you see."

"Who's he?"

"You haven't met him have you? My hobgoblin friend, works on all the horses here. Sometimes rides them too. You'll have seen him definitely, though you probably won't have known his name. Anyway, he was there and he told me that the man, the dead man, was new and a bit of danger. Mostly to himself, as he tells it. Well, they were out patrolling on one of their usual routes it seems. Just the six of them, this one included. I don't know where the commander and the rest of them were. When they encounter a troop of the King's men. Twenty of 'em! Normally they have an understanding see, not to interfere with each other's business. To leave each other alone like. But the man didn't want to leave it alone, did he? He starts goading them a little. Talking about their horses and their mothers and such like. The others tried to get him to stop of course but it was too late by then, wasn't it?"

"What happened?" said Sam.

"I'm telling ya, I'm telling ya! Then, see, some of the King's men start talking back and not in a friendly way neither. As you would expect. Well, then you'd think he'd calm down and think himself outnumbered and to take the shortest way home wouldn't you? No, their words only encourage him to make more of his own! Then he gets out his sword see and challenges any one of them. Right then and there! Well, this didn't go down well at all. Least of all with his companions who wanted no part of it, and aren't permitted of course, even if they wanted to. Besides, it's beyond them at this point as the man was fixed on a fight, and so were some of the King's men. There were fewer on their side who spoke calm words see. Well, the man, with his sword out, turns his horse to approach the nearest of them...and he goes for him, doesn't he? Well, he missed! The one he chose to swing at wasn't wanting a fight and hadn't said nothing to him neither, so he moved back out of the way. Well, when the King's men saw one of theirs having a sword swung at his head and not escaping by much...they went for him."

He paused a moment as some people walked past. They peeled diligently until they had gone and John had had the chance to catch his breath.

"They went for him didn't they? They circled around him. Our men weren't able to do much I guess. So Muresh tells it, I don't know do I? Anyway, a big fella, one of the King's best men, gets off his horse. He had the axe that finished him. The man did his best to protect himself but they were all around him. With a swish and a scream he was down in the dirt. They backed away and left the poor man on the ground covered in blood and moaning terribly he told me. They stepped back and let them come over to pick him up and bring him back, but he'd still have died even if the doctor had been there with them. Then see, the commander and the rest of them suddenly turn up and see what's happened. Well, with their number against them the King's men looked to be in trouble. And they were, for the commander, not knowing what had caused the matter charged at them straight away when he saw his men surrounded and one of them bloodied on the ground. The King's men weren't ready for it you see. He chased most of them away but quite a few got chopped up with just a few cuts and scrapes for our men. On the way back though the commander gets wind of what started the matter.

When he learns the nothingness of it he turns purple and screams that he's started a war over something so pathetic and about it being not proper behaviour for a soldier and all. Anyway, he sends Muresh and the others back with the man, so that's all I know of it."

Samuel had stopped peeling by this point and was staring at John.

"A war?" asked Sam, with a distinctly panicked look on his face.

"Well, I don't know."

"God, we'd better learn to fight pretty quick. Either that or you help us steal some horses."

*

Bird song and a chill right through to his bones were the first things that Gurgle became aware of when he awoke. He decided it was still dark but changed his mind once he realised he could slide back the sack cloth from around his face and see the light. There weren't any sounds to hear beyond the twittering of birds. He looked around carefully as the thoughts of his situation flooded his brain once more. He hands were still tied. Tirgu was not there.

Slowly he wriggled free of the covering in which he was confined. Sneaking towards the flap of the tent and freedom he supposed he began to move. He looked through the small slit of light coming in. Mist. Grey gloom.

He struggled with his bindings but they wouldn't budge

in the slightest degree. He turned his head back around but could see nothing of any use to him in his present state. Outside his control he suddenly began to slide head first out of the tent and into the light.

"Good morning!" said Tirgu enthusiastically.

He looked down at Gurgle who was without expression. Gurgle could see the breath coming out of this hobgoblin's mouth in curling drifts.

"Ready for some work?"

Gurgle did not reply to this but instead begged frantically to be released. Tirgu smiled gently at the idea and after some thought he responded. Kneeling, he untied Gurgle's hands and stood him up, though he was not unaware that Gurgle meant more than simply being freed from his bindings.

"I'll release you the moment you no longer wish to leave. You're going to work for me, and you'll learn a lot. After a while you'll become used to your situation, and believe me, you might even come to rely on it. I know you'll want to escape for a good while yet but I won't allow that. You'll find that all your attempts get you nowhere. Wherever we go I'll know the place better than you, and besides, I can run a lot faster than you."

He looked into Gurgle's eyes for a few more moments.

"You hate me now, I know. You'll soon get used to me. Then you'll realise you can't get away and that you need me to stay alive. In a while you'll accept that you're here to stay. Then you might even start to like the things you'll be doing."

92

Tirgu laughed to himself.

"One day you might even save our lives. What do you think of that?"

"Not likely," came the quiet but defiant response.

He laughed once more. Great puffs of warm white smoke emerged with each chuckle. He stepped quickly inside his tent and came out with something. He brought Gurgle a thick looking cloak which he then placed about his shivering body, clasping it together in the middle of his chest.

"Hey, I haven't asked you your name yet have I?"

Gurgle looked at him and decided to use this sudden little moment of power. He didn't respond.

"Come on, what is it? You can tell your uncle Tirgu now can't you?"

Realising that Gurgle wasn't going to say his name easily Tirgu decided to use some gentle persuasion. He never liked to ask a question and not receive an answer. Putting one hand on his shoulder he stared at Gurgle and took away his smile instantly, allowing a grimace to grow on his face instead. This was more than enough and Gurgle gave up his secret.

"Thank you," his smile returned. "Gurgle, help me pack away the tent. We need to be off. In fact, forget that, just stay there and watch me."

And so he did, standing there in a little cloak as a gang of strangers all about him began to dismantle their tents and pack up their belongings. One or two glances came his way, though no smiles accompanied them, not that he was expecting any. This was quite an alien situation for Gurgle and his previous knowledge of things seemed little use in it. Within his new cloak, behind his back, he gently nursed the worn skin on his wrists with alternate hands. He closed his eyes for a moment and thought of home. He opened his eyes and thought about when he would return there. He knew that he would.

Skilfully, with practiced ease, Tirgu and the others shut down and packed away their tents into their little packages. The few fires that were still alive were extinguished. Food, if it was needed by them, was eaten quickly and whilst other tasks were conducted. One by one they became ready to leave.

"Let's go," said Tirgu calmly and everyone obeyed.

Following his lead, though in fact another member of the group actually walked out in front, Tirgu led his band of men and one goblin through this stretch of forest. Gurgle noticed that the trees were not familiar to him. The species were different from those he knew. This was a very different place indeed. He soon began to notice interesting things about the way these people moved about. They did not walk together but rather walked on their own but in the same direction. They tended to stand apart from each other and when one looked one way his colleague was sure to be looking another way. He also noticed that they said very little to each other. They were careful not to step on twigs or branches, nor were they keen to kick through the piles of leaves as he liked to do. He wisely resisted the temptation of this and instead tried to do as the others did.

He could sense that they were a very serious type of people. He had to confess to himself that they were impressive.

After a while the man in front slowly came to a halt, though not after signalling for the others behind to come to a halt also. Gurgle stopped too. The man in front pointed cautiously in some direction ahead of them and was looking at Tirgu as he did so. Gurgle looked past the point of the man's finger but could see nothing. Tirgu moved slowly up to join the man and after a few seconds of observation and quiet conversation they were all motioned to move forwards, though in a different direction to that in which they were previously going. Tirgu fell back towards the middle of the group once again and put his arm around Gurgle and gently guided him in the new direction with the others. After a couple of minutes he leaned down towards Gurgle and whispered in one of his little green ears.

"A little lesson for you. Unless you've arranged to meet with someone avoid people you don't know."

Gurgle considered this for a while as he nibbled on a piece of bread that another member of the group had handed to him. Thoughts of escape were still in his mind of course but looking about him he knew it was impossible. He would be grabbed within ten feet. If they were all discovered however and forced to defend themselves or flee he might well have a chance. They stopped their observations and continued on.

Gradually he noticed that the thickness of the trees around

them was diminishing. They could all see much farther ahead of themselves and accordingly they moved faster and more freely, though not so much as to abandon their former careful habits.

He had no idea of their destination and it seemed they were unlikely to tell him. It occurred to Gurgle that perhaps even they did not know where they were going. He smiled to himself. A few of them looked quite nervous. Strangely, he did not feel the same way. He felt quite safe for some reason. He wasn't sure why. Whatever or whoever they might meet on the way he had no reason to fear anyone. After a while he started to question this idea a little.

He looked down at himself. He was relieved that he had decided for no particular reason to take his toughest pair of boots with him to the river. He appreciated this decision with every step he took. His blanket was gone though. He knew that this would be some clue as to what had happened to him at least. He wondered just what his family would be doing now to try to find him. With a sickening feeling he suddenly realised that they would think he'd fallen into the river! Oh no! And that he had drowned! They might even be having his funeral right now! What a thought! His whole family would be walking along behind an empty coffin, all of them wearing black, crying and wailing, he hoped. Our little one, swept away by the water, oh lord, oh lord, and not even a body so we can say our proper goodbyes, woe, woe, they would say, probably. Gurgle Sycamore Roundtop, explorer, hero, crime fighter, leaf kicker, porridge eater, rock lifter, snail examiner, taken before his time.

He laughed suddenly, safe, unsurprisingly, in the knowledge that he was not dead. A swift slap found the back of his head. He turned to express his anger and to see who it was. It was Tirgu.

"Concentrate!" he whispered viciously.

Gurgle rubbed his head and his attention was very quickly turned back towards where he was and all that was happening.

"I think we should give you a little test," thought Tirgu out loud, still speaking with a furtive hush.

He looked around carefully and felt confident then that they were all alone. He spoke to his men.

"Fan out, and conceal yourselves," he commanded.

Surprised and uncertain at first perhaps, they obeyed. Tirgu watched them for thirty seconds or so as they moved away. He looked back to Gurgle and suddenly stripped him of his warming cloak. He was back to his lighter clothing. The chilled air found him again.

"Now you should be able to run faster. You're free! At least for a little while. Let's see how far you get. You've a minute before we're after you. Go!" he said, motioning to Gurgle with both his hands.

Gurgle was still a little dazed and knew straight away that there would be no chance that he could get out of their reach. He thought about it a little more. It was foggy. Maybe he could hide somewhere! Perhaps he might find some other people about. Perhaps they could rescue him!

He decided.

He turned and charged off directly away from the group. Tirgu smiled heartily and clapped his hands together with great satisfaction and stood perfectly still, waiting.

Gurgle didn't think about looking behind himself. He searched with frantic eyes through the undergrowth and in the far distance as he ran. He was frustrated by the fact that there seemed only more trees in his way. There was little foliage in which to hide. He looked up hoping to find verdant treetops. He found nothing but bare tree trunks that he could not climb unaided. He charged on, putting as much distance and difficulty in their way as he could. The earth was very hard. In one corner of his eye he spotted a wild carrot or two, which ordinarily he would have stopped to pick. The ground was covered with leaves and quite uneven. It was dangerous to run so fast, as he might easily break an ankle on this terrain. He could not resist the urge to run however. He soon found that he was tripping and stumbling and his hands and elbows were getting dirty. Damn it. A few birds were scattered as he fell once more, flapping loudly as they do.

His desperation rose. He felt useless. He wished he'd had more dignity and refused to run. They would have respected him at least.

He looked up from his crouching position to see a goat looking back at him from about ten paces away. It stared at him with those strange crossed pupils they have. Its lower jaw rubbed casually against its upper counterpart. Beyond it Gurgle could suddenly see a trail of smoke. A chimney! A house! In the forest! He couldn't see anyone about. The goat shook in fright as it looked above Gurgle's head. It darted away from whence it came. Heavy footsteps followed. Gurgle felt a tight grasp upon him. He yelled out as he was lifted up. His cries were quickly stifled by Tirgu's sweaty hand. They were surrounding him. No-one emerged from the door of the house.

Several of the men were angry that they had come so close to an inhabited place. Tirgu merely laughed and told them to calm down and to withdraw quietly. Once they were safely away he whispered in Gurgle's ear.

"That was close. Lucky you didn't get their attention," he paused a moment. "Lucky for them at least."

CHAPTER 4

The smoke from dozens of sickly, smouldering torches drifted around the Hall of Goblins. This building marked the geographical and administrative heart of Milton Greens. The wooden beams within it were first assembled and laid to form the structure three hundred and fifty years ago but the age of the beams themselves could only be speculated upon. Some of the larger beams holding up the main hall had over a thousand rings in them. There was cool red sunshine reaching up and over the clouds. Uniformed workers were extinguishing the torches to mark the transformation of night into day.

Many people were about even though it was still early in the morning. Thump and Screech Roundtop were stood at the head of a queue of goblins. This queue began near the main entrance to the Hall. They had numerous people waiting behind them. Some leaned casually, holding papers and when necessary shifting from foot to foot. Some were dressed in their finest clothes, desperate to maintain their dignity amongst the rabble. Some sneakily tried to edge themselves forward in the queue, coughing as they did so. Gaps were few and temporary or accidental absences were ruthlessly filled by those behind.

Thump and Screech had come to petition the Council to authorise the raising of an army to look for Gurgle and the others and if not that then hopefully a search party of militia at the very least. They had been waiting there since the previous night, narrowly reaching the front ahead of an eccentric old couple who were there to make an official complaint about the lack of tree-lift facilities at the central library.

They had also arranged to meet Lieutenant Chirp Tilestain once again. He would speak on their behalf, and on behalf of all those affected by this terrible assault upon their community. Publicly and officially what had happened was known to all but this was no reason not to go through the proper channels or to approach this matter in a haphazard fashion. The wheels of justice would turn. They had been assured of this. Who would turn them, the speed at which they would turn or the strength needed to turn them was an issue conveniently not mentioned.

The increase in day light brought with it an increase in the noisiness of those in the queue. Soon the petitioners would be granted access to the Hall to make their claims in the order in which they queued. Thump was anxious that the Lieutenant was nowhere to be seen. Thump had not spoken in such a setting before. For Gurgle's sake of course he would speak to the best of his abilities and he would make sure he said all that needed to be said. He knew that these Councillors were not going to feel as passionately about his son as he naturally would and he didn't want to be too demanding or aggressive, if, as he suspected, they would be less than enthusiastic about sending a goblin army out of the forest.

He glanced about as whispers spread through the crowd behind him. The whispers were concerning the Council Leader, who it appeared was the official looking goblin slowly making his way from the official looking sedan chair, carried by four official looking goblins with their official looking uniforms gleaming in the official looking morning sunshine. The Council Leader paused a moment whilst his attendants removed themselves from their chair carrying duties and began their cloak holding duties. They took up his cloak and kept it clear of the dusty ground. Once he was happy that this had been done with sufficient pomp he began to move gently up the slope towards the main entrance. It should be noted that at no point did his worship deign to glance at those arranged below who had put up with all manner of hardship to seek only a moment of his attention.

He slithered inside and a minute or two later a great gong went off somewhere above them. This signified that the Council was now in session. Various officials came down from the entrance and approached the bulging queue. Thump and Screech were rightly identified as the first of the day's petitioners. A velvet rope which had somehow held them all back was unhooked. They were beckoned forward and the rope was quickly hooked behind them. They followed on as instructed and went up the steps to the main entrance. This was a huge wooden archway. Finery was all about it. Inscribed in the main beam buttressing the top of it was the following message for all those who came below.

'From Little Acorns Mighty Societies Grow'

Gloved hands of emotionless persons guided them inside. Shadow swallowed them until their eyes adjusted to the gloom. They felt a distinct chill in the air. This was no surprise. There was no heating inside to speak of. This would cause no complaints as most goblins would regard the huge cost of heating such a public building as a waste of money when visitors could simply wear an extra jumper.

Plush gentle carpeting began to caress their feet. Dirty boots were not permitted in the main hall. They found themselves in a large open arena with a small wooden platform nearby. This it appeared was the place from which persons would make their address to the Councillors. The room was rectangular with the longest sides running parallel to each other on either side of Thump and Screech. The ceiling appeared taller from the inside than from without. It was deep, dark and ornate. It had curved crossbeams which held things up. The crossbeams were covered with carvings that detailed the history of things, but since they were, so to speak, wood on wood the details were hard to resolve from below.

Back on the floor these two humble petitioners were prompted forward and they took their places alongside each other on this small wooden platform. They looked ahead of themselves and saw that the Councillors were not yet fully assembled. The Councillor's seats were elevated some ten feet from the carpet, protected by a heavy wooden barrier. They were to sit together, side by side, each with their name and official title displayed below, and indeed how it was displayed! Below each of them, of those that had so far assembled at least, stood a young but smartly dressed servant. Around each of their necks there hung a wooden panel held with a golden chain. On the panel was written the name and title of the Councillor that sat above.

One more Councillor emerged from somewhere in the back, beyond Thump's sight. As the Councillor slowly stepped to his seat a young servant, chain around his neck, watched him eagerly from below and tried to mirror his movements so as to not get too far ahead or behind. Once satisfied that the Councillor was at the right seat the servant turned his attention away from his master and took his place between two of his colleagues. Once in position and with the correct posture and checking finally that the name around his neck was correct he suddenly stopped moving, as if turned to stone.

Steadily, the remaining few Councillors came out and took their seats. All the seats were filled except one. In fact this one was strictly not like the others, for it was higher and set back and it must be said the loveliest and most comfortable looking chair in all of Milton Greens. It was huge, covered in soft velvets, made of the finest polished walnut and big enough to sleep on. It belonged of course to the Leader of the Council. This time there were two servants who held a large panel between them with his name written on it in gold lettering. It was quite a sight.

'The Most Honourable and Venerable, Croak Hebdo Uniross, Leader of the Council of Milton Greens.'

Screech glanced about. She saw behind herself a wall full of wooden panels. Many hundreds of names were placed in great rows up and down the wall. The panels were exactly like those held around the necks of the servants. It appeared that some measure of immortality was the reward for service to the Council. She was not impressed by this show of grandeur and pomposity, particularly when her son was gone and facing unknown perils whilst it slowly continued.

Arranged about the hall were numerous officials and staff, invariably well dressed. There were one or two other promontories from which certain officials had the duty to stand and address the Councillors. Thump growled to himself under his breath. Where was the Lieutenant!?

Whatever subtle conversation there was in the main hall came instantly to a halt. Everyone stood. For Thump and Screech there were no seats from which to get up. This they suspected was to encourage the petitioners to not become too comfortable whilst making their requests. With great ceremony the Leader of the Council, whom Thump had already nicknamed in his mind as 'Old Croaky', approached his chair. An underling checked that all was well with it and gave it a thorough brushing. Only then did he take his seat. He sat and for the first time he looked at Thump and Screech. He then looked below and to his left. He nodded to someone.

An official standing close to the Councillors, but free to go about, moved forward and onto a little wooden step. He began to address everyone.

"The Council of Milton Greens is hereby welcomed into being once more this day! And none other Council may

speak in its stead! All others are but grass! Be upstanding!"
Everyone was already upstanding, except the Councillors
of course, upon whom there was no duty to stand. A few
moments of silence followed, plus a cough or two, then
everyone sat down again. A paper was handed to the
goblin who had just spoken. He read it and then looked at
Thump and Screech. He looked back at the Councillors
and spoke again.

"My honourable Council, may I give you the first. These
persons here to petition you are Thump Roundtop and his
good lady wife Screech Roundtop. They wish to request
that a force be raised to answer that recent and most
frightful kidnap of eleven goblin souls by person or
persons unknown. Amongst that number they count their
son, one Gurgle Sycamore Roundtop, as missing."

The Leader of the Council suddenly grumbled into life.

"Ah yes, I see, a frightful business indeed," he seemed to be
speaking directly to both of them. "The Council has been
made aware of this matter and it has been in consideration
by us now for some time. Rest assured, when the time is
right the necessary actions will be taken. I thank you for
your patience."

With that and a gentle flourish of his hand towards an
official all eyes turned to the next petitioners who were
waiting feverishly beyond the open door. Several of the
officials moved that way. One moved towards Thump
and Screech and he seemed eager to escort them out.

"Wait a minute!" bellowed Thump suddenly.

All eyes turned to him and then to the Councillors to

106

gauge their reaction to this outburst.

"Sir," began one of the lesser Councillors, "this matter is being given our most urgent consideration. There is nothing more we can say or do on the subject until that is concluded," he looked away, expecting his wise words to do the trick.

"What do you mean!? Our Son is out there in the hands of criminals. He's in danger! The others too. We can't wait another day!" said Screech frantically.

This same Councillor continued, though with increasing irritation.

"We are considering which is the best course to take. We understand your position but we mustn't put our fellow goblins in unnecessary danger through excessive haste, now must we?"

"What are you waiting for? We've got to get out there and start looking for them!" said Thump.

"Please, Sir, try to remember where you are. There is no call for agitation. When we have the full report we will make a decision."

"Report? What report? I'll tell you whatever you need to know!" said Thump, causing a few winces.

"The full report of this incident! Of what took place by the river! We have not received it yet," he replied angrily.

At this point the Councillor saw that a hand had been raised by a colleague of his. It was a gesture for this more senior Councillor to interject. This new and more approachable sort of person took over the conversation. He spoke in a friendly and comforting fashion, bordering on condescension.

"Now, my dear Sir and Lady, I want you to know that we are doing everything we can to find your son, and the others. We await merely the full facts of what occurred so that we can see the best way towards retrieving them. Sending our troops out into the world prematurely might lead to troubles that could put the whole forest in greater peril than your son is in. I know this is hard to accept but until we know all the facts we cannot throw our best and bravest to the wind."

"But Sirs" said Thump, "it's been three days of torture for us and for the other families I'm sure. Three days and nights. Not to mention what our little Gurgle is facing...in with all those hostile hands. What are we to do? Can we not go as a search party ourselves, taking whoever is willing and able to go?"

"But where would you go...except into danger yourselves? We would be out searching for you as well! There's constant danger beyond the safety of the forest and we must venture there only with the utmost precaution. What you ask is perfectly understandable but it would be foolhardy of us to allow it. I am very sorry."

Upon hearing this Screech laid her head against her husband and started to cry. Thump responded by comforting her but he did not lose his composure in the same fashion. Her crying was of such a shrill and blubbery nature that it caused much discomfort amongst the Councillors and officials. Many turned their heads and pretended not to notice, hoping that someone would escort them out as quickly as possible.

Noises started at the door. Thump turned to see what he thought were more petitioners trying to push their way in. He was prepared to shout at them for their selfishness and insensitivity. But instead, to his great surprise, he saw that the Lieutenant was trying to push his way inside. The old couple who were concerned about the lack of tree-lift facilities at their local library were not making it easy for him. From their point of view he was a pusher-inner, as brazen as they come! Fortunately, they were no match for him and he swiftly got past them.

The Lieutenant looked forward at the Councillors, arranged against him at the end of the hall. He stopped a moment and seemed to pay his respects with a nod towards them. He looked around for the appropriate person to speak to or the correct place to stand. It seemed he was eager to address the Council. He spoke to the nearest official to him. They had a short conversation whilst the rest of the hall remained silent, waiting to find out who this person was. Whilst the Lieutenant was talking he glanced to his side and saw Thump and Screech standing together. He nodded and smiled. The official directed the Lieutenant to another little platform that had not been used until that point. He stepped onto it.

"Honourable Council. I am Lieutenant Chirp Rideau Tilestain of the 11th Milton Greens Militia. I wish to address you in regard to the matter of the recent kidnap of eleven goblins and to make my official report."

After some grumbling amongst themselves, from which

Old Croaky remained aloof, the Councillors agreed to hear the matter now and they requested for the Lieutenant to continue.

"Thank you. Shortly after dawn on the morning of the fifteenth of this month, some three days ago, I received an urgent communication from a member of the public. This was to the effect that there had been a serious incident of some kind on a stretch of the river which fell within my area of responsibility. I had little information beyond this at that time except that we had been told that several persons were believed to have been kidnapped by boat. I immediately made my way to the area mentioned with all my colleagues that were on duty at that time of the morning. There were seven of us...and I was the first officer at the scene."

He paused for a moment to catch his breath and to consider his notes a little further. This allowed time for a question to be asked by one of the Councillors.

"And who was this member of the public? One of these two persons petitioning us?" he enquired.

"No Sir. That part of the forest was much alarmed by what had happened and many persons were about looking for help. It was one of those persons that raised the alarm."

"Ah, I see. Thank you Lieutenant, please continue."

"Yes Sir. Well, as I said, I was the first officer on the scene. We were at the slight bend in the river, between marker posts ninety one and ninety three. Once there we found many persons wandering about on the eastern side of the river, where there's most habitation. Some were frantic, others, just sitting quietly. One or two had injuries."

"Was it one or two? And how many altogether? Be exact now!" barked a different Councillor.

"Sorry Sir. Two persons were injured, to my knowledge." He continued once he felt settled.

"There was great alarm amongst the people. I counted some twenty four persons that were in the vicinity and a further two that came shortly after. They were the two petitioners here today Sirs," he gestured towards Thump and Screech then continued once more. "I did my best to calm people down so as to get a clear answer from them on what'd happened and at the same time I instructed my troop to search the area for any clues as to who'd been there. Well, I began to question the people thereabouts, though some indeed began to question me. Saying such things as why had we not been there to protect them and the like. They were very upset and it came as no surprise when they reported to me what had taken place. Over the next thirty minutes several people informed me of many things, which, when the similar parts were taken together revealed the following. Namely, that during the previous night, sometime between midnight and one o'clock in the morning, a force of human men, numbering not less than six...and one hobgoblin, had with stealth come down the river by boat from the north. At some point they had disembarked for a period, and then had, I regret to say, stolen by force some eleven goblins from their homes and nearby places. These men it seems did not travel far from their boat shown by the fact that only persons living nearby or travelling through the area were affected…and I might add they used great speed and brutality in their activities."

"And," a further Councillor gently interrupted, "…the individuals who were taken. You have their names and all the relevant particulars?"

"I do, Sir. I'll provide these after if I may," replied the Lieutenant.

"Of course you may. Are we to conclude then, err, that some outside group has stolen these people? Why would they do this?"

"So far, I can say with certainty that none of the missing persons has returned, nor has there been a single sighting of any of them. It does indeed appear that these people were stolen, though for what purpose I cannot say at this time. My more unhappy instincts can only suggest that they were taken to be put to enforced labour of some kind. I also suspect that they will have been separated from each other and will have little idea of which way to travel to get back to the forest."

"Let *us* establish the facts Lieutenant, that is our business. After that *we* may speculate about why this occurred," said one of the grumpier Councillors.

"Tell us a little more about the missing people, and how came a child into this matter? Did they really come here to steal children?" asked another Councillor.

"Well Sir, it seems to be an accident that this one missing child, Gurgle Roundtop, the child of the petitioners, came to be involved," replied the Lieutenant.

"He was not taken from his home then?"

"Oh no, Sir!" yelled Thump and Screech together.

"Then how did he end up by the river in the middle of the night?" came the short tempered response, directed at the parents.

"Gurgle has a little habit of sneaking off," ventured Screech. "He's a good boy, he is. He's a lonely sort though, not many friends. He likes to go down to the river some times and other places too."

"Yes, thank you, thank you. Lieutenant, please go on."

"Yes Sir. It appears that this boy happened to be in the area at the time and was taken off with the others. We know this as his blanket was discovered at the scene. An unhappy accident as I said."

"Most unhappy, most unhappy," said the Leader of the Council suddenly but very sagely, "though, how can we be sure, much as it pains me to suggest, that this child did not fall into the river or simply go to some other place as yet unknown?"

"I suppose we cannot be sure that he did not, Sir. Nevertheless, some were indeed taken away by force and this child was definitely there at the time and now is missing like the others. It stands to reason that he has been taken too."

"You are right I am sure," continued Croak. "Now, tell us what you know of the people that did this terrible thing."

"I'm afraid there is not too much to tell. We know from eye witnesses that at least six adult human men were in the

113

boat along with one hobgoblin. Quite possibly more were on board...and who knows what other people outside the forest may also be involved."

"But who are they and where are they now?" said yet another Councillor.

"The answer to both your questions can only be speculated upon. There have been a few suggestions, from sources independent of each other I should say, that point to a certain group of men with a hobgoblin as their leader being those responsible. They are in service to a man Lord called Spikepoint. Whoever these men were and whoever they were attached to, if attached to anyone at all, I suspect that they were acting on their own initiative just to make money for themselves."

"What do you know of these men and this hobgoblin?" said this same earnest Councillor.

"I know nothing but I've heard some things. I've heard that they and their man Lord are serious, well organised warriors and should not be insulted...or underestimated."

"Where do you think our people are likely to be now?"

"I can only suggest that they will be spread about in various camps, towns or villages, or on their way between such places. Amongst human people I would say and not the best and friendliest sort I'm sure."

"What do you think would be the best way to get them back?"

"Well, that's the question isn't it Sir? It won't be easy since they are all likely to be separated. I don't believe a proper army would be able to achieve very much. We should try to cause as little attention to be drawn to ourselves as possible. Too much and we would harm our cause and put fright into those that we are seeking to trace. With a small, secret troop we can find out where they are and when it's needed we can use strength in numbers to release them and punish those who have them."

"I see, so you're recommending a quiet approach?"

"I am Sir."

"And how many troopers do you think would be necessary for such an adventure?"

"I would think that, on and off as needed, one hundred would be necessary."

"I see, thank you very much for your report Lieutenant. You've been most helpful," said the Council Leader. "I think that we have heard enough on this matter for the moment. We will consider it further and make our decision in the usual way."

"When will that be?" interrupted Thump, who had been anxious to speak for several minutes.

"That will be at the end of the Council's business tomorrow!" he responded angrily. "Next!" he bellowed, looking towards the door.

The next petitioners were at this point finally admitted entrance. They quickly approached the platform where Thump and Screech were still stood. This old couple had an expectant look on their faces. They clearly had been in this place before. They swapped positions with Thump and Screech who started to walk out. The Lieutenant approached as they were leaving and patted Thump on the back.

"That wasn't too bad. They seemed friendlier than usual!" said the Lieutenant positively.

"If you'd arrived a moment later they'd have thrown us out with nothing!" said Screech.

"Yes, I'm sorry about that. I was on other duties, as they say."

"When will they make a decision?" asked Thump.

"They'll hear all the petitioners first, which they'll get through today most probably. Then tonight and tomorrow they'll make decisions on all the applications. You being first this morning they'll consider that first...and besides it's the most important anyway. Tomorrow sometime they'll put up notices outside with a list of the petitions and the decisions made. Should be tomorrow as he said."

"I was thinking more on what you suggested down by the river," said Thump.

"Oh?" he replied.

"I want to be involved. Where should I go?"

"Hold on a minute there," he said laughing. "Assuming they authorise anyone to go they'll almost certainly want only regular troops. I couldn't get you in, even if I wanted to."

"But you said..."

"I know what I said. I don't make the decisions though do I? And I'm not so sure it would be such a good idea to be honest. Forget I said anything."

"Hang on, I have to get involved, I have to go!" he

116

responded angrily.

The Lieutenant looked directly into Thump's eyes for a moment and smiled.

"If fate wants you to get involved she'll make it happen. I won't."

He then stepped away quickly and left them together. They were back in the sunshine once more. Screech grabbed his arm and addressed him angrily.

"What's this you're talking about? You think you're going out of the forest and leaving the rest of your family to it are you? Thinking of going off on an adventure? Not likely, not bloody likely Thump Roundtop."

"Calm down woman, I've got to do something haven't I?"

"You're no soldier. What'll you do, hit 'em with your mulching spoons?"

"Behave yourself, we're in public."

They walked together down the slope at the entrance of the Hall of Goblins without saying another word to each other. They were both naturally upset and very anxious for the outcome the next day. Their home was not a full one so their minds could not be at rest until it was put right. They returned home and had yet another difficult night with barely any sleep.

The following day they returned to the same place and found that the Council had been unexpectedly efficient overnight. Several public notices were displayed with more well-dressed attendants on either side of each large sheet. With anxious eyes and nervous stomachs they looked at the top of the first page. There were their names!

And details of the petition! And the decision! Where was it! Screech noticed it was on another sheet. She read it out to Thump, whilst he held her arm for their mutual support.

"The Council of Milton Greens...hereby authorises and requires the...formation of a troop of able bodied...and motivated soldiers...of at least one hundred in number to assemble together and make ready...to retrieve those goblin souls so infamously taken from us by...outside forces. All those with soldiering experience, and who are willing to risk their safety and liberty for such a duty...are requested to appear and make themselves known to the Council...in the great field...one week from this day."

Thank God, they said to each other. Screech grabbed his hand and stepped away with him. One week though! What would they do in the meantime! Find a way to join up thought Thump to himself. He scratched at his beard. His aging limbs were not as confident as his mind was.

It was bad news on the tree-lift however.

*

Sometime in the late morning of their fourth day at the garrison Sam, Joe and John were introduced to a new activity. This promised them a great deal of excitement but in the long term considerable danger. The day had started slowly in stark contrast to the previous two days of anxiety and talk of war, which had come about as a result of the foolishness of their colleague whom they last saw near cut in two on the surgeon's table. Many had come and gone in the last two days, some to strengthen an outpost here or a patrol there. There were many new faces but almost as soon as someone new had arrived they were off again to parts unknown. Such was the way of things.

The three of them had settled in as well as could be expected. John in particular seemed most content with his new position, one that he was intent on solidifying and calling his own. Sam and Joe were more suitable for and therefore more likely to fall into the main occupation of soldiering. In any case the situation about them being as it was made it almost a certainty.

As far as today was concerned and this new activity in particular all three would be expected to participate. They were all dressed in light clothing and stood together in front of a long table covered by a white cloth. There were numerous objects beneath the cloth, but what they were was being kept secret. Behind them and spread out generally inside the garrison were most of the soldiers and their commander amongst them. Their general attitude was good natured and they were friendly towards the three but if they felt it necessary they could suddenly demand strict obedience.

The commander approached the table and whisked off the cloth to reveal an array of shiny new weaponry. From left to right there was arranged a wooden sword, a dagger, a small metal sword, a broadsword, a wooden axe, a one handed axe and then a very frightening looking double handed axe. None of them appeared to have been used before except for the two wooden weapons, which had numerous stains and cuts in them. The commander was smiling at them but there was devilish intent behind the smile.

"One of you, I don't care who, pick up a weapon, any of them you like," he said.

The three looked at each other for a moment seeing if anyone wanted to take the lead. John was the most reluctant and was more than ready to allow one of his fellows to pick ahead of him. Joe was in the middle and just decided to grab at one of the weapons, a moment ahead of Sam who had had the same impulse. Joe picked up the wooden axe. It felt light and handy.

"Very good. Now step back from the others into the middle here." He motioned for Joe to move into the space that had opened up behind them. "You two, same again please."

Sam and John moved closer together and smiled at each other. Again John allowed another to go ahead of him. Sam looked carefully at the weapons and soon picked out the small metal sword. Without needing to be prompted he turned and moved into the open space behind them. This left John to consider what weapon to take. He looked anxiously down at the table in front of him. His right hand moved towards the dagger since it seemed discreet and the easiest to handle. He eventually picked it up after touching it a little to gauge its weight. He turned around and tentatively moved forward to stand with the others.

"Thank you gentlemen. Just stay where you are for the moment. Now, what can we tell about them from this little exercise?" his question being directed to the soldiers standing all around.

They didn't respond much at first. The commander prompted them a little. Their voices were generally quiet but he heard them and announced each suggestion as they came to him from all around.

"What do we think about the first one? What? He picked the *wooden* axe because...because he doesn't want to harm anyone? Maybe. Why would he pick first then? Anybody? Because he wants to get it over with?"

There was a mild eruption of laughter.

"No, no, I don't think so. Any other ideas? Because what? Because he's not confident with the real thing? Yes, I think that's much closer to the truth. But why the wooden axe and not the wooden sword? Trickier question this time isn't it? Because it was closer? Well, maybe, maybe. Someone suggest something else! Because...it felt the more natural of the two? Yes, I'd agree with that. But why? Come on, use your brains for once...no one?"

After a pause.

"Alright...well what about Sam with the short sword? Why do we think he picked that up? Because...he's used one before? Quite possibly. Something a bit more imaginative please. Because? Because he wants to learn the basics first. Hmmm, not sure what you mean by that. Something else? Anyone? No? Well, I think it's because he wants to be a regular soldier. He wants the simplest weapon, nothing too complicated or too heavy. He wants to do things the simple way, I think. He picked second because he's too sensible to go first and rush into things and he didn't wait till last because for all his caution he doesn't want to appear indecisive or weak. He wants to take part obviously. Am I right?" he said, directing his last question at Sam.

Sam felt that his commander had read far too much into his choice but he sensibly nodded back to him all the same. He was right about his good sense at least. The commander continued, excited by his shrewdness and the sound of his own voice.

"Good, good...and what of poor little John, taking his choice last. What do we all think of that? Come on...he...he's what? Far too nervous of fighting? Yes, that seems likely. But what about his interesting choice of the dagger? What? He wants to what? To stab me in the back and run away?"

At this the commander laughed as well as the others.

"Yes, maybe, I hadn't thought of that. Alright, settle down, something sensible please. Because...it was the smallest on offer? Maybe, but give me something more interesting. Because...come on...because he wants to kill people from...from where? Behind...rather than face to face? Ah, now that is interesting! What do you think of that John?"

John shrunk at the suggestion and hated all the sudden attention drawn to him. Unexpectedly, most of all to him, his courage and imagination somehow found each other and he shouted something out.

"Who said that? I'll stab him where he sleeps!"

This was much appreciated by all, even by the person to whom it was directed and John was deeply relieved to hear laughter as a reward for his risky outburst. These festivities were quickly ended by the commander who barked for quiet and directed the three of them to put down their weapons on the table. He suddenly shouted out to one of his men without moving his eyes.

"Beatty!"

From the crowd emerged an average looking soldier, neither large nor small, though slightly older than the rest. He had dark brown hair which was wild and unkempt, though not particularly long. He had no hair on his face. Sam had noticed him before a few times but the other two did not recognise him. He displayed no emotion and seemed to know what was wanted of him. He stepped forward and stood next to the commander who then withdrew. So now, the three of them were facing this one man. The commander spoke once more.

"Alright you three, we've misled you a little as you won't be using any weapons today. The first and most important thing you'll learn is how to fight without weapons because they're rarely laid out for you so conveniently as today, though you're welcome to grab the wooden ones if you think it'll help! Where's the bag? Beatty, have you got it?"

"No I don't," Beatty replied.

From somewhere in the back the commander was handed

a small cloth sack that seemed to contain a few bulky items. He stepped forward again and spoke once more whilst lifting the sack aloft.

"Gentlemen, you all remember this I'm sure! Let's see what's inside shall we?" he said excitedly.

He picked out the first item and announced what it was for the benefit of Sam, Joe and John.

"Some...no, wait. A chunk of...salted beef!" which he sniffed, lifted and waived about. "Very nice! A piece...a *large* piece, of cheese. Hope this doesn't get squashed! And three apples! Hey, one for each of you! Pretty good overall I think. You're a lot more generous than last time boys. Well done."

The commander approached Beatty and tied the bag tightly with some narrow rope and made a loop, then placed the loop over the man's head allowing it to hang behind him. Beatty made it comfortable with one or two adjustments. With a slap on Beatty's shoulder the commander turned and looked at the three of them stood just ten feet away. They were unsure of what was happening but once the bag was tied around the man's neck it quickly dawned on them what they would be expected to do.

"Alright you three. If you can get the bag what's inside is yours. You can go it alone if you wish and if you get the bag it's yours alone. I'd recommend you work together and share the contents, assuming you get anywhere near them. Beatty, how many times have you lost the bag?"

"Never," he replied ominously.

"Come on, you know that's not true. Once I think, though it was probably torn open and you disputed it," said the commander.

He directed his attention back to the three youngsters. He asked them if they were ready and if they knew what to do. They reluctantly nodded then looked anxiously at each other. Beatty became hunched and ready and beckoned them to come and get their prize if they could. The commander stepped back into the crowd at which point a great roar of excitement shot upwards. The three of them were in the majority in this little arena but seemed a hopeless bunch compared to the man facing them. Their training began now it seemed, though not as any of them had anticipated. Beatty did not approach them as it was their responsibility to approach him. He stood waiting. After a few seconds in which they moved hardly at all the noises of the crowd started to grow a little hostile. They wanted a show but weren't getting one.

Sam looked to Joe to help him. They didn't say anything to each other but both smiled and seemed to understand what the other was thinking. The two of them separated and gently edged towards Beatty but neither made any sudden movements. Beatty constantly grimaced and growled at them and dared them to attack. Without any real coordination Sam and Joe suddenly lunged at him, one at each arm or thereabouts. They both managed to get a firm grip around his arms and for a moment or two it seemed that they had Beatty under control. Joe yelled at John to come and grab the bag while they held him. John

125

saw the sense in it but was too slow in coming forward. By the time he was near to them Beatty had bettered Sam and freed his arm. He grabbed the poor boy's neck and lifted him almost from the ground. He swung him around and threw him into Joe who had so far done well in restraining Beatty's other arm. Joe was forced to let go by the weight of Sam crashing into him. They both fell tumbling onto the ground and once in the dirt heard a huge yelp of satisfaction from the crowd.

John meanwhile was stood still in the middle of the open space. He did not feel as bold as he did when making his little joke. He wanted the bag however, and by getting it earning the appreciation of everyone there. He favoured a sneak attack when no one would expect it. He knew he would fail in a direct battle of strength so he kept his distance while the other two got to their feet. Sam and Joe were both angry now though Sam was better able to control it. As soon as Joe got to his feet he surged straight at Beatty who had correctly predicted whom his next attacker would be. He easily grabbed Joe and tossed him off his feet once again. He landed hard and was winded for a moment. He cursed himself with what little breath remained.

Sam tried to distract Beatty by circling around him, for he knew that he could not observe the three of them simultaneously if they moved around far enough. Beatty was aware of this but was not worried. He carefully arranged himself between the three of them so that he was constantly moving and giving none of them a sustained chance of grabbing the bag. He generally kept his back towards John, whom he thought with some justification to be the weakest of the three. Joe dusted himself down as he readied himself for another move. This time he would definitely work with the others. He held his hand on his right leg and looked at Sam to try to signal that that was what he would go for. Sam saw the nod but wasn't sure if the signal was that he should go for that leg or that Joe would. The way Joe shifted himself suggested that Sam should go for the other leg. Sam nodded back and instantly ran for Beatty's right leg, grabbing it with such speed and with so much force that Beatty yelped in pain despite doing his best to deflect Sam. The crowd showed their appreciation and shouted all the more, some for Beatty to punish him, some for the brave young Sam to succeed.

Joe followed his lead and went for the other leg, taking a firm hold after a brief struggle. Beatty punished them both for their boldness, belting them mercilessly with his fists and arms. But he was not free from them and he felt himself being turned over. He was in the dirt but struggling viciously. Sam yelled to John to help them. He didn't move. The shouts from the crowd increased. They could see the bag was vulnerable but neither Joe nor Sam could release their grip or do anything constructive whilst such blows rained down on them. They struggled on the ground in a pile. Beatty was about to get the upper hand. There were only seconds left for John to do something. He did something.

Rather theatrically John charged over the pile grabbing the exposed bag as he went. He held it as he jumped over them but his grip was destroyed as it pulled taught around his neck. It could not be removed so easily as that. The skin on his hands stung sharply from his failed contact. He tried again but did not jump over. Instead he leaned as far as his balance would allow, being a little too cautious not to step on anyone beneath him. He touched the bag again but Beatty was aware of him this time and wriggled away. Joe was thrown off, and Sam, despite his fiercest efforts, was also bested. He received a painful boot in the back as he was forcibly rolled over and kicked away. Beatty stood up and away from them. He was tired and ruffled but not nearly as much as his attackers. He had deep red marks around his neck caused mostly by the rope rather than the rough grips of the others. His hair was completely messed up however and his cheeks were flushed and scratched. Both Sam and Joe nursed painful limbs and grazed skin. Both had dust in their throats. After just a couple of minutes they were panting heavily. John was untouched apart from his sore hands.

"Come on! You can do better than that!" shouted the commander above the tumult. "Go get him!"

At this point it was not looking like they would succeed in getting the bag but not one of them was prepared to think the contest at an end. In his frustration Joe walked straight to the table past Beatty who stepped back as he felt Joe was going for him once again. At the table Joe looked quickly about and grabbed the wooden axe that he had picked before. He turned it around so that the head of the axe faced away from whom he might swing it at. He thought to use it as a club. A big cheer rose up from the crowd at this unexpected act. Joe stood for a few seconds, almost foaming at the mouth from breathlessness. He ventured to step closer towards Beatty, not sure what to do with his new weapon. For his part Beatty was not too concerned. He'd had many an encounter like this before with new recruits, though rarely three at a time. His skin and body had been toughened through many an arduous encounter. Nevertheless, this challenge to him would be met with a little more than he had so far given in retaliation. He spat aggressively on the ground.

Beatty altered his stance a little. He was ready to run at Joe, who was still edging slowly towards him. Sam could see the danger Joe was in and decided to run at Beatty just at that moment. This put him onto the back foot and he was forced to put both his arms around Sam as he was dived into. Sam growled as he tried with all his strength to push Beatty off his feet. It wasn't working and he could feel powerful hands reach down and grab him under both arms. He began to feel his feet loosening off the ground but just as he could sense he was about to be thrown one of the hands that held him suddenly stopped holding him. Sam was almost on his knees and was looking down at the ground but he now felt able to shake himself free. He could hear Beatty struggling with someone else. Sam fell to the ground and turned his body around to break free. He looked up to see Joe trying to hit Beatty with his club but it was instantly batted away. Now, Joe had lost his weapon and his composure. His wrists were gripped tightly by Beatty who then twisted them viciously, forcing the rest of Joe with them until he was on the ground and screaming for his arms to be released, which Beatty had little inclination to do. Sam stood up and jumped on Beatty in an attempt to release his friend. In the heat of all this Sam noticed that his feelings of support and protection for his fellows grew with every moment they were in pain.

Neither of them had much success in getting the better of Beatty. John meanwhile was stood off from the rest wondering when would be the best time to mount a sneak attack. If he was to impress the others he'd better do this impressive thing soon, whatever it was. The commander was going to stop things if they could get no further. The rest of them were still struggling desperately together. Once again it seemed that an opportunity for John was presenting itself. Joe was on the ground and held uncomfortably. Sam was around Beatty's neck but was doing little beyond that. Beatty himself was distracted but was slowly getting the better of his two assailants yet again. Before this could happen John had something of a brainwave. He rushed to the table and grabbed the dagger whilst the crowd held its breath wondering at the meaning of it. Stepping up behind this lump of people he reached at what he thought was the weakest part of the knot holding the bag around Beatty's neck. As quickly and as carefully as he could he sliced through the rope and to his great surprise it cut cleanly. He grabbed at the bag and it came loose. He had stolen it!

John stepped away from the others just as the crowd roared its approval. The commander stepped in to release the others from their conflict. Joe lay on the ground in some pain and Sam staggered away. Beatty was gently patted on the back by the commander. He stretched his body and regained his composure. He had a little blood trickling from his nose. The commander quietened the crowd by gesturing with his arms so that he could speak to everyone.

"Well done John, well done!" he said warmly. "You have the bag and I think it's yours alone. Anyone disagree?"

The crowd and the combatants remained silent. He continued.

"Good. But what about the other two John? They seem to have fought much harder than you. Don't you think you should share with them?"

"No, Sir," came the reply from John, surprising everyone. Sam and Joe were too tired to say anything.

"No?" said the commander, genuinely shocked. "Is that how things are John? Will you really keep everything for yourself...when they made all the effort?"

"I'm just following your rules Sir. If I could grab it, it's mine."

"You should be careful you know. I might put the bag around your neck and let your two friends fight over you," said the commander menacingly.

"I think you won't...Sir," he replied, with surprising

tenacity.

Surprised at this response the commander thought about just such an idea for a few moments. But John was right, that would not be fair considering what he had told them to begin with. He said nothing further on the point.

"Alright everyone! Get back to whatever you were doing!" he shouted. "Sam, Joe, come here. I'm sorry about that you two. You both did well and it's a surprise to me you've nothing to show for it," he said, turning to John who was within earshot. "Go and clean yourselves up. Get something to eat. Tell the cook that I said to fetch you something good. Tomorrow we'll try a little with the weaponry. I think I know someone you'll enjoy practising on! Off you go."

The commander watched as Sam and Joe moved slowly and painfully away. He turned his attention to John who had moved not at all from the spot where he had held up the bag for all to see. John watched him as he approached. He was not sure that he had made the right decision. The commander put his arm around him and began to talk quietly with him away from the attentions of everyone else.

"Very foolish of you. I can't believe you'd be so selfish and in front of everyone too. Why'd you do it John?"

"I didn't intend to deprive anyone. I just wanted what was mine, since I got the bag."

"Yes but you only got it because Beatty was occupied dealing with your friends."

"They were doing their thing, I was doing mine."

"But don't you think they would have offered to share with you if they had got it?"

"I have no idea," said John dispassionately.

"Well, in one way I admire you for standing up to me and having the courage to run off with the spoils, but you've no friends left now my boy, no friends at all. Will they run to help you if you're in trouble out there somewhere? I doubt it very much, don't you? I think you should go and see the other two and split up the food between yourselves. If you're wise that is? Go on. I've got other things to be doing."

The commander stepped away and left John standing on his own. He could see Sam and Joe sat together some distance away. By now everyone was back to their business. John felt very isolated and resolved to share his bag of things with the others. He went over and stood in front of them to gauge their reaction to him. They both looked sore in body and in mind.

"Now I know why you picked the dagger," joked Joe.

"Do either of you have a knife?" asked John.

"Why?" replied Sam.

"Because I'll need some help cutting up this juicy meat," he said, smiling warmly as he spoke.

John reached into his bag and pulled out the beef. He motioned that he wanted to sit down next to them. After a few moments Sam moved to make some space for him and they all ate together.

*

Dusk was falling upon the tops of the trees. Gurgle was not welcoming another night of this. He found that despite the natural progression of night and day it was hard for him to keep track of the passage of time. He slept poorly as you might expect in uncomfortable and alien surroundings and amongst hostile strangers, though as things continued he found little hostility was directed towards him. The hostility it seemed was all on his part. The men in the group were generally indifferent to him, concerning themselves with their own business. He watched their activities very closely. They tended to be silent unless prompted. They did not laugh too much or chat idly with each other. They were content in their own company since when they were together they were still apart.

There wasn't much to say about their appearance - quiet, dark, functional clothing. Their features were sunken and dirty, even when they emerged from a river after washing. They carried so many of their things in a multitude of small pockets. One of them had a leg pocket in which there was a little practical knife. He could always be seen cutting or whittling on something useful. Others held in their chest pockets little pieces of food that they periodically lifted and bit upon. They were all lean. None had any fears of the forest and sat and stepped wherever they chose, though to be honest, Gurgle could not say that he was in a forest anymore. They had travelled so far now that his limbs ached in ways and places that he didn't know they could. He felt always tired and generally hungry. He felt his passion for escape slipping into the background. That required sustenance as much as he did and without it faded quickly.

He was sat against the stump of a small tree. He ate upon some stale bread. From where it had come he didn't know, one of the others, and he hadn't looked at who'd handed it to him through the gloom. As he chewed at the hardened crust he laughed to himself thinking that it'd been baked in its oven before he'd been baked in his mother. His saliva gradually soaked inside and softened it.

The darkness of the evening grew and it seemed to Gurgle that once or twice he could see bats flying not far above him. He remembered an old proverb, or tale, or something about bats that a friend of the family had once told him. He couldn't remember who it was but he remembered the saying well. Never try to follow a bat because...how did it go he thought to himself...because bats always fly in circles, that was it. He laughed to himself once more. He wondered for a moment if bats were poisonous.

They were all encamped on gently sloping ground at the edge of a wood. The tree stump against which he was leaning was in the centre of a clearing and was surrounded by the tents of the men. A warm and generous fire crackled and spat nearby. Up above and behind them Gurgle could see the shadows between the trees in the wood. Below them open grassland stretched for miles. It seemed the others were more relaxed than they'd been in the previous few days. None of them were patrolling the camp in its defence as before. They were generally sat around the fire and eating as he was. This, suspected Gurgle, meant that they were in safe territory and not far from their homes.

Sometimes, when Gurgle looked around himself he felt that he was not really there and that he was dreaming somehow. He knew that he wasn't but something about what was happening just couldn't seem real to him no matter how real he knew it to be. Even though these people had taken him and used violence in doing it now that he was here he wanted contact and conversation with them and an understanding of why it had happened. He'd felt in the first few hours that he would deny and resent them the merest word from his lips. He would refuse to do even the smallest thing for them, even at the cost of his own life if need be. He would be like a stone. How dare they do this to him and all of them? He wondered where the others were. But now he felt simply that he needed to talk and be with people once more, even these people. He looked at them, trying to catch someone's eye so they would pay him just a little attention. It didn't work. Nobody noticed him.

Slowly, he thought and considered his situation a little more. He didn't know where he was. He didn't know the country he was in or what the people in it were likely to think of him. He wasn't going to be set free anytime soon nor would he have any real chance of escape and he had an unknown destination ahead of him. What was he to do? It was at this point that the inevitable thoughts of cooperation began to enter his head. His imagination suggested all kinds of sweet possibilities to make the idea palatable to his conscience. Perhaps some of these men were taken against their will and grew accustomed to it. Perhaps Tirgu himself was once as he was. Perhaps this is just what happened to people sometimes and that it needn't be so terrible. They weren't going to eat him! They didn't beat him or sell him or make him do things that put him in any danger. No, it was true they did not. But still, he was hungry, uncomfortable and most upsetting of all he was their prisoner. Nevertheless, he had no choice. He had to make the best of things. That also seemed to him to be a goblin proverb of some kind but not one that he could place in his memory. He looked around again. They were all fairly quiet and the night was drawing in.

Soft footsteps came from behind him. Tirgu and one of his men had returned from the wood. They had with them what looked like handfuls of wild vegetables and some mushrooms, no doubt recently picked. The man picked up a small metal cauldron and placed it onto the edge of the fire. He filled it with water then sat down next to it. Until the water inside began to boil he kept peering over the rim to see how things were going inside. With one of his little knives he trimmed and sliced the vegetables and mushrooms and threw each piece into the water. Apparently he felt there was no reason not to cough over everything that he was doing.

Tirgu came around Gurgle and sat opposite from him but also near the fire. Gurgle expected him to say something to him but he did not. He glanced quickly at Gurgle but that was all. Tirgu was silhouetted by the fire light against the dark blue background of the evening and Gurgle observed him properly for perhaps the first time. He was sat quietly and seemed quite tired. He stared, mesmerised, into the fire. Looking at him now Gurgle thought him to be not as old as his father but not too far short. This was something that he could not be sure about however since he knew that goblins and hobgoblins and men aged at different rates. Someone once told him that some of the very oldest men can be nearly twice the age of the oldest goblins.

Tirgu had one small scar on the front of his neck. He couldn't think what had caused it because it had such a strange curve to it. What little hair he had on his head was short and bristly. His ears were longer and more pointed than his own but they were not as large. The skin on them was light brown as opposed to Gurgle's own dark green colour. His skin looked sweaty and dirty and was the same colour as his ears. His eyes were sunken but this did not diminish from what Gurgle felt was his very deep and penetrating gaze. Up close his eyes looked right into you as though he was studying the inside of your skull.

Tirgu coughed gently and scratched at the top of his chest which was exposed to the cool air. He did not look up at Gurgle whose eyes were ready to look away in an instant if he did. Gurgle continued to study him discreetly. He was wearing his usual leather waistcoat under which was his usual grimy dark shirt. He could see the curvature of his arms and body. He was lean and fit, though in some respects worn out by use. Nevertheless, wisely and not even for a second did Gurgle doubt that Tirgu was the most dangerous creature he had ever met, not only because of his line of work but because of his obvious and instinctive willingness to put down those that opposed him.

Tirgu picked something up that was near to him. It was a piece of some root or other. He began to chew it slowly and with some effort. He looked around at the men one by one. He stopped on the man who was cooking the vegetables and mushrooms. He said something quietly to this man which Gurgle could not hear over the crackle of the fire and general conversation. The man responded and this Gurgle could hear.

"Ten minutes I think. You got anything else to put in it?" he said.

Tirgu shook his head.

"Anyone else got anything good?" said this same man with more volume to all the others.

One or two of them came over and showed him little bits of things. Some were wrapped in cloth. These were unwrapped in front of him. He waved away most of it but selected some of what was shown to him and put it in the pot. He noticed that Gurgle was paying attention to him. "Have you got anything young man? If you put something in you'll get something out!" he said, with a light heart.

Gurgle shook his head. Tirgu's attention was drawn to the two of them and he watched them talking.

"I'm not a man and I've nothing to give," said Gurgle disconsolately, whilst looking down at himself.

"Oh really? Why don't you go and have a look for something in the wood there. Be quick now! If you can find just the smallest thing that's good enough to go in my pot then you can have a bowl full of the stuff. What do you think to that?"

Gurgle smiled and jumped to his feet. What a generous idea he thought to himself. He had smelt the soup in that pot for a while and it was the best thing to enter his nose for days. His gurgling belly was probably responsible for that. The man smiled at him and nodded his head towards the wood.

"Hurry up! It'll be ready soon," he said.

Gurgle stepped as quickly as his tired legs could carry him. The dark trees were soon around him and he thought about what to try to find for the pot. He kicked about with his feet through the undergrowth. He looked up into the trees to see if there were any fruits or berries on offer. They were not those kinds of trees. The light was almost gone and little that seemed green was on display. It occurred to him to look for the same things that they had found. There must be more somewhere. Vegetables or mushrooms he whispered to himself repeatedly. With more focussed eyes he peered about and soon found some interesting types of mushrooms living on the sides of the trees. He picked them and also picked what he suspected were herbs of some kind.

He returned to the camp within a few minutes of leaving. He had both hands full of lovely good things. He approached the man in front of the pot and placed all he had in two small piles on a large piece of linen that the man had laid out on the ground next to himself. He looked cautiously at the two piles of things and then looked cautiously at Gurgle. He had hoped for a better reaction from the man.

"What this you've brought?" he said, eyeing the things in more detail. "Tirgu! Come take a look at what your little friend wants to feed us."

Gurgle was now starting to worry that what he'd found wouldn't earn him a proper meal as he felt he deserved. Tirgu stood up and approached the two of them. The attention of some of the others was also aroused. The man picked through the things on the cloth and then handed one or two of them to Tirgu as he arrived. They both laughed once Tirgu could see what they were.

"You know what you've found Gurgle?" said Tirgu calmly.

Gurgle did not respond.

"You've found some pretty poisonous stuff here."

He handed him one of the mushrooms that he'd picked and told him to take a good look and to have a sniff but not to taste. He beckoned him towards the fire so they could see it more clearly. Tirgu turned back towards the man and told him to pass him all the other items that definitely could not be eaten.

"Is this all of it?" Tirgu asked of the man, once he had been passed a few things.

"Yep," he said quietly, without looking up from his pot.

"Is there nothing you can use?" asked Tirgu again.

141

"What? The moss or the twigs? Which d'you prefer?" he answered, his voice laced with sarcasm.

"Shush!" replied Tirgu, "Give him a bowl."

"Fine. I was going to anyway," said the man, smiling.

Tirgu turned his attention back to Gurgle. They sat together at his request so they could examine the mushrooms where the light was better. Gurgle held what appeared to be a very nutritious looking thing and he'd been tempted to nibble at it back in the wood. He was now deeply relieved not to have done so. It had a slim stalk and was generally a dirty brown colour. Its cap was conical and dry to the touch. Gurgle looked at it for a while and seemed not to notice that Tirgu was now so close to him. He was startled when he suddenly heard Tirgu's soft whispering in his ear.

"This one I forget the proper name of," he began. "I've always known it as 'the worm's wife'. You can see it's very pointed...and also the stalk gets narrower as it approaches the cap...and the underside smells sweetly."

"Why's it called the worm's wife?" asked Gurgle, not sure that he was telling the truth.

"It's because of the way the stalk looks as it enters the cap. They're common where I come from."

Gurgle couldn't see what he meant and didn't question him further on it.

"How poisonous is it?" Gurgle asked again.

"Well, if you'd eaten the whole thing you'd have been sick for...at least three days. You'd probably foam at the mouth. You might even hallucinate a little bit."

Tirgu paused to allow himself time to think of some extravagant nonsense to try to frighten and amuse the young Gurgle.

"You'd change colour from green to purple! Then your arms would shrink, your legs would fly off and your head would swell to twice the size!"

Tirgu looked seriously at Gurgle without saying anything else. Gurgle looked back at him, not sure what to make of it all. He knew he was joking. He humoured him with a smile and Tirgu smiled back warmly.

The man in front of the pot announced that it was ready. He found a stack of bowls, enough for all of them to eat from. One by one he filled them. Some he left at the flap of those tents that were occupied. Others were collected by those still energetic enough to answer the call of come and get it. Gurgle and Tirgu had a bowl placed in front of each of them. The steam from both rose up, joined forces, and did battle with the smoke from the fire. Tirgu allowed Gurgle to eat, lending him a spoon, while he continued to look through the objects that Gurgle had collected from the wood.

Gurgle immediately slurped at the soup. It tasted good. He could see all sorts of things inside it including some mushrooms that did not look particularly different from the worm's wife. He isolated a whole one on his spoon to show to Tirgu. It trembled and shimmered in its warm little bath.

"This looks the same as the worm's wife!" he said to Tirgu.

"No, that one's a different colour, don't you see?" he responded. "It's a much darker brown."

"Are you sure? It looks the same colour to me."

"Maybe it's the sauce," said Tirgu after a moment, resisting the temptation to become impatient with Gurgle. Gurgle looked at it again. Maybe it was the fire too. The orange flame put everything in the wrong light. He decided to eat it. It was fine. For the next minute or so Gurgle made the soup disappear. He was so hungry that he would allow nothing else to occupy his attention. The warmth from the fire and the flavours in the soup made Gurgle feel good once again. It had been several days since he last felt that feeling and it was strange to him that he could feel this way with these particular people around him. What was happening to him? Was he settling in? Was he beginning to enjoy himself? Was he being accepted? His inner thoughts were interrupted. Tirgu was looking for his attention once more.

"See this one, Gurgle? This one's a different kind of mushroom. This is called a Grey Foe. They're always very moist and sticky. Do you see the grey fan on the underside of the cap?" asked Tirgu.

"Yes," responded Gurgle, after a close look.

"This mushroom is not to be eaten under any circumstances. This one can kill. The liquid you get from squeezing them can be made into a paste. You put it on knives and arrow heads. Once it's dry it stays toxic for weeks. Nasty stuff."

"Why are you telling me all this?" said Gurgle carefully.

His soup was by this point all but gone. Tirgu was surprised by the question and looked at him directly for a moment, unsure of his meaning. He had thought that Gurgle was interested in all this and that he was taking the first steps towards being a part of his team. He was thinking of reconsidering his friendly approach.

"I'm telling you because it's useful and could help you some day. They won't teach you the things I can teach you in school you know. Besides, if you don't learn you'll poison yourself, or starve."

"I'm sorry. I'm interested, I am, but..." answered Gurgle.

"But what?"

"What do you want from me? Why'd you take me away? Where are we going? I want to go home! You stole me from my family!" yelled Gurgle, the blood rushing to his head.

"Settle down, Gurgle, settle down," he said, trying to reassure him. "I know it's difficult. You'll have these thoughts for a time. You hate me and us and all of this but you're starting to find things that interest you now and we're willing to make you one of us, aren't we?" he suddenly bellowed to the rest of them.

To their credit they responded well and straight away.

"Calm yourself Gurgle. You'll start to feel good again once we're up and running. You'll learn things and do things and once you're confident and one of us then you won't worry about home anymore. I promise you that."

"You're wrong!" said Gurgle angrily.

"Easy my boy, easy. What d'you put in his soup?" he

joked with the others. "Listen. Tomorrow, I'll show what we can eat from the forest and what we can use from the forest. I'll give you the guided tour. Don't worry, you'll soon see that what's happened to you can help you. You'll become someone far stronger and cleverer than you would have become stuck in Milton Greens. Just you think about that."

Gurgle didn't have much to say in response. Arguing would have got him nowhere. Defiance just seemed pointless since it hadn't helped him at all so far. He lowered his head and looked into his empty bowl. It suddenly occurred to him that he'd missed a wonderful opportunity to escape when he was looking for food in the forest. Why on earth hadn't he realised it?

He then looked up at the sky. The stars were out and they over sprinkled gloriously.

CHAPTER 5

Trumpets bellowed - of the kind that are long, thin and golden, and have little flags hanging off them. Four men in bright decorative tabards held one each to their lips. They needed to use both their hands to hold them up in the air. This sharp flatulent noise reverberated over the town square in which they were stood. Those people that understood the meaning of this noise and had an interest in what might be announced gathered in front. Those that couldn't care less continued on about their business. This second group were more numerous.

From behind the four trumpet players there emerged another man, similarly dressed, though without any trumpet to speak of. He held a small scroll in his hands. He unfurled it and began to address the crowd in a slow, clear and particularly loud voice.

"Hear Ye! Towns people of Grumbleweed! Hear Ye! The King, in his majestic wisdom, has decided that a banquet is to be held in his honour two weeks from today. Before that date all trades people, farmers and the like persons interested in doing him service are requested to attend at the castle gates, where they shall be informed of all the necessities that will be required for the feast. Manufacturers of furniture, bakers, meat men, vegetable growers, wine makers, and entertainers are all in the King's mind. The King thanks you for your attention and looks forward to your attendance. That is all."

Once his speech was completed he withdrew behind the

four trumpeters who gave another blast to signal that there would be no more announcements. The instant the man had stopped talking many in the crowd had quickly left to avoid being blasted by the noise. One of those that had scurried away was a middle aged man by the name of Thomas Medon. He was a farmer and had a particular interest in this matter as he was reliant upon the court for custom. He'd had notice that something like this was being planned. He was glad for this final confirmation. Here was another opportunity to earn some much needed cash and perhaps for him to make an impression with the fine foods that he could provide.

He puffed and panted through the streets. He was overweight and did not help himself by insisting on wearing a heavy coat and a tight shirt collar. He was rushing home because he wanted to begin preparations as soon as he could. By working quickly he and his daughters would prepare a cartload of the very finest foods that could be pulled from the ground.

After setting such a blistering pace through the town his body convinced him to take it easier on the longer stretch back to his farm. His muscles relaxed as he slowed. He journeyed on one of the winding grassy approaches that met with the town. The countryside started abruptly with overgrown fields and pathways, more wind and sunshine than before, the odd sheep and cow staggering about, twittering birds, greenery and rocky debris by the roadside.

On his way back he saw numerous people, though none of

them were as well dressed as he. He met a neighbour of his by the only bridge on the route. He was waylaid there for a while, talking about this and that. He took the opportunity to refresh himself with a drink from the stream that flowed beneath the bridge. He informed the man of the announcement in the town but the man was not too concerned since he'd managed to sell the bulk of his produce the week before. They were in different lines of business. Thomas shortly bid his friend farewell and finished the remainder of his journey home to the farm. Once there he found little activity. His youngest daughter, Constanza, played quietly with her little black and white pig by the front door to their cottage. He noticed this and was not amused. He stepped by her and into the cottage. There he found his eldest daughter, Dora, preparing lunch for all four of them. She stood at the stove which was charred and blackened with decades of carbon. In front of her she was chopping chives and tomatoes together. In a pan beyond many eggs were being fried. They bubbled and spat as the fat swam over them.

"That smells lovely my dear," he said.

"Welcome home. It's almost ready," said Dora.

"Where's Sarah?"

"She'll be back in a minute. She's outside doing something or other."

Thomas poked his head back through the entrance, looking for his youngest.

"Constanza, come inside and eat with us."

"Can I bring Truffles with me? I'll keep him on the floor,"

she asked sweetly.

"No, don't be silly, leave the pig here."

Constanza grumpily complied and set Truffles down on the ground. Truffles looked around at her for a moment or two then wandered off, sniffing at grass and stones as he went. She followed her father back inside and took her seat. It had a cushion on top of it to allow her to sit comfortably at the table. At the table were four place settings and a half eaten loaf of brown bread and a bread knife. A few pieces of fruit joined it. Next to these things was a jug full of fresh and foamy apple juice.

Thomas stepped outside through the back door in search of Sarah, his middle daughter. He could not see her so he chose to shout for her to come instead. A shout came back at him but he could not tell from where. The voice said that she was coming and for him not to worry. He turned and went back inside. Dora had now finished her cooking and was placing the eggs onto a large plate. She then followed this with the salad of tomatoes and chives which she placed in a bowl nearby. She carried both of them to the table and placed them where she found space. Constanza smiled at Dora and said to her elder sister what a good girl she thought she was. Thomas came over and took his seat. With a great huff he settled himself into position. He leaned over the table and picked up the bread knife. He cut several thin slices and placed a slice onto each of his daughter's plates. He then cut a larger slice for himself. Without being requested and without much choice in the matter Thomas placed a fried egg onto

Constanza's plate. She looked up at her father and a little frown spread across her features.

"Eat both parts of the egg! Not just the yellow part. You need them to grow properly and I won't have food wasted in my house," he said firmly.

She was tempted to reply but had nothing worthy to say. He then spooned some of the tomato salad next to the egg. This she did enjoy so she began to eat. He also filled a wooden cup with some apple juice and placed it next to her. He turned back to his own plate and scooped up a couple of eggs whilst they were still hot. Dora took a seat opposite him with Constanza to her right and the one remaining empty chair to her left. She waited for her father to finish filling his plate before she considered her own food.

With a clatter the back door opened and Sarah swept in. She kicked off her boots and joined the others at the table. Once she was settled and all of them had food on their plates their father told them about what he'd heard that morning.

"We've a lot of work ahead of us. The King's having another banquet. If we can take our cart there tomorrow full of our best then we'll get a good price for it."

"Another banquet? What's he celebrating this time? His dog's birthday?" asked Sarah sarcastically.

"Quiet Girl! Without his trade you'd have a lot less than you do now," replied Thomas.

"I know, I know," said Sarah.

"What will we take?" asked Dora.

151

"As many apples and tomatoes as we can fit inside...and only the best ones, be strict now. We'll also put in some carrots, parsnips, plenty of herbs. How many eggs do we have left?"

"Not many. A few dozen," answered Dora.

"We'll take a few dozen with us then," he decided. "Maybe we'll kill a few of the hens so we have some meat to offer them as well."

"No!" they all seemed to say instantly, each at a different frequency.

"What difference will a few extra chickens make to their banquet table? Don't do that. We need them all," said Sarah.

"Fine. Fine," he acquiesced. "The hens are lucky they have you to protect them."

"Is it an early start tomorrow then?" suggested Dora.

"Yes, I'm afraid so. How are the marrows looking? A few of those will look good on the cart."

"They're huge, big enough to put a pig inside and then to roast it! Do you know of any pigs around here?" said Sarah, smiling across at her younger sister as she did so.

"Stop it! I'll put you in a marrow and roast it!" replied Constanza angrily.

"Behave you two," barked their father. "If the marrows are really that big then it's due to that good fertiliser you found Sarah. Where did you get it?"

"Oh, the mulch you mean? That's from my friend."

"What friend?" asked her father, his attention suddenly concentrated.

"Squelch," she replied after a moment.

"Squelch?" blurted her father, and he laughed. "What kind of a name is that?"

"It's a goblin name."

"A goblin!?"

His face became red like the piece of tomato skewered on the fork hovering in front of his mouth.

"Yes, a goblin. Well, he's a half goblin actually. I think his father was a man, though I'm not sure."

"A half goblin? My God, what do people get up to? I can't believe it."

"He lives in the forest not too far from here. You know about all of them in the forest, of course you do."

"Yes, but I didn't know you knew about them. What are they doing around here?"

"I don't know, maybe I'll ask him the next time we meet."

"Listen Sarah, do as I tell you...don't associate with creatures like that."

"Creatures? He's nice. He's good company. It's boring around here...some of the time."

"Do the rest of you know this Squelch person too?"

"No, it's the first I've heard of it," said Dora, looking anxiously at her sister.

Constanza just laughed at the name and obviously knew nothing of the matter.

"Sarah, you're but thirteen years old. You're not old enough to look after yourself yet. Let alone go off and be friends with some dirty tree frog!"

"Stop it! Don't say that, that's a horrible thing to say!

What could I do with him that would be so terrible?"

"Sarah! Listen to me! I'm your father and I know best. Stay away from the forest. Understand!?"

Sarah was stunned by the sudden anger she had provoked in her father. She calmed herself down a little before speaking again.

"Fine, but you can say goodbye to your big marrows then, can't you?"

This seemed to put an end to the conversation. After lunch they all separated. Dora packed away the plates. Sarah found a quiet spot by herself to think. Constanza looked around outside and found Truffles sat patiently waiting for her. Thomas went to tidy up the cart ready for the food and the journey the next day. He did the best he could with it.

The following morning Thomas was the first to wake. He was ready to go almost before the roosters welcomed the day with a cock-a-doodle. He dressed quickly and began to consider the best way to organise his family for the tasks he expected of them. His faithful mule that would pull the cart was also awake and was gently munching on grass below his bedroom window. He decided to do as much as he could by himself for the moment. That way he would not waste time arguing with his daughters for them to get out of bed, nor to coordinate them all through their sleepy haze. With his gloves and a knife he went out into the fields that were his. Carefully he selected root vegetables and picked and dusted them off. This he did, painfully, for an hour or so until Dora joined him. She had come without being prompted. She was his most faithful and attentive daughter, though he would rarely admit it to her. Soon they had several large boxes filled with fresh vegetables and herbs. Together they also cut and lifted three of the best marrows and placed them in the cart. Once his other two daughters had slowly emerged from the cottage they all began to pick apples and tomatoes from their places. Similarly, they made many boxes full with these things. At the end of their morning's work they made up a full cart load of their best things as they had intended. Thomas decided it would be better for him alone to take the mule and the cart to the castle gates. Dora was well able to accompany him but he would not wish to leave the other two alone together unsupervised. Sarah might also come with him but she was too unpredictable and Constanza was just too young for such a journey. Another part of him was also reluctant to expose his daughters to the rough type of men that might be found in that place.

He set off clear and happy and wished his daughters well and that they take care of themselves and each other. He led his mule by a harness which he held in his hand as he walked alongside. The cart clattered and staggered along behind them. The fruit and vegetables bumped and bounced. Together they retraced the route to the town.

Beyond the town stood the castle. It was plain to see as it stood well above the tops of the tallest buildings in Grumbleweed. Even a mile or more from where he now was he could discern the shape of it. Three turrets it had with thin purple flags trailing from a spike on each one. Dark grey stones made up the outside walls, greened up by primordial moss. The town itself seemed to be just a dingy afterthought that the castle could not shake off.

The people that lived in Grumbleweed were rarely separated from trades that depended on the King's favour. At least half the town's folk made their living either working there or in some related activity. Thomas Medon was one of those that depended on the income from the King's extravagance as well as from his necessities. Without it he would have a farm full of rotting fruit that could not be sold for the lack of demand. This was often on his mind and he wished for a more secure situation for him and his family. He and his mule continued their journey up the road to the town. He wondered if any other farmers had been able to ready their produce in so short a time. Probably not. He hoped to be the first to offer such things as he had.

He circled around the edge of the town and took the path towards the castle. On this route the land quickly became more manicured and presentable. There were straight lines, flat ground and flowers in neat rows. The King clearly had a talented gardener somewhere amongst his retinue. He'd made this journey before so he knew to avoid the main entrance at which he would be rudely turned away. He diverted and made his way to the place where tradesmen such as he were received.

From a distance he could see there were a few people dotted about. To his alarm he saw that there were several other carts already there. To his relief he could see that none of the things inside them matched his. He saw that the men with the carts were in heated discussions with the men that stood protecting the entrance. An official of some kind seemed to be in charge of things. As he approached, Thomas could overhear a little of the conversation.

"It's not my job to give you a living" said the official.

"But your lists there say you need joints of mutton and beef!" said one of the men standing by his cart.

"Yes, but only if they're up to the necessary standard of course...of which I am the sole judge."

"I've been selling my meat here many times these past three years. I've always been met with civility and honest trade. There's nothing wrong with these joints."

"That's for me to decide, isn't it? I'm not going to buy them. Now clear off!"

This upset the man considerably and he growled at the official and motioned towards him. At this point the guards all around them, of whom there were four, approached and suggested that the man follow this instruction, however damaging to his pride it might be. He had little choice but to comply. He took his cart and walked past Thomas giving him an icy stare. He mumbled something to him but Thomas could not make it out. Perturbed by this but still confident that his cart would not be turned around in such a manner he walked up towards the official. He looked towards the other men and their carts but they did not seem to be willing to stand in his way. They minded their own business after nodding for him to proceed.

"Vegetables is it," said the official, unimpressed, "and apples?"

"Yes, that's right. I've got all kinds of vegetables for soups and stews. The freshest herbs. Some rare ones too. Eggs. As many tomatoes and apples as I could carry. All of the finest quality, and...three of the biggest marrows you'll ever see!" laughed Thomas.

"Fine. We'll take the eggs, the vegetables, not the herbs, we have our own gardens for such things. Tomatoes, yes, not the apples, we don't need them. We've already got fruit. Alright?"

"Oh...alright. Well what about the marrows?"

"What do we want marrows for? Archery practice maybe but for eating I don't think so!" replied the official, scoffing at his own wit.

"Alright," grumbled Thomas, "for all those then...it would be..."

"Err, yes," interrupted the official. "Have you sold to the castle before?"

"Yes, many times, why d'you ask?"

"Well this time the King expects that we take these things on credit."

"Credit!?"

"Yes, I'm afraid so. I don't need to remind you of course that the Royal accounts do not enjoy being indebted to anyone and who better to assure you of a bill being paid than if it is the King to pay it?"

"But why can't he pay now?"

"Now, Sir," said the official, adopting a more sinister tone, "to answer that would be to pry into the private affairs of our Lord and master and that I cannot do. Rest assured that the King appreciates your assistance and understanding at this time and that this account will be settled properly in due course."

Thomas couldn't believe it. He was relying on this money to live. He looked up to the sky, but instead of distant blue he caught a glimpse of many well dressed persons standing on the parapet of the castle observing all that was on display below. The official spoke to Thomas once again but he did so a little more quietly.

"These other gentlemen behind you have been discussing amongst themselves whether to agree to this condition. I hope very much that they do. If not then I suspect very strongly that they will have great difficulty selling their goods here in the future. I shudder to think what impact that might make on them and their families. It would be a great shame if that was to happen."

His meaning could not be clearer to Thomas. He looked over at these other men conversing quietly and chose not to join them to discuss something that he could decide alone. He let out a sigh upon realising that he had no real choice in the matter. He could little afford to be alienated from his most important customer even though he could little afford to wait for the money. He was a shrewd man and knew the delicacy of men's honour. He began to doubt that he would receive the money for a long time and only then at great insistence by himself, an act also likely to harm his reputation as one of their suppliers. Nevertheless. He looked at the official and gently nodded. The man smiled and nodded back. A voice suddenly spoke behind Thomas.

"We've decided," said one of the other tradesmen. "We're taking our things back with us. We don't do business like this...on credit...even if it is with the King."

"I'm very sorry to hear that. We'll just have to get what we need from your competitors. Good day gentlemen!" replied the official.

"Don't give in to them friend!" said this same man to Thomas. "They're just trying to take advantage of you. Think you'll be able to get your money out of them? Not a chance. Believe me. If they pretend not to know you who'll get your money back for you? What's to stop them?"

"You're no longer welcome here, Sir!" said the official suddenly and loudly. "Leave immediately!"

"We're going! And we'll be sure to warn others of the generosity of your master! And the wisdom of the men he picks to speak for him!"

The day was not going as Thomas had expected. He understood the man's plea but he could not risk his long term business because of this short term difficulty. He stood quietly waiting for them to leave. They looked at him hoping he would join them. Once they realised he would not they continued, cursing at all of them as they went.

The official thanked Thomas for his patience and for his

loyalty to the royal person, as he put it. He was asked to sign a paper and to write upon it all the things that he was selling, or for the moment, giving to the King. The official examined it. Then, once he had made a copy he gave the copy to Thomas as a receipt for the goods rendered. Several kitchen boys came scurrying out from somewhere. They grabbed at the boxes on the cart and quickly took them inside. They were told to leave the apples and the marrows. Some of the herbs were accidentally picked up but neither Thomas nor the official was worried about it enough to correct the error.

With much disappointment Thomas tidied away and secured the marrows and the remaining boxes. He was frustrated with himself for allowing his mind to lull him into relying on the money he was to have received for all this. Numerous plans had been formed by him and were founded on the expectation of having enough in his pocket to spend in the coming days. All were aborted now and it would take some embarrassing explanations to avoid the various unhappy consequences. He returned home.

Inside the castle kitchens where his produce had been taken and stacked a chef examined the content and the quality of the things very carefully. He pored over and grappled each piece or item as he lifted them clear of their containers and onto the wooden surface in front of him. Like a culinary detective he smelled and investigated everything. Only when satisfied of the merits of each thing did he decide to segregate them for preparation. The general quality was very high as Thomas had said, so only the occasional bit was rejected. The chef then put the chosen things onto another table and called over one of his junior counterparts and instructed him to place them into one of the various pantries until needed. As this instruction was being given a shout came from across the kitchen. Someone upstairs had requested some boiled eggs. They had no information as to whom it might be for. Their attitude was that anything may go up to the King so therefore everything they served had to be fit for a King, as indeed the very great majority of their output was.

A sudden double clap of hands occurred. The chef that had just examined the produce requested from his various underlings a pan of boiling water and for some toast to be made. It would be made by holding a thick slice of bread, baked thrice daily of course, the correct distance from the open fire at the heart of the kitchen. The chef then looked for eggs and found them in the stack that Thomas had given. He selected several of the biggest and best, not before checking their integrity, and popped them into the pan of water that had just been placed on the stove in front of him. As they bathed he grabbed a large flat metal dish. He placed three porcelain eggcups on it. He then took a pat of the finest butter and using a peculiar little knife he expertly curled delicate yellow shapes onto the dish. He took also a small metal vase and placed in it several fresh flowers that he selected from the large bunch close by that had been picked that morning. He put the vase next to the egg cups to provide an attractive little shade for the eggs. "Toast!" he shouted. "Where is it?"

Hot crusty brown slices were placed in front of him. He approved and took them to put on the metal dish. In transit he removed the crusts and sliced them into thick soldiers then placed them carefully between the buttery installations. The masterpiece was almost complete. With exquisite internal timing the chef picked the boiling pan up from the heat after four minutes. He plunged the eggs into cool water so they stopped cooking and so they could be handled comfortably. He put the three eggs into the three eggcups. With another double clap of his hands a waiter came over and carefully picked up the dish. Off he went out of the kitchen. He negotiated his way past all the other chefs at work on other tasks. He left the smoke and noise and chaos behind. He then went up a long set of stone stairs and out into a very formal looking hallway with swords and paintings adorning the walls. Here the dish was handed to another person who was more senior and better dressed. He then took it up another flight of stairs into a private set of rooms from whence the order for the boiled eggs had come. He stepped softly on the carpeted floor towards one of the rooms. He knocked at a door. Permission to enter then came. The person inside the room took a long look at the dish as it was placed in front of her. She picked the flowers out of the vase and turned to address the servant that had brought them.

"What the hell are these flowers doing here?" said she, in a very demanding tone of voice. "I asked for eggs, not the garden of bleedin' Eden!"

A strong sun shone down on Sam, Joe and John. Without any fuss or favour they had been thrust into the excitement and difficulties of training. In front of each of them stood a very solid looking wooden pole. Each pole had been lazily decorated to mimic a man. The three of them had plenty of room between themselves to swing whatever weapon they were given and they would be given all of them. Before they had the chance to attack these figures as it was obvious that they should other more senior soldiers demonstrated the proper technique. Without technique these weapons and any weapons in fact were perfectly useless.

They watched attentively as men much stronger and fiercer than they charged and swung at these poor parodies. They did not use as much force as they had expected. Perhaps their first lesson was that these men were not superhuman and that one should conserve as much energy as one could especially when in the heat of combat. John was breathing deeply and was the most anxious of the three. He felt the weight of a simple sword in his hand and he thought to himself it was much too much to even carry than to swing in anger, let alone thrust into a man's body. He seriously doubted that he would have the strength for such an act.

The commander overseeing it all understood how they would feel going through this process. He knew it well from once having to do it himself. At first they would experience feelings of weakness and inadequacy when using the weapons for the first time. These feelings would be removed by simple exercise and repetition. Soon they would feel confidence from discovering that they could control and use them. Then they would become stronger and more skilled from repeated training sessions until they were ready for actual real life use. He felt that Sam and Joe were the most naturally capable. He felt John was physically weaker than the other two but he knew that people in such a position very often made up for their deficiencies with other talents. He hoped to discover them. Steadily, the three of them were encouraged to advance on their arboreal enemies and to attack them as they saw fit. Steadily, the errors which they demonstrated were exposed and corrected. Beyond this education the soft vibrating clunk of metal against wood was their only reward. This continued for half an hour or more. One object of the exercise was to wear a person out so that they could be taught to control and pace themselves and so not to fall victim to a blade simply by virtue of exhaustion. As time passed the pace inevitably slowed and the clunks became less frequent. All three were using a standard sword to make their cuts. Sam found that at first the sword was heavy and awkward. After a while, despite his growing tiredness, he found that it was not so awkward and that he could achieve results with it he did not expect. He gathered his strength and his breath between each sideways blow, which he made every ten seconds or so. He approached cutting both up and down steeply, imagining that he was attacking at the neck and shoulder when swinging down and attacking under the ribs when swinging up. He resisted the temptation to try extravagant swings and instead kept to the simple instructions given him. He recognised the value of them.

Joe was having a little more difficulty in maintaining his rhythm. He was obviously not as fit as he thought he was. He was regularly forced to stop, panting feverishly for breath with his hands on his knees, but the blows he'd inflicted on the pole when he began were the most impressive of them all.

The commander looked over them from his high vantage, sat on one of the upper platforms on the inside of the garrison. As he watched them he sliced off little chunks of flesh from an apple and put them into his mouth. He was thinking about the meaning behind a simple message that he had received that day. It had come from his commander Lord Spikepoint. It had read simply - prepare your men as soon as you can.

He pondered the state of mind of the man that had written it and the delicate forces which he might be attempting to control. In fact he knew little of his Lord on a personal level. He was not a member of his intimate group of subordinates. He was not involved in any of the larger decisions which affected him and his garrison. He was rarely invited to any of the regular celebrations and functions that attended with real power. What he did know was that only with political cunning or success in battle could he hope to draw his Lord's gaze upon him. He

166

had been able to occasion neither thus far.

He'd heard little of the consequences of that fateful engagement with the King's men the previous week. He'd reported to his superiors all that he and his men knew of the encounter. They'd not given him any information in return as to the response from the King's camp. Negative he was of course certain, but the real question was whether his master or the King wished to press the issue and make an excuse of it to provoke something further. Neither could do so without the proper resources and neither would do so unless he felt his opponent's resources significantly inferior to his own. With a pessimistic groan he realised that conflict would not be too far away. To him battle was like an old friend that would mysteriously keep reappearing when he least desired it. His friend was long overdue for another visit.

Frustrated by these thoughts and by the obvious lack of sophistication displayed by his three newest recruits the commander jumped down from his position to give some personal tuition. He now needed to speed things up. He suspected he and his garrison might be suddenly called upon to fight. He didn't want any weak links in his chain. "Right! Put the swords down. Get a drink of water and then gather round. That goes for the rest of you too."

The three of them staggered over to a barrel full of cool water and spooned as much into themselves as they could whilst they had the chance. The men that had supervised and assisted them sat around on straw bales as their commander had instructed. Once they'd had their fill of water they returned and sat amongst the others. The commander stood in front of them with his back to the tattered totems.

"What are you people doing?" he said with a resigned expression on his face. "You look like a bunch of donkeys! And I'm not going into battle sat on your back, which may be sooner than you expect."

He paused for a moment to think. He paced around and then continued speaking.

"I'll let you in on a little secret. You don't need all these weapons. Well, to cut someone's head off, yes you need them but defending yourselves you don't need them. Can I have a volunteer please?"

As he said this he unhooked his belt which held his sword and he wrapped it and placed it on a far table.

"Come on, I'm going to show you all how to behave in a fight. No one want to find out?"

Upon realising they were all either too tired or cautious he pointed and demanded for one of them to get up and approach him. For a sickening moment John had felt that the finger was pointing at him but it was not and a man stood up behind. He walked out to the front and stopped some eight feet or so from the commander. The commander looked at him, altered his position to face him and then winked.

"Thank you for volunteering," he joked. "Now, grab a weapon from behind you, anything, doesn't matter."

"A wooden one?" answered the man, smiling and with proper concern for his commander.

"Any you like. Don't worry, you won't get hurt."

The man picked up the broadsword. He gripped it tightly and lifted it up and around his head to remind himself of the feel and the weight of it once more. The commander remained unarmed but everyone in the audience could tell that he was much the more confident of the two. The man suddenly let the sword drop down at an angle to his side. He knew what the commander wanted from him but he chose to do it without being asked in the hopes of catching him off guard. He drew a deep breath and ran full tilt at the commander lifting the huge sword up in the air as he did so ready to swing it down on the man's head, at least in theory. The commander saw it coming and quickly sidestepped clear of any danger as the sword slammed into the dirt where he'd just been standing. The commander was now facing the man's right side. He lunged at him kicking the sword away. Simultaneously he put his left arm around his far shoulder and his left leg behind him and swung him with enormous force off his feet. The man fell in an instant and yelped in distress as he struck the ground. The commander picked up the sword and pointed it at the man prostrate in front of him. Neither of them moved for a moment or two.

"Someone else," said the commander. "You!"

He was now looking at Joe, who peered around hoping that the commander meant another. He did not. Reluctantly he stood and made his way towards the same dusty spot. His place on the straw bail was taken by the man that had been so easily defeated. He nursed his sore shoulder and dusted himself off.

"Again, pick anything you like Joseph," said the commander once more.

He moved to the table to pick up the same short sword that he'd been using for the previous hour or so. It was the only one that he knew even a little of what to do with. He turned to face him. The commander managed somehow to combine paternal affection in his facial expression with a psychotic lust for combat. He beckoned Joe closer. He came forward but without much enthusiasm. Just as he seemed to be ready to punish and hurt Joseph, as he had the last man, he relaxed and began to speak.

"Come on boy, how will you defeat your enemies with an attitude like that? Get me! Get me! Get me!"

Joe suddenly thought it best just to get it over with. He swung at his commander who now was quite close to him. In a moment his thrust was stopped by a solid hand against his wrist that held the sword. He felt paralysed and helpless. He closed his eyes and braced himself for a blow to his exposed body, but it didn't come. He opened his eyes to see that the commander was holding him there in this awkward position and was just using him as a tool for the demonstration.

"The most important thing you need to know is how far away your man is from you. It doesn't matter how big or small he is or what weapon he has because there's always an answer to variations like that. If you know how far your man is away from you you'll always know what to do. If he's out of your range when he attacks then you get out of his way. If he's in range, which is less than a stride, when he attacks you've time to stop him before he can do so," professed the commander.

He looked at Joe then let go of him.

"Stay there a minute," he said quietly before addressing the crowd again. "Make a constant assessment of the distance from you to him. Keep it the same when nothing is happening. If he approaches back off, if he withdraws step after him to maintain that same distance. The distance varies of course depending on the weapon being used. Let him make the first move. If he's too far away when he does so, get out of his way and then kill him when he's exposed and off balance. If he's close to you when he strikes use any simple blocking technique you wish. But be quick! Again, he'll be off balance. You can throw him, stab him with a free hand, anything, he's yours. Understand?"

A general murmur announced that they all did.

"Alright. I want you to remember. It doesn't matter if your opponent is a seven foot savage or your five foot sister, maintain that distance...and all you need to do is wait for him to make his move...or her if it's your sister," he laughed and so did a few of the others, "and then block or move out of the way, either way you win and that's what matters. Questions?"

A hand suddenly shot up from the audience. It was John who'd been listening rather incredulously to all this. The commander was pleased to have such a swift response and he beckoned him to speak.

"What do you do if you're in the middle of a battle and

everyone around you is screaming and running around and you haven't got a clue from where you might be attacked next?"

The commander laughed at this but considered it an important observation nonetheless. He responded after a moment of reflection.

"Get somewhere safer! If you can't do that...just hope that I'm nearby...and if I'm not nearby then fight with every ounce of strength you have left to stay alive. Think of home, think of life, think of eating juicy joints of beef with fried potatoes. Just fight with everything you've got to stay alive! Scream and shout and say that no one is going to put you in the ground! Fight! Kill! Survive! Make sure that you do...or *I'll* kill you," there was a pause, "any other questions?"

*

The history books held within the central library of Milton Greens state that there have been a total of nine historical conflicts in which a goblin army has taken part. Putting aside the debatable definitions of a 'conflict' and a 'goblin army', all the goblin historians of note agree on this point. The most significant of these was the first such conflict. Few physical remnants of this time remain in existence. Let it be said however that the effects of it are still felt to this day, for this conflict was a single battle in which the very future of the forest was determined. At that time there was not too much forest to speak of, even so, some considered it worth fighting over. These were the goblin people that had settled in it and the hobgoblin people that wanted to settle in it. The dispute was simple; we saw it first so you get out. That was how the hobgoblins saw the matter at least and in fact how many today still see it. Naturally, the historians are as divided on this issue as the original combatants were and along the same lines of nationality as you would expect.

The battle was by all accounts an unexpectedly bloody one, most unexpected of course to those that were caught up in it. It was also remarkable for the fact that such long odds were against the goblin army that defended the forest from the invaders. It is a celebrated story that the forest was saved for future generations of goblins only by the preparation and cunning of the first and most celebrated Goblin General. He enjoyed so much favour by his actions that he became also the first Goblin King. His name was King Rustle and he is sometimes known as 'The Saviour of the Goblins'.

The Goblin Kings are few and far between in the pages of the history books and only arrive when an individual warrants such a nomination through great merit and exceptional achievement. Goblin Kingship is not passed on from father to son. Goblins see no reason why a King's son should be any more likely to reproduce his father's successes than any father's son. This is more goblin logic.

Future historians would regard the present band of goblin warriors that now stood as a crowd awaiting processing in response to the Council's recent request as not sufficient to merit the term 'goblin army'. Nor would they consider the fighting that they would soon be engaged in to be a 'conflict', in the proper historical sense. But, not one of these goblins, at least those that would prove to be worthy of participation, would regard themselves as part of anything other than the toughest goblin army that ever walked the highways and byways of their beloved forest.

It was now a week since the decree had been issued by the Council. Much rumbling and excitement had been created by it. From one side of the forest to the other there was scarcely a place that had not heard the call to arms. The present crowd of eager young warriors, though some appeared not so young, numbered easily in excess of three hundred. Consequently, each goblin had to perform better than two of his fellow applicants to gain admittance to this select band.

For all this time since the decree the forest had talked of little else. Almost everyone knew someone or had a neighbour who knew someone that intended to put themselves forward. Such an event summoned up the blood and filled even the meek with courage. From premature youngsters (some of whom painted fake stubble on themselves to appear older) to creaking elderly gents (some of whom shaved off their greying beards to appear younger) all walks of life were represented. A great crowd had gathered to answer the Council's call, and all were there because their collective honour was at stake, as well as a good few lives. If they did not answer this challenge how long would it be before the raiders came looking to take more of them? To a brave young goblin this was an intolerable prospect.

They were a motley crew indeed. Most were clad in homemade armour and carried with them clubs, short swords, axes and shields. Those that were a little slight in body bulked themselves up by packing their jackets with straw. Those that wished to make an impression before the formal process of selection occurred wandered around slowly and with little subtlety, demonstrating their prowess with their weapons. They swished and poked at the air. If they were not careful with each other's space it was just possible that a battle might break out. That would make Lieutenant Chirp Tilestain's job much easier. He could simply select the survivors.

The Lieutenant was pleased by all that fate had given him in recent weeks. Whilst the recent kidnap of loved ones was a tragedy for all those directly concerned it had not been such for him. He was enjoying the high tide of good fortune which had placed in his way a glorious opportunity to advance his military career. In two and a half weeks he had progressed from being a minor troop leader to a key participant in the biggest assault on the forest for years. He had performed so well in front of the Council that they had awarded him with the command of this brigade. He was smart enough to know that his position was not secure however. It was his idea that was being played out in front of him and he knew that if it went wrong he would get all the criticism and he would never get another chance to progress. It had to go well.

Naturally then he would pick only the very best to accompany him out of the forest on this very dangerous mission. There would be no loudmouths, no show-offs, no weaklings, no drunkards, no clonks (goblin slang for daft, stupid or otherwise mentally inferior persons) and definitely no family members allowed.

The Lieutenant stood on a raised platform with his quartermaster sat at a large table below him. He had already picked some of his most trusted comrades to make up the core of the brigade. Looking out over the healthy crowd he decided that he had more than enough goblins to choose from. If he waited much longer they might be there all night. He put his hands to his mouth and shouted for their attention. It didn't work and only those at the front heard him, who then became even more anxious to be admitted. He tried again but the general hubbub was too great for him. From below his quartermaster suggested that he throw a powder bomb in the air. He took one from a box and handed it to the Lieutenant who accepted it gleefully. He leaned down to scrape the fuse along the rough wooden surface at his feet. This was sufficient friction to spark it. He held it at arm's length for a few moments, judging when would be the best time to throw it in the air. These powder bombs would not do any harm to you but they would go off with something of a bang. At the right moment he threw it high and forward into the air above the ignorant throng. It dropped to within about ten feet of the crowd when...

Bang!!!

The whole mass of them shook as one! White powder then drifted casually down onto their heads. The Lieutenant made ready to speak once more but instead he faced a wall of shouting. They were complaining loudly at such a shock. At least they were all now looking in his direction. He motioned with his arms for them to quieten down, which they steadily did. At last there was enough quiet for him to address them properly. A few of those show-offs at the periphery of things put away their swords and decided to try to barge their way to the front in fear of losing out.

"Thank you all for coming," began the Lieutenant. "We all appreciate the efforts you've made. But as you know we won't need all of you."

He paused a moment to allow his point to sink in.

"Unless you start a war!" shouted one of those at front and a great laugh surged up.

"Yes, that's right! If there is a war we'll contact you! For now we don't need your help. Thank you. Goodbye," responded the Lieutenant angrily.

He instructed the quartermaster to deny that one his chance, who groaned and complained loudly at the decision but was eventually escorted away by one of the Lieutenant's colleagues.

"This is a serious business!" said the Lieutenant. "No jokers need apply. We're going to get you to line up in four rows then we'll get you to answer some questions. If you meet the basic criteria then we'll consider you further. We're going to whittle you down until we have what we need. Right! Get into four rows. It doesn't matter who's at the front, you'll all be seen. Line up!"

With the clatter of armour against shield and shield against armour several hundred goblins quickly rearranged themselves. The Lieutenant stepped down from his platform and sat next to his quartermaster and two of their colleagues. The four of them now sat at the table and in front of each was a row of goblins. They also had pencils and paper in front of them to make a record of each applicant.

"Alright, let's begin," said the Lieutenant to the other three.

He then turned to face the first goblin in his particular queue.

"Yes Sir, your name?"

"Slap Canopy's my name."

"Age?" asked the Lieutenant, just as he looked down at a piece of paper and began to make notes.

"Thirty five."

"What equipment d'you have?"

"Two swords, shield, good armour, water bottle."

"Any military experience?"

"Some. I was in the Flat Top campaign."

"Really? Are you sure?"

"I am. Why?"

"I think you'd need to be a little older for that. What's your real age?"

"Forty," replied Slap, after a contrite pause.

"Well, I should bin you for that...but you might be useful. Go and wait behind the platform, on the bails. You're through. Go on."

Simultaneously, the three other judges began asking the same questions of those standing in front of them.

"Name?" asked one of the Lieutenant's more junior companions.

"Slurp Silverfrog."

"Age?"

"Twenty five."

"Equipment?"

"Good pair of boots, an axe."

"Military experience?"

"None."

"In that case why do you want to join up?"

"To protect the forest! Sir!"

"Fine. Go on then, behind the platform."

"Wonderful, thank you. By the way what's the pay like?"

"Five nuts a day."

"Oh, good."

The quartermaster spoke to his first goblin.

"Name?" he asked.

"Grate, Grate Twigstick."

"Age?"

"Sixteen."

"Equipment?"

"I thought *you* would provide it?" he replied after a pause.

"In exceptional circumstances perhaps. I take it you've nothing with you."

"No Sir."

"No military experience either I'm sure."

"No."

"Why should we take you then?"

"Because...I'm...I'm good at fighting?"

"Sorry son, off you go," said the quartermaster, who pointed his pencil and began poking holes in the air with it, aiming to his right.

This repetitive task continued for more than an hour. Each of the four had a stack of papers in front of them covered in various scribblings. As tedious as it was for them it was more so for those stood waiting. Behind the Lieutenant and the others quite a crowd had settled themselves in. Well over a hundred had been permitted to stay and would soon be considered again for formal acceptance. Very soon the crowd behind outnumbered those still queuing in front. The Lieutenant noticed this and quietly whispered to the other recruiters to be a bit stricter with the remaining fifty or so. They found this difficult and eventually the Lieutenant just stood up and announced that they had had enough, in every sense. It was not much of a sacrifice thought the Lieutenant, the rest were a pretty shabby lot and had been the last to arrive. He also noticed one or two that had joined the queue for a second time despite being rejected the first time. He thanked everyone for their patience and apologised to those genuine persons that had queued for so long but had not had the chance to give an account of themselves.

As the unhappy ones grumbled away he turned to take a closer look at the others in all their glory. Perhaps glory was not the right word. Whilst surveying this bunch the seriousness of the task ahead suddenly hit him. With this group of goblins that he alone had the responsibility to train and command he would hunt for those kidnapped. He hadn't the power to foresee that he and his goblins would soon face various enemies and would enjoy successes as well as failures.

"Well done everyone. I guess you're the best that Milton Greens has to offer? Am I right?" asked the Lieutenant.

A lukewarm groan of approval was heard in response.

"Quartermaster! How many goblin souls do we have?"

"One hundred and thirty eight, Sir."

"Good. In case you haven't heard, my name is Lieutenant Chirp Tilestain. Just call me Sir, it's much easier to remember," he paused, allowing time for a laugh that did not appear. "Now you all know that one hundred is the number we need as we're on a budget. Even if you don't find yourself amongst that number we'll keep your names and details so we can contact you if we need replacements or extra troops. So, I think it's likely you'll all get involved somehow. Please don't be disappointed whatever happens."

He looked at them in more detail for a few moments and considered the best way to trim that surplus thirty eight.

"Before we find the final one hundred I think one or two formalities are in order. Here's a little tradition I know. Would the youngest soldier please step forward?"

One or two fresh faced and very eager recruits did so. The Lieutenant asked them both their ages. One said he had just turned fourteen, the other said he was thirteen and a half. The one who was fourteen was asked to sit down whilst the other was told to stay where he was.

"Now, would the oldest soldier please step forward?" asked the Lieutenant once again.

This time there were many candidates for that title. Ten or more of them stood up. The Lieutenant told them to stay standing and to lift up their hand when he announced their age. He confirmed to his relief that none were over forty five.

"Forty four?" he said, but no arm went up. "Forty three? Forty two? Forty one?"

A hand went up sharply.

"I remember you. You're...erm...Slap something!"

"Slap Canopy."

"Yes, and you said you were forty!"

"Yes, I know Sir, I was lying again."

The Lieutenant smiled and looked up to the sky, then at his quartermaster who smiled back at him.

"Alright Mr Canopy. It's tradition that the youngest...oh, what's your name?"

"Growl Bonetone, Sir," replied the youngster.

"It's tradition that the youngest and oldest members come up with the name for our brigade. I want you two to disappear for a while and come back and tell us what you've come up with. This is an unofficial title we want now, something inspiring, nothing stupid. This is what people will know us by. It's important. Off you go! Good luck!"

They both nodded and walked away from the rest of them

and stood together against some trees. After a moment or two they sat down and began talking. The Lieutenant looked back at all the others and told them how he was going to find his one hundred.

"As you know our job is to find all those goblins that have been kidnapped and we're going to do that with speed and stealth. Stealth I can teach you but speed I can't, especially since time is so short. We're likely to be doing a lot of running out there. That's why we're going to have a little race. Naturally, the first one hundred will be chosen. Those of you that aren't fast enough will have to go home I'm afraid. Is that understood?"

They all understood and said to the Lieutenant that they did.

"It's not going to be a sprint so pace yourselves, nor is it a marathon so don't get left behind. If you're too tired then stop...and take off your armour! I don't want any heart attacks thank you very much."

"Where to?" shouted one of them.

"I was just about to tell you. Listen very carefully. This is the Great Field. We start here. You then follow the main road to the north east for two miles. Take the second left turn, heading west, it's very obvious. That leads to the market area after another two miles. Then you go south west on Oak Road for three miles then turn east on the Highway that brought you here. Don't worry, by the time you return the finish line will be set up."

"It's a bit complicated isn't it?" asked another.

"Yes. All the better to test your navigating skills then,

wouldn't you say? If you get lost you won't be chosen, and don't try to cheat, we'll be watching! Don't worry about your belongings they'll be safe here. Right! Let's have you! Oh wait! We haven't heard from our two friends yet."

The Lieutenant wandered over to where Growl and Slap were sitting. They appeared to be still in discussions. They saw the Lieutenant approach and stood up to greet him.

"Well, what have you come up with?" said the Lieutenant pleasantly.

"Slap's Scumbags!" announced Mr Canopy, with no lack of confidence as he did so.

"Awww listen, I don't need jokers in my brigade! You're lucky to still be here after lying to me twice today. You were probably lying about your military experience too. You'd better have come up with something decent, otherwise I'll..."

"The boiled mice!" said Growl suddenly, perhaps to protect his new friend.

"The boiled mice? Where d'you get that name?"

"My great grandmother was a hobgoblin Sir. Boiled mice are a very popular dish. It was her speciality."

"The boiled mice. Ha! I like it. Well done. The boiled mice. Alright, come back with me. We have a race to run. Finish in the first hundred and you'll officially become a boiled mouse. Don't worry about the route, just follow the others. It's about ten miles so don't charge off at the start."

The three of them walked back to join the others. They all had smiles on their faces as they approached.

"Right everyone! Follow me to the start. If you want a

drink or to leave something else behind do it now. Last chance! If at any time you want to stop, please just stop and come straight back here to report yourself as dropping out."

Quickly everyone did as instructed and abandoned their things or swigged one last swig from their bottles. The Lieutenant checked with his quartermaster and his other two colleagues that all was well. It was, and they prepared to go to their various appointed positions in the forest to stop any cheaters finding a short cut. The Lieutenant decided he would begin the race to keep some order and discipline amongst them and to get them going at a suitable pace. They all moved with him as he walked down to the start of the road that they would follow first. Several went out in front hoping to get ahead of the others. The Lieutenant told them to hold their horses and that it wouldn't make any difference whether they started at the front or the back. All but the most eager listened to him.

The first road they were to take was fairly wide, as were each of the roads on the route in fact. Two huge trees one hundred feet apart marked the natural beginning of it. The mass of goblins was quickly assembling in front. They were stripped now of all their armour and weaponry and most looked like serious trooper material, much to the quiet satisfaction of their commander. He backed out of their way and intended to find his place somewhere in the middle of the runners so as to keep his eye on as many of them as possible.

"Right!" shouted the Lieutenant. "Everyone ready?"
They murmured something back that was good enough
for him.

"Then off we go!"
Like water rolling down a gentle slope they began to move
forward as a single body past the start and into the race.
He joined them at the back and gradually moved forward
to keep an eye on the whole thing. He was pleased to note
that none of them rushed away and that none fell over
themselves. The weather was just right for this. There was
sunshine through the trees but along with it came a cool
breeze to dry the sweat from their bodies. The Lieutenant
was also surprised that there was still a metallic clattering
noise coming from somewhere as he'd instructed everyone
to leave their armour and weapons behind. Ah well, on
their own heads be it he thought.

Back in the Great Field the quartermaster casually spun a
line from one tree trunk to another at the entrance to the
field that was opposite the place where they had just
started. He instructed one of the others to stay and
supervise the return of the runners and any other stragglers
that returned in the meantime. He and his remaining
colleague ventured northward into the forest to keep an
eye out for any creative types that might claim to have
mistaken the route in their favour. Also, he suspected that
one or two of those that were rejected at the first stage
might try to hang around and join the race towards its
end. As it turned out no goblin would attempt to worm
his way into the brigade by either method.

The idea for the race had come from the quartermaster, a goblin by the name of Flap Phosphor. His surname was a nickname gained from his familiarity with explosive powders. He was a veteran of the highest quality and would have been of value on any campaign out of the forest. He was as solid as a rock in his body, moulded by many years of active duty. He had in fact trained the Lieutenant. This was something the Lieutenant had asked him to keep quiet about. He thought the Lieutenant a little too sensitive at times but a good leader nonetheless.

The first and the last mile are the hardest so they say. In this case it seemed that each mile was as hard as all the others. The general standard of the runners was pretty good, although many were eating into reserves they didn't have, simply to keep pace with the main group and avoid becoming one of the stragglers. As you might expect the younger ones and those with some training and experience found that steadily they put some distance between the older and flabbier ones. It seemed that word of this spectacle had gotten around and many goblins came to take a look at them all. The route itself was a naturally busy one and on more than one occasion a trader with his barrow became surrounded.

The Lieutenant was starting to enjoy himself and the weight of his responsibility escaped his mind for a little while. He would stay with the runners till the end. His eye naturally examined them to see who if any would stand out. He would not use the entire one hundred straight away but instead would favour thirty or so as a scout party. Once they were on the trail of those kidnapped he thought he would then summon the rest should they be needed to help liberate the captives. Therefore he wanted the brightest and best individuals to form that core. Quickness on their feet would be an essential characteristic for membership of a scout party. But, he didn't want anyone that would outrun him too easily since he would definitely be out there with them and he didn't want to have angry humans chasing them with himself as the slowest runner.

Soon cheers and encouragement from the spectators came their way, especially for those that were in danger of making up the unlucky surplus thirty eight. The ground was dry under foot and quite hard so it was tough going for those that had brought basic shoes or heavy boots and had not anticipated an event like this. But that was what faced them out there, uncertainty and difficulty, so they had better learn to adapt. The pack lengthened considerably as the miles slowly dragged by. The better runners were safely past halfway whilst some were still to complete one quarter of the route. The Lieutenant managed to stay somewhere in between the two groups. Behind him it was obvious that certain faces would not make into the first one hundred and he fully expected them to stop and call it a day. Despite their red faces and anguished expressions he was surprised that none had so far done so. He was glad he had listened to Flap about having a race. It was an excellent excuse to train them and to see who was really ready for this adventure and who was not. This important question was being answered for him most conveniently as the day wore on.

The Lieutenant was also pleased to discover that the youngest and eldest members of the troop were amongst the front runners. It would've been quite embarrassing if they'd come up with the unofficial name for the brigade but then were sent home for being too slow. That Slap Canopy character was clearly a very fit forty one year old, if indeed that was his age. He hoped it would not rise again, at least no faster than everyone else's. He himself was tiring a little but was more than capable of maintaining pace with all but the fastest, as was necessary since he was in command and had a reputation to uphold. He could not allow his own weaknesses to dispirit the others and damage their faith in him.

After a while he saw the quartermaster join him for a little part of the way. They managed to have a short conversation as they kept pace with the main pack.

"Any...given up...yet?" said the Lieutenant, his words emerging after each stride and each breath.

"None Sir," reported the quartermaster, not in the least out of breath.

"Any cheats?"

"None Sir."

"Good. Keep an...eye out...will you?"

"Yes Sir."

"Go to the...front and...make sure...they're going...the right way."

"Yes Sir," and with that he charged ahead, putting some

distance between him and his commander.

The Lieutenant groaned as he noticed that a couple of little yappy dogs were chasing him. As discreetly as he could, without alerting their owners wherever they were, he incorporated a savage little kick in his stride as they sniffed and yapped around him. They yelped and snarled as they were hit but this had the desired effect and they ran off into the forest. He laughed at the success of this nifty little trick and he wondered if their enemies out there might be dealt with as easily.

"Wouldn't that be nice?" he whispered to himself.

Soon the long westward stretch was coming to an end for all but the slowest runners. This part of the forest housed the market area. All along their right side they could see the stalls and produce on offer. Everyone got a good look at each other as the fruit and beer for sale, amongst other things, were tantalising to the runners, and for the market people the sight of so many running idiots was not to be missed. As the Lieutenant passed by it suddenly occurred to him that he had not thought to provide a drink on their return. He might have some very thirsty goblins on his hands and he certainly didn't want any of them to die of dehydration. He thought of the stories that would appear in the Milton Green's Pamphlet. *'Several die in foolhardy race!'*, *'Blood on the racetrack!'*, *'They wanted to save innocent goblins but were killed by their own!'*, *'Inexperienced Lieutenant blamed for tragedy!'*, *'Councillors meeting to consider his fate!'*, *'Idiot's public execution is approved!'*

He decided on a quick diversion and ran over to the nearest drinks stall.

"I hereby confiscate these two barrels of water in the name of the Council of Milton Greens!" he said to the goblin stallholder, with as much bravado and authority as he could muster.

The goblin said nothing back to the Lieutenant but instead scoffed and folded his arms.

"Alright, alright! How much!?"

For the runners at the front it was getting close to the end of the race. They were generally relaxed and each knew that they were safely assured a place in the first one hundred, so few of them were particularly anxious to be first through the finish line. The inevitable show-offs charged away when the finish line came into view. Those that did so found little advantage from it as they were simply counted as they came in and were barely looked at beyond that. The rest of the field stretched back for over a mile and by now several aging or unfit goblins had indeed had enough, though without withdrawing from the race properly. They had simply gone home after thinking better of their ordeal.

The numbers passing the line increased gently at first. Ten, twelve, fifteen, you can imagine the pattern I am sure. When the total reached fifty the Lieutenant crossed the line. He had carried two small barrels with him under his arms for the last mile or so, although he had taken some convenient shortcuts as was only fair. He approached those that had finished the race and cracked open the first barrel. He anxiously gave some water to those that appeared to be the most likely to fall over and get him into trouble. He smiled when he realised that possibility was now remote.

The Lieutenant's colleague, a young but normally reliable goblin called Crunch Tone who had been entrusted with counting them in, reached seventy in his count. He could see yet more approaching and decided that he would venture a little up the route to announce just how many places had been taken.

"Seventy five finished!" he shouted.

This caused a moment of great anxiety amongst those runners that were within earshot and had not yet finished. They suddenly surged and he had a little trouble maintaining his count. He cupped his hands around his mouth and shouted even louder back up the lane.

"Eighty five finished!"

Those at the edge of his vocal reach and in serious danger of not being in the one hundred started to sprint. Some even grabbed at each other to get past. This was a poor decision by the young Crunch. Now he would have to count about twenty in a few seconds. His eyes blurred over the runners and he suddenly jumped out behind what he sincerely hoped was the one hundredth runner. He held his arms up, waved them around and shouted frantically at those still to finish in front of him.

"That's it! One hundred! No more! That's one hundred!"

Many did not want to listen and started arguing with him about his counting and his attitude. Others just rushed past him and ensconced themselves into those that had already finished. Fortunately for him the quartermaster had been observing and keeping his own count. He approached Crunch, dragging with him two of the late runners that had naughtily tried to become a part of the one hundred. He also brought with him his natural authority.

"We'll have no misbehaviour here! We've one hundred and we'll take no more! If you've not made it ther. go home. I'm sorry but we've got to be strict! Collect your things and go home. Thank you very much."

He waved his hand dismissively after letting go of his two goblins. He took his young colleague back with him and made sure that they had a final count of one hundred. Then he formally confirmed this to the Lieutenant. This was good news and the Lieutenant allowed a broad smile to break out on his face. He looked around and saw that the headlines he'd feared would not come to be written. He now had in front of him a distinguished group. Even the hardened quartermaster enjoyed the scene. Not one seemed inferior and they were a good blend of the young and eager and the seasoned and wise. Even in their tired and drained condition they still looked a useful bunch. He stood on the platform which he had occupied a couple of hours earlier. He had achieved the first task assigned to him, to make a suitable troop of goblins. This he had done well and he allowed himself a moment of pride. He began to speak.

"Well done, all of you! Thank you for your efforts! And

welcome to the fold!" all said with a smile on his face. "Now...another duty for me to perform is to properly inaugurate our brigade. Our official title is the...One Hundred and Seventh Milton Greens Special Militia Brigade. Our ceremonial commander is technically the Leader of the Council. If he shows up though I'll tell him to bugger off 'cause I'm in charge."

To his relief he got his first laugh.

"But, as you know, by convention we'll use an unofficial title. Our youngest and eldest friends performed that task for us this morning and came up with something good. At least I think so. Our brigade shall be known as...'The Boiled Mice!'"

There was stunned silence, which the Lieutenant had not expected.

"What? You don't like it?"

CHAPTER 6

Two very succulent and well manicured pink feet poked lazily beyond the fine sheets that covered them. They moved slowly and the toes on one foot curled and stretched a little. Some five and a half feet away from these feet a contented princess dozed by herself in an enormous bed. Outside the sun was making a great deal more progress with the day than she was. It was not her responsibility to do anything at this moment in time however so she was happy to stay in bed. The gentle rumble of deer scattering about the castle grounds could be heard through the open windows in her room. This noise woke her sufficiently to make it impossible for her to doze off once more. She turned over onto her back and pulled herself upright in the bed. She sat and looked around for a few moments after which she was attacked by a huge yawn. She reached over to her bedside table and picked up her favourite pipe. It was long, slender and pure white in colour. Not, in fact, too different from her. She quickly stuffed a little tobacco inside it and grabbed a match nearby. She scraped the match against the stone wall above her bed and it burned into life at the first attempt. The moist brown fibres in her pipe glowed and crisped nicely.

She got out of bed and walked over to the window with a trail of smoke billowing behind her and down her exceedingly long blonde hair. Before presenting herself at the window to take in the view she wisely decided to put on her robe which had lain on the floor beside the bed. The sight of a naked princess at the window might put the lower orders into something of a swoon she thought to herself. Outside she could see verdant neatly trimmed lawns, frolicking fauna and fountains and flowers all around. It was quite a sight and would have impressed all but the most indifferent and hard hearted of princesses. She was not impressed. For her it was all an annoying contrivance designed to interrupt her beauty sleep.

"Fenton!" she bellowed behind herself.

The door creaked open a touch, and her servant presented his voice but not his person.

"Yes my lady?"

"What time is it?"

"It is noon my lady."

"Ah, breakfast time! See to it will you. I want some more boiled eggs but tell them not to put flowers on the plate this time!"

"Yes my lady."

She watched the door suspiciously as it closed.

At the many castles and courts of the time this princess, by the name of Ursula, was a frequent visitor. For the benefit of any royal watchers reading this her full title was Princess Ursula Ekaterina Tinklestrop, daughter of King Simon the Nonentity and Queen Sarah the Overpowering, of the distant Kingdom of Phyla. At whose invitation she originally came was a matter of some debate. As you will come to understand once her welcome had rapidly been extinguished no one wished to volunteer this information. She was possessed of great vitality and had a keen eye for finery and things of quality (especially when they belonged to other people), a talent for music (and its impassioned recital at any hour of the day or night), a powerful voice (with an opinion rarely very far from her lips) and a fine length of strong blonde hair tied always in an ornate plat stretching down to the back of her knees. However, never let it be said that she was not a beauty, for whatever qualities she may have lacked in taste, warmth, discretion, courtesy, generosity, self restraint, embroidery, frugality, and sobriety to name but a few, the princess more than compensated for any other disadvantage with her prettiness. With the liberal use of her physical charms she easily created whatever support and affection she required from the many princes that moved within royal circles. This was true at least of those that did not know her particularly well.

She owed her current position to her royal parents, who, having it in mind to get rid of her for as long as humanly possible had persuaded her to write to one of the many princes to try to get an invitation to visit the King's castle. Naturally, being of royal blood and travelling under her own inflated reputation, the request was readily accepted. She was received with great ceremony and allowed the use of certain private rooms for her stay. At that time the length of her stay remained undetermined; a few weeks estimated the King's officials. A few months had almost elapsed. But, one does not just tell a personage of royal descent that they have outstayed their welcome, unless it is another personage of royal descent that does so.

Her timing had been excellent as recent events had caused great distraction to the King and his ministers who were all very busy. The lesser royals had their own suites to retire to whenever they chose and so did not particularly care about any difficulties or offence the princess caused to the staff; and caused it she did. Consequently, there was no one in a suitable position to tell her to go home or if there was someone they didn't care enough to do so. She was appreciated by some however. Her great beauty brought many an admiring glance and even though the unfortunate prince that had invited her had long since vowed to avoid her as if she were swollen with one of the less attractive plagues there were numerous young men of condition that were still swayed by her.

The princess was so eager to stay that she wished to ensnare one of these young men in the hopes that she might be granted a more permanent position here. After all, this was the King's castle, where the greatest Court in the land resided. It was far ahead in terms of grandeur, excitement and influence than was her parent's crumbling back water pile. Soon she would attempt to impress herself upon a person none other than the King's nephew. He had been away on military exercises for all the time that she had been there so they did not know each other. He was therefore virgin territory, in every sense. He was a pompous and prickly creature and had but one virtue, his proximity to the throne. From what she had heard about him she believed he would easily submit to her dominating nature.

She turned and smiled at a creature over which she held as much power as she would like to have over the King's nephew, and every other man for that matter. This creature sat at the end of her bed and had had the pleasurable habit of biting her toes during the night. He was a white long haired cat whom she had christened 'powder puff', though on ceremonial occasions she referred to him by his proper title - 'King Hairy the First'. He stared up at her but did not move except to scratch gently at the fine sheets beneath him. He was splayed out on the bed like a sphinx that had melted in the sun.

The princess turned back to the window and thought about what new and diverting pursuits she might try today.

In the similar sized room directly above Ursula's bedroom several men were at work. It was not noisy work. In fact it required silence for the men to properly concentrate upon what they were doing. They were all mapmakers and had recently returned from certain specialist missions given only to them. Each carefully drew up the results of his efforts into large individual maps on his own separate table. One for instance was drawing in the very finest detail a series of gentle slopes approaching a group of low craggy hills, beyond which a certain castle lay. He included the walls and fences of farmland. He included every conceivable pathway and usable route. He even included crumbling old buildings in case they might be useful as shelter from bad weather or from other more immediate dangers. Another had been given the task of drawing a map, one edge of which bordered the forest of Milton Greens. This forest, from the King's point of view, was a very minor piece of ground. Nevertheless, the forest was close to several important trading and re-supply routes so might prove to be of some strategic importance to the King.

The windows to this room were shut and the only sounds inside came from the soft scribbling and scraping noises of quill against parchment and the mumbling noises coming from an adjacent room. One of the men was about to finish his map. He had coloured all sections in the appropriate colour, he had checked and rechecked that the scale was consistent, he had compared his field maps with his new map and they were exact and he had put on all the proper signatures and explanations at the side of it. He now blew upon it to speed up the drying of the most recently applied ink. He stood up and gently began to roll up his map. It measured some four feet by four feet and provided it was approved by his superiors would be duplicated many times.

He carefully approached the door linking this chamber with the next one. Beyond, voices could be heard. He knocked gently against the heavy wood. The voices stopped. Footsteps began. The door opened and the man was invited in and told to place his map on the large table in the centre of the room. He did so. Conversation did not resume till he had left the room and the door had been closed behind him. He was given not a word of thanks.

The map was unrolled and examined by five men standing in a circle around it. Two of the men were dressed in fine velvets. They were members of the King's ministry and each was as fine a judge of human behaviour as the Kingdom could produce. The other three were senior Captains dressed in light armour, and each had many hundreds of men under their command.

Together the five were debating the merits and demerits of various military plans that were in consideration. Once they had decided on a solution they would show it to the King for his approval. This approval would be just a troublesome formality as, sadly, the King was suffering from a disease of the mind. He was becoming senile in his old age. This was the best kept secret in the Kingdom. Whenever the King had appeared in public at a function he would be sedated beforehand so that he would remain silent and docile throughout. This was explained away by those in the know as a short melancholy from which he would soon recover, or as excessive tiredness brought about by the great burden of his duties as King. Privately, his physicians could do little to remedy the disease. Left untreated, or perhaps I should say left unguarded, the King would start to demonstrate his delicate grip on events. The Kingdom itself would be put into peril if it all came loose.

It was fortunate that those close to the King by reason of family or duty would be in as much danger as he if this matter came out. As a result they willingly helped to conceal the facts of his illness. The danger to all of them lay not from within but from without. Despite all the many people obliged to the protection and sustenance of the King the whole organisation would be vulnerable if other powers knew of the weakness at its core.

As it happened the King's ministers were doing an excellent job in controlling things. They hoped for a gentle transition of power, at least in the eyes of the public, from the King upon his death, which his physicians agreed would not be more than a year away, to his only son Frederick. However, this would solve one problem only to replace it with another, for Frederick could be disposed towards his own brand of derangement when the mood took him. As a result, the prospect of his ascension to the throne, though expected as the natural heir, was welcomed by very few, either with power or without. The men in this room had the considerable and unenviable task of protecting the Kingdom and its future as well as their own positions within it. In truth, these five men were just part of a clan; a clan that would outlive any person that was a member. The strength of the clan itself protected them, not any individual within it. Their loyalty to their King was in fact a loyalty to their clan, that which sustained them and gave them real power. If the King was no longer a relevant part of the clan then it was as if he had never been a part of it at all and he could therefore be put aside as though he meant nothing.

They faced threats of many kinds but the largest and most pressing was that offered by the King's former favourite Lord Spikepoint. This group of five looked closely at the map on the table because it showed a large part of the territory between them and his area of influence, at the centre of which was Spikepoint Castle. It was therefore essential to study this map due to the likelihood of a confrontation. Natural light bathed them and the hills and valleys on the map seemed to have their own shadows because of it. The rhythmic sounds of the heart pounding battle drums did not seem far away.

These men did not want war with Spikepoint because it would be at too great a cost to themselves in terms of men and money, and they in their considerable experience felt that such a conflict would be decisive for neither but very painful to both. Sadly, despite their best efforts it was becoming unavoidable. It had become known to them via numerous channels that Spikepoint was consolidating his territory and expanding his forces. They needed little analysis to comprehend why. He was preparing for an offensive of some sort but they could not say when it would come or where it might be focused. They thought aloud that somehow it might have been discovered just what a weakened condition the King and his Kingdom were in. There could be spies and traitors everywhere it seemed. This all added to their sense of insecurity.

The enemy lived beyond these western fells, written in clear blue ink on the map, but it was within the rooms and corridors of this very castle that the war might be won or lost. Each of these five men knew Spikepoint personally and all had reason to suspect that any of the other four might have made some arrangement with him. This climate of uncertainty was a test of a man's loyalty. If the fear grew too great for some they would switch allegiance. This was a mental rot that afflicted the political person more than the military person, for loyalty was the driving force of the latter and necessity of the former. As a result there was a barrier of suspicion between the three Captains and the King's ministers. The tension in the room strained them all.

They continued their discussions for a short while. Gradually they were coming closer to an agreement on how best to make the defensive preparations. The youngest of the three Captains, a man by the name of Starling Dodd, was it seemed the man least affected by the threat that faced them and was the only one to suggest any offensive strategy. As they talked further they began to hear footsteps from another room. This room was one of those which belonged to the King and the thoughts of all five were that the footsteps could belong only to him. The door swung open, creaking slowly, and the King emerged cautiously into the company of the others. He wore a sad and hollow expression on his face. He had some armour on his chest but his feet were bare. His hair had been cut short. He carried nothing and his hands flexed and his fingers wandered. He closed the door behind himself and moved away from it. He said nothing to the others who simply stared at him, unsure of what he was doing or the state of mind he was in. He looked at no-one and behaved as if he was the only one in the room. The light from outside suddenly attracted his attention. He moved over towards the windows and then opened them. A gust of wind came inside and disturbed the map and the other papers sat on the table, which Captain Dodd then quickly held firm. This prompted one of the ministers to speak to his King.

"Sire...are you alright?"

It took several seconds before the King seemed to hear what had been said and he turned, startled, to the source of this strange noise. He looked at them all suddenly as if for the first time. He then began to speak, though much strange noise came from his mouth before any proper words fell out.

"Where is this? I wonder where is this...and these people where are they? I wonder, where are they?" he said, pointing at the few people wandering around outside.

"Sire," said his minister again, "do you not recognise us...and this place?"

"Gavelrigg? Is that you?"

"It is Sire," he said, relieved, "Gavelrigg."

"And what of my Kingdom?"

"It is...still here Sire!" he said, chuckling nervously.

"Fool!" bellowed the King, and at such a volume and in so unexpected a fashion that the others all jumped in surprise and alarm. "Is a jester in charge of my Kingdom? Where is Gavelrigg? Gavelrigg!"

"I'm here Sire, it is me."

"No!" he bellowed again. "You're that idiot son of his. Where is the father?"

"My father died many years ago Sire. You appointed me

in his place. Do you not remember?" said his faithful minister, with growing exasperation.

The King stared suspiciously at Gavelrigg for a few moments. He seemed to accept what he was being told, though not without resentment. He grumbled quietly. He then turned his back on the men and looked out of the window.

"Is there anything you need Sire?" asked one of the other Captains, gently and sympathetically.

"Fresh air...that is all."

He continued to look out onto the fields then suddenly seemed to remember something.

"How go the preparations for the banquet?"

"They are well underway Sire," said Gavelrigg.

"And the pigs! The suckling pigs, we have them?" asked the King.

"Yes indeed Sire, many suckling pigs," he replied, though in truth he had no idea about any pigs and was now just humouring his King.

"And the entertainments! The musicians and colourful jesters!"

"All in hand Sire, I believe," this time Gavelrigg was more cautious in his assurances for he knew pigs were easier to come by in an emergency than musicians or jesters.

"And the magician?" asked the King.

"The magician?" responded Gavelrigg.

"McCranahan!"

Gavelrigg had not heard this name before and thought his King was in a land purely of his own making. He turned to the others and they looked equally baffled.

"Zebulan McCranahan!" said the King again, staring at each of them in amazement that he was not being understood. "The fire for hire! The greatest magician alive!"

"Oh, I think I've heard of him!" said one of the Captains suddenly.

The others looked at this Captain, thinking he was also humouring the King like Gavelrigg had done, but it seemed he was serious.

"If you find him and bring him here for the banquet I'll make you one of my Captains!" offered the King excitedly.

"I am one of your Captains Sire."

"Congratulations!" said the King, after a pause. "Bring him anyway."

"Yes Sire," he replied, wishing he had stayed quiet.

"How are my armies?" continued the King.

"We were just discussing them now Sire. What would you like to know?" said Gavelrigg.

"What I would like to know," asked the King angrily, "is why you are all here discussing business which concerns only me?"

"Well, we're simply doing our duty and protecting the Kingdom Sire...as you instructed us to do."

"I gave no such instruction! What are these papers here?" said the King, pointing at the table in the middle of them. He rushed to the table and picked up the map. He squinted at the fine detail upon it and seemed as though he was about to speak several times but became distracted each time by some new feature before he could do so. His forehead and his mouth were in a wild state of activity and the skin on his face wobbled and trembled with a manic excitement. Suddenly he recognised the land described on the map.

"Ah, Spikepoint, my friend, how goes your business?" the King paused awaiting an answer. From somewhere in his mind it came. "Wonderful. Wonderful. Such a rocky existence you have. I can see you there in your little castle! Hello!" he was now waving at the map. "Is it cold in there? So very grey in your castle, is it not? When will we see you again here in our castle? We miss you and your lovely wife so! A charming giant of a woman I remember, and your nineteen sons and daughters, delightful little souls but so ugly! The poor little creatures! They'll never touch anyone in my family I can tell you! I can see you in your little window there! Yes..."

The King seemed to become bored with this and he turned to leave the way he had come. This came as a relief to the others except that he was still holding the map tightly in his hands. Gavelrigg was losing patience with this display and he moved around in front of the King to block his exit. "The map Sire, may we have it back?" he said, as calmly as he could.

"Why? You don't need it?" replied the King.

"We do need it! We have important business to attend to! Leave it here!" said Gavelrigg, losing his temper for a brief moment.

The King stopped in his tracks and stared at Gavelrigg.

He was boiling now at being spoken to in such a fashion. Uncertain of reality he may have been but forgetful of his supreme position over other men he was not. He growled and snarled at the man.

"What possible business could you have with the map that would come before mine? You...you impudent little snake! You understand nothing! You are a waste of flesh! I should have you boiled and fried!" he turned to the others and addressed them, "Have this one roasted on a spit so I can eat him at my banquet!"

He motioned again to leave but Gavelrigg was undaunted and put his arm directly in his King's path.

"Leave the map with us Sire," said Gavelrigg quietly but firmly, and staring into his eyes.

The King was at a loss at such a challenge and felt the power ebbing away from him. He could not understand what was going on.

"Everything in my Kingdom belongs to me, does it not?"

"Yes Sire, but the Kingdom is in trouble and we need the map to protect the Kingdom."

"Trouble? What trouble? I am the trouble to others not the other way around."

"Lord Spikepoint. He means to attack us...and you Sire. He wants your crown, your Kingdom!"

The King looked at Gavelrigg with a strange expression. This last statement made no sense to him at all. He laughed at the idea but it was a nervous laugh and he did not lose the uncertain look on his face while doing so.

"That is not true," said the King, in way that even he

209

seemed to doubt, "he is my most loyal Captain. He could not do such a thing even if he wanted to."

"It *is* true Sire, and he *is* capable of it, *and* he's planning to do it at this very moment," said Gavelrigg.

"It's true Sire, we're discussing our tactics now," said one of the other Captains.

It seemed that these words were slowly sinking into the King's mind. His shoulders slumped but he did not loosen his grip on the map. He looked around at all of them.

"What are we to do then?" he said, showing genuine fear.

"We must have a conference, and bring him here. I can persuade him to be loyal once more. I'm sure he will listen to me."

"That won't work Sire, it's far beyond such things now," said Gavelrigg dismissively.

"I am still the King! You will do as I say or face the consequences. Do you understand Gavelrigg?"

"I do," he replied, but not meaning it.

"We should invite him to the banquet. It's not too late to arrange," said the King.

"He wouldn't come!" said the other minister.

"Why not? He might you know," said Starling Dodd. "If he's confident he can take over then he wouldn't refuse the chance to see the state of things here and to see all that he might try to take."

"He would think it a trap!" said Gavelrigg.

"No, he would not," said the King. "He knows me. I am a man of honour who would not play such a cowardly game."

"But what would we achieve by it?" asked Gavelrigg.

"What would we achieve?" said the King, and for the first time he seemed to speak like a King. "Here is what we would achieve. I would get to stare him in the eye and see what the man is made of and he would see what I and we are made of! He would quickly lose his confidence. What do you think?"

The others could say very little on seeing their King so energised. They did not respond so he considered the matter settled.

"Make the arrangements. I want to see Spikepoint and McCranahan at my banquet next week. Thank you gentlemen."

The King smiled and handed over the map to Gavelrigg. He then withdrew, whistling a tune as he went. Gavelrigg closed the door behind him and turned to the others.

"He won't come but we'll send the invitation anyway. If he is such a fool as to come then we'll just arrest him and put him in the dungeon."

"I know what we'll do," said Starling Dodd, "we'll sit him next to Princess Ursula. She'll take care of him for us. On second thoughts, maybe that would be a little too cruel."

After a moment or two for the others to imagine such a scene there came raucous laughter.

*

As each day passed Gurgle learned more about himself and more about the people with whom he was travelling. He found that he was settling in well to the routine of tents, walking and foraging, enforced though it was. He had developed his own style and had adapted his clothing somewhat. Most of the clothes he wore had been given to him by the others. If you were to look at him now compared to before the only thing you might recognise would be those sturdy boots of his. Tirgu had also given him a very nifty little blade for cutting and whittling. Some of the others had quietly questioned the wisdom of doing so considering that Gurgle's memories of capture might still be too fresh. They were not as trusting as he in this instance and they suspected he might wake up and find the blade in his back one morning. However, Tirgu was not in the least bit concerned by their caution. He had grown very fond of his little green scout and felt relaxed in his company. For his part Gurgle had lost all his fear of them and was ever so slowly starting to enjoy himself. He still thought of home every day, many times a day in fact. But for some reason the further away they travelled from it the less important it seemed to him. He no longer had regrets for himself, for his daily life was exciting and full of surprises. His only regret was for his poor mother who he knew would be sick with worry. This saddened him so much that he hoped he might be thought to have died so that she could grieve and move on with her life. He thought of the pleasure it would bring her if he suddenly appeared at their tree door once more, in the months, or maybe years to come.

Naturally he was still in two minds about his situation. If he had had the power to transport himself home immediately then of course he would have done so but he was a sensible and practical child and he knew the difference between what was possible and what was not. He could not ignore what his situation demanded of him and so he followed the maxim taught to him by his father. Wherever you are and whatever you're doing, make the best of it. He wondered if his father would approve of his cooperation with these people. That was unlikely but what else could he be expected to do? Was it his duty to escape by any means necessary, even if it put him in danger of his life? No, he thought to himself, and besides, it's my decision to make.

Tirgu no longer felt that Gurgle was a risk. He was perhaps a better judge of behaviour under pressure than most. He knew that what was in front of you was of far more influence on you than what was in your head. He had engaged Gurgle's energy and imagination not just through what he had told him and arranged for him to do but also because of what he was - a strange, dangerous and intelligent creature that fascinated Gurgle immensely.

Tirgu was ready to try another level of education for Gurgle. So far he had shielded him from real danger and responsibility. Now he felt he could begin to teach him how to be a scout, his scout. How to observe, how to move about, how to communicate quietly, how to hide and most importantly of all how to listen to things at distances that he and his human men could not. This exercise would not be achieved quickly, not only because of the complexity of the training but also because other priorities came first. They were returning to Spikepoint Castle. This was Tirgu's base of operations and from where he received his orders. Their recent excursion into Milton Greens was not as a result of any order Tirgu had received, it was a journey of his own making and he had been ordered to return to the castle once his business had been concluded.

The land through which Gurgle and the others now moved had very few trees in it. In fact the number of buildings exceeded the number the trees. Gurgle's attention was grabbed by practically every other thing that he saw for so much of it had not entered his eyes before. His presence also grabbed the attention of all the people that were out and about, for very few goblins tended to pass this way. The place was a collection of scattered houses and outbuildings. Some had thatched roofs made of straw and some had roofs that were made of earth. They all had stone walls around them which marked the perimeter of each property. Gurgle could see that nearly all of them had small fields and allotments full of growing food.

Tirgu and his group were walking casually down the path that led through this part of the world. The path was a wide one and there was dry mud underfoot. The weather was cool and breezy. Gurgle was wrapped up to protect himself from the elements. Ahead of him he could see a little black and white cat sat upon the end of a wall belonging to one of the houses. It watched them approach with wide eyes then darted away behind the wall when they came close. Those few people that were walking around were all human men and women, and each was as anxious as the cat to avoid contact with Tirgu and his group. That would not have surprised them for they had a mean and menacing style and cultivated just such a reaction wherever they went.

Gurgle turned his head around and looked for the little cat that had run from them. They exchanged a look as the cat poked his head from his hiding place at the foot of the wall. They were strolling almost. None seemed in a hurry to get anywhere. Tirgu controlled the pace and walked in front, occasionally turning to see that Gurgle was still with them, ensconced in the middle of the group. Several of the men around Gurgle were talking to each other and smiling at what they were being told. He listened discreetly.

"How long has it been since you and she were together last?" said one of the men.

"Three weeks. I know she'll be missing me. She always does," replied his companion.

"And how old is your little boy now?"

"Three, in a month."

"Will you get the chance to take them somewhere for a little while?" asked another, to the same man.

"No, you don't think we'd have time off at the moment do you?"

"I have. Four weeks."

"What!? How d'you get that?" asked the first man angrily.

"Oh, it's been arranged for a good while now. They can't cancel it, can they?"

Tirgu turned his head again and decided to have his say.

"Don't be surprised if they do," he said, "we'll all be needed soon I can promise you."

"How soon? And for what?" asked the man, who had the leave arranged.

"As soon as we get back," Tirgu replied, "and for business of course. What else do we need you for?"

"Great. Thanks. You know, that's what I like about you Tirgu, your caring and sympathetic nature."

"That's right," said Tirgu smiling, "I have to set an example for my boy here, don't I?"

Tirgu laughed and turned to look forward once more. More than one of them recognised the familiar way in which Tirgu had referred to the goblin.

One of the men went forward and matched his pace with Tirgu so that he could speak a moment with him. The man pointed up ahead of them and Gurgle could see Tirgu's head move to look at what was being pointed out to him. He listened and then nodded. The man turned his head and smiled at the others.

"Who fancies a drink then?" he said.

The rest instantly agreed and became as happy as he was. They diverted away from the path and down a gentle slope between two farmhouses. Ahead of them Gurgle could see what appeared to be the largest building around.

It also appeared to be the most worn out. As they came near to it some gentle rays of sunshine hit them, which felt warming, and encouraged them to decide to sit outside. Gurgle could not understand what they might want to do here. Perhaps a friend of one of the group lived here. It seemed this friend was a popular sort as his house was full of people.

Gurgle did not like the look and atmosphere of the place at all. His instinct was to hide himself behind the others but they were all too busy trying to get inside. To his relief Tirgu came over to him and guided him with his arm. The two of them took a free table and sat together. Gurgle could see inside the house by looking through the window nearest to him. He could see several of the men gathered at some kind of wooden bench talking to a lady and a man wearing an apron. He could also see others sat around inside. Some were drinking. It looked warmer in there but the people looked frightening and dirty. Gurgle thought that on balance he was better where he was.

The men soon emerged carrying many clay beakers in their hands. These were put on the table. Gurgle peered over the rims and saw the same liquid in each. He could see bubbling white foam with little purple oases. He wondered what it was. Whatever it was, it would not last long as they sank them down their throats very fast. He reached over and took one of the beakers, supposing naturally that one was meant for him. He brought it closer to himself and leaned forward to take a sip. They all laughed at Gurgle and he stopped before his lips reached the edge.

"Stop! Don't drink that!" said one of the men.

"No, it's fine. Leave him. Let him have it," said another.

"You can't let him drink it, he'd fall over," said the first man again.

"What's wrong with it?" said Gurgle suddenly.

The others laughed again.

"Have you been to a place like this before Gurgle?" asked Tirgu.

"No, well, it's just someone's house isn't it?" he replied.

"Yes, sort of, sort of."

Tirgu smiled and looked at the others who all smiled back at him. Tirgu pointed upwards and directed Gurgle's eyes to a square wooden sign hanging above them. A large five pointed star was painted on it with writing underneath. The star and the writing were painted bright red.

"What does that say?" asked Tirgu gently.

"I can't read it."

"It says...The Pentagram."

"What's it mean?"

"It's just a name, but people know the place as that and they come to here relax and have a drink."

"A drink of what?" asked Gurgle.

Tirgu had not had a drink so far so he reached for the beaker that Gurgle had taken for himself, and he took a hefty gulp from it.

"Hmmm, gritty. Not beetroot brew again? It's such foul stuff."

"What juice is it? Can I try some?" asked Gurgle.

218

Tirgu looked at him for a moment or two and saw that he genuinely wanted some.

"You'll regret it. But, if you want to become one of us this is the quickest way! There you go."

As Tirgu and the others looked on, all with smiles and laughter, Gurgle held the beaker in both hands and took a quick sip. His first feeling was that it wasn't bad; thick and tangy, with a nice residue on the tongue. It was much like the vegetable juices he had all the time back in the forest. This was slightly different in one way though. He couldn't quite say how but the drink had a rich sharpness in his throat that he hadn't expected. He tried a little more and considered the flavour once again whilst staring deeply into the dark purple liquid. He coughed.

"What do you think of it Gurgle?" asked one of the men.

"It's good," he replied with a smile.

He took a large gulp. This prompted Tirgu to take it away from him and with Gurgle's best interests in mind he finished off what was left of the drink.

After half an hour or so and after several more 'juices', some of the men decided they were feeling hungry. To solve this problem they requested some food of the lady inside. Shortly thereafter they were brought a large dish full of fried potatoes and onions. It steamed gently and with all those delicious crusty brown edges to the potatoes Gurgle could not resist staring at it. Alongside they also had many pieces of bread and a pot of garlic sauce. To his relief Gurgle was invited to help himself as there was plenty to go around. He tentatively picked off a few

219

potatoes from the pile and began to eat. One of the men grabbed a big piece of bread, nearly half a loaf, and hollowed it out. He piled some of the potatoes and onions into the hollow and then liberally splattered some of the sauce on top. He bit into it savagely. He made such a mess but he obviously didn't care. Gurgle laughed as he watched him out of the corner of his eye.

Once all these things had been consumed and a little more time had passed the mood of Tirgu's group shifted from relaxed and happy to bloated and irritable. Tirgu and Gurgle had not touched much of the juice and as a result were relatively normal in their manner. However, some of the men could not be said to be in a similarly stable condition. A couple of them seemed queasy and jumpy. One sat motionless, cradling his head. It was at this point that it occurred to Gurgle that the drink might have been responsible for the change which came over them. He examined his own responses and feelings to see if he felt alright. Apart from a feeling of warmth in his legs he seemed fine.

Gurgle did his best to stay quiet and just to let things happen. He was uncomfortable with all this but he felt they would be leaving before too long. He was also in a warm spot that was protected from the cool breeze by the large bodies of his companions. So there he remained. He looked up at Tirgu next to him who also appeared to be reacting normally. He had not eaten much of what was in the dish, though he had dipped his finger into the garlic sauce a few times.

They were all sat about ten feet from the main entrance. The men had their backs to it but Gurgle and Tirgu and another man, sat opposite them, could see all who came in and out. With a clatter the door suddenly burst open. A human man staggered out. He was uncoordinated and clumsy and he seemed to have difficulty getting completely through the doorway. Once this complex task had finally been achieved he began to step gently forward. He seemed to be set on making his way home but he decided to look around first. He saw a large group of persons to his left. He identified one or two unusual creatures in it, a goblin and a hobgoblin.

Tirgu noticed him immediately and the drunken man diverted his stagger towards them. With bloodshot eyes and a dribbling lip he stared at Tirgu and Gurgle.

"Oi!" he blurted loudly, "get out! You get out! Go on! Off with you! We don't want your stinkin lot 'ere! Back to the bloody woods!"

He continued to stare, expecting them to move and in all honesty was surprised that his heartfelt request was not immediately complied with. In the heat of his indignant passions it had not occurred to him that they might object. Tirgu put his hand on Gurgle's shoulder and pressed him in his seat.

"Stay here," he said calmly.

Tirgu looked at his men opposite. They would not move until he moved. He nodded to them as he stood. They also stood and quickly turned to face the man that had challenged their leader. The man was so emboldened by the drink that he did not shrink at the sight of them. He continued his verbal assault.

"What're you still doin' here? Get out of it! This is where I live see!" he said, poking his own chest with his finger. "I've got a right to live here and I don't want it polluted by the likes of you."

This was a shameful display of hostility. The man was boiling with anger, caused as much by this no doubt as by the rest of the problems in his life. It was such a surprise to Gurgle as well. He had not seen people behave in this way before. Each new day seemed to contain a dozen things to confuse and frighten him.

"Listen to me," said Tirgu calmly, but with menace dripping from every word, "shut your mouth or it will be done for you. You understand?"

The man's eyes scrunched up and he bared his teeth. His grey stubble flared up like an animal alarmed.

"Don't you threaten me...I've handled your sort before. Back in my day we'd just flog you lot if you even dared come into our territory, now here you are treating the place as your own! Get out! Get out I tell you!"

Tirgu managed to control himself. He nodded to his men that now nearly surrounded this man. They seemed to know the natural thing to do and they swarmed upon him and picked him off his feet. Tirgu marched out ahead of them and his nose led him around the back of the building. He smelled water and decided it was better to soak the man in this fluid than the red one he would have preferred to soak him in had they been alone. His grandfather had been a victim of people like him and for all he knew this man might have a few unpaid debts to the hobgoblin race. The commotion of all this had caught the attention of everyone there and very little of the response was favourable towards Tirgu and the others. Shouts of objection and disapproval came as soon as the man was taken off his feet but because no other groups were as large as Tirgu's no practical help was offered to the man. He writhed and struggled furiously but it did him no good. Each limb had its oppressor.

Casually, they made their way around the building and took their prize down the grass verge to the edge of the babbling river. Gurgle followed them but tried not to seem a part of it all. He didn't know what to make of it. He had been frightened by the man's anger towards them but hadn't seen any reason why they should do this to him. He'd seemed harmless despite his offensiveness. Gurgle held his ground some distance from the others as he didn't want to become involved. He watched as Tirgu and the four men carrying the man chucked him without ceremony straight into the water. He threw vicious insults at them even as he was still moving through the air. It was not much of a splash. He yelped as his head fell beneath the water and groaned as he emerged for breath a moment later. This humiliation did seem to cool his anger though and he crawled to the opposite bank and pulled himself out of the water. He sat there with a very surprised look on his face and held his shoulder as though he had injured it on the rocks under the water.

From where Gurgle stood he could still see the front of the building and he noticed some activity and conversation. The man he'd seen inside wearing the apron came barging out. He was a fat man and his presence seem to coordinate and encourage the others standing about. He waved his arm in an arc behind himself and they began to follow. They all passed Gurgle and as each did so he received a dirty stare. He shrank from their attention and felt that now there was genuine danger. He yelled out.

"Tirgu!"

Tirgu heard the call and turned his attention from the wet man and back up towards the building. He bounded back up the grass verge as boldly as the man wearing the apron bounded down it.

"Don't worry, we're leaving," said Tirgu to the man in the apron.

The man in the apron said nothing but once he was within a few feet of Tirgu he suddenly swung a club at him, which Gurgle had not seen. It was desperately close to hitting him as Tirgu was surprised by it. It all seemed to be in slow motion for Gurgle. To his amazement Tirgu had somehow instinctively moved clear just in time. The man in the apron was now off balance after hitting only air and Tirgu simply grabbed him by his neck and twisted him off his feet using his weight against him. He stumbled and fell forwards, rolling to a stop at the feet of Tirgu's men. They kicked away his bat that had fallen with him.

"Shall we wet this one too?" asked one of the men.

"No, let's go," replied Tirgu.

Tirgu and the others made their way back up the slope and gathered Gurgle in with them. They did not hang around and they walked straight back to the lane. They faced no difficulty from the others, for with no leader to follow they instantly lost their courage.

Gurgle was once again in the protected heart of the group. He heard laughing from some of the men around him. Tirgu was walking in front and seemed to be stretching and flexing his hands and arms, presumably to see if they were still working well. He turned to address his men.

"Next time I'll pick the tavern."

The men all laughed and agreed. Tirgu turned his attention to Gurgle.

"Thanks for the warning Gurgle. You were a good lookout! Wouldn't you agree boys?"

They instantly cheered the fact and several hands reached down to pat Gurgle on the back.

"I think Gurgle should get a medal for his bravery and loyalty. Don't you think?" said one of the men.

"Yes! That's a good idea! Gurgle, have you ever been awarded a medal before?" asked Tirgu.

"No," he said, naturally.

"Well, I shall have a word with Spikepoint and I'll see what I can arrange. Would you prefer the medal mounted on your left tit, or your right?"

Gurgle did not answer, knowing the question to be a foolish one. Tirgu laughed loudly anyway.

*

The garrison commander sat quietly at a wooden table. He was alone. He was waiting in a large empty room with a stone floor. There was a huge charred fireplace behind him. He was dressed in his light armour. He rubbed his hands around his neck to please his sore and tired muscles. He had with him several folded pieces of paper. One of them had the order written on it for him to attend here. It was from his master Lord Spikepoint, via an underling. It was a standard summons meant not just for him but for all the commanders at his level. The other commanders were waiting elsewhere. He had been with them a little while before but was asked to sit separately and wait. It seemed someone wanted to speak to him alone. He expected to be reprimanded for his decision to attack the King's men.

It was very quiet and he supposed that he wouldn't be disturbed for a while. He decided to stand and take a look out of the narrow window through which the only light in the room could enter. He approached the window carefully as he did not enjoy being in high places. With a gradual dip of his head he slowly looked at the view below. Small helmeted figures walked their repetitive routes around the grounds of Spikepoint Castle. He saw a group of around seven people approach the main gates, which were almost directly beneath the window. He recognised one of them as a worthless, mean spirited hobgoblin. He knew him when he had been stationed at the castle many years ago. He tutted and screwed up his features at the thought that he may bump into him again.

He didn't like this new situation at all. Spikepoint was planning a big and decisive move and he was worried that he would be caught up in something beyond his control. He had become increasingly disgruntled over the years as he had been kept isolated in his garrison by his enemies and rivals. The natural opportunities to progress seemed to have passed him by despite a fine military record and an exemplary reputation amongst his men. As a result each trip back to the castle was a humiliating reminder of how far his conniving colleagues had travelled upwards in his absence. Each order he received was proof that the undeserving and ingratiating people in this world were progressing and not him. Yet, when battle came around once more it would be men like him that would take all the personal risk, leaving his superiors to benefit from his efforts, with their accolades and promotions.

He looked again at the order written on the paper.

'Under Seal;

To be delivered to the hand of the recipient only;

'Low Rise' Garrison;
Haine, Robert
Commander

Sir,

Report at once to Spikepoint Castle. No escort or

preparation is necessary.

Sincerely,
Levant, Alexander
Chief among Officers.'

Low Rise was the proper name for his garrison but the
name itself came not just from the topography but also
from the long history of the unfortunate officers that had
spent their careers there. He knew the author of the note.
A coward, but a clever and ruthless one, named Levant.
Neither of them had any time for the other, for each
recognised in the other the qualities that might destroy
them.

It was a lonely journey that he had taken to get here and
he never felt as lonely as he did when at this castle. As such
his trips here were few and with mutual consent. As he
leaned his arms on the small window ledge he noticed a
creature struggling on the outer ledge. It was some kind of
waspish thing and he wondered quite how it had managed
to fly so high. It seemed injured in some way and fluttered
and buzzed aimlessly. It was going nowhere. He watched
it for a few moments then decided to give it the soldier's
way out. With his thumb he made a dirty yellow smear
on the ledge. Perhaps he should have blown it into the air
he thought, a moment later, to give it a chance. Maybe it
was still summoning the courage to take flight, as he was.
He stretched his arms and looked around, wondering
whether he had been forgotten about. He had not, as

gentle footsteps began to be heard. A small discreet door opened into the room. It was not one of the doorways that he had noticed before. It was a secret one that he had missed and which opened next to the fireplace. He smiled when he realised that he had overlooked it completely.

He expected someone to walk through but no-one did. Instead he simply heard a voice from the darkness beyond. "Come along," the voice said, "his Lordship is ready for you."

Carefully he followed the voice and stepped into the shadow. The passageway inside was narrow and cool and after a few moments his eyes began to adjust and he could see the slim figure of someone ahead of him. The voice and size and motions of this person suggested that he was a she. After only twenty or thirty steps she suddenly stopped and turned to her left. She tapped lightly against what in the dim light seemed to be just a part of the stone wall. Another small discreet door opened and she stepped through. The light from this room illuminated her face a little and this allowed him to catch a glimpse of her for the first time. Her face looked lean, angular and elegant. She was beautiful to him. She distracted him enough that he walked into the wall as he followed her and scraped his shoulder painfully.

Inside this new room he was greeted by a large man sat at a large table. It was covered with maps and papers. There were no windows to this room. It was illuminated by candles only.

"Commander," said the man sat behind the table, "come

in and sit down."

His voice was calm and welcoming. The commander did so, on the only available chair.

"My Lord," he said, "how can I be of service to you?"

The man opposite him smiled patiently.

"Oh, don't worry about that for the moment," he said, seeming very relaxed and friendly. "You have been one of my most loyal and dedicated commanders. I expect nothing further from you."

"I am pleased that you think so well of me," he countered, smiling in return.

"Miranda, fetch a drink for our thirsty guest," he said, motioning to her.

"What will you have Sir?" she said to the commander.

He turned to face her and smiled nervously upon seeing her clearly and, as he might describe it, in her full glory.

"Water...please," he eventually replied.

She nodded and smiled at him and left the room. Lord Spikepoint regained his attention.

"Commander!"

"Yes!" he said, turning his head rapidly. "My Lord."

"Something has caught your attention?" Spikepoint smiled at him and continued. "She is very nice to look at is she not?"

"Yes."

"We discovered her in one of my more distant villages. She'd survived a raid on it you see and the poor thing had nowhere else to go."

He looked at the papers on his desk then began to speak

once more.

"Why do you think I wanted to see you?"

"To question me about the attack I made?" he said, after taking a few moments to think.

"No! To congratulate you on it!" said Lord Spikepoint excitedly.

The commander was stunned and replayed the words in his mind to confirm that they were as his ears had suggested.

"But, it was a disaster and shouldn't have happened."

"Under normal circumstances perhaps but for my purposes it was just what I needed. Because of your punishing attack I could judge their reaction...and there was none!"

"Yes, I was surprised by that too."

"They showed themselves to be weak as I'd suspected. The King I know would never have allowed such a thing to happen without a proper response."

"Could there be another explanation?" asked the commander.

"Such as?" replied Spikepoint, after a moment or two.

"Perhaps they are examining our reactions as well."

"Naturally, but that was not what they intended beforehand. Otherwise they would have behaved normally to show that they were not examining us. The man that started the fight which you so admirably finished...you hadn't known him very long had you?"

"No, he was a new transfer and was with us for only a couple of weeks."

"Yes, well I transferred him to you and I told him to behave as he did."

"What?" said the commander. "You did that?"

"Yes, I needed to provoke a reaction and to get things warmed up."

At this point Miranda returned quietly and placed a glass of water in front of the commander. He looked up and smiled at her and thanked her. She did not reply. Spikepoint quickly motioned her away again and she left the room immediately.

"They didn't react so they're vulnerable and we're going to attack. We'll have them! What do you think to that?" said Spikepoint.

The commander could not help releasing a little groan, which he tried to stifle behind the glass of water held in his hand.

"What does that noise mean?" said Spikepoint. "You're not enthusiastic about it, are you? I need brave and enthusiastic men Robert and I was hoping that you would be one of them. I don't want an army full of disinterested mercenaries. Such armies always lose against a motivated defence. I want dedicated fighting men that believe in what they're doing."

The commander thought carefully for a few moments. His conversation now could divert his future in a dozen different directions.

"I agree with you," said the commander, "but..."

"Say what you think, don't worry," interjected Spikepoint.

"I think we would lose in a war with the King."

There was a moment of silent reflection by Lord Spikepoint.

"Why?" demanded Spikepoint flatly.

"I'm a believer in the idea that the side with the most to fight for usually wins. I don't think that's us."

"Do you have a less philosophical reason?" said Spikepoint unpleasantly.

"I also think we would have little or no support amongst the people for us to build on."

"The people!?" he blurted loudly. "The people will do as they're damn well told! Don't mention the people again unless you want to join them in their stinking hovels."

The commander had obviously touched a sore point and decided that he would not question his Lord's plans any further.

"My Lord," the commander began, "you must do as you think fit. I am your servant and go where you say I should go."

"Now you're being insincere. This isn't going too well for you is it? But don't lose your confidence, you can still impress me."

"What would you have me say?" asked the commander, who felt he was already fighting a losing battle.

"I want you to use your head to think of things that will make our endeavour work!"

"Yes, of course, forgive me."

Lord Spikepoint looked at this humble soldier in front of him. A man of some thirty five years. Slim, dark haired and worn out. He sat waiting for him to show some real enthusiasm. He knew that remaining absolutely silent was an excellent technique for getting another to speak and he used it now on the commander, who soon felt compelled to fill the void. Eventually the commander spoke.

"I think...depending on the weaknesses of the King...we can defeat him and his armies," he said cautiously and slowly.

"How?" responded Spikepoint after a few moments.

"By ignoring his outlying bases where he would anticipate us...and attacking him where he lives."

"Excellent, excellent," he laughed, "wonderful! My thoughts exactly."

Lord Spikepoint stood and stepped out from behind the table. He put a hand on the commander's shoulder and stood next to him.

"I know you've had a dull and difficult time out at Low Rise. It was no coincidence that I chose your garrison as the one to provoke a fight with the King's men. I knew you to be a brave and reliable commander and one that I wanted to protect from all the politics and duplicity here in the castle. I want you to come back into the fold. I want you to lead a part of my army and take your orders directly from me. What do you think to that?"

The commander turned to face his Lord but could say nothing at first.

"Have you lost your voice Robert? That would be a shame since you'll need it on the battlefield."

"No my Lord, I haven't lost my voice. I'm just very surprised."

"Not as surprised as those men were when you cut them to pieces, I'm sure."

CHAPTER 7

"Wuuh wuh hah! Wuuh wah! Wuuh wah! Gah! Ugh!"
said Croak Hebdo Uniross, the Leader of the Council of
Milton Greens, as he sneezed loudly whilst sat in his
elegant ceremonial outdoors chair. An underling
immediately offered him a handkerchief to attend to
anything that ought to be attended to, but it was refused.
He looked out over the 'One Hundred and Seventh
Milton Greens Special Militia Brigade' or as they preferred
to be known 'The Boiled Mice'. They were a full brigade
now and stood in formation for his satisfaction. In five
rows of twenty they were, all facing him and all in their
full armour. Lieutenant Chirp Tilestain stood in front of
them with his quartermaster and their two assistants. The
front goblin in both of the end rows held up a large flag on
the end of a wooden pole. The design on it was a simple
trio of black mice in a circle and nose to tail, superimposed
on a grey background.

Once the silence had returned post sneeze a bellow came
from the quartermaster for the brigade to begin a
formation march. Their legs began to move up and down
one after another on the spot. After another bellow from
their quartermaster they all quickly turned and started to
move forward together. For a few minutes they marched
around holding a tight formation and looked passable as a
disciplined military force. All of them held serious
concentrated expressions and there was no foolishness.
The Leader of the Council of Milton Greens looked on

236

without much obvious enthusiasm. He leaned to one side as another of his underlings respectfully requested his attention.

"Sir," he whispered, "would you sign these documents to authorise the brigade's pay please?"

He looked carefully at the papers presented to him. A pen was also presented.

"Once I am satisfied I shall ask for the pen," he said grumpily, and the underling withdrew it.

He scanned the papers and found that the figures though higher than he had hoped were still acceptable.

"Pen!"

It was given, used and then returned.

"Have you their wills?"

"Yes Sir. I have a copy of each in our records."

"Excellent. Well then, let's try to get out of here as quickly as military dignity allows shall we? Is there any other business we need to conclude?"

"Yes Sir, the farewell speech Sir!"

"Oh God, yes alright. Get their attention would you?"

The underling attracted the eyes of the Lieutenant and they spoke together as the brigade marched happily behind them. The Lieutenant listened and then spoke to his quartermaster and asked him to bring the marching to a close. The brigade came to a halt and they stepped back to where they had begun. Some simply walked whilst others tried to march there. It wasn't pretty.

Croak stood up in his chair and steadied himself for a moment. He read from a sheet of paper that was suddenly thrust at him by yet another underling. He had no idea who had written the speech. He began to speak using his most powerful and inspiring tone of voice.

"Brave goblins of the One Hundred and Seventh! I salute you!"

A cheer erupted and many hands were waved. He continued once they had quietened down.

"You have one mission and one mission alone - to rescue your brothers and sisters. Let nothing stand in your way. No human man, no hobgoblin, no river, no storm, no mountain, no weakness on your part. You are the best that Milton Greens has to offer to the rest of the world. Acquit yourselves well. Act with courage and dignity and above all give the others a good opinion of us. When you find the ones that have stolen our brothers and sisters make sure they can never do such a thing ever again. Follow the river out of the forest and search in every place you can think of without fear of anyone or anything. Our brothers and sisters are in great distress and are waiting for you to find them. Go and satisfy their dreams of rescue. You will face danger out there. Beyond the forest danger is a way of life. So I want you to thrive on danger! To seek it out and live on it! Make danger your companion, your ally. Make it drip from the points of your swords and give danger to those that committed this terrible assault on us. Remember that heroes are not the ones that charge off in search of glory and get themselves into trouble. Heroes are the ones that obey orders and do their duty wherever it may lead them, even if it should lead to their deaths.

Goblins past and present will watch over you. I thank you. The forest thanks you. Good luck...and farewell!'

The Boiled Mice cheered triumphantly. Their noisy approval was the signal for Croak and his attendants to leave. He sat back down just as his huge chair began to bob and dip due to the four stocky goblins beneath it struggling to their feet. His other officials and underlings crept along behind as they withdrew. The Lieutenant realised that these would be the last friendly faces they would see for quite a while. He turned to his brigade and yelled at them to calm down and to get themselves ready.

"Now! Is everyone sure they have everything they need? It's your last chance to speak up. We won't be back in Milton Greens for a long time," shouted the Lieutenant.

As he spoke Croak and his group disappeared behind the thick trees at the edge of the forest. Beyond the Boiled Mice there were open plains and poorly kept fields. The river ran along nearby and followed the downward flow of the terrain into the valley below them. In the far distance at the other end of the valley the deep blue shape of hills and mountains could be seen.

"No? You're all happy?" he said. "Good, then we're going! Follow me!"

He waived an arm in the air and his goblins fell in behind him. It was a wonderful feeling to have them at his side and for all of them it was a wonderful feeling to be underway at last. The clumping of boots and clattering of plate armour accompanied the Boiled Mice as they followed along by the river down into the valley. The flag bearers stood together at the back of the brigade and held their flags fixed on the side of their chests with a special harness. They had both volunteered for this honourable duty and had not been the only ones to do so.

The Lieutenant saw the valley stretched out below. It was a sight new to him and he felt for the first time in his life a feeling of being in a real open space. As he led his goblins along the river he sucked in the air unfettered by the leaves of the trees and the scents of the forest. It tasted very different. There was thick grass beneath his feet which was such a change from the dirt and leaves he found beyond his doorstep every morning. The land was very pleasant indeed but it could not remove the trepidation he felt in his heart. Outwardly he appeared confident and positive but this was just for the benefit of his brigade so that they would feel the same. In this place and with the noises of so many goblins in his ears he suddenly felt the full weight of the responsibility on his shoulders. His quartermaster had advised him on what he knew of the typical problems of leadership and would no doubt continue to advise him as the mission went on. He had said that once the initial fears of the situation had died down he would start to feel a growing confidence, once he received from his troops the admiration and deference that was his due. After that, provided he had the proper qualities of leadership within him, he would find things relatively easy. The trick to being a successful leader was apparently to find the right balance between being a bully and a friend.

As the Lieutenant pondered these thoughts his

quartermaster stepped up alongside him.

"Lieutenant, how are things with you?" he said.

"Things are fine. We're on the right route and I think we'll try to get at least twenty miles under our belt before we set up camp for the evening," replied the Lieutenant.

"Very good Sir."

There was a moment or two of silence and it occurred to the Lieutenant that he may have missed something important that his quartermaster was waiting for him to mention. The Lieutenant looked at him carefully.

"Anything else?" said the Lieutenant.

"Oh, not really Sir, but if we get the opportunity we should fill our pouches with water while we're next to the river and later on we should look for food. It should be easy picking."

"We have rations for ninety days, don't we?"

"Yes Sir, but I think such an exercise would be useful to sharpen their senses and keep them occupied, and I always find fresh food is much more enjoyable than the dried worm bricks we've got in our packs."

"Yes, I suppose you're right. I think we'll fill up later on though. I want to camp close to the river so I think we'll let it carry our water for us."

"Yes Sir."

"Flap?"

"Yes Sir?"

"How many times have you been out of the forest?"

"Oh, too many times to mention."

"On a mission I mean."

"Well then, at least twice, depends on what you call a mission though doesn't it?"

"When you got into a fight then."

"Hah! Are you sure you want to hear about that?"

"Yes, definitely."

"Back when I was your age I was not too different from yourself, though a little more handsome as I recall," laughed Flap at his own wit.

"Hmmm, I think your memory is failing you!" said the Lieutenant, and he laughed too.

"Yes, anyway, at that time there was a lot of trouble from a certain hobgoblin by the name of Grim. I don't know whether that was his real name or not but it was appropriate I can tell you, for that was exactly what he was like and so were your prospects if you got into a fight with him. I remember that he was particularly upset by goblins. It didn't matter much beyond that. If you were a goblin he would despise you and be a serious danger to you....and he was terrible for stealing horses too! He was never off one to be honest. He always used to sleep in the hay with them. That led to quite a few rumours and not of the kindest variety either, but, that's another story. He had few loyalties and he was able to attract a lot of independents to fight alongside him. He had quite a nasty set of friends believe me. Anyway, he was basically a mercenary so he would often be found in this battle or that battle and would usually be on the winning side. Naturally he built up quite a reputation."

"So how did *you* get involved with him?" interrupted the

242

Lieutenant.

"Ah well, that's easy. We fought on the same side."

"The same side! What?" blurted the Lieutenant.

"Yes, shush, keep your voice down. They'll think we're arguing."

"We are!" he whispered. "What were you doing fighting with hobgoblins?"

"I needed a bit of money didn't I? It was just the once. Keep quiet about it! You weren't there at the time. There were lots of problems in Milton Greens then. You were just a youngster."

"Alright, but who were you fighting?"

"Oh, I don't know. A mixed bag of men and hobgoblins. It was a confusing time."

"Hobgoblins were fighting each other?"

"Oh yes, they're a treacherous bunch. If we end up fighting them on this mission you'll need to be as ruthless as they are."

"Where did this happen?"

"Oooh, now that's a tricky question, somewhere not too far west of Brown Root. You know it?"

"Brown Root Forest? Yes, that's where all the hobgoblins live. I know that."

"That's right. Well, they don't all live there."

"You ever been there?"

"Once or twice."

"What's it like?"

"Dark...humid...smelly...not as nice as Milton Greens obviously. I guess that would explain why they're such bad tempered creatures."

"And the battle?"

"Yes, the battle. Only about six or seven hundred on each side if I remember correctly. Open ground. It was muddy. There was a thick wood to our right I think. Yes, I remember now. Grim was right up the front on his horse shouting and screaming and doing his best to scare the hell out of them. Hah! What a lunatic he was! He didn't take to me at all for obvious reasons but at the end of the battle he had to give me his grudging thanks. I was in the back somewhere and on foot by the way. Oh, and I wasn't the only goblin there. I had some good friends with me, most of whom survived I'm glad to say and I think there were several goblins on the other side too!"

"No!?"

"Yes, 'fraid so."

"What happened to them?"

"Oh, killed, definitely, though not by me."

"It's hard to believe."

"I know, I was there and I found it hard to believe too!"

"How did it start?"

"That's a good question. I'd like to know that myself. I was at the back so I didn't see too much of the early stages. Everyone who was there knew what to do. There weren't any weak links in our chain."

"Who was commanding you?"

"Errrr Captain something or other, a human man. I forget his name. Close to the King he was and a good commander it has to be said."

"Tell me what you did."

"Well, to start with I was happy to watch! It was a slow start though. Battles often start slowly. People are usually in disbelief that it's actually happening or they're so stunned or frightened by it, it takes them a while to get stuck in. Not Grim though, he'd be ready to fight as soon as his eyes opened in the morning. I've no doubt that he was amongst those that started things rolling. I seem to remember it was very quiet where I was stood, so much so that I could hear the moans and groans of those fighting about two hundred yards ahead of me. Our Captain was stood not too far behind me and I remember that he was using some kind of eye tube to observe the battle. He didn't say too much except settle down now and again. Every ten minutes or so another wave of us would be ordered to walk forward into the fray. We were just ordinary infantry, nothing special, but we knew what we were doing of course. When our row's turn came you can be sure I was feeling all kinds of sickness in my stomach. There was this one human man stood in the row in front of me. All I'd seen for over an hour was the back of his head and his broad shoulders, which kind of filled up my view. I remember he had long brown hair poking out from under his helmet. His row went out just ahead of ours of course. As they advanced I kept an eye on him. When he got near to the front he and the two hobgoblins on either side of him started to run forward with their swords raised up. They were swallowed up by the fighting and I lost sight of him, but a minute or so later I suddenly spotted him. He was staggering away from the battle and he looked hurt. He didn't get very far. I saw this other human man walk up behind him. I tell you, I've never felt such anger in my life before or since as I watched that man be murdered with one casual stroke of a sword."

The quartermaster paused a moment to stifle a wave of emotion that surged up within himself.

"Suddenly revenge was my motivation to fight that day, but I didn't know his name or anything about him. It was just that he was on *my* side. The wind was blowing over the battlefield towards us and you could smell the blood and sweat in the air. It was awful, disgusting really. Some of us were sick, and once one started everyone had a go. But when you're in a situation like that you just have to get on with it. We started to move forward, though not very fast as we weren't in a hurry to get there, but not so slow as to be accused of cowardice. I've discovered it's best to just get it over with. On we went. We were all packed in very close together. I felt this weird combination of terror, excitement, anger, it's so hard to really describe. It was life on the very edge of death...and never do you feel so alive."

"What weapon did you use?" asked the Lieutenant, absorbed and transfixed by this tale.

"Weapon? Just my trusty half sword. You just need one decent weapon that's all and maybe a spare if yours gets broken. That happens quite a lot to be honest. As we got closer we could see just how vicious the whole thing was. Fortunately, by that stage the battle was turning nicely in our favour. Battles are never fought until the last man is left. People are always very sensitive to how things are going. If you can get a clear advantage over the other side then they'll run for their lives. If you can frighten them enough with either numbers or fearlessness they'll lose the will to fight and the day will be yours. That's the way to win a battle."

"What happened? Go on!"

"Steady, I'm trying to teach you something here! But, if you insist, yes well, we suddenly all started to run towards the fighting. It wasn't my idea I promise you. But what else can you do in such a situation but join in? Besides you look tougher when you run into battle instead of just strolling. I remember my heart thumping in my throat. I remember bumping shoulders with my fellows beside me about a hundred times, though most were taller than me of course."

By this stage some members of the brigade had moved up to listen to this exciting account and the Lieutenant suddenly realised that discipline was not being properly maintained. He turned around to see most of the brigade bunched up behind them.

"Oi! What's all this?" he shouted.

They did not respond and just looked sheepishly at him. Flap held his Lieutenant by the arm and pulled him to one side. They spoke quietly together.

"Why don't we stop here to refresh ourselves for a while? They're only trying to listen to the story. I may as well finish it off by telling everyone. Then they can have some of their rations and fill up their pouches. What do you think?"

"Good idea. Do two things at once."

The Lieutenant turned his head to address the brigade.

"Right, we'll stop here for a while. Fill up your pouches in the river and we'll have something to eat. Then the quartermaster will finish his story."

This was just what they wanted to hear and they did exactly as instructed. This was where he was behaving as their friend. He wondered how and when the bullying would come in.

After a little while they settled themselves down on the soft green grass by the side of the river. The setting was very fine and the weather was equal to it. They could see for several miles in each direction and not a soul was to be seen. In fact they had seen nobody at all since leaving the forest. The quartermaster sat on a large rock in the middle of the group and watched them all as they started to eat with each of their eyes fixed upon him.

"Where was I?" he said.

"Charging into battle!" said one of the brigade.

"Oh yes!" said Flap, laughing, "a frightening moment which I hope you'll never have to experience. But if you do I hope you'll be as fortunate as I was. Charging into battle, that's a strange phrase. I didn't feel like I was charging. I felt like I was being pushed or dragged along. I don't think anyone really wanted it to happen and we would have avoided it if we could. That might sound like cowardice or fear but it's just natural and you would feel the same in my boots. Unless you're a savage lunatic like Grim! But there are very few like him, or *were* like him I'm glad to say. I didn't see too much of him at this point. He was on the other side of the crowd somewhere. Once you're inside a battle your zone of awareness drops to within about ten feet and I had plenty to concentrate on. I had a strange dilemma just as I was about to meet the enemy, though it was hard to say where my friends stopped and the enemy began as you can imagine. I remember thinking...who should I attack first? It was a difficult question, not only because of the chaos and who was who but because I couldn't say who deserved my sword the most, or the least! It's a very serious thing to kill someone. It's the worst thing that you can do in life...to take life away from another. Sadly, there are many people who wouldn't agree with me, which makes them very dangerous. Anyway there I was, *reluctantly*, charging into battle when I suddenly see the very same human man that had killed the other human man, the one with the long hair and whose sweat had filled my nostrils for an hour or more!"

The quartermaster stopped for a moment to cough, take a drink of water and to regain his train of thought.

"Yes, there he was, larger than life and much larger than I. My skin suddenly felt cold and wet, despite the heat of the day and of the battle. I can't remember what he was doing exactly but he wasn't fighting with anyone and strangely he seemed to be just wandering around. I couldn't possibly describe my feelings, I was just all emotion. I went straight at him. With the help of one or two others nearby, who I hadn't asked to help me, we quickly took him down. His body was very tough, very muscular. He didn't appreciate me sticking my sword into him, not at all. I put it in the middle of his back. It was hard work but I managed it. He screamed terribly. He didn't see me but he saw one of my fellows that was also attacking him and he belted him viciously with his club. He fell down unconscious and he didn't wake up until several hours later the lucky devil, though he was covered in dirty footprints! That became his nickname afterwards. Footprints!"

The quartermaster laughed loudly.

"I wonder where he is now. Yes, well, there it is. That's what battle is like. Dirty, vicious, terrifying, not to be recommended. We won't face anything on that scale but there could be some nasty fighting so prepare yourselves for it."

"What happened to Grim Sir?" asked one of the younger members of the brigade.

"Grim? He survived of course. Thanks to me in fact. Yes, I forgot to mention that, didn't I? He preferred to do his fighting on horseback but in this battle he lost his horse early on. All that achieved was to make him angrier than he already was at the start! I think it was just after the turning point of the battle, when they decided they couldn't win and would retreat. Not everyone gets the message you see and several big nasty creatures were after Grim, determined to kill him. He brutally convinced one of the three to reconsider by nearly slicing off his leg. The other two were undeterred though and they joined forces to try to overwhelm him. They were powerful and all he could do was parry and deflect them. He needed help otherwise he was dead for certain. I'd seen the way the battle was going and there weren't too many individual fights left. Most people had retreated so I had an easy route over to him. I came up behind them both. Grim saw me. I hacked at one of them, in the buttocks I think. He yelped and turned around and fell over in the mud. The other was distracted by this and Grim took full advantage. When he was dead Grim turned to the one I'd attacked who was still stuck in the mud. I think you can guess what he did to him. That was pretty much the end of the battle. I'd managed to avoid its most dangerous moments. I was exhausted like I'd never been before in my life! My legs felt like the soggy mud that clung to them. I was alive, relieved of course but very frightened and sad at what I'd seen...and done...and still am I suppose."

"Where's Grim now Sir?" yelled the same brigade member.

"Oh, he's dead. Not too long after that battle in fact. He fell foul of another hobgoblin. Tirgu I think he was called. I'm sorry to say that's probably the same hobgoblin who's behind our kidnapping!"

The Lieutenant's green ears pricked up at the mention of this name as did those of the rest of the brigade.

"Hang on, you can't be sure about that!" said the Lieutenant anxiously.

"No Sir," replied the quartermaster, "I can't be sure it's

Tirgu who's behind the kidnapping. That's the rumour. But I am sure he killed Grim and I've never seen a more dangerous creature than Tirgu. Let's hope he's got nothing to do with it."

"Alright everyone!" interrupted the Lieutenant. "Let's be on our way! Come on! Off your arses and on your feet!"

The brigade grudgingly stood. The Lieutenant disguised his sudden fear and insecurity with harsh words.

"Get into formation! We've a lot of ground to cover before we set up camp. Come on! Let's move!"

This was where the bullying came in.

*

Zebulan McCranahan walked into Grumbleweed via its southern approaches. The people of this little castle town were filling the streets, busy with their business. He was dressed in a long black coat that was plainly trimmed. His shoes were also black. He wore no colour at all except for a little yellow slash of silk stitched to his collar that was cut into the shape of a bolt of lightning. He was carrying a large black cloth bundle over his right shoulder and in it he kept most of his things. His many pockets bulged with the remainder of his possessions.

He was a medium sized human man with long black hair that hung all around the top of his body. He was suffering a little of late with a bald patch but this problem was a mere trifle to someone of his abilities and it was well disguised with dark powders.

He scanned the crowds in front of him hoping that he might be recognised. He was not. He approached a stall holder selling fruit and vegetables. It was manned by a plump gentleman and three pretty young girls. Zebulan stared at them all for a few moments trying to make an impression on them. He looked down at the produce on offer.

"Fruit and vegetables," said Zebulan, in a needlessly eccentric fashion, "just what I'm after."

The youngest girl laughed and Zebulan smiled at her.

"Yes indeed Sir, grown locally, the very best you'll find," said the man.

"Excellent. I'll have six apples. Will you give them to me for free?" asked Zebulan, trying a special suggestive tone of voice he'd been working on.

"No! We don't give anyway food for free Sir." replied the man.

"Oh...alright," said Zebulan, disappointed by this embarrassing failure in his powers. "I'll take six apples...and six eggs too. How much will that be?"

"Seven pennies if you please," answered the man as he bagged up the food.

Zebulan fumbled in several of his pockets and managed to assemble the necessary funds which he then handed over. As he left he winked at the youngest girl who giggled at the sight of him. Then up the main street he walked, carefully putting the eggs away in his bundle. He started to eat one of his apples.

His reason for coming to Grumbleweed was to come to

the castle that towered over it. He had been invited to perform at the King's banquet that was due in the next couple of days, and considering his poor financial position he could not refuse the chance of such well-paid work.

The usual place in which he earned a living was in a street such as this one. To the relief of his ego he could avoid such a drab and difficult existence for a while. Now he was heading to a dignified, privileged and above all wealthy place. Despite his lengthy and impressive magician's *C.V.* he could not conjure up cash, unless he held it to begin with.

Soon the streets became less busy as he ascended towards the castle, and if such a thing were possible he stood out more than he did before. Now that he was well into his middle age the walk was a tiring one but he knew it would be well worth it. A chance to impress the King and his Court was of undeniable value. He went over in his mind the illusions he would like to perform. He would begin with the 'Bouncing Flames', then move onto the 'Glowing Cloth', then 'Dragon Flame' to finish - a world of possibilities!

He made his way up the gradual incline which led to the castle itself, grumbling to himself all the while in an attempt to frighten and disturb the people he passed. Out of his capacious sleeves he steadily dropped little pieces of paper. This was the way he advertised his presence. Each piece of paper had 'Z' and 'M' written on it in large black lettering with a picture of a bolt of lightning sandwiched between.

He thought to himself about how to make a proper entrance at the castle. It would be amazing to wake the King up in the morning with a drink perhaps, baffling the King's guards at his method of entry. A good idea definitely but he couldn't think of a way to do it. Perhaps some explosion of smoke and flame from which he could emerge in front of the castle gates? No, that might make them think they were under attack. Some kind of disguise! To make them all think he was someone else entirely! Then, when they called his name expecting him to appear he could stun them all by revealing himself as Zebulan McCranahan, and not Princess whatsherface from wherever.

"Oh damn it," he said to himself, "I left the spare clothes bag at home!"

The upward path he was taking widened due to the needs of the large vehicles that made their way to the castle from nearby farms. It was rutted and muddy. This was the route that he'd been instructed to take in his invitation, but Zebulan rightly suspected that this was not the direction from which the royals and other privileged persons normally approached the castle. Clearly the entertainers were about as well respected as the dung men. A dung man! What an excellent disguise that would be!

"Ah," he mused, "how would I get into the banquet hall smelling like manure?"

His train of thought was halted by a group of people approaching up another road that connected to Zebulan's. He quickly looked them up and down to make sure that there were none amongst them from whom he needed to hide. Many a tradesman and fellow entertainer wished Zebulan harm for one reason or another, so much so that he now relied merely on remembering their faces, as the causes of their anger were too numerous and varied to recall. He didn't recognise any but slowed his pace to allow them to walk ahead just in case. They wandered on to parts unknown.

The castle somehow managed to sneak up on Zebulan, for he was in a world of his own as he continued his journey. A great dirty archway loomed up. This was indeed not the main entrance, but he knew instinctively that it was the one meant for him. From a distance nobody seemed to be guarding it but as he approached a couple of armour clad figures emerged from the gloom inside. They stood on either side of the arch and gave Zebulan a look up and down that did not fill him with confidence.

"Stop there please," said the smaller of the two.

"State your business," said the larger of the two.

"I'm here to perform at the banquet. Do you know who I am?" replied Zebulan hopefully.

He passed them his invitation bearing all the proper marks of authenticity, which they viewed but were not impressed by.

"Nope, never seen you before, though if I had I'm sure I'd remember," scoffed the smaller of the two.

"Right you are Raglan, right you are," giggled the larger of the two.

"Can you let me inside please? I need to prepare."

"Oooh I'm not so sure about that Sir. I worry you're one of those crazy beggars that come wandering through these parts sometimes," added Raglan, and to which his colleague giggled further.

"Hey! I'm Zebulan McCranahan, the magician," he said indignantly, "I'm more talented than your whole family and all their friends! I've got an invitation...there it is...now let me inside."

"Did I hear you right Sir? Gardner, remind me of what he just said would you please?"

"With pleasure Raglan. He seemed to say that he was more talented than your whole family and all their friends. A most curious statement, wouldn't you agree?" said Gardner.

"Yes I would, most curious, considering he'll get nowhere with an attitude like that," replied Raglan.

"Look, the King himself wants me here. If he finds out that you two messed me around like this he won't be too pleased."

"Well I never! The King himself wants you, you say. Gardner, I know our King is fond of them but haven't we our fill of jesters at the castle?" asked Raglan, and to which Gardner burst out laughing.

"Out of my way you two!" commanded Zebulan as he stepped forward between them.

Two huge metal pike blades pranged together in front of his face.

"Now then! You just stop there! We'll have none of that! You'll enter this castle with our permission or not at all.

D'you understand?" said Raglan forcefully.

Zebulan held his arms wide and stepped back with a frustrated look on his face.

"Drop that sack of yours so we can inspect it," said Gardner, "and empty your pockets!"

Zebulan groaned and grimaced at the two of them. His mind raced. They stared at him for a few seconds in complete silence, waiting for him to submit. He did not, but in the silence gentle footsteps on the stone floor behind the two guards began to be heard. They turned to look at someone inside. Two hands came out of the darkness and each took a shoulder of Raglan and Gardner. A face and body followed soon after. This man was well dressed and seemed very patient in his ways.

"What is all this?" asked the man soothingly.

"Sir, this man...I mean we were just allowing this man entry. His letter of invitation Sir, look," said Raglan, noticeably nervous.

The man took the letter and unfolded it carefully. His manicured fingers glided efficiently around the corners of it. He understood it instantly and then looked at each of the men and then at Zebulan.

"All is well I see. Please escort this man to appropriate quarters and let us hope his reputation is well earned."

No sooner had the man appeared before he was gone. The two guards anxiously watched him withdraw, eager to see that he was indeed gone. They turned back to Zebulan, keen to punish him for their embarrassment. Before they could throw a little vitriol in his direction a voice came out of the darkness.

"Now Raglan!"

Raglan grudgingly backed out of Zebulan's way and beckoned him forward. He slapped at Gardner's armour for him to make space.

"Alright you! Come on," said Raglan, "You're lucky, very lucky."

"Yea, very lucky," added Gardner.

"Shut up you bloody parrot!" said Raglan.

"Oh please, after you," said Zebulan, with a growing smile on his face.

The three of them went inside with Zebulan bringing up the rear. Once inside he found very quickly that the darkness was frightened away by candlelight. They had stepped into a small hallway that had swords and shields adorning the walls. As his eyes adjusted he could see that there was no natural light at all. He followed them both as they trotted alongside each other. They moved quickly and he had to run a little to catch up on their fast walking pace. At the end of the corridor they were met by double doors, beyond which Zebulan could hear many people. There was great activity nearby. Zebulan could feel the vibrations flowing through his bones. The doors were pushed open and daylight surged into all six of their eyes. Zebulan was looking upon the banquet hall. It was *very* large. From this entrance it was much wider than it was deep and all along the opposite side there were tall glass windows through which the sunshine entered.

The guards continued inside and Zebulan fell behind a

little as he took it all in. There were dozens of attendants milling around. Some were putting fruit and flowers onto the tables, of which there must have been fifty and all capable of seating at least ten; other attendants tidied, arranged, and assembled. There was a space in the middle of the hall. It occurred to him that that was the place for the entertainments. It seemed to be larger than he needed. It had a wooden platform in the centre with a few boxes and adaptations on it that were obviously there for other performers. It was a big stage and he would do well to fill it.

*

Commander Haine mounted his horse with ease. Once in the saddle he shuffled his bottom to make himself comfortable. He gently tugged at the reins to get his beast's attention. Around him there were a dozen men supported by a dozen horses and each was as shiny and as finely clad as their mount beneath. The commander turned to his companions and nodded to show them that he was ready. They ignored him, instead turning around to look at another horse approaching them. It was muscular, white and with a gentle speckling of grey. Sat upon it was the undoubted leader of this little expedition. Lord Spikepoint slowed his horse as he joined the group. They parted the way to allow him to move to the front but he declined to do so. He looked to the commander and from under his golden helmet began to speak.

"Robert, will you take the lead...you know the way I trust?" asked Spikepoint.

"Aye my Lord, I will, and I do," replied the commander.

He prompted his horse, a gentle and obedient creature, to move to the front of the group. She stepped lightly and rolled her head as she was redirected. The others looked on quietly, some with veiled suspicion of this new man. Numerous eyes, hiding in the shadows of helmets, watched as he moved to the front to lead them. The commander was anxious that they might not follow and he checked behind himself to see that they were. They stepped from the rocky ground onto the wide wooden bridge that connected Spikepoint castle to the other side of the river that cuddled it. The hooves of his horse touched lightly onto the beams, as though she were sensitive to the deep waters which ran beneath. The thud and clatter of the others came soon after.

This would prove to be a nervous journey for the commander for he was not a commander here, merely an interloper, given his entry against the will of everyone except Spikepoint. Underneath the noises of their travel he could swear several times that he heard his name mentioned, with not very pleasant words following it. Perhaps this was just paranoia. He had to control it. Paranoia unchecked can break a mind, a home or a nation. They were all headed to the banquet at the King's castle some thirty miles distant. Besides Spikepoint and himself they were accompanied by Miranda, resplendent in flowing crimson robes, a few attendants that he didn't know, half a dozen of the biggest looking guards he had ever seen and close by Spikepoint's ear as always that snake Levant. The commander suspected that none of them was the least bit interested in the celebrations on offer, though indeed what man would refuse to fill his belly at another's expense? He could not think why Spikepoint had consented to go. He feared the reason was that Spikepoint wanted to throw his weight around and quietly gloat over the King's recent losses, thanks to himself of course. He knew in his bones that it was a mistake. They might even find themselves as prisoners, but as Levant had insisted, to refuse to go would be considered cowardly. That was a hard argument to refute. "Robert! Let's pick up the pace shall we?" yelled Spikepoint suddenly, "I don't wish to spend all day on the road."

The commander turned and nodded anxiously. He had obviously slowed as his mind had drifted. He prodded his horse and she snorted as she sped up a little. The others followed suit.

The commander felt the heat of the day slowly fading as the time and the rocks passed by. He had not spent much time in this part of the world despite it being a place where many people lived. It seemed he was used to the quiet of his distant garrison and all the sights and sounds of the castle were having more of an effect on him than he had expected. He retreated into himself a little and made the wise decision to keep as quiet as he could this evening. He smiled as he imagined asking Spikepoint whether he and

Miranda could take a table together away from the rest and pretend not to know them. It occurred to him suddenly that he in particular might have been included as some sort of provocation to the King, and that some survivors from that day might be there to be offended. He groaned at the helplessness of his position.

"Are you unwell commander?" asked Levant.

The commander was caught off guard and turned to see Levant riding close by and looking at him none too impressed.

"No...Sir," he replied, "I'm just thinking."

"About what may I ask?"

"This foolish adventure," said the commander grumpily, unwisely letting his guard down.

Levant turned back to face the others and yelled in amusement.

"Here's to a foolish adventure gentlemen! So says our man here."

"A foolish adventure!" many of the others replied.

"So sorry to draw attention to you Robert, but you must remember we're presenting a united front tonight. We can't have you showing us up in front of the enemy. You do understand I hope?"

"Of course I understand, now go back with the others...leave me be," said the commander, forgetting himself once more.

"Hah, you're just as I remember you to be. Bitter and disappointed at your lot. Well, I've no time for you but I tell you this, behave properly tonight and don't shame the rest of us or I'll punish you personally."

The commander turned and glared at Levant, who gave no reaction. After a long pause the commander spoke.

"I look forward to it."

*

Inside the bedroom of the King a couple of attendants were cowering in a corner. The King was agitated and almost in a frenzy. He paced up and down at the end of his huge oak bed with a dagger in his hand. The two young men protected themselves by staying clear and out of sight as best they could. One of them had the idea to reach for the rope above the bed and call for attention. He went for it and pulled as hard as he could whilst the King had his back to them. The sound of the bell alarmed him and he turned and yelled at the man on his bed.

"Hah! You little devil! Come here I say! Spies everywhere! Interfering in my business!"

The man scampered back to his companion and hid behind the furs they had brought for their King. He had not objected to the furs as such, more to the demonic intent with which his injured mind had imbued those that brought them. He returned to his pacing at the end of the bed. The two young men watched him carefully, glancing this way and that for a way out.

"Who sent you?" asked the King suddenly.

"We were sent to bring you clothes Sire, nothing more!" answered the less terrified of the two.

"But who sent you?"

"No one Sire, we do this often! Don't you know us?" pleaded the other.

He motioned towards them and they shrunk from him. He stopped just inches from their faces and kneeling down peered into each of their eyes.

"My boys," he said sympathetically, "my dear boys, you're lying to me...I know."

"No Sire, no," they both said.

One of them began to cry at his predicament and pleaded with the King to let them leave. He seemed immune to their obvious distress. Fortunately for them the door burst open and one of the King's ministers came barging into the room.

"What is all this noise!" he yelled, before noticing the King and the others on the far side of the room.

The King turned to look and seemed to hide for a moment. He then stood up and came towards the man with his dagger brandished.

"So you're a spy too are you?" said the King.

"Stop this! Put the dagger down! I've no patience for this, not now," said Gavelrigg firmly.

The King laughed and move towards Gavelrigg with the blade in front. Gavelrigg backed away toward the door. He opened it and shouted down the corridor for some assistance. Heavy footsteps soon followed as two members of the private guard entered the room. They saw their King with whose safety they were entrusted, and it seemed they were required to protect him from himself.

"Take the blade away and restrain him...be as gentle as you can," commanded Gavelrigg.

Naturally they were a little slow to react, not only because of their duty but also because of the King's alarmed state. As they grabbed him Gavelrigg quickly left the room to search for the King's physician. He moved from nearby room to nearby room shouting for him all the while. There were only a few hours until the banquet began and this was not a frame of mind in which the King could be presented to his guests. It was at a time like this that Gavelrigg missed the Queen and the useful supervision she used to provide. Her absence had made all the difference to the King's health.

The man Gavelrigg sought came bounding upstairs after hearing of the commotion. He carried his wooden box full of drugs and potions and nodded to Gavelrigg as he charged past. The two of them went to the King.

Back inside the bedroom the two youngsters had fled. The two guards had easily got the better of the old man. He was disarmed and held down on the bed. He shivered and shook at the indignity of it and snarled curses at them both. The physician, Doctor Brand, opened his box after placing it at the end of the bed. He quickly produced a glass tube full of liquid and moved alongside the King. Gavelrigg settled himself at the back of the room and watched, shaking his head at the ridiculousness of it all.

The King turned his attention to the Doctor and closed his mouth in anticipation of what was to come. This was not the first time they had had to do this. He got the

King's mouth open by squeezing his nose, forcing him to breathe. When he inevitably gulped for breath the potion was expertly poured inside. The King choked and strained to be released. The guards relented a little and he was able to turn and cough heavily. He closed his eyes and began to moan at his persecutors.

"Aaah...treachery," he said softly into his pillow, "what treachery. I'll have you all rotting on the castle walls by this time tomorrow, I swear it!"

The King's mind was furious but his body seemed to calm down a little, though indeed more from exhaustion than the drug. The others watched him for a minute or two as his energy slowly flowed away. They all relaxed as the drug took over the job of restraining him.

"What can you do for him this evening Doctor?" asked Gavelrigg.

"He'll sleep for a few hours. No more than that. Then it's up to you I'm afraid."

"You can do better than that I think! We need him stable and talking, tonight more than ever. After that it won't matter."

"I'm not a magician. He'll be groggy when he wakes and I dread to think what state his mind will be in."

"Just do your job, and stay with him until he wakes, and you two can help him dress. Where did those other two disappear to? It doesn't matter. I've got more important things to organise. If you need me...well, you'll just have to manage things yourselves."

"Fine, we'll watch him, off you go," said the Doctor.

Gavelrigg left the room and moved swiftly back to his previous duties. Downstairs he was organising the banquet and making sure all was ready. You have no idea how much he had to do. Outside he needed to sort out the torches that lit the way, enough stable space, the numerous grooms and servants, preparing the balconies from which some of the entertainments would be staged, not to mention dealing with the threat from certain guests in particular.

Inside he had to manage all the food and wine, all the tables and arrangements, the central stage and all the performers and the very delicate task of deciding where all the guests ought to sit. He had decided to put Spikepoint's group in the centre of things, partly so they could get a good view of the entertainments but mostly so they would feel surrounded.

Some had suggested that Spikepoint might be influenced one way or the other by how things went. In Gavelrigg's mind it was all nonsense to try to influence their sad slide towards war. His gut suggested that it would be better to cover them in arrows as they rode in. The soldiers at the castle numbered more than five hundred.

CHAPTER 8

Below stairs, in the heart of the kitchen, the bulk of the food was ready to be assembled. Smoke and steam filled the atmosphere in equal measure. All the little windows high in the walls were open and from ground level outside it might have appeared that a fire breathing dragon was on the loose. Great cauldrons of boiling vegetables were being stirred whilst at one end creature after creature rotated slowly near the huge open fire. Young boys stood next to the roasts and poured stock over them to keep them moist. They were being browned by the fire almost as much as was the meat. Dotted here and there were the cooks doing their best to control and organise the crowd. Twenty or more servants stood at the main doorway to the kitchen all eagerly anticipating a tray piled high with good things.

In the main cellar close to the kitchen several burly men were being organised by the chef. He directed them to certain barrels and casks. They rolled them out into the candle light so he could examine them in more detail. With a snoot and a nod he selected the various wines and beers to be served upstairs. The guests would make a serious dent in his reserves for which he did not thank them. The men rolled and carried the barrels out of the cellar huffing and groaning as they went. The chef looked on disapprovingly and was saddened by the empty spaces in his collection.

Above stairs the activity was just as intense. Dozens of

269

servants buzzed around the banquet hall checking and rechecking that every place was ready and that all was where it ought to be. The guests were not expected for at least an hour but so much seemed still to do.

In a room next to the hall various entertainers and entertainments were being prepared. Zebulan was here and sat by himself rummaging through his sack. He was in a world of his own and was hostile to those around him. He didn't want to be disturbed. In the far corner of the room all he could see were jugglers. Zebulan hated jugglers. He believed that they were stupid, talentless creatures that thought their 'skill' superior to his. All they did was throw things in the air and then catch them again. Pathetic! Zebulan had an even more terrible opinion of them but I could not mention it for fear of causing offence. Closer to Zebulan there were other kinds of entertainers. There was a band of musicians for instance. They seemed reasonable enough. Next to them were several garishly dressed people. Jesters damn them. Zebulan could never understand what kind of 'entertainment' they actually provided. He sniffed at them disapprovingly. On his right side were a group of players, poets, storytellers and the like. Boring! On his left side several singers warbled quietly. Nightmare! He would show this lot of amateurs what entertainment was all about.

He continued to rummage in his sack. Carefully he withdrew several small glass bottles. These had within them various solvents and quickeners. He also pulled out a handful of white paper packets. They were full of

270

explosive powders that when ignited would produce different coloured flames. He also brought out the eggs he had purchased earlier. He laid them...in a tight pile at his feet. Using a delicate little spiked knife he made a hole in the top of the first egg. With practiced skill he enlarged the hole and poured the contents into a bowl. To this gloop he added a little of the liquid in one of his bottles and mixed the two together. The yellow and the white seemed to lose their cohesion and soon what was left was a pale and sickly mixture. Zebulan added the contents of one of the paper packets to it. He stirred it all together and then *very* carefully poured the mixture, or as much as could be accepted, back into the egg shell. He covered the hole with a little piece of the paper packet, which he painted with glue from yet another bottle.

"What's that you're making?" said one of the jugglers suddenly, after noticing this delicate operation from across the room.

"Aaah! Don't sneak up on me like that!" replied Zebulan angrily. "If this went up you'd never be able to throw anything again. Bugger off!"

"I was just asking. No need to be rude!" said the juggler, who walked away muttering unpleasantries.

Zebulan stared at the man as he backed away. He turned his attention back to the special egg which he placed inside a wooden box. He gave the same treatment to the other eggs, each with a different powder inside. Once this was done and all were safely stowed he leaned back on his stool and tutted once more at the company he was forced to keep.

*

In a distant part of the castle Princess Ursula was also sat on a stool, though this one was not made of hard gnarled wood with two and a half legs. This one was plush, comfy and elegant.

Hairy the First looked at his Princess and purred gently under her soft touch. The cat was sitting on the table in front of her. She carefully examined the pots and little glass vials lying beyond. This was the place where her great beauty was enhanced. All manner of rare perfumes and special waters were available to her, not to mention the choicest of regenerative powders from all corners of the known world, and from a few corners unknown as well. She looked into the mirror in front of her and began to sing a little song to the cat.

"Who's the loveliest of them all little one?"

The cat did not reply.

"Why, it's me of course! As if you didn't know! Ah my sweet, you are finer to me...than all the birds in the tree...you'd like that wouldn't you, birds in the tree for you to eat before they could flee! Oh, that rhymes!"

Once again the cat decided it was best to stay quiet.

"Who should I pick for myself tonight? Have you any thoughts my darling? A Prince as handsome as he is foolish...as brave as he is stupid...as rich as he is generous...or as fluffy as you perhaps? Of course not. Oh,

272

where is my handsome Prince? I suppose I haven't met him yet. But I'll never have as good a chance as I will tonight. Half the Kingdom shall be here and I'll have my pick. Yes I shall. What do you think to that?"

For cats too, the better part of valour is discretion.

"I know my darling. I won't pick a Prince that has a dog. I wouldn't do that to you."

The Princess picked up a jar and unwound the top. She sniffed at the contents and closed her eyes as she smiled to herself. Lovely she thought. She picked up a little delicate brush and rubbed it inside the jar. Plumes of dust emerged. Quickly and expertly she battered her face with the fibres of the brush. Her features contorted and grimaced to allow the powder to reach every part. The poor cat suddenly caught the tail end of one of these dust plumes. His back arched on the table. His whiskers twitched and his eyes slammed shut. His mouth opened and his tongue fell out in distress. He sneezed a big feline sneeze and dived off the table.

"Oh sorry sweetheart," she said, chuckling to herself, "I didn't mean it, but that'll teach you for trying to be as beautiful as me."

The Princess looked about herself and decided to turn her attention to the dress she would wear for the evening. A healthy selection had been laid out by her maids for consideration. She chose a warm yellow dress that would stretch to her ankles. It was in elegant satin and had a figure hugging quality that would catch many an eye. She put it on.

"What do you think?" she asked of her companion.

The cat sneezed again. He obviously did not care for it.

*

The commander, still at the front of his group, moved gently up the slope towards the castle. The light of the day had faded to the point where the sun was a pleasure to observe rather than a pain. For quite a while nothing had been said by anyone. Whether this was due to the length of the journey or the difficulty at the end of it he could not be sure. However, he was happy to be silent.

After several hours in the saddle his thighs were very sore. He looked forward to arriving at least, if not to the banquet itself. The evening might be a pleasant one though as the commander did not expect any show of anger from their hosts. All those feelings would be safely contained, ready to boil over when the time came. This last climb was over muddy ground. Obviously a great deal of water and traffic flowed down it. At the castle ahead of them a low rumble of noise became audible. It was the sound of many people talking and moving around. As they drew nearer the flicker of flames showed the shapes of people.

Several nervous looking youngsters appeared and seemed to want to take the horses from the commander and the others. Lord Spikepoint came forward and stepped beyond them but none had the courage to object to such an imposing figure. He led his horse a little further into the courtyard that emerged from the gloom. He turned his head to the nearest boy.

"No one is here to greet us?"

"I wouldn't know Sir," was the meek reply.

Spikepoint growled and dismounted. The others followed suit, though without growling. They removed their helmets and seemed at a loss as to where to go next. This lack of official welcome was instantly interpreted as a snub by Spikepoint. Various other guests were nearby and also seemed to be newly arrived. They said nothing and kept well away from this fearsome looking group.

The commander quickly realised that they would have to follow the others into the castle and that they would have no official to guide them. He felt like saying something to try to calm his Lord but thought better of it. That would only direct his anger towards him. Once the horses had each been taken they began to walk to what seemed like the proper entrance. Torch lights flickered on the inside walls. They could hear the sounds of many people somewhere ahead. About twenty yards in front of them two double doors opened and a well-dressed person came through. He seemed to know Lord Spikepoint, or at least of him, and he quickly adopted an apologetic manner.

"My Lord, many apologies for not greeting you at the gate but I was not informed of your arrival until a few moments ago. Please come with me and we shall see that you are all taken care of."

Spikepoint simply nodded and took these words well. He turned to Levant at his side and smiled with a wink. He looked behind him and motioned for Miranda to come to the front. She did so and took the arm that was offered by her Lord. The commander was disappointed by this as it seemed she had naturally chosen to walk near to him after they had dismounted from their horses. He was obviously not the only one to find her a soothing presence.

They all stepped forward together in the wake of this well dressed person. The corridor was a narrow one and they walked two abreast. Ahead of them were more doors and in between a shaft of light and noise came through. The man opened the doors and stood to one side to allow them all through. They were entering the banquet hall, a place that was familiar to Spikepoint but not to the commander. As the others filed in the commander stopped to look at the ceiling. It was high and appeared to be made of huge wooden beams that he estimated would need a hundred men to lift a single one. He caught up with the others as they snaked between the outer tables to the centre. Their table was long and everyone sat on one side. There was extra space between it and all the others, as if to isolate it. They each took their seats, which were not designated personally, giving first choice to Spikepoint. He sat with a flourish and took a menacing look at the other people close about.

Twenty feet ahead of them was an uninterrupted view of what the commander presumed to be a stage for performances. To both the left and right of the stage and beyond it were other tables of the same type as theirs. They were not fully occupied and there was no sign of the

King. This was natural enough thought the commander. He would be expected to make everyone wait. In front of him and the others were metal dishes without anything on them. The rest of the table was fully laid but no food or drink was to be seen. This was surprising as behind them other guests were enjoying little bits to eat and all seemed to be supping a drink when it suited.

The commander was suddenly startled by the voice of one of Spikepoint's personal guard seated next to him.

"Where's the wine?" he whispered, but for such a big man his whisper carried someway.

"Is that all you're interested in?" whispered Levant reproachfully.

The man said nothing further. Spikepoint and Miranda stared straight ahead maintaining a dignified silence, though Spikepoint tapped his fingers on the table nervously.

*

In another part of the castle, far from all this unbridled excitement, the King opened his eyes and coughed gently. Doctor Brand was distracted from his box of drugs and moved over to attend to him.

"Sire, how do you feel?" he enquired.

His mouth opened but there was no answer to put into words. The King blinked a few times and began to move. At first the doctor thought to hold him there but then changed his mind. The King moved from the bed and got to his feet. He did not appear as groggy as the doctor had predicted. He looked around himself and spied the doctor. He nodded, but not to him, more as an acknowledgement that all was well.

"It is evening," said the King.

"It is Sire, how do you feel?"

"Not too bad, not too bad. What time is it?"

"I'm not sure Sire, but it is an important evening, many people have come...for the banquet."

"The banquet! Yes! Is everything ready?"

"Shortly, I believe Sire. May I help you dress and prepare?"

The King seemed more energized than earlier and responded enthusiastically. The doctor was much relieved. The King fetched a bowl of warm water from nearby and placed it in front of himself. He took a small blade from his things and offered it to the doctor.

"A shave Sire, or a wash first perhaps?"

"A shave," replied the King, "will you do it for me?"

The doctor nodded as the King clumsily splashed his face with two handfuls of water.

*

Zebulan was becoming anxious and excited. It would soon be time to perform. He was sat with the others but still doing his best to sit apart. It was reasonably quiet in the room now as most of them were ready and waiting to perform. The sounds from the throng next door were louder than anything in the room and this seemed to focus everyone's attention on why they were all there. Fortunately there was food and drink on offer and Zebulan was an enthusiastic recipient. He had a little pile of little pies cradled in his lap and a drink of beer with which to wash them down. He sniffed at each before biting into them as each seemed to have a different filling - meat, fruit and pastry, delicious, and he had apples too, much like the ones he'd bought from the market. He checked continuously on all his belongings. Delicately and excitedly he seemed to touch everything about himself with his fingertips. He munched and smiled simultaneously whilst the others nibbled nervously if they nibbled at all.

He picked up the wooden box containing his special eggs and peered at them unnecessarily once more. At the same moment he sank his teeth into another small pie, though this one was of an inferior construction and half of it fell away, landing audibly on top of one of his eggs. He spluttered at the danger and crumbs exploded from his lips in much the same way as a sneeze might explode from a nose. But, fortunately, there was no eggplosion. He removed the fragments of pie and examined the egg for cracks. To his great surprise there were none. He breathed a long sigh of relief and the eggs were treated to yet another shower of crumbs. He looked about himself to see if anyone had noticed how close they had come to an early performance of his act. He met the gaze of one or two inquisitive souls but they only seemed to look at him disapprovingly rather than in alarm. He turned back to look at his eggs and began to speak quietly to them.

"Well done boys, that was close," he whispered. "Very foolish of me, I should...eggcercise more care."

He tapped the box gently and they wobbled as he had anticipated. He began to speak from the corner of his mouth on behalf of his eggs.

"Zeb you lunatic, you nearly killed us! And stop with the bad yolks. Jokes we mean!"

"Ha ha, you said yolks, you can't eggscape the truth!" he replied, whilst pointing at them.

"Please Zeb stop it, have mercy!" shaking the box a little more vigorously this time.

"Ask me nicely!"

"Oh Zeb, master of most of the universe, handsomest magician that ever there was, foolmaker by royal appointment, the juggler crusher, will you please stop the jokes?"

"Is that your act then?" joked one of the jugglers suddenly, interrupting the scene. "Talking to eggs?"

People laughed loudly. Zebulan wheeled around and glared at the man. He looked him up and down for a few moments.

"Shut up! You...juggler! You're lower than the lowest of the low!"

"Really? Well I'm looking down on you my friend and I can see a rather worrying bald patch. Are you here to perform or to be laughed at?"

People laughed loudly again. Zebulan growled and

thought for a few moments on a suitable response. He suddenly waved his spare arm theatrically at the man.

"I hereby cast upon you...the ugly spell! Pish! Pash! Poosh! Hey look everyone it worked!"

People laughed very loudly and many a pie crumb was ejaculated through the air.

*

Lord Spikepoint shuffled uncomfortably in his seat. He and his companions seemed to have been left out of the celebrations as they were sitting quietly with nothing to do whilst everyone else seemed lively and contented. He leaned to one side and began to speak with Levant, who leaned also, almost in anticipation of the question.

"What are they are up to?" said Spikepoint.

"Too early to say my Lord. I think they are just playing a little game with us. It shows they don't have the nerve for anything more so they settle for this childishness."

"Hmmm, I think you're right. But I'm hungry. Let's see what we can do. Send someone."

Levant thought for a moment and looked further down the table. At first he considered asking one of the guards but with a smile it suddenly occurred to him to ask the commander to handle this tiresome little task. Over the shoulders of the guards a conversation began between Levant and the commander.

"Robert!" said Levant venomously.

"What's the matter?" replied the commander, already

made tense by the tone of his voice.

"Don't just sit there, arrange everything for us."

"Arrange what?" he replied, irritated by this condescension.

"Get up and fetch us some food!"

This last command was loud enough for the whole table to hear and each person looked at the commander to watch his response. Though he would have preferred to grab Levant by his hair and shout in his ear for him to do so he stood grudgingly and looked around for someone to speak to. He wandered away from the table but looked back and noticed two faces turned around keeping an eye on him. Levant and Miranda. He deliberately smiled at one and grimaced at the other. A young man brushed past him carrying a tray of food. The commander stopped him. "Boy, will you bring us some food. To that table there," said the commander, pointing.

He seemed to hear him and nod but he continued on to another table and the commander felt he had not made himself clear. He looked around for someone else to speak to. Beyond the edge of the farthest tables he spied a few attendants doing nothing, stood by a table full of food. He moved towards them and between two narrowly separated tables. A hand suddenly grabbed his thigh. He reacted quickly and shook himself loose of the hand. Several men stood from their seats and circled around him.

"Is this him?" said one.

"That's him. He's the one. I remember him very well," said another.

"What's all this?" asked the commander, startled.

A large man moved in front of the commander and stood inches from his face.

"See this?" said the man, pointing to a particularly large scar down the left side of his face.

"Yes, it's a beauty. Who gave you that?" replied the commander, unfazed by the hostility on offer.

The men growled as a pack and the man facing him widened his eyes in shock.

"You did!" he barked, and grabbed a fistful of his tunic.

The commander looked at him more closely this time. For the benefit of his companions he decided to be a little more diplomatic.

"Oh...well...let me apologise to you," were the only words the commander could put out.

"Apologise!? I want more from you than that. A lot more."

The others laughed knowingly. He was put on the spot once more.

"Gentlemen, I don't believe this is the proper time or place," said the commander patiently but with a note of impatience in his voice.

"Why not? It seems pretty good to me," said the man.

Before the commander could think of a response to defuse the situation he noticed the eyes of these men turn away from him. A member of Spikepoint's rather large guard walked casually over to them. He put a hand on the commander's shoulder and on the shoulder of the man with a scar on his face. He stood at least six inches above his nearest rival. He looked at all the other men and gave them a sinister smile.

"Anyone know where I can find some wine?" he asked jovially.

Nobody answered him but he guided the commander through the pack and the pack quickly made way. They reached the table that the commander had originally spied. He breathed a sigh of relief and thanked this man and asked him his name. The man looked at what was on offer and grabbed several jugs of what he hoped was wine.

"Help me will you?" said the man to the attendants standing nearby. "Pick up a few trays and follow me. We're hungry."

The commander also grabbed a few things and they all trailed back to the centre with their hands full. The commander could feel the tension as they walked past the tables with the other men. They all stopped their conversations and stared. The man, laden with his wine, suddenly stopped within earshot of these men and stuck his nose in the air. He coughed.

"Ugh, what's that stink?"

The commander anxiously pushed him forward and the man laughed.

*

Upstairs the King was almost ready. He held out his arms as his servants slid a great warm cloak over his body. Gavelrigg stood some distance away and smiled as he saw his King in a good condition once more. Despite his advanced age he still had some size to him and a certain grace not often found in ordinary men.

"Are you ready Sire?" asked Gavelrigg.

The King turned to face him and smiled in return.

"Let's go and greet my old friend Spikepoint shall we? Lead the way Gavelrigg."

With a flourish of his arms and a shiver of adjustment he began to follow his minister out of the bedroom. The two of them stepped unhurriedly down the corridor as the eyes of the guards kept watch.

The King wore his long burgundy cloak, one that was once much favoured by his Queen. Around his waist he had a simple black belt with a golden buckle. Over his shoulders he wore his great bear skin, a trophy from his golden youth. On several fingers he wore several rings, not one of which failed to sparkle with rare mineral brilliance. Gavelrigg was much the plainer dressed.

The two men made their way below and into the banquet hall. Most of the guests did not notice at first. Gavelrigg had decided to dispense with the usual noisy announcement. With a gentle confidence the King simply made his own way to his table overlooking the main stage. A little further around the stage Spikepoint and his entire group watched the King carefully. He was hard to miss as several servants and attendants had attached themselves to his trail and most of the hall had fallen quiet. The King paid little attention to those around him. He sat smoothly, lifting his bear skin over the back of his large chair. He looked straight ahead with a surprisingly calm air about him. He lifted a glass of wine and took a sip.

Spikepoint was closer to him than he had expected, easily within shouting distance. Now that they were so close Spikepoint found that he could not think of anything to say. Gavelrigg sat next to the King and looked over at them. Recognising them he stood up again and walked over. He nodded to Levant as his counterpart of sorts, but began to speak to Spikepoint.

"My Lord. Thank you for coming. Have you been treated well?"

"As well as I expected I suppose," replied Spikepoint, somewhat ungratefully as he chewed voraciously on a bone.

"I'm glad. It is good to see you all again."

Gavelrigg turned his back and started to move away but was not given time. Levant spoke up.

"Gavelrigg, my old friend," he said, trying as hard as he could to seem sincere, "won't you speak to me?"

"Alexander, so it *is* you. I didn't recognise you without a glass of wine to your lips. How go your plans for the world?"

"Hah, beautifully as always. It's been too long since we last saw each other."

"Has it? I'm not sure I agree," he replied coldly and returned to his seat.

Levant was not pleased. He grabbed at a bone on his plate and angrily tore the flesh from it.

"Have you and he history?" asked Spikepoint quietly.

286

"It seems so," he replied.

"Anything I should know about?"

"He dislikes me, but when has that ever concerned your Lordship?"

Spikepoint smirked into his food. He then swallowed the last of his beer. He held out his beaker into the air, without even looking. Moments later it was refilled. At that moment they all became aware of music. They looked up to see two women playing pipes, one on either side of the stage. In between them a man played a small drum and sang gently. The music was slow and patient and had a soothing quality. Most of the guests quietened their conversations in order to listen.

The King sat impassively. Gavelrigg kept a close eye on him and would intervene in a moment if he took sick or behaved as he should not. So far he seemed well but this was a guarantee of nothing. He tried to engage him in easy conversation.

"Sire, are you enjoying your food?"

"It's good. Too much spice though, for my liking," said the King.

"Ah, it is hard to please everyone with spice," replied Gavelrigg amusedly.

"Stop blathering."

Gavelrigg stopped blathering at once.

*

Zebulan was waiting patiently in the back room, or in

fact, the others around him were waiting patiently whereas he was forced to wait impatiently amongst them. By now an orderly queue had formed of the participants. Some rather forgettable musicians had been out shortly before. Some wizened old geezer and his companions would be next. Then it would be Zebulan. It seemed that the various jugglers were wandering in and out and didn't have their own special show, as was appropriate in his view. Perhaps they were to entertain the horses outside he thought.

Beyond the doors Zebulan could hear the music come to an end. The wizened old geezer suddenly became rather energetic and flapped his long sleeves. The doors in front of him opened and he stepped through. He moved slowly out into the hall and towards the stage. He had two young boys with him that each took an arm as escort. Into the middle of the stage he was led and once there placed on a small wooden chair. His two boys crept back into the shadows and sat at the edge of the stage.

The old man gave his throat a generous clearing. He stood and crept forward. All around the stage were various long candles, spaced apart. He proceeded to blow most of them out save one, which he picked up and carried with him. This created a certain atmospheric gloom, adding to the drama of his appearance. He held the candle close to his chest and began to speak.

"Hark, all of you! I have a story. Not a tale...not a happening...nor an anecdote...but a story. For story it is, call it what you may. I have been alive for nearly one hundred and thirty years."

There were chuckles from the audience to which the man reacted angrily.

"Hush! Hush! Hush, those frightened doubters amongst you! Come here and stare me in the eyes and you'll see the truth of it. I come from a land suited to long growth where nay sayers are swallowed whole by their own foolishness. I've travelled through more places and seen more pain and peril than you could bear. I've seen trees come crashing to the ground. I've seen empires do the same. I've seen nations wither on fortune's vine. I've seen grown men weep at the ways of the world and others rejoice in them. I've seen my babies born...and die. I've seen through my own bones because of hunger and I've lived off the fat. Hush."

He stopped speaking for a moment and moved slowly about the stage. He looked out at the candle lights on the many tables and continued.

"I come to tell you a story...told to me when I was young by a man who was older then even than I am now! Doubt me not. He told me of a time long ago. When all our society, even this castle itself was mere dust and dirt, unformed and the land hereabouts was wild and overrun by valueless people, who battled with each other ceaselessly. Such was life then. Mud...and blood."

He glared and pointed out into the audience.

"I want to tell you how our world formed and how it finally managed to stand on its feet and how it can so easily fall back into the mud once more. In the beginning our world was born from darkness, pure black darkness.

The trees and mountains cracked up through the surface as we drifted, pilotless, through the void. There were no animals to amuse the world so the world began to weep at her lonely state and the tears formed rivers in which little creatures could begin to grow, and so they did! In a multitude! And they grew and explored the world and amused the world with their ingenuity and resilience. And the world loved her new inhabitants and sheltered and fed them."

He blinked slowly and seemed to lose concentration for a moment. He found himself again.

"Oh, what a paradise it was when all the world was full and all the animals were happy. When gentle sunshine fell and slow, easy lives were lived. The world continued like this for an age and would have continued like this for another, but an unhappy mistake occurred, when the world was too content with herself to take notice. A few imaginative animals changed from four legs to two legs and with their increased height they saw more of the world, and in the seeing of it they began to desire more of it. And so, slowly, quietly, these two legged animals looked around and imagined marking out parts of the world for themselves. One day, one of these animals saw a very nice part of the world that no other two legged animal had seen and he began to mark a line between it and the rest of the world and the world cried out in pain for she was not whole anymore. But the world could do nothing to stop the two legged animals from carving up the world except weep once more, which only served to make the rivers flow greatly and the two legged animals prospered, thinking themselves rewarded by their actions."

Some people in the audience were starting to find the performance a little heavy going but the food and refreshments kept coming, and apart from gentle slurping noises the audience listened quietly.

"The world continued in her drift and she wept daily for each new day's pain. The two legged animals became so numerous and strong that there was little room for all the other animals and they became scattered, and when they strayed onto land marked by the two legged animals they were chased away and sometimes eaten. The two legged animals took control and enjoyed the feeling. But, as long as the two legged animals were able to tell the difference between the qualities of one piece of land and another they continued to be restless and unhappy. Eventually, the world had no more tears to shed and the mighty flow of the rivers dwindled to a fraction of what they were. The two legged animals, seeing their lands in peril, put their heads together to find a solution. But because there was not enough water to satisfy them all, there was no solution to satisfy them all and so they turned on each other. Such is the nature of the two legged animal."

He grumbled and cleared his throat. He slowly moved back to his seat. He looked up into the dark ceiling above him then at the crowd once more. He continued, in a sorrowful tone.

"And he we are, all of us two legged animals, masters of

the world but not of ourselves. But fear not for we are not to blame. We come and go as all things do, and we cannot be expected to act except as our nature instructs us to. So be it. Let what pain there is to come, come, because that too, one day, will go."

He chuckled and rose to his feet once more. His mood seemed lifted.

"Ah, fear not you brave fighting men, for what you desire is coming. You always have the power to make it happen. Fear not you calm and gentle souls, for the peace you crave will soon wash over you. Fear not you patient men in the middle, for you are ready for any outcome. Fear not you old folks, for the dark screen is near. Fear not you young ones, for you know not fear."

He went quiet for a few seconds and dipped his head. His two young assistants crept towards him and it seemed to most observers that the performance had reached its end. As they neared him he opened his eyes once more and motioned them away.

"One thing the world nurtured in her animals was the capacity to surprise, as that was what gave her most joy. As my decades have drifted by I think I am closer to understanding it all. But my doubts grow with the years as does my hair and the vision fades. No more smoke comes from my chimney you understand. I think just one thing now. How peaceful will my peace be? Soon I will discover. How peaceful will yours be and how soon will you discover?"

He raised his arms slowly but with a relentless purpose.

"Oh world, spin, turn, move! Shake us off! The four legged animals have enough grip to remain. Shake us off and you can be back to your happy state once again! Cry tears of joy! Cry tears of joy! Cry tears of joy and wash away the stain!"

He crumbled back into his seat, exhausted by his display. His assistants came by and helped him off the stage. Modest applause occurred spontaneously once it was clear the performance was done. Zebulan and the others opened the doors for him and welcomed him back inside. Around the stage several people worked in the shadows in rearranging things for the next performance. To fill the void music and singing began again as the candles were relit.

Gavelrigg was keeping a close eye on his King. He seemed quiet and contented and had said nothing during the old man's talk. Intermittently he sipped wine from his goblet, which had been slightly watered down. The King seemed to enjoy it nonetheless. He also nibbled at the various interesting things on his plate.

Across the way, Spikepoint and his party had relaxed somewhat and were enjoying the food and drink that was being lavishly offered about. Spikepoint's personal guards had been instructed not to touch the wine, within reason, and so they remained alert while many of those about them drifted smoothly into warm senselessness.

Zebulan was prepared now. Much of what he would use in his show was concealed about his person, but he brought with him a dark coloured box, lacking any

293

pattern, as he walked out onto the stage. He put the box to one side and moved to the centre. It was largely surrounded by candles about waist height but there was a clear section about a metre wide in front of him through which the King had an uninterrupted view.

He bowed, first towards the King then more generally. For all his previous enthusiasm the King did not seem to recognise this man, much to Gavelrigg's frustration; and much to Zebulan's frustration his welcome was distinctly calm. This would not be the first time but he didn't care. He was in a perfect zone and he knew his act would be good and would get them shouting his name.

"Mortals!" He bellowed suddenly with his fists in the air, "I am Zebulan McCranahan...behold!"

He threw a short puff of explosive powder towards the nearest candle, though to the observers no powder could be seen and it seemed as though by his will alone a great green streak of flame erupted into the air above a rather shocked section of the audience. They gasped and laughed. Immediately he threw another short puff, held between two different fingers, in another direction. This time another section of the audience cowered beneath a hot crimson cloud. He wheeled around and those that were previously behind him were treated to a brilliant yellow flame, delivered by swinging an arm underneath his raised leg. In this moment of shock he scrunched the remaining powders into one fist and then spun around, letting them escape bit by bit so that a continuous but smaller and multi-coloured flame followed him around the tops of the

294

candles. He came to rest facing the King and kneeled, bowing his head forward.

All eyes were focussed on him now and there was instant applause. The King too seemed to recognise from all this excitement what was happening in front of him and his eyes lit up and a smile opened across his face. Zebulan noticed this reaction and smiled also.

Out of sight of the crowd, or rather in their view but not to their attention, Zebulan fixed a thin and dark rod to his waist belt and a special loop to his right foot that enabled him to adjust its height. Between him and the candles a couple of metres distant there was a distinct shadow of which he took advantage. As he rose to his feet he raised his arms as part of the show but mostly as misdirection. He played with his fingers and looked up at them as though he were manipulating something in them. In reality he was carefully positioning his waist so that it faced the first candle in front of him and to his left. He suddenly moaned in pain and pulled aggressively at his hair. People looked on fascinated at this unexpected act. He pretended to stumble and stagger then seemed to be still for a few moments. Then he leaned forward and began to choke.

"Help!" he groaned.

People were a little unsure about how to react and no one immediately leapt to his aid. Before anyone could consider practical help he moved his arm towards a candle and borrowed some fire, which burned gently in his cupped hand. Moments earlier he had rubbed his hand against the side of the box, which had been coated in one small section with flammable grease. It burned comfortably but did not injure him, as the layer was thick enough to insulate his skin against the heat. He continued to choke as he brought the flames in his hand closer to his face. With one motion he put his hand to his mouth and pretended to swallow the flames. He groaned and winced in pain and made a dry hacking noise in his throat. With wide eyes he slowly moved around to face his King. He seemed to be choking again but it seemed more exaggerated this time. He drew a huge intake of breath and coughed a fireball towards his open hand and it lit up once more. He breathed a loud sigh of relief and the audience clapped.

He moved towards the first candle in front of him and to his left and he positioned the unseen end of the rod close by it. Gavelrigg also shared the same uninterrupted frontal view that the King enjoyed and he began to suspect that he could see something hanging off the magician's waist. With the flame in Zebulan's hand he pretended to cradle and protect it, as he placed it on the flame of the first candle, thereby enlarging it. He moved his head back a little and allowed the largely unseen rod to touch the flame. The moist tip was lit. With a tap of his foot the rod moved quickly back towards him and he opened his mouth. To the observers it seemed the flame had suddenly jumped at him. He held his foot in place so the flame stayed just an inch from his face. He kept his mouth open so it seemed he had the flame in it. He lifted his foot and the rod and flame moved back to the candle.

"Hey...hup," he whooped theatrically.

He began to rotate his body to his left whilst still making the tapping motion with his foot. The effect was impressive and the flame bounced back and forth from his mouth to each successive candle as he turned, giving the impression that he was spitting flame and drawing it back. Once or twice the flame missed a candle or came a little too close to his mouth for comfort. This could not be avoided however and he just continued like the professional he was. The progress of the flame took more than a few seconds and the crowd cheered him on once they saw his intention. As he came around and towards the last candle he held the rod and flame there. He held his ground for a few moments and breathed another loud sigh of relief. Then he looked at the flame once more with a hungry look in his eyes. He reached out with both hands grabbing the flame and then scoffed it down excitedly. The flame was thus extinguished. He laughed heartily for a few seconds and many in the crowd joined him.

"Aaaaaah!" he said smoothly and with pleasure.

He felt happier now because the crowd were happier. He turned once more towards his King and bowed, to which the King smiled and nodded slightly. Zebulan did not rise immediately however. He grabbed at his chest and stumbled suddenly, arching his back painfully.

"Aaaaaah!" he said, though not smoothly or with pleasure. "Too hot!"

He dived backwards and laid himself out flat on his back. He lay still for a long time so as to give the impression that he was dead. The crowd eventually quietened down, though few people genuinely thought he was hurt. As arranged previously, a couple of boys came forward and placed a large white sheet over his body so that he was completely covered and that there was plenty of excess in all directions. There he stayed, motionless, waiting for complete silence. There was too much munching and slurping for that however. After at least a minute on the ground a hand seemed to rise from within the cloth and stay there. In fact, Zebulan had raised a particular rod, another, and fixed it there. This allowed him some space in which to use his actual hands. He poured a thick liquid from one sealed pouch in his cloak around his prone body. Then he did the same with another thick liquid from a different sealed pouch in the same motion. From the perspective of the crowd all this occurred undercover and out of sight. The two liquids mixed and began to glow and Zebulan let out a long low moan.

The crowd giggled in their delight. Another hand shape emerged under the cloth, though this one was real. The cloth took on a rich red hue as the liquids mixed and followed their interaction. Zebulan moaned even louder and unhooked the rod. He began to roll in the cloth and shake his body, covering himself in the liquid. He trembled and wobbled and bounced on the ground, moaning and groaning all the while. Eventually he became motionless and quiet again for a few seconds before slowly rising to his feet. He put out the candles by trailing his arms, from which liquid dripped, around himself in a circle. This allowed his glowing appearance to become clearer.

In the relative darkness this weird red shape stretched out his arms and bowed once more in the direction of his King. Whilst in this position he untied his cloak from around his neck and lifted it off his shoulders. It glowed now, separately. He began to run towards his King but at the last moment he turned, though not before throwing his cloak high over the King and his table before grabbing it again as he raced around it. He moved through the crowd, now preferring the darker spots, holding his cloak in the air behind him, which still glowed a strong red. They clapped and cheered and some tried to grab at his cloak as he raced past them. After tiring himself out Zebulan turned his route back towards the stage. Once there he folded his cloak and put it away in his box. There was no more red glow, and the candles were relit by the boys as arranged. Zebulan was now down to his body hugging undercloak. It was black, like most of his attire, and had small yellow stars on it.

"People!" he yelled. "What do you think of the show?"

The response was enthusiastic.

"You won't see a real magician and sorcerer like me every day!" he yelled again.

The enthusiasm continued.

"Now for something really special!"

He moved towards his box and opened it slowly, for to build anticipation. Inside were his eggs, manufactured earlier, amongst a variety of other bits and pieces, most of which would not be used. He kept them there as he didn't feel confident to leave any of his things backstage, especially with those thieving jugglers about. He had also in his box a bottle of water and half a dozen plain wooden bowls. He put the bowls around himself in an array of six on the floor of the stage. He took out the bottle, removed the stopper and then proceeded to pour the contents into the bowls, doing so to some considerable bemusement from the crowd, but as Zebulan knew, this was no ordinary water.

Zebulan returned to his box and then peered over the top of the lid at a table to his right. He didn't know any of them sat there but they seemed important and well to do. One of them was a strikingly pretty lady dressed in red and Zebulan thought to amuse and impress her. He held her eye and she held his. He raised one of his special eggs from inside his box and held it in his hand. During the old man's chat he had taken the opportunity to paint them all red, and though they were the same size and shape as ordinary chicken eggs, in the gloom of the setting it was not immediately obvious from a distance what they were. "Do you know what this is?" said Zebulan, addressing his words in her direction.

She smiled and shook her head.

"This is a dragon's egg."

She smiled again and those about her began smiling also.

"You must be very careful with them. Baby dragons can breathe fire too you know. Why don't you come up and see?"

She looked to Spikepoint seated to her left. He gave her leave to stand. This she did and all eyes turned to watch her as she stepped away from the table and moved the few metres towards the stage. The commander kept an especially close eye on her. Zebulan motioned her onto the stage and she stood with him, both now illuminated by the candle light. By gesture he invited her to take the egg, which she did.

"Now, you must be very, very careful. Do you understand?"

She nodded.

"What's your name my dear?" asked Zebulan.

"Miranda."

"Miranda. Do you know my name?"

"Ah...Zim...Zar?"

"Can anyone help her?" he yelled to the crowd.

Some in the crowd obliged in near full voice, including the King.

"Thank you," said Zebulan. "Now Miranda, what you have in your hand is very special. Do you know how special it is?"

"No," she said, giggling.

"It's very special. I had to climb a mountain to get it and struggle up a sheer cliff face at the top of the mountain. Then I had to wrestle with its mother. Have you ever wrestled with a dragon?"

"No," she said, smiling still.

"I thought not. When I had finally won, because you know dragon's don't give up their eggs just like that, when

301

I had finally won I had to carry them all down the mountain very, very carefully. Because, you see, if you drop them...they'll explode! Look!"

As he spoke his last word he brought the other eggs out of his box and held them in his cupped hands. One of the five was sitting on top of the other four and he looked at it closely, inviting Miranda to do the same. Through subtle movements he caused it to teeter and he suddenly looked at her with a look of shock in his eyes.

"It's falling," he yelled. "Catch it Miranda, catch it!"

She stood motionless holding her dragon's egg and simply copied his expression unable to react in time. The egg fell away from its fellows and turned earthwards. Zebulan had in that brief moment shifted his remaining four eggs to one hand, leaned and caught it expertly with his spare, and once the full motion had been witnessed by the audience to considerable applause. He looked up at Miranda and made a circular shape with his lips, blowing air through them, in much the same way that a chimpanzee might, upon discovering that his secret stash of bananas had not, as he had for a moment suspected, been stolen.

"That was close!" he gasped. "I think we'd better put them back."

With that he put his five eggs back in the box and collected the other from Miranda. On this last egg's route back to the box however he deliberately scraped the top of the egg, that which he had previously covered with a small thin piece of paper, against a roughened corner. It sparked into life and a small green jet of flame began to emerge to about six inches from the hole.

"Ah! It's alive!" he screamed. "The dragon!"

Miranda jumped in shock for a moment then laughed and ran back to her seat. Zebulan charged about pretending to be at a loss as to what to do. He left the stage in a contrived panic and tried to hand off his flaming dragon's egg to members of the audience, who invariably declined the offer. He came to the King and offered it to him, though by now its flame had died a little and would only last for a few more seconds. His eyes lit up and the King happily snapped away the egg against Zebulan's expectation. He held it aloft and out of Zebulan's reach laughing childishly whilst doing so. Zebulan realised the danger should the King accidently tip or crack the egg and the hot contents come pouring out on top of him. Fortunately, he held it firm as its flame died away. It was still very hot even so and Zebulan could see the King beginning to realise this as his expression changed. His hand had been insulated with grease unlike the Kings, and Gavelrigg, also sensing the problem, helped Zebulan get it back from him.

Spikepoint and the others looked on at this rather unexpected behaviour from the King and seemed to be having as much trouble as everyone else in understanding it. The King was a little upset by this treatment and he moved away from his former gentility.

"Stop! Don't touch me!" he bellowed. "That's my dragon's egg! Give it back to me."

Spikepoint watched with increasing surprise at this bizarre

303

and childish display. Zebulan and Gavelrigg naturally backed away but the egg shell was too hot to return. Gavelrigg, with a wave of panic, could see what mood was suddenly taking over the King. He tried to encourage the King to sit again but he could not be manipulated.

"I am your King! Do as I say!" he said, directing his command to Zebulan and brushing Gavelrigg away.

Zebulan seemed unsure what to do. He knew all of a sudden that his performance had come to an end. He looked at Gavelrigg, who seemed frozen and unable to react.

"Come now. This is my banquet," said the King again. "Indulge me."

Zebulan quickly dipped the egg in one of the bowls of water to cool it down. The King approached him and stepped onto the stage. Zebulan shook off the water from the egg and handed it to him. The King took, held and examined it in detail as though searching for the dragon inside. He turned to see Spikepoint watching him intensely. The King smiled and moved over to his table and stood in front of him.

"My dear captain. Spikepoint. Have you and your friends enjoyed the banquet?" said the King.

Spikepoint said nothing but simply glared ahead.

"Take this egg shell," said the King as he proffered it. "Let it be a symbol of my feelings for you and how I wish things to be whole between us and not broken."

Lord Spikepoint decided it was time to speak. He put his arms firmly on the table in front of him, lifted his head and arched his back. He sucked in a great lungful of air that caused the small hairs on those people close by to tremble and by this action their attention was immediately drawn to him. He smashed the egg away and it crumbled to pieces on the stone floor.

The room dropped to silence and Zebulan quietly started packing his things.

CHAPTER 9

Gurgle sucked in a lungful of fresh, early morning air and opened his eyes.

"Go!" whispered Tirgu, standing above and behind him.

Gurgle stood and leapt from his concealed position and moved to a run as quickly as his muscles would allow. He was to get to a distant rock and then return within one minute, and Tirgu was keeping time. He charged along the flat grass training area at the back of Spikepoint castle, his muscles quickly beginning to complain at the exertion. The lumpy granite boulder that marked the halfway point soon loomed up and appeared much more interesting up close than from far away. His hands reached out and touched the yellow blob of paint on its nearest protrusion and he dug his foot into the ground to slow himself and then to turn. Back he bounded, though with less fury and coordination, and soon into the hollow from which he had emerged approximately one minute earlier.

"Awww, very close Gurgle, but no," lamented Tirgu.

"I'm not so sure, it seemed just on the minute to me," said an observer.

"No, he was too slow," replied Tirgu, correcting him sharply. "We've tried this every day for a week now Gurgle and you still can't do it."

Gurgle looked at him nervously.

"You have to do it Gurgle. You've got to pass all these trials or I can't use you...and don't think if you fail I'll send you back to that forest of yours. I'll send you to mine to work as a slave for my sister...and that you don't want I promise you."

Gurgle understood but kept quiet.

"Since your legs are tired let's do something with your arms. You need to practice your climbing. Did I tell you I was once the champion climber of Brown Root?"

Gurgle shook his head but believed him.

"Not had a chance to compete for a while though. Come on, let's go to the wall."

Gurgle, Tirgu and the few soldiers that had taken a break to watch his trials moved to one corner of the castle. This corner had fallen into a state of disrepair and was somewhat dangerous. Not the sort of place one would recommend trying to climb. However, from Tirgu's point of view this was an excellent challenge for young Gurgle. So far he had not managed to climb the entire way, up to a ledge from which he could get into the castle through an opening and in which a guard had been instructed to welcome him. The total height Gurgle found hard to estimate but it was probably about the height of his tree house back in Milton Greens with perhaps a little extra on top. The first few steps were easy. A pile of crumbled stones that had once been part of the wall formed a nice little platform to get started.

Gurgle had climbed trees before but had never been a natural at it. Walls felt much harder for him despite the numerous cracks and empty spaces where mortar once held the stones together. He looked up at the wall from below and spied the guard looking down at him from above. The man smiled and chuckled to himself and seemed to gesture for Gurgle to begin.

"Remember Gurgle," said Tirgu, "climb with your legs, not your hands. The hands are just there for stability. Get both hands secure then step up with your feet, find new hand holds get them secure and then repeat...and don't look down!"

Tirgu might have been able to rig up some safety rope if he'd wanted but he felt you couldn't train people properly to face danger if you trained them in safety. At least he chose to stand beneath Gurgle once he left the ground so that he would have a fair chance of catching him should he fall. Once Gurgle had scaled the crumbling stones and stood facing the vertical part of the climb he hesitated, quite naturally.

"Come on, you can't climb it with your eyes. Be bold, be brave," demanded Tirgu.

Reluctantly Gurgle made his first grips on the wall, jamming his fingers into familiar places. He could hear Tirgu walking up the crumbling stones behind him and felt reassured.

"Keep your body close to the wall as much as you can," said Tirgu.

Gurgle did as he was instructed and slowly started to leave the safety of the ground. As he breathed in and out dust was alternately sucked into his mouth and blown away in the air. Without looking down he raised a leg. Knowing that the stones had a fixed height it was easy enough to find the gaps with his feet. He began to gain height and he tried to keep focussed on each move and not on his predicament. Tirgu was stood beneath him and held his arms aloft. Gurgle was beyond his reach now and with his eyebrows and other body parts Tirgu silently gestured his young charge upwards.

Gurgle had about another ten metres to climb and the guard above continued to look down at this keen young goblin, admiring his ability. Gurgle managed to find good places for his hands and feet to fit into and made steady progress. There was one section though in which the mortar between the stones was still good and there were only tiny little ledges for him to use. This bit had stopped him before and he had fallen before, though fortunately without injury as he had been safely caught. Now he was determined to succeed, but not to please Tirgu, just so that he wouldn't have to do it again. His muscles were managing but would soon tire and he knew that you couldn't hang about in the middle of a climb; you had to keep going and the longer you waited and struggled with a difficult section the less likely you were to climb it.

He could see this difficult section looming close above him and he tried to look for a different place to put his hands. The guard above him was much closer now and if he had been hanging down by his toes from the ledge he could have patted Gurgle on the head. Tirgu could see all this happening and he could also see the solution.

"Gurgle, try going around that bit, to the right, go to the side!" he shouted.

Gurgle struggled to concentrate on what was being said,

but once the guard above him repeated the suggestion he heard it and understood. Looking to his right he could see a way in which the poor condition of the mortar continued. He moved in that direction with a very careful shuffling motion. The only problem was that it led to the corner of the wall and the view that greeted him as he pulled his face around it was so startling he almost lost his grip. He saw from a fresh and frightening perspective just how high he was and Tirgu was not in a position to catch him if he should fall. His muscles tightened and his lungs shrank. He gasped and clung to the wall. Tirgu recognised the signs.

"Gurgle! Stay calm, focus. Look back to your left and into the wall. Turn your body and move back a little."

"I can't," murmured Gurgle, "I can't move."

"Yes you can," said Tirgu, combining support and menace in his tone of voice. "Raise your left hand and put it into the crack above your head."

Gurgle opened one of his eyes whilst trembling and looked in that direction. He saw that it was a way up and he slowly reached for what seemed a generous space. He jammed his fingers in as demanded from below and then shifted his body to the left, also as demanded. Gurgle was shallow breathing now and his nerves were jangling. He was rapidly approaching a state in which he could no longer command his body to climb. He reached up with his right hand and found another crack, though it was less generous than that which his other hand enjoyed. He had no obvious place for his feet and Tirgu shouted from below that he would simply have to walk up the wall. At first this seemed an impossible suggestion but then he realised that with one last serious pull on his arms he could just push against the wall with his feet and bring his body up. He managed to do so but felt terrified. He looked up and found a better hold for his right hand and suddenly felt that he could pull himself up. The guard above was excited now and hadn't seen this goblin so close to succeeding before. He was anxious to put out a hand to grab at him and did so.

"Leave him!" bellowed Tirgu, and the guard pulled his hand back.

Gurgle had just a few more feet to go and was close enough to see drops of sweat on the guards face. Somehow he managed to scramble up the last section with reserves of energy he didn't know he had and placed a hand on the ledge, which protruded from the wall. With the last of his will he reached up with his other hand and pulled himself inside, collapsing at the feet of the guard. In his haze he could hear cheering from outside. The guard picked him up and presented Gurgle at the window. The crowd below yelled his name and smiled and clapped. Tirgu had a warm smile on his face.

"How was that?" he shouted from below.

"Easy," said Gurgle, shouting from above.

"Really? Why don't you climb down then?" asked Tirgu.

Gurgle smiled and disappeared inside. The guard that had helpfully collected him brought him back down but by a safer method. Tirgu and the group with him walked around to the front of the castle and went in by the main entrance. There they came across an unexpected scene. Assembled there were a group of about a dozen people on horseback, looking somewhat tired and dishevelled. Tirgu recognised his Lord amongst them, who recognised him in return.

"Tirgu, a word with you now," said Spikepoint.

Spikepoint dismounted, as did the others immediately after him. He approached Tirgu with his arm outstretched and enveloped him, pulling him away from the group and into an alcove near the main gates. Spikepoint removed his golden helmet and Tirgu could see the dried sweat on his face and soon heard the tension in his voice.

"It's begun. Get the men ready. Organise the defences. We'll have war on us soon."

"My Lord, how long do we have?" asked Tirgu.

"No time, not even for questions," he replied.

With that Tirgu was away and to work. Gurgle came down with the guard at this moment and soon felt the chaos in the air. Tirgu winked at him to follow. He did so and followed him at great speed through various parts of the castle, much of which he'd not seen before. He was now witness to yet another side of Tirgu. He ran about yelling, pushing, threatening, goading, organising everyone he could find that did not outrank him, and of those there were few. Within the space of five minutes helmeted guards began to congregate and stand at their posts and from a distance the top of the castle seemed to grow a head of hair. Shortly after, dozens of men came streaming out of the main gates and stood in formation on the far side of the babbling river that they had just crossed via the drawbridge. Once all had emerged the drawbridge was raised and bolted. Tirgu continued to prowl around, making sure that every pair of arms was at work. Those few men that were idle were quickly belted around the head and into action.

Gurgle was struggling to keep up with Tirgu and to understand all of what was happening. He wisely decided to wait until there was a pause in the action before asking any questions. Once Tirgu seemed satisfied that everyone that could be put to use had been he noticed Gurgle standing behind him.

"Well, let's agree that it was one minute after all," said Tirgu, without smiling. "You're my scout now."

*

Lieutenant Chirp Rideau Tilestain was away from his brigade, seeking a few moments peace. He was squatting over a hastily manufactured hole in the ground and checking anxiously that the leaves and fronds of the plants all about him were giving him sufficient privacy. With a gentle thump his kindnesses were welcomed by the soft earth.

"Lieutenant!" came a voice suddenly, but softly.

Exasperated by this fellows timing he replied angrily.

"What the hell is it!?"

"People Sir, about half a mile away," answered the goblin.

"What sort of people?"

"Human people, a mixture, men and women, about twenty five."

"Are they heading this way?"

"No Sir."

"Can you see any goblins amongst them?

"No Sir."

"Then let them pass and give me some peace."

"But Sir, they might have information to help us."

"Really? Then why don't you go and ask them where the goblins are? That'll work nicely."

"Are you sure Sir?"

"No, you clonk! If I wasn't busy I'd throw a rock at you! Get out of here!"

The goblin disappeared and what remained for the Lieutenant to do he did. After he was tidy he emerged from cover and saw most of the troop lying on the ground observing this group of people in the distance. He noticed they were nervous and not very skilled at controlling themselves or keeping quiet. He caught the eye of his quartermaster, who saw a not very satisfied look on his face. He beckoned him over and began whispering.

"What's the matter with them?" asked the Lieutenant.

"Most have never seen human people before Sir. I think it's mostly curiosity rather than fear. Even so, it's not very inspiring."

"No, it isn't. We need to be off shortly. Can I see the map again?"

Flap reached behind himself and pulled out a small scroll,

unrolling it in the same motion.

"Where's that town you mentioned?" asked the Lieutenant.

"The one I suggested we avoid?" queried Flap.

"Yes."

"Here Sir," said Flap, pointing at the map. "It's not very far away, about a mile and a half."

"Thinking about it," thought the Lieutenant out loud, "perhaps that's the kind of place where we'll be more likely to find something out."

"Hmmm, I'm not so sure that's a good idea," ventured Flap, gently.

"Why not?"

"Well, I think we'll not be welcome and we'll stand out like a very sore thumb."

"What if a few of us go in quietly and try to find things out? You can stay here and watch the brigade."

His quartermaster frowned at this last suggestion but didn't really have a good reason for saying no to the idea of having a discreet look around the town. They did have long warm cloaks for the chill evenings and could wear them to keep a low profile.

"It's a plan I suppose."

"I'll take two others with me. Do you think we should wait till nightfall?" asked the Lieutenant.

"No, even though you'll have the cover of dark you won't be able to see too much, and humans often get a bit excitable in the evenings. If there's any of our goblins in the area then they'll be under lock and key at night but might be put to work during the day. I'd go shortly."

"Good thinking. I'll get some gobs to come with me."

One of the few goblins not lying on the ground was Slap Canopy, the eldest of the brigade. He was leaning against a boulder and nibbling on a root of some kind. He seemed quite relaxed and saw the Lieutenant coming, giving him a modest wave.

"Slap, I have a job for you."

"Okey dokey. What sort of a job would that be then?" he replied inquisitively.

"I want a couple of people to come with me and take a look around this nearby town."

"You sure?" he asked.

"Yes. Why, have you got another idea?"

"No, no. Seems a fine idea. Just checking that you really wanted me to come."

"I do."

"Count me in," he said, simultaneously resuming his nibbling on the root.

The Lieutenant looked around for a third goblin to make up his party of spies. He caught the eye of another member of his brigade whose name had escaped him. He began pulling his finger towards himself and this goblin got to his feet and walked towards him.

"Yes Sir," said this goblin enthusiastically.

"Fancy a trip into town?" asked the Lieutenant.

"Yes Sir."

"Might be a bit dangerous."

"That's what we're here for Sir. I'm ready."

"Good, good. Remind me of your name son?"

"Rustle. Rustle Blacknose, Sir."

"Rustle eh? Fine name, fine name. Get your stuff and follow me."

The quartermaster had been watching this scene and had already given words of warning to Slap. Once the Lieutenant was attending to his own possessions the quartermaster approached Rustle and had a word in his ear.

"You just watch out. Have a look around. Don't stay there after nightfall. Keep yourselves to yourselves and behave. If you're spotted by the enemy you're likely to share the fate of the other goblins or get yourselves killed. Keep your eyes open...and come back safe. Got that?"

"Yes Sir," replied Rustle.

"Off you go then."

The quartermaster gathered the rest of the boiled mice and instructed them to keep quiet and not make a scene. They were to wait in secret and to wait all day if necessary. The Lieutenant, Slap and Rustle were soon ready and dressed in their long cloaks. Underneath though they carried little and were prepared for speed, should it prove necessary. They each carried a weapon concealed upon their body and the Lieutenant carried some coin money for use abroad. He could imagine many reasons to carry it. The three of them nodded quietly to the rest of the brigade and set off on their journey.

The quartermaster stood silently, watching them leave. A wave of sickness suddenly bubbled up inside him but he stoically ignored it until it passed. He turned back to the rest of the brigade and collected them together. He made sure they kept a low profile.

The three goblins followed their own path towards the town, making sure not to follow the main road as it was often occupied by one group of humans or another. This ground they covered was full of features. There were many rolling fields, sandy tops and soggy ditches. Plenty of cover for them had they needed to make themselves invisible. It was somewhere around the middle of the day but because of the impenetrable cloud they could not make exact measurements from the sun. It did not matter.

Rustle was the first to identify the looming shape of the town ahead of them. He asked the Lieutenant what it was called but he had to confess that he didn't know and that the quartermaster had not told him its name. Slap suddenly spoke up and dispelled the ignorance of his companions.

"That's Roper. I've been there a couple of times."

His two companions looked at him, surprised. It seemed he had been this way before.

"Why didn't you say earlier?" asked the Lieutenant.

"I didn't realise that's where you wanted to go," replied Slap, "I would've told you if I'd known."

"What can you tell us about it?" asked Rustle.

"Well, it's not too bad. Bit smelly, but it has its friendly parts. I know a farmer there. He might help us. Then again he might not."

"What sort of people live there?" asked Rustle again,

getting his questions in before the Lieutenant.

"Locals," replied Slap, with a smile on his face.

"Come on," prompted the Lieutenant, irritated by this poorly timed witticism.

"Well, you know, farmers and such. Who else would live there? It's a bit of a dump, but it's between lots of places so somebody might have seen something."

Without anything needing to be said they all noticed the man that suddenly came over the rise ahead of them and they ducked to the ground and kept out of his sight. Six eyes then emerged tentatively from cover and took a look at the man. He seemed inoffensive enough and when a flock of sheep followed him over the rise it was confirmed. They felt more confident and stood up only to flop down again once a large dog followed where the sheep had come. Goblins and dogs have never been the greatest of friends you see. The six eyes appeared once more and soon met the two glistening brown eyes of the dog. So rarely had they seen any dogs that they had little idea of the breeds and whether this one might be at the more vicious end of the scale. Their eyes met and little reaction was encouraged in the dog. Its tongue fell out and it returned to watching the sheep.

"What should we do?" asked Rustle quietly.

"Stay here and wait for them to pass," said the Lieutenant.

"Let's go and have a word, shall we?" said Slap.

With that he was up and waving at the man. The Lieutenant slapped Slap on his legs frantically but did so in vain. Slap called out warmly.

319

"Waaaay!"

The man heard the sound and turned in their direction. He stood still for a moment or two to examine who had called at him. Upon realising the lack of a threat he smiled and walked towards them. The Lieutenant did not like this at all.

"Slap! Stop it, send him away."

"Bit late for that I'm afraid Sir."

The man approached to about ten feet and to their credit the sheep gradually did also. The dog was off skulking in the background somewhere.

"Who's that there then?" said the man, in an accent unfamiliar to goblin ears.

"Good morning to you," said Slap.

"Thank yu for yur greeting, but its afternun."

"D'yu know a farmer by the name o' Cronin?" asked Slap, doing his best to mimic the local lingo.

"I duz."

"He about much?"

"Why? Yu nose him?" asked the man.

"I duz," replied Slap.

With that the man laughed out loud. He also noticed two other strange creatures keeping an eye on him.

"Thems yur frends?" he asked Slap, who turned to look at them.

"Come out. It's fine," he said.

They slowly did so and the man gave them each a little nod as their eyes caught his.

"Where d'yu nose Cronin from then?" asked the man.

"Frends from his campaign days," replied Slap.

"Frends yu say. Sure o' that, are wuz?"

"Wuz are."

"Hah. Which campaigns we got in mind then?" said the man with a cough and a smile.

"All sorts."

"All sorts? Yu ant convinced me yet sun."

"Eken. Five yur ago."

"Eken, yer I nose it. What of it?"

"Cronin and I wuz init. Met um then."

"Not many o' yur sort fort in Eken."

"No...jus' me."

With that the man leaned back and gave Slap a good look up and down. He grumbled in his throat and looked about himself and at his sheep. With a mad look in his eye he suddenly released a piercing whistle that startled all three of them. His dog came charging up out of nowhere. Slap stood his ground but the other two recoiled. The dog came to an immediate halt at the man's side and looked up in his direction. The man spoke once more.

"Dog's tend not to be too fond of forest dwellers such as yuz. If yuz been much out o' the forest yu'll seen dogs and nose how to treat em. Has yursel a pat on um."

Slap understood and cautiously approached this man and his dog. He had spent a lot of time out of the forest but hadn't used too much of that time getting friendly with dogs. The dog turned his attention from his master and towards this goblin. His tongue stopped flopping about and was snapped back inside his mouth. Their eyes met

321

and Slap held out his hand, topside first and hanging down. He'd seen human men doing that with unfamiliar dogs. The dog didn't react much beyond giving him a casual sniff. Slap went further and gave him a pat as requested. The dog seemed disinterested.

"Well then, I nose um. He's me cusin. Got sum bisnis with um, have yuz?" asked the man.

"Just passin this way. Hoped to see im again."

"He ain't too well. Urt imself last yur. Heez livin in tha town now, 'bove the bakers."

"Thank you. You helped us a lot," said Slap, reverting to his normal speaking voice.

The man just nodded and turned back to his sheep. They all drifted away. Once they could speak privately again Slap expected a pat on the back but got something rather different.

"Never do anything like that again! Do you understand me?" demanded the Lieutenant.

"I got us a place in town and a safe contact to meet."

"I don't care. You could just as easily have given us all away and gotten captured."

"He's a gentle old soul, I recognised him...I think."

"Listen, I'm in charge here. That means if things go wrong I get blamed. Not you for opening your mouth, not the quartermaster, not anyone else, I get the blame, just me. So you'll damn well do as I say and follow orders then won't you? 'Cause I'm not taking the blame unless I make the decision that leads to it."

Rustle stood between the two of them and felt that things

were not quite going according to plan. Then it suddenly occurred to him, mid gulp, that there was no plan.

"Understood," said Slap contritely, hardly able to look in his Lieutenant's direction.

The Lieutenant was justified but nonetheless felt he was overreacting. He cooled himself down and took a deep breath before speaking once more.

"Let's go see this friend of yours."

*

Back at their not so skilfully concealed camp the Boiled Mice were huddling together due to there being little cover to hide so many goblin bodies. They had retired from their previous position and were close to the river that they had more or less followed since leaving Milton Greens. They were over a day's full march from safety now and as such the Mice were on edge. The quartermaster sought his own spot, ostensibly so that he could keep watch for the brigade, but mostly so that he could have some solitude away from the multitude. He had his back to them but kept glancing around to check that all was under control. For the moment it was. He sank his teeth in the corner of a worm brick, or at least did his best to do so as it was decidedly firm and chewy. He couldn't help thinking that somewhere between the official procurement of rations for the troops, and the goblins that dug up the worms, someone was making a lot of money they shouldn't.

"Sir?" came a soft voice from behind him, to which the

quartermaster turned in response.

"Yes?"

"Sir, we've finished our watch. Can we be replaced?"

"Fine. Get some of the others and send them out."

"Yes Sir."

After the quartermaster turned again this goblin went off and selected some others and passed on the quartermaster's instruction. However, they either didn't believe him or didn't care and a row soon broke out. The quartermaster was losing his patience with some members of the brigade and was getting increasingly worried about what he'd gotten himself into. Back in his day fighting goblins were exactly that and there was no tolerance of any fannying about. He waded into this embarrassing little fracas and settled it in no uncertain terms.

"Stand up! The lot of you!" addressing those few goblins sat on the ground and reluctant to keep watch.

They did so but seemed unafraid of his angry manner and expected no repercussions.

"Get out!" he demanded. "Get back to Milton Greens this instant! Stick to the river and keep out of sight."

They looked at him, open mouthed.

"Go on! Get out now! Take your stuff and get out," said with real menace in his voice.

"But Sir..." said one of them.

"No more words! Out!"

With that he drew his sword and proceeded to hit one of them with the flat side of the blade on his back and they began to move.

"Anyone else who just wants to fanny about pack your stuff and get out now! I've had enough of boys like you! I want fighting goblins that do their duty!"

He watched, unperturbed, as the five of them reluctantly and slowly left camp. For the others sat and stood around this was a clear and undeniable message. They had not seen their quartermaster behave like this before and it was a sobering spectacle. For many this event brought with it the realisation that this was no relaxed jaunt into the countryside, this was war and war must always be taken seriously.

*

Their overland and hopefully discreet route into Roper seemed unavoidably to be trending towards the main road into the town, much to the Lieutenant's alarm. It did not seem too busy though considering it was in the middle of the working day. Many figures could be spotted in the fields outside the town but all seemed too tall to be goblins. The Lieutenant thought a little more and decided to abandon any notion of a sneaky approach, since it was almost inevitable they would be seen by someone and he thought it better that when spotted they should not appear to be engaged in any bad business. The three of them changed their route and walked unhurriedly into the centre of Roper. Slap was right, it was a dump. But strangely the Lieutenant felt that this was a good thing, since such a quiet, dirty little place, was just the sort of place the goblins might have been brought through.

A few people wandered about and even fewer paid any serious attention to the three of them. Rather than ask for directions Slap thought it best to just follow his nose and try to find the bakers directly. Through shrewd observation he looked at the plumes of smoke coming from many of the buildings and identified the largest, supposing that might be the bakers. They followed the edges of various old wooden buildings and did their best to avoid getting stuck in the mud.

The smell in the town was frightful. The Lieutenant had smelled a few unpleasant things in Milton Greens before, as part of his duties, including the time he discovered a sweet old lady that liked to hoard turnips inside her tree, who then promptly died amongst them. The smell in the town however was something else entirely and was a new experience for his nose. He looked around to try to find the source and noticed it trickling between his feet. At first he heard the trickle then perceived a gurgling sound and saw that this rancid stream emerged from the far edge of the building they were walking past. Then he noticed the sounds of men close by and realised where he was.

"Hey," said Slap to the Lieutenant, in a hush. "You don't want to go that way."

The Lieutenant backtracked immediately to where Slap and Rustle had halted but where he had not.

"That's where they do their bisnis," whispered Slap, and the Lieutenant nodded.

Slap gestured that they should take another route and the

others followed. The Lieutenant could sense a little embarrassment and saw that in practical terms they were a team in which he was not the leader, no matter how hard he tried to be. He was unsure of the situation and what to do and so followed the one that seemed to know what he was doing. Soon the air cleared and they made good progress through the town. Human people wandered here and there and the Lieutenant was surprised at how easily they moved through them. The town didn't have a guilty conscience it seemed.

Rustle was fascinated and frightened at the same time. He saw shops and homes and businesses and none of them resembled those in Milton Greens. Even though his mother had always told him he was tall for a goblin few of the humans looked at him eye to eye, and he was starting to get a pain in his neck from having to look up at everything and everyone.

A rumble in the distance greeted their ears. They couldn't identify it but they could see the human people ahead of them spreading to the sides of the street and making way for whatever it was. A herd of cows came swiftly down the street towards them and they made way for them also, hugging the walls. A farmer stood at the back, doing his best to shout at and corral them into doing what he wanted. He didn't seem all that effective and there was a hint of stampede in the air. Thankfully they lacked coordination and just stumbled forward, past Slap, Rustle and the Lieutenant who sheltered in a doorway. The door in the doorway opened behind them as the cows went by and a rather gruff and overweight character emerged.

"No loitering! Off with you!" said this man.

The three goblins in his doorway were a little alarmed at such a demand, since it was impossible to satisfy. He understood their predicament but pointed rather unrealistically to a gap between the wall and the cows that he meant for them to use.

"Come on, off with you!" he repeated.

"D'yu know a baker's nearby?" asked the Lieutenant, above the din.

"Aye, next street over. Off with you!" replied the man.

At this stage the cows had passed and so did they, towards the next street over. After a few moments of close inspection they spotted the bakers, though whether it was the right one was hard to tell. It did have a first floor at least. For the first time in this town a pleasant smell entered their noses. They walked inside the shop, which had no door, and pretended to be interested in buying bread. The pretence soon proved unnecessary, as they were hungry and the bread seemed worth the expense. The Lieutenant nodded to Rustle, who then picked out a few fresh buns and brought them to the counter. Slap kept his distance from the other two and looked about for any signs of his friend. He quietly left the shop and took a look around the back, finding steps up to the first floor and a doorway. He returned to the shop to pass on the news.

"I've got something," said Slap quietly.

"So have we," replied Rustle, as he bit into his bun.

"No, I mean the other something."

The Lieutenant prodded Rustle and out they went to the back of the bakers. They were in a small alleyway and they could see stairs going up to where they presumed this Cronin man to be. It was a murky, misty spot as the smoke from the chimneys thereabouts preferred to sink than to rise. An old human woman poked her head out of a window on the first floor of a building opposite. She didn't seem too concerned by their presence and just kept an eye on them with her lids half closed. The Lieutenant hoped that she would dip back inside but she didn't. He didn't care in any case and walked up the stairs to the first floor of the bakers.

"I'd better knock," said Slap, as the Lieutenant moved in front and raised his knuckles.

Without answering he stepped back and Slap stepped forward. Thud, thud, thud. They waited a few moments and listened. There was some sort of shuffling sound and then a cough and then a latch being unlatched and then a scrape as the frame of the door was pulled inwards by the human man inside.

"Wut?" said the man, bleary eyed.

"Cronin? That you?" said Slap.

"Yup. Whose you?" he said, blinking and squinting at the daylight.

"Slap Canopy. Remember me?"

"Yerr," said Cronin laughing, after a moment's reflection. "How d'yu find me?"

"Bumped into yur cusin today."

"Ah, but...wut yu doing 'ere?"

"Need a bit of 'elp."

"Spose yood best cum in then."

"I'm with a couple of frends, that alright?"

"Yup."

Cronin made way and swept his arm out to invite them inside, but because of the modest size of the room his arm did not have too far to travel. As he shuffled backwards it became clear to Slap what sort of injury his old friend had suffered. He walked with a painful looking limp and could only move slowly. The room was sparse and barely furnished. There was a bed, a small table and beneath the only window there was a box with a few stained cushions piled on top and from which it seemed he spent a lot of time looking out.

The three goblins went inside and did their best to not appear uncomfortable. Cronin slumped back down on the bed and sighed with relief that his physical ordeal was over.

"Bull got me last year," he said quietly. "Up 'gainst a wall. Can't wuk na more."

"Oh...I'm sorry about that old friend," said Slap gently.

"Nay bother. Want owt? I ain't got much."

"Short o' stuff these days, Cronin?"

"Aye. Cusin helps me a bit. A live modest now."

"Maybe we can offer you something?" suggested the Lieutenant.

Slap and Cronin both turned and looked blankly at the Lieutenant.

"What brings yu this way?" continued Cronin after a few

moments silence.

"It's a delicate business...concerning some goblins," said Slap.

"It usually does wi' yoo."

"Well, not me personally," replied Slap.

He turned and walked over to look out of the window.

"See much out o' this window?" asked Slap.

"Sometimes. That's my winda' on the world that is," said Cronin jokingly.

"Bet you can smell a lot too," said Slap, whilst drawing a lungful of air in through his nose. "Smells good that does. Meat pies is my guess. Fancy one?"

"Might do. Whose paying for all ten o' them then?"

Slap smiled and nodded to the Lieutenant. He took Rustle with him downstairs, closing the door, and left Slap and Cronin to speak privately. Slap moved over to Cronin's bed and sat on the edge of it with Cronin laid back looking up at him.

"You heard about the kidnap from Milton Greens?" said Slap softly.

"Aye, I 'erd."

"Were after 'em."

"Thought u might be."

"See anything?"

"Aye. It's not a popular subject at the mo' tho'. Not safe to talk about it."

"Come on, what d'yu know?" pressed Slap.

"They were in Roper for a couple of nights. While back now."

"Where'd they go?"

"Baintha took um."

"Baintha?"

"Baintha Brakk. You not know 'im? Bad sort, 'obgoblin."

"Yea, I know him. Bad sort is right. Any idea which way?"

"Back to Brown Root I suppose, where else?"

"How d'yu find all this out?"

"Lotta big mouths in town, s'all ways the way."

Slap paused and looked away to have a think about what he had been told.

"Just you three is it?" asked Cronin.

Slap looked at him again for a few moments and then replied.

"Aye, just the three of us."

"Yu'll have a job getting 'em back then. They been gone a while now. Least a couple o' weeks. Yu'll need an army to get 'em off Baintha, soomin 'e ain't sold 'em off yet."

Slap nodded and at that moment Rustle and the Lieutenant came back up the steps and opened the door. They both carried a pile of pies in their hands and plonked them down where Cronin instructed. The Lieutenant looked expectantly towards Slap as he was eager to leave.

"Got what you needed...have you?" asked the Lieutenant.

"Aye," said Cronin, who then proceeded to turn over on his bed and face away from them.

Slap nodded to his Lieutenant and the three of them left. As Slap closed the door behind himself he quickly said goodbye to his friend, who mumbled something back at him.

Outside, on the ground, Slap whispered the gist of the matter to the other two and they resolved to return to camp. Within half an hour they were approaching the place that they had left just a couple of hours earlier. The quartermaster came out to greet them and they soon exchanged their stories. The quartermaster listened intently and once the Lieutenant had laid out the day's events there was only one question in his mind.

"Great...but where's *my* pie you clonks?"

CHAPTER 10

In the only enclosed and quiet space at Low Rise fort Commander Haine threw off his sweat soaked tunic and stood in front of a bowl of warm water. He cupped his hands in the grey liquid and brought steaming relief to his face, head and neck. He leaned backwards once this was done and stretched and arched his back, moaning lightly at the pleasure of it. In the corner of the room one of his Lieutenants watched the scene, pleased to see his commander returned.

"It was ridiculous," said the commander suddenly.

"But they fed you well?" came the reply after a few moments.

"Aye, they did. That wasn't ridiculous, it was Spikepoint."

"What was he up to this time?"

"Ah, before I get to that, he had some news for me, and I for you."

"What?"

"Well, I've been promoted."

"How'd you manage that?" said his man, scoffing slightly.

"Spikepoint's decision. Seems he's been keeping an eye on me here for a while."

"Hmmm, I do all the work and you get the rewards."

The commander turned to face his friend and smiled. He turned back to the bowl and dipped in a knife. After wetting the blade he put it to his face and began to slowly shave, holding his fingers in strategic positions to prevent it slipping.

"Hard work brings its rewards, you know that. Anyway, I don't look forward to it. We're all in trouble now. War's coming...and he wants me to take a part of his army and my orders directly from him!"

"That is a quite a promotion," said his man, trying to stifle his surprise.

"Promotion is one word for it. An invitation to complicate my life seems more accurate. But it doesn't matter, we'll all be mixed up in what's coming I'm afraid. There's no quiet route out of it. This place will be all but emptied."

"We can leave the chickens in charge if you like."

"They already are," laughed the commander. "Would you like to stay? I can arrange it if you want."

"No, what would be the point? My place is at your side." The commander thought a little more, and appreciated this loyal sentiment. He continued his shaving and was finding it easy enough despite the difficulty of his journey back to the fort and the dirt he had collected along the way.

"So tell me about the banquet."

"Ah, yes, what an experience," said the commander sarcastically. "They didn't seem all that welcoming. We had to serve ourselves half the time. Nearly got into a spot of bother over that business from a few weeks ago."

"I was wondering about that."

"Yes, it was brushed off though. Spikepoint's got some big guards around him. Food and drink was pretty good though, nice meat and decent wine. It's a different world that place."

"Did you think about staying?"

"Shush. No. I couldn't really do that after what happened."

"Did you see Starling Dodd?"

"No. Didn't see him. That would have been good. He's busy no doubt, planning to take us on."

"You think it'll go that far?"

"Oh yes. You didn't see Spikepoint and Levant. They've wanted this for a while and they made it happen."

"Made?"

"He took all their food and hospitality...then spat it back at them," turning and looking indignantly at his friend.

"Not literally I hope."

"He may as well have done. The King's clearly gone mad in his old age, but to be honest Spikepoint's not far behind him. Is that door closed?"

"Yes, I closed it."

"Yes, so, after a relatively calm and sensible evening...good magician they had by the way," turning again.

"Oh yes? Who?"

"I forget his name. Anyway, after a nice evening Spikepoint goes and ruins the atmosphere by slapping an egg out of the King's hand."

"Slapping an egg from his hand?"

"An egg, yes," said the commander laughing.

"An egg? Are we at war over an egg then? I can think of better things to fight over."

"Hah! It may as well be an egg. Why not?"

"Why was the King carrying an egg and why did Spike slap it away?"

"If I had a penny for every time I've been asked that question I'd be a rich man," replied the commander light heartedly and whilst gesturing with his blade.

"Come on Robert."

"The egg came from the magician, which the King had grabbed at you see," said the commander, pointing to his temple and frowning, indicating the King's loose grasp on the world. "Then he proceeded to walk around with it while we all watched with no idea what to think. He could have been part of the act come to think of it! That hadn't occurred to me."

"How old is he now?"

"Pfff, oh, at least twice my age."

"And twice the man!" he joked.

"Yes, you have me there. Right, stop distracting me. In his confusion, let's be generous and call it that, in his confusion he wanders over to Spike and offers it to him, with kind words you see, as a gift."

"A peace offering?"

"Something like that."

"Let me guess what happened."

"Exactly, but he didn't just catch the egg he caught his hand too. You'll never guess what the King did then?"

"Threw a drink over him."

"No, he started crying, and not just teary eyes I mean full blown sobbing, within moments. I've never seen anything like it. No one knew what to do."

"You must have done something."

"Yes, well I expected us to be arrested right then and there."

"Hmmm...but you weren't. Did you fight your way out then?"

"No. One of his ministers came over and tried to smooth things over, to my relief."

The commander dropped his blade into the water and a drop or two of blood followed it into the turmoil. He picked up a cloth and dried his face.

"So, he said a few words of comfort to the King and to Spike, not that he deserved them, and suggested we all leave."

"And you shoved a few chops into your pockets and off you went."

"How'd you know that?" replied the commander, surprised.

"I know you, and I can see the grease on your clothes."

"Well, I'd just got them on my plate. What was I supposed to do?"

"No threats made as you went? No curses or promises of revenge?"

"From us or them?"

"From them?"

"A few, as you'd expect, but not from anyone that mattered."

"So what makes you so sure of war?"

"Spikepoint."

"What'd he say?"

"Next time I'm here the banquet will be in my honour."

"Ah."

"Ah indeed."

"How soon do you think we'll need to leave?"

"As soon as were ready. Which will be how soon by the way?"

"Six months?" he said flippantly.

The commander turned and looked at his friend and spoke seriously to him.

"We have six hours to get under way...still sure you don't want to stay?"

*

On an area of scrub land in front of the current King's castle a lightly armoured man examined carefully the troops arranging themselves in front of him. An aide said gently to him amidst the clattering that this particular group were ready to be inspected. Captain Starling Dodd sucked in a chest's worth of air and bellowed at the men in front of him.

"What the hell is this?" he shouted.

There was no response, except that communicated by embarrassed body language. He charged in between the various rows, in and out and around, and systematically battered anything out of place - arm, leg, stomach, weapon, shield, attitude. They soon shivered into formation. Once he had made his point he returned to face them and began yelling at them some more.

"For God's sake, is this the best you can do first thing in the morning?"

His face was beginning to turn a strong red colour and he started pacing from side to side.

"Tomorrow we could well be in a battle and look at you! If you can't even stand in a line properly with your bodies straight what use will you be to me as fighters? Why should we even bother turning up? Just to get slaughtered!? Not me! Not me! Definitely not me!"

He was starting to tire himself out with this display and was running out of intellectual steam as well. He had nothing more to say for the moment. In his mind he knew not to expect great things but always at least to demand them. He signalled to his aide and seemed to suggest that he should take over. He began to walk away and back towards the castle. The other captains each had their own men to muster and were doing so in the castle grounds at the same time. Captain Dodd was happy to leave his men and his duty in the hands of others for a little while.

He stepped gracefully but swiftly in between the people milling about at one of the side entrances to the castle. He was after Gavelrigg and soon found him in one of the state rooms on the first floor. The man was engaged in various small but necessary duties, directing men and materials to where they were needed and making decisions that no other had the authority to make.

The captain was happy to wait for these duties to be dealt with. Only a few people still queued for his minister's attention. Once he had signed, advised and approved where necessary he glanced in Dodd's direction and beckoned him over to take a seat next to him.

"Captain, how are we today?" he asked gently.

"I'm fine."

"And how are the troops?"

"I'm preparing them as quickly as I can."

"What can I do for you?"

"It's a delicate matter."

"Yes?" said Gavelrigg, moving closer.

"I need to know who is in charge now, truly," he said under his breath.

Gavelrigg thought for a while and was unable to dislodge his gaze from his youngest and most daring captain.

"Though the King is kept out of sight and our secret is free we cannot openly control things, even if we did all see eye to eye. Frederick..."

"No, not Frederick."

"*Frederick* will nominally be the figurehead and will take over the King's duties."

"No, he won't see himself as just a figurehead, we'll never be rid of him if you do this."

"This is the way it's done my lad, no other, I'm sorry."

"He doesn't have the slightest interest in military matters, beyond the clothes. He's totally capricious, unpredictable..."

"Sometimes a good quality," interjected Gavelrigg.

"He's not even here!"

"Keep your voice down...and settle yourself if you please

Captain. He returns soon. This is the only way things can go, but what I will assure you is that he will take no decision that I do not approve of," said Gavelrigg, pointing to himself earnestly.

"Hah, how will you do that? Especially on the battlefield."

"In that place I will rely on you and your fellow captains to use your advice and influence."

"It's just not going to work Gavelrigg."

"Not with that attitude young man. You must trust my judgement on this. We need a figurehead and there can be only one. How can we announce to the world how things have been run in the castle so far, with you, me and the others arguing amongst ourselves? This is how our power will continue," gesticulating with a fist landing on his open palm, "with all of us working beneath his tunic...if you follow me?"

The captain nodded but was not happy. He blew air through his mostly closed lips and they rasped together. He leaned and put his arm around his minister and long standing friend.

"I'm still no closer to an answer to my question. Who's orders will I follow, yours or his?"

Gavelrigg smiled at him and nodded knowingly.

"How could you ever doubt it?" he replied warmly.

*

Gurgle sat waiting for food on a long wooden bench in

Spikepoint castle. He was flanked on either side by a variety of soldier types, interspersed with other members of Spikepoint's retinue. The bench faced the kitchen and it could be seen just how much progress was being made with their food. Half a dozen sweaty men toiled in the heat and humidity and did not appreciate such an audience, with so many piercing eyes examining their movements.

A couple of heads away to Gurgle's left a man unknown to the young goblin picked up his beaker and started to bang it on the bench slowly and rhythmically. After a few seconds others began to mimic him and soon a tinny chorus had been brought up, much to the irritation of the head cook. He came forward from the steamy interior and had a few words for the individuals in front of him.

"Shut it! Or you'll get nuthin'!" bellowed the tired looking man.

Most of the beakers became still again, which helped to reveal the ringleaders of this little protest. The man focussed on the head two heads to Gurgle's left and moved towards it.

"Go and help if you're getting impatient," suggested the man.

"No thanks, no one can cook slop quite like you," replied the other, causing many to laugh.

"Oi, because I didn't hear that, I'm not going to spit in yours. Understand me? You'll wait!"

Gurgle was getting impatient for food too. He had worked hard this morning and could literally feel a hole inside his stomach that echoed and amplified his desire for food. The men on either side seemed to tower over him and his eye level was their shoulder level. Gurgle followed the movements of the men inside the kitchen. The head cook was in fact the only permanent cook there, so he had heard, and the other cooks were just soldiers taken on rotation. They were obviously unhappy at this duty and seemed to be sweating more than they would on exercises. The smell that bombarded his nose was not all that pleasant and left a greasy feeling in his throat.

Gurgle felt a hand on his shoulder all of a sudden and turned to see Tirgu standing over him, who then clicked his fingers in a way which seemed to cut through the noise of cooking and conversation, and caught the head cook's ear. He turned, saw who wanted his attention, and came immediately.

"Tirgu," he said plainly, but slightly nervously.

"Make sure my friend here is served first and with the best stuff."

"Alright, I will."

This request caused a little stir amongst those nearby and all eyes turned towards Tirgu and then to the cook to see his reaction.

"Make sure he gets a man sized portion as well...and that he eats every bit of it."

With that Tirgu walked away and was soon out of Gurgle's sight. He felt intimidated by such big people around him and knowing hardly any of them. One or two faces were familiar to him from his recent trip but none that were close by. The man to his right looked down at Gurgle and wondered out loud what on earth he was doing here. The man to his left reproached him and nudged Gurgle with his arm in a heartfelt but clumsy attempt to make him feel welcome.

Another of the cooks had been informed of this special meal request and came out of the steam with a dish in his hand. He did not have to look hard to find the goblin it was meant for as he stood out from the crowd in both size and colour. He placed Gurgle's dish on the bench, rather than chuck it as he would soon do for the other patrons, and rotated it a little so that it was perfectly positioned. He placed a metal fork and spoon within easy reach. Then he filled Gurgle's beaker with water. The food seemed unusually clean, tidy and separate from the other food in the dish. This was something of a change from his usual experience of cuisine at the castle, which consisted, as his fellow diners would soon be reminded, not of such decent looking food but of an awful, greasy mess, the constituents of which were known only to God and to a lesser extent the cooks.

As Gurgle tucked into his carrots, dumplings and sausages the others received their dishes and looked at them with disgust. He bit and chewed it all up, and if it was a man sized portion so then must he now have been a man as it was soon got down his neck.

Tirgu walked up a set of stairs in a quieter part of the castle. He had been summoned to see Spikepoint and was not accustomed to keeping him waiting. The corridor that he joined was deserted and he made his way down to the far end along a faded and worn out carpet that ran down the middle. Rather than knock on the door, which might seem natural to you, Tirgu waited at the door and signalled his presence by coughing. Spikepoint preferred more subtle methods of communication, especially with his special staff members like Tirgu.

The door slid open and Tirgu nodded to his master. He was invited in and told to take a seat. As soon as he had done so Spikepoint began to talk with him.

"Tirgu, what have you to tell me?" he asked.

"We're ready for defence and attack," he replied.

"How soon can we engage in either?"

"Defence immediately, attack tomorrow morning."

"That's fine."

"Should I expect either?" asked Tirgu.

"What do you think?" responded Spikepoint, whilst laughing.

"How soon do we move?"

"Let's get another meal inside them tomorrow morning and then be on our way."

"Fine."

"I have something different for you and your band though," said Spikepoint, and at that Tirgu's pointed brown ears pricked up.

"You don't want us in battle?"

"No," said Spikepoint flatly, "not that I wouldn't value you by my side, of course I would, but I want your special talents employed elsewhere."

"Doing what?"

"Sabotage, sowing seeds of confusion, general chaos and the like...your speciality," said Spikepoint with a smile.

"I'll see what I can do," replied Tirgu, matching his master's smile in width.

"How was your recent excursion to Milton Greens? I noticed you brought back a little trophy."

"Yes Sir, little Gurgle. I think he'll make a good replacement."

"Any trouble from him or the forest?"

"None that troubled me, so none to trouble you."

Spikepoint nodded and stood from his comfortable chair. He moved to the window and looked out at the organisations of his men below.

"What do you intend once we are victorious my Lord?"

"What would you like to see?" replied Spikepoint, after a few moments thought.

"You King, of course, and I..."

"Yes?"

"I want Brown Root."

"Oh," said Spikepoint, as he continued to stare out at the world, "how would I cope without your valuable assistance?"

"You would have me as a valuable ally instead."

"That's true, that's true. How do you intend to take Brown Root, or for me to give it to you, assuming it was within my power?"

"There's just one hobgoblin in my way."

"Brakk?"

"Brakk."

"Surely his little fiefdom can be smashed with your cunning and skill."

"He's more powerful than me for the moment...but with your help."

"I understand. I'll see what I can do. I've never met him. How dangerous is he?"

"He's clever, shrewd, careful and very smelly. That sums him up."

Spikepoint laughed out loud.

"Sounds like an ideal replacement for you," he said.

Tirgu didn't react but his Lord still felt that he ought to apologise for such a remark.

"Forgive me Tirgu, I'll help you get what you want. You've been very loyal to me and that will soon bring its reward, I assure you."

"Thank you my Lord."

"What will you do with Brown Root anyway, if you take it over?"

"Whatever I want...whatever I want," replied Tirgu, with a gentler but more sinister smile on his face.

*

With a hiss and a crackle a small pocket of air inside a log popped as the heat finally penetrated and released it. The log rolled slightly from the modest force of the explosion but was prevented from moving any further by an iron placed in the way by a goblin. She was prodding and maintaining a fire in the household of a hobgoblin family that had recently acquired her services from Baintha Brakk, the local hobgoblin chieftain.

By the family that now owned her she was simply referred to as 'goblin' since, through some unconscious universal tendency in all creatures, they needed to destroy her identity before they could use her as they did. She wearily poked at and managed to enliven the flames as instructed by the matriarch of the household, who had recently given birth. Her other children were sat behind goblin and keeping an eye on her, as they had just been instructed, whilst their mother stepped out. She was going to see Brakk to give him the second half of the money for the use of the goblin. It was customary when buying slaves from Brakk to pay half the price up front, but only pay the second half once it was clear that the slave worked properly and without complaint; something of a guarantee. Very few were ever returned though, as you can understand the amount of pressure put on such poor creatures.

She carried her brown baby bundle wrapped securely around her shoulder. Soon she was at his door and gave a knock. For someone that was so well known and influential around these parts his home was surprisingly ramshackle. He did have a number of runners and assistants working for him though, and he would never be expected to answer his own door. One of them did suddenly open the door, and listened to her explanation for why she was there. He invited her in and told her to wait and that Baintha would be with her in a little while. Baintha or Brakk, together or separate, his name seemed interchangeable.

She began to notice that his appearance of living modestly from the outside (a hollowed tree and simple wooden building attached to it) was not quite the whole story. There were hatches and latches in the floor and from time to time they opened and nimble little assistants would emerge and run off to an errand of some kind. Clearly there was some subterranean activity and that was probably where most things were being done, as little seemed to be happening where she was. There was also a strange musty smell that she couldn't quite discern. She had not been here before. It was her husband, a business associate of Brakk's, who had arranged for the goblin to be sent to her. She looked down and to the side, into her child's eyes, who dutifully looked back and gurgled at her. At that moment a great coughing noise startled them both and she turned to see a figure approaching.

This figure was fat, or at least had the appearance of being fat since he had so many layers of clothing around his body. He was about half way through his life, assuming it would be allowed to proceed to its natural conclusion, and he had thinning dark hair, a wide face and deep set eyes, which overall gave him the impression of being less intelligent than he actually was. He didn't worry too much with pleasantries.

"You brought me money," he said.

"Yes," she replied.

"How's the goblin working?"

"Fine, a little slow but fine."

"Really? Pick o' the bunch I thought."

"She's fine," repeating herself nervously.

She then placed the coins in his hand. He momentarily glanced in their direction and counted them in just that fragment of time. He smiled at her and she smiled back, noticing for the first time the source of the musty smell.

"If she gives you any trouble I'm sure your husband will take care of matters. Do you know of anyone else that might need some help? I've a few more goblins still in my possession."

"No, I don't, I'm sorry," she replied, coughing a little at the odour that she imagined was starting to stain her lungs.

He nodded and looked at the door, a message she gratefully understood and away she went. Once confident that he was alone he looked up and spied a panel in the ceiling that only he, and none of his staff, could reach. He stretched his arms and pushed it aside with one hand and with the other reached inside for a small wooden strong box which tipped and rattled as he brought it down to his level. It was full of coins but not so full as to refuse admittance to a few more. From one of the many pockets in one of his many waistcoats he fumbled for the right key with which to open the box. With ease he poked the key into the narrow lock, opened it, made his deposit then locked it again and put it once more out of reach. This was not his only store of coins by any stretch of the imagination, as he rattled gently whilst walking out of his door into the unsettled afternoon air beyond.

His stomach was bubbling at him and demanding attention, which it did many times a day regardless of how much he gave it. Looking about he oriented himself in the direction of the market and made his way there at a brisk walking pace. Soon he was upon it and examining the various dingy stalls and pondering what would be worth his pennies. The market was extensive and made up mostly of vegetable stalls and stalls of griddled meats. Hobgoblins are great fans of grilled meat and in Brown Root forest the life expectancy of anything small, not particularly fast and unable to fly was probably about two days.

He gravitated towards one stallholder that he recognised and was welcomed as he approached. He set his eyes upon two unusually plump looking rats that were splayed out on the grill plate. They were both facing outwards towards Baintha and each had a cherry in its mouth, something of a local speciality. The flames beneath had the effect of heating the fluids inside them to the point that their skin puckered and bubbled, an indication to Baintha that they were fresh kills and not leftovers, preserved in brine for another day's trade.

Their fate was sealed and Baintha handed over the money. It was received with a smile and a word or two of thanks. The skewers on which they had been so unceremoniously impaled were slid out of their bottoms and they were wrapped in leaves, folded for the purpose, and handed over. Rather than move out of the way of other potential customers, some of whom were mingling about, Baintha immediately sank his teeth into the first of his juicy rats. With tongue and teeth in unison he devoured it in about half a minute. As he was doing so a runner of his came up, seeking his attention, and tugged at him from behind on one of his many waistcoats.

"Sir, sir!"

"What is it?" replied Baintha, in an attempt to calm this lively youth of his.

"They're restless Sir...can't keep 'em quiet. They won't listen to me or do wot I say. They're going mad!"

"Mad!? I'll show them who's mad," he said, splurting fragments of viscera from his mouth with each syllable. "Come on then."

The two of them returned and bounded indoors. The little one opened the hatch to the underground and allowed Baintha in first. He found another of his runners sat in near darkness with just a few candles going. In the back of this chamber he could hear the familiar groans and curses of his remaining goblin captives.

"Woh-oi! Be'ave! Or I'll 'av ya!" shouted Baintha, completely intolerant of any nonsense.

He approached his other young charge and demanded to know why the oil wasn't lit, the usual way in which the room was exposed to his view.

"Sir, it must be blocked somewhere," he replied unhelpfully.

"Well get upstairs and plunge the pipe. You know what to do!"

353

"Yes Sir."

Brakk took the candles in his spare hand and wandered over to his purpose built goblin storage facility. The pale, creamy light revealed to him a mass of unhappy looking creatures and revealed to them the glare of a malevolent hobgoblin beast that, for their liking, couldn't die soon enough.

"How are we all feeling today?" enquired Baintha sarcastically.

He received more of a general hiss than a reply and continued.

"Hmmm, but listen, it's a very serious point. If you don't behave yourselves then I can't sell you...and if I can't sell you, that's a problem because I can't keep you either...I think you all know what that means."

He kneeled down a little so he could speak to them on their level.

"It might not be so bad though, thinking about it. If I'm forced to do it then I'll just have to do it. I won't let you all go to waste though. It'll save me having to buy any dog food for a while at least. S'up to you lot I suppose."

*

Lieutenant Chirp Tilestain stood alongside his quartermaster and a little way ahead of their brigade of Boiled Mice. In the distance his quartermaster had pointed out the looming shape of Brown Root forest, a sight new to the Lieutenant. They stood upon a raised mound of

354

earth and took in the scene.

"There it is," said Flap calmly.

"It looks dark," observed the Lieutenant.

"Colour of the wood I suppose...lotta dark trees and much denser than Milton."

"Big too."

"Aye, it's big. Easy to get lost once inside, as I know from experience."

"Is this another thing you forgot to tell me?" asked the Lieutenant.

"No? I told you about coming here, didn't I?"

"It doesn't matter...what can you tell me?"

"Narrow criss cross paths, lots of trees as I said but they're generally thinner and not much use for living in. A few trickling little rivers. The water supply's not very reliable. There's a general smell in the air too. As a place it's not well ventilated."

"And the locals?"

"You've never met any?"

"No."

"Well, you'll probably be surprised. Most are not as bad as they're painted out to be, but when they're bad, they're really bad."

"How are they as fighters?"

"Much like us. A little bigger of course but only a few are properly trained. The one's we'll meet will be ordinary and nothing to worry about, with a few exceptions of course. We'll have a lot of trouble with them."

"Where will we find this Brakk character?"

"Hard to say...Slap's got no idea sadly. Though if I remember correctly last time I was here I heard his name mentioned a few times...and not in the friendliest terms either. What did they say to me?"

The quartermaster looked up into the sky and closed his eyes in an attempt to recall useful information about their target. The skin between his eyebrows scrunched up and he started wagging one of his fingers in front of him. His eyes opened then he looked at his Lieutenant excitedly.

"He's the real chieftain, the real chieftain, that's what they said to me, of course! He's..."

"What? He's what? What's the real chieftain?"

"This whole place, it's not run like Milton Greens, no Council, no politicians, it's run like a business."

"And Brakk's in charge?"

"Yes, he's the real chieftain."

"Fine, how does that change anything?" said the Lieutenant, not impressed by this gleeful revelation.

"Errr, it doesn't I suppose."

"What's the plan of attack?"

"Isn't that your job Lieutenant?" said Flap mischievously.

"Come on. How do we get our goblin's back!?"

"What do your instincts tell you, Lieutenant?"

"Tonight, sneak in, scout around, find the goblins..." his voice trailed off, realising the obvious limitations of his plan and wishing he'd kept quiet.

"Sounds flawless," replied Flap.

"Don't get sarcastic. I'm still in charge around here! What's your bright idea!?"

"Lieutenant, calm yourself. They can see us arguing and probably hear us too."

They both turned to look back down the slope to the assembled Mice about ten metres below, looking up at them expectantly. The Lieutenant did as he was told and caught himself before getting out of control. Looking into their eyes he was reminded not only of his great responsibility but of their loyalty to him, something he could not allow to become tarnished. He turned back to his quartermaster and spoke a little more quietly.

"Alright. Let's think seriously now."

"Right," replied Flap, now equally focussed and determined.

"Three teams, one big, one medium, one small. The small team is the scouting party, no more than half a dozen. We go in tonight in heavy garb and try to pick up the scent."

"Right."

"The medium team is the quick strike team, thirty goblins, fully armed, concealing themselves at the edge of the forest...ready to intervene at a moment's notice."

"Right."

"The big team is the main force, held in reserve in case of emergencies."

"Right. What sort of emergencies?"

"What do you mean exactly?"

"When should they move in I mean."

"Right, well, if we need them."

"Yes...?"

"If I or you call for them."

"Right. Where do you want me?"

"In charge of the quick strike team."

"Right. You?"

"In charge of the scouting party of course! Where else should the leader lead from but from the front?" said the Lieutenant, almost tripping over his own words.

"Say that again," said Flap jokingly.

"I couldn't if I tried."

"Who'll look after the main force?"

"I'm happy for you to choose someone. We'll split the ordnance between us, taking ten smoke bombs each."

"Right. How will we signal each other?"

"Use the gongs and drums?"

"Gongs and drums, right."

"Three quick whacks on the gong means we're in trouble and we need you."

"Right."

"Three quick beats on the drum means we're on our way out."

"Right."

"And if we're not out within thirty minutes, something's wrong, come and get us."

"Oooh, are you sure that's enough time, especially if you get lost?"

"Slap'll be with us. He assures me he's knows Brown Root well."

"Let's make it an hour."

"That seems too long."

"Well, they won't be able to organise anything significant

in that time. We'll still have them by surprise."

"Alright. I wouldn't want you charging in while we're on our way out somewhere else, a few minutes late."

"An hour it is."

"Let's select our teams, come on."

The two goblins retreated from their vantage point and rejoined their eager Mice. Without explaining their plans openly they went about looking at the various goods on display, trying to select the fastest, fiercest or sneakiest looking goblins, according to their needs. Those goblins, the majority, that were not ultimately selected by either the quartermaster or the Lieutenant felt quite left out. They were not to be disappointed however as every one of the Boiled Mice soon set off towards Brown Root and the inevitable danger and excitement that awaited them.

*

Tirgu fiddled with the buckle that was wrapped around his horse. He pulled at it hard, once the metal prong was through the eye, and grimaced as he did so. His horse barely reacted. Gurgle was standing behind him with a little pack on his back. Tirgu had given him this present a few days previously and had instructed him on the only things that he would ever need to put in it. He would only ever have use for the following - food, water, a reliable blade and spare, strong waterproof blanket, compass, needles and twine for repairing clothes, a collection of little objects that make sparks to light fires and a spare pair of boots.

Gurgle was also the proud owner of two new blades; one for whittling, cutting food and general use, the other, much bigger and for protecting himself. Tirgu had told him not to get the latter blade out unless it was necessary to use it, though if it was necessary Gurgle had little ability to use it. Both blades were now nestled in special pockets in a dark brown waistcoat that was another recent gift. In fact, much of what Gurgle now carried or wore was arranged or made for him. It seemed Tirgu was not exaggerating when he had described him as a member of the team.

The other members of that team were already on their horses and eager to be on their way, pleased as they were to have avoided being used in Spikepoint's army. Once Tirgu felt everything he needed to do with his horse was done he unceremoniously picked Gurgle up and swung him around on to its back and then moments later huffed his way up to a seated position in front. He looked behind himself to check on his small companion and without saying anything he saw that all was well. He nodded to the others around him and they set off.

Spikepoint had ordered Tirgu to leave early, ahead of his main army, and do some scouting. The intelligence he expected Tirgu to provide on the enemies movements would be invaluable in deciding where and when to commit his forces but Tirgu was not the only one sent out for this purpose, a fact well known to him.

Gurgle was a little unsure of what was happening and

what to expect. The whole experience of the past couple of months had been so overwhelming for him that in some ways he'd had no time to break down but had simply come out the other side. He was fragile no doubt, as Tirgu could tell, but he spoke less and less about home and goblins and so he must have been thinking about them less and less too. Tirgu made sure his days were busy and allowed him no indulgence in talking about the past. Tirgu only talked about his future and after a while, with Gurgle hearing it and seeing it every day, it was becoming his future. If his mother could see him now she would be relieved and horrified at the same time.

It occurred to Gurgle, whilst holding onto Tirgu's midriff, that the events overtaking them all might put him close to Milton Greens. The country that surrounded him was alien but he might be able to follow his nose back home, should a suitable opportunity arise.

In one of those unexpected little ironies of life he realised that all his negative expectations of the men that had taken him had been consistently unfulfilled, excusing the initial unpleasantness of course. That event set his view of them to be sure but since then they had only moved away from that extremity and as the days had gone by he found himself liking and relying on them, more and more. He found the gentle brush of the short hair on the horse's backside against his legs to be an interesting and soothing sensation.

They kept an easy pace, time ticked, and the day shifted into evening.

Furtively, secretively, sneakily, clandestinely, whichever word you might like to use, the 'One Hundred and Seventh Milton Greens Special Militia Brigade,' such as it now was, approached one edge of Brown Root forest in search of their brother and sister goblins.

The Lieutenant was relatively pleased with the progress they had made so far. Even though they had nothing solid to show for their efforts he felt they were close to their objective and he only hoped that he would find them all in one place. In his darker moments he conceived of a near endless search for one goblin after another and all the hopelessness that that would engender in his troops.

The main body of the brigade had found a useful hill to occupy the far side of. From there they could observe the quick strike team further ahead, and any signals they might send, in relative obscurity. The evening was drawing in though so they agreed to rely on setting small fire signals. The Lieutenant, the quartermaster and their various team members, amongst them Slap Canopy, Rustle Blacknose and Growl Bonetone continued to the edge of the forest. They slid gently through the long grass and kept their heads down. They had not seen a single hobgoblin in the area but that was no guarantee that one had not seen them.

The quartermaster and Slap led the way, alternatively nodding or shaking their heads at each other, indicating the best route. They were only a matter of metres from the nearest tree and they all seemed to flop instinctively onto all fours for the final approach. They crawled into position and kept themselves flat. The conditions were good in that it was cloudy, keeping light levels low, and that it was windy, agitating the trees a great deal and thereby providing a screen of noise that would cover much of the noise they would make.

Soldiers all they were, motivated now, muscles blood filled and firm, eyes brimming with light, from inside and out. Like a dirty carpet they covered the ground but unlike a carpet, dirty or not, they slowly crept forward. The Lieutenant's scouting party had naturally followed him and were close by. He signalled towards the quartermaster and beckoned him over, which he did, scuttling like a frightened crab over other goblins.

"What do you think? How's it look?" whispered the Lieutenant.

"Seems quiet. I think we're here undetected," replied the quartermaster.

"Right, it's time to go in," said the Lieutenant, summoning up his courage and lifting his body.

"You got everything you need?" asked the quartermaster, breaking his leader's momentum and causing him to shrink back down.

The Lieutenant nodded and turned to face his team, and saw them nodding in unison to the same question.

"Have you got everything tied down? We can't have anything clattering about," asked the quartermaster of the scouting party members, who all nodded once more.

"We're ready. Don't worry," said the Lieutenant.

"How can I not worry?"

"Wish us luck."

"You just need to be careful, luck's a bonus. By the way, aren't you forgetting something?"

"What?" asked the Lieutenant.

The quartermaster pointed to his face and tilted his head slightly in an expression of surprise.

"The face paint!" exclaimed the Lieutenant under his breath.

"The face paint, right. Here," said the quartermaster, proffering a small tub filled with brown paste.

The Lieutenant extracted a great gob of the stuff, slapped it onto his face and then passed the tub onwards to those behind him, each of them doing the same.

"What's in this stuff anyway?" asked the Lieutenant.

"Nothing that won't wash off, I promise. Don't forget the backs of your hands as well. Come on, off with you!"

With that last whisper the Lieutenant rose to his feet but did not lift his back, and moments later the others mimicked him, resulting in a series of right angled creatures entering the forest. For the first few minutes the Lieutenant seemed to think that the best tactic was to move rapidly from tree to tree and then hide, before doing the same thing again. He hadn't done this kind of thing before and failed to realise that rapidly moving things more easily catch the attention of others than slow moving things. Slap, from behind, threw a small stone at him which caught him on the leg. He turned, startled, and showed his angry face to Slap once more, annoyed that his concentration had been disturbed. Slap sneaked over and whispered in his ear that he ought to try to relax and move more slowly. They had the gloom of the forest on which to rely and didn't need to do their back bones a serious injury by moving in this way, a precaution of particular relevance to Slap. The Lieutenant thought for a few moments, looked off into the distance and decided to acquiesce. They all stood and began to walk naturally, though not without the precaution of wearing their cloaks and hoods with which it was hoped they could move anonymously through busier areas.

The other members of the team were each in their own way absorbing the sights and sounds and, in particular, the smells of the forest. Growl Bonetone, who had become somewhat attached to Slap and who'd been given the task of carrying the gong and drum (in his backpack and on his shoulder respectively) sniffed at the air and decided that everything negative he'd heard about Brown Root had been severely understated. The desire to cough and spit out this nasty flavour was strong but he controlled the urge, knowing the great seriousness of the task in which they were engaged. He would not be the one to get his fellows goblins into trouble. He was there to be a hero and he fully intended to grow old and tell stories of his deeds to the young ones he fully intended to be alive to create.

Slap and the Lieutenant walked side by side and in front. The other four goblins also paired up and the whole group did its best to be uninteresting. They moved at a steady pace, following Slap's instinctive directions, and were soon coming across seemingly abandoned habitations. Their style was a surprise to those unfamiliar with them. Few trees were used as homes it seemed and they had the habit instead of making little wooden huts and buildings. Many were decrepit and had clearly been scavenged for materials. A glance inside confirmed this, along with the presence of thick green moss covering the floors and walls.

On they went, still without seeing a single hobgoblin. After a while they began to wonder if the forest was inhabited at all. This pleasant suspicion was soon dispelled however once they arrived at an intersection of paths and a horse and cart approached from another direction. The two hobgoblins sat upon it seemed to pay little attention to their surroundings. One of them looked asleep. When they passed by this group of six however the more awake of the two gave them a lengthy look up and down, keeping his eye on them for longer than they felt was justified. The horse was moving fairly swiftly and his own business was obviously more important to him than enquiring into the business of others so he looked away and continued on. Their disguise seemed to be holding up well enough.

The six of them looked at each other nervously and smiled once they felt they had passed this first little test. The Lieutenant faced forward once more and in the distance his brain discerned some movement. He peered and focussed, then drew Slap's attention to it. He saw it too.

They could see not just one hobgoblin but a swarm and

where they looked the forest seethed with them. This spectacle was still some distance away but it was more than enough to stop them in their tracks and reconsider the wisdom of this entire exercise. Then their ears suddenly became attuned to the noise, as though their eyes had prodded them in action. A rhythmic thumping could be heard and at the same time torch lights were being lit. The Lieutenant realised that any drum beats they might make would be defeated by such a noise. In any event, the likelihood of needing to bang their drum, signalling a safe and successful trip, seemed increasingly slim now.

Slap put his hand on the Lieutenant's shoulder and began to reassure him.

"It's just the time. Eight o'clock. Listen, there'll be eight beats. The torches are lit in the evenings at this time."

Sure enough he was right and eight beats were all there were.

"It's the evening market. They're not after us, just after something to eat. Let's keep moving."

"Which way?" asked the Lieutenant.

"We'll go around them this way, to the right," he replied. They followed the path as it wandered its way further into the forest. It was impossible to avoid coming close to the hobgoblins now and from time to time they were passed by some generally disinterested and unhealthy looking creatures. Growl looked down at his hands and saw that as they passed the pale orange torch lights his brown coloured skin looked a little shinier and greasier that it ought, when compared to the locals. He assumed his face would also share the same aspect. He glanced at the faces of the others, only partially concealed by their hoods, and saw what he suspected. They were looking increasingly vulnerable and he gulped at the prospect of what might await them if discovered. Not only were they conspicuous because of their reduced size but also because of their hue. Anyone looking them directly in the eye and paying attention would surely detect them.

The Lieutenant was also getting anxious, though for different reasons. If they had each been aware of the full list of reasons to be anxious they would all have turned around and left as quickly as their little legs would carry them, but ignorance kept them going forward. He was anxious about just how to find their goblin brothers and sisters. They would not be just wandering about and they could not easily enquire as to their location. So how could they be found? That was the question that rattled around inside his head without resolution. Slap had no easy confederate to bribe for information and perhaps the information they had been given was total nonsense and they were therefore putting themselves in danger for nothing! Well, Slap seemed a shrewd character, and if he felt the information from his friend was good so must they.

Brown Root seemed a lot bigger than Milton Greens but a lot less well arranged. They were going to need a considerable slice of good fortune to pick up the scent. On they went, their hearts fluttering like elderly humming birds and their skin dripping with sweat. The humidity was considerable and the wind could no longer penetrate this far into the forest.

The hustle and bustle of the market was to their left now and much of it reminded them of markets at home. It did seem more frantic here though, with more jostling, voices and argument than they would typically find in Milton Greens. There were no young ones around either, much to their surprise. Did hobgoblins grow up so quickly?

Slap suddenly stopped dead in his tracks and the Lieutenant walked several paces onwards before noticing. He turned and saw him staring at something plastered to a tree. It was a sheet of paper, partly tattered but much of it legible. He could see Slap's eyes flicking from side to side and his mouth opening further and further as he read.

"What is it?" asked the Lieutenant.

"Advertising," came the reply.

"Anything we can use?"

"Oh yes."

"What's it say?" asked Growl quietly.

"Brakk's Emporium. If you need something, I have it. Domestic services, personal services, tracking services, import export. Everything is my speciality. Come find me before I find you!"

"That's it. Where is it?" said the Lieutenant.

"Hang on, I'm looking," said Slap. "They're dotted about. There isn't just one."

"Try the head office," joked Growl, earning only a slap on the back of the head from a colleague.

"There's a sort of a map, but it's torn. Let's try to find

another one. Look around," said Slap.

Their heads instantly sprang in different directions, looking for other trees and other posters. The Lieutenant gave them permission to fan out and off they went but not out of his sight. Growl was the first one to find another likely candidate and he quickly tore it from the tree and brought it to his Lieutenant. This was it and he ordered everyone back. He studied it on the ground and encouraged everyone to join him, just to keep out of sight as much as possible. The diagram in the corner was small but fairly clear. It was a series of red circles connected by a series of red lines with one larger circle in the centre, clearly signifying a base of operations, or head office as Growl might have put it. Most helpfully one of the smaller circles was filled in and with an arrow pointing to it. This was clearly nearby and the arrow showed the way.

Using their noses and best guess they tried to work out which way to go and found that it took them slightly back on themselves but not any nearer to the market. The brush underfoot was getting thicker but the trees were less frequent so it was not such a problem for our adventurers. The Lieutenant thought to himself how much time they might have left. The drum beat of eight o'clock was a most useful guide for them and if they should hear the drum roll of nine then he knew Flap would be on his way in. He thought seriously about leaving now, since they had good intelligence, but decided to carry on for the moment and see what was to be seen.

Back at the edge of the forest the quartermaster was

waiting with his quick strike team. He was doing his best to keep an eye on the time as well. His small hourglass was not really suitable for this kind of outdoor use and he had to keep rotating it, trying to remember how many times it had been turned. The others were becoming restless and as each minute went by they felt closer to action. Flap could sense this and cooled their enthusiasm.

"Not even half an hour yet. Stay calm, stay quiet. Keep your eyes and ears open and your mouths closed."

Meanwhile, near one of the arteries coming from the heart of Brown Root the scouting party was nearing the red circle they had identified on their map. The building they approached seemed isolated but had the size and style of a store and they felt confident this was it. One or two hobgoblin souls wandered about but none seemed to come from there or have any business with it. There was a flame flickering inside and shadows flickered on the inside walls as a result.

The six ensconced themselves in bushes to the rear of the plot and waited for a few minutes, observing the shadows. The Lieutenant was sure that there were two individuals inside. He could see the hobgoblin head of one but the other was shorter, or bent over, and working at scrubbing the floor. He prodded Slap and whispered that he was going in for a closer look and asked him for his help. Slap agreed and they crept forward together from the undergrowth. They slinked up to the side of the building and sat below the opening. The Lieutenant slowly got to his feet in order to observe those inside. On the other side of the wall the one at work was still scrubbing away. The Lieutenant's back straightened and he stood on his toes. He glanced inside and looked down. The individual looked up at the same time unfortunately and let out a very understandable moan of shock. Before the Lieutenant had time to think he reached inside and grabbed this individual, hauling him straight out of the window. The hobgoblin on the other side of the room could not fail to notice and he rose to his feet grabbing a club from nearby. "Hah!" he yelled maniacally, and came charging out of the door and round to where they were.

The Lieutenant was the first goblin he saw and his arms were full, holding another equally startled goblin, and he could not react as the club was waved at him. Slap Canopy had anticipated this hobgoblins approach and had waited behind the door for him. With timing, determination and a brutality that surprised those still frozen in the bushes Slap stabbed him straight through his body from behind. The creature was dealt with so effectively he barely had chance to look down at the blade protruding from his chest, before being pushed off it with a hard thud into the dry ground. Slap was emotionless and acted quickly, dragging the body under the wooden boards of the building. He looked around and tried to see if anyone had spotted all this but he saw nothing. He ran back inside the building and examined the papers to see if there was anything useful. Nothing leapt out at him. He flung the torch to the floor, then piled various papers on it and smashed a bottle of spirit alcohol that his victim had so recently been enjoying. He then rejoined the rest of his party. They had gathered around the Lieutenant and were looking to see if this really was another goblin. His green skin and wretched appearance were more than enough to convince them that he was. The Lieutenant had but one word of instruction for his team as with a great whumpff the building caught fire.

"Scarper!"

Growl and Slap held this goblin on their shoulders and helped him along. Their flight was covered by the fact that they were soon away from the scene, and as the flames became more prominent the attention of the forest was drawn to it rather than them. Putting out a forest fire was naturally a priority. Within another ten minutes they could glimpse what little daylight remained through distant trees. They were close to the edge.

The quartermaster knew he was less than ten minutes away from the hour and was getting anxious, particularly when he spotted a plume of smoke rising above the canopy.

"Oh bugger," he said. "Get yourselves ready, something's happened."

"Sir, Sir!" said another. "There they are!"

All eyes flicked to their right and they could see the six, no wait, the seven of them!? They came bounding, stumbling, exhausted from the forest and piled into their group. The quartermaster breathed a huge sigh of relief. The Lieutenant, panting, came close to him.

"No time to explain. Let's get back before they get wind

of us."

The quartermaster was stunned and went along without thinking. He stared at the new goblin, surprised and pleased. They all stood and like a swarm of green bees swiftly buzzed off. Once back on the far side of the hill they took time to rest and had a good look at their find. The smoke from the forest was dying down by this point so the fire had been extinguished. The Lieutenant hoped that the body would not be found straight away. A crowd gathered around this tired but relieved looking goblin and the questions soon began.

"What's your name?" asked an enthusiastic Mouse.

"Sigh Stratton," he replied. "What's yours you cheeky pup?"

The others laughed and the Lieutenant crossed his name from the list of kidnapped goblins. He would send this prize back home with an escort as soon as possible. First thing in the morning he thought. The forest would be delighted and they would say his name with pride...and that of the brigade too of course.

CHAPTER 11

Like the deafening thunder of a rock fall, Spikepoint's army began its march. The hooves of horse thumped into the ground and the gentler but more numerous clumps of armoured footprints added to the scene.

From each of his garrisons as well as his main castle his forces had been drawn and stitched together and they began their journey into the unknown. Without it even needing to be said Spikepoint rode from the front and held by his immediate flanks his senior men, with whom he would secure his life's ambition. That is, to replace his golden helmet, forged from the treasures of vanquished foes, with that simpler crown of iron and wood, which carried so much more power. That other crown, held by the aged and rapidly withering King, would soon be passed on, though to who it was not yet decided. That was what this entire spectacle was about, bringing force of arms to achieve what persuasion and politics could not.

Amongst these senior men Commander Robert Haine was now present, fulfilling his master's wish to join them and become a key player suddenly in this great drama. His previous force at Low Rise garrison, typically of between thirty and forty men, was now amalgamated into his new battalion of fifteen hundred men. As he turned his head to keep an eye on his force he smiled to himself about how life, just when he thought he had it figured out, found it so easy to surprise him. He looked again to his master, Lord Spikepoint, and wondered where all his ambition would lead him and just what consequences there would be for the roughly six thousand souls trudging behind him and his immaculate horse, not including staff or camp attendants.

The castle and the modest numbers of men left to its maintenance, including Levant, dwindled slowly from view. The sight of such a force of men and beasts, and many with characteristics of both, had the effect of shrinking all other objects around it. Spikepoint, a man of few doubts, particularly in regard to himself, felt a stillness amidst the tumult. He knew the great prize that awaited him and he knew not to grab for it in panic but to walk calmly towards it, place both hands firmly upon it and then take it. No other rival had his power and resources and he knew his future better than any oracle.

Ahead the sun was rising high and the intensity of the light above the horizon caused smudges of red and green to follow his vision wherever he looked. He breathed low and smoothly through the gap in his helmet and allowed his horse to dictate the gentle pace, moving his body where his horse caused it to go. He had but one destination, unless intelligences came through indicating the sense of another course, and that destination was all that filled his mind. He had spent his indentured youth there as a simple soldier in that castle, doing his King's bidding. He thought back to those times and remembered his King as someone fierce and fearsome, not the laughable shadow of a once great man that he had now become. In many ways that man had been his mentor and role model. Well, no more, and Spikepoint was intent on surpassing the old man and his legacy. The full purpose of his years of planning and preparation had come to life and now the ground softened and sank at its presence.

Spikepoint turned and looked at each of his chiefs in turn, starting with Haine. He caught his eye and they nodded to one another. Haine took this as an invitation to step forward, which he prompted his horse to do. The two men rode along together for a while and discussed any concerns that Haine wanted to raise. He had nothing of great import on his mind. Spikepoint did this in turn for his other two chiefs and they, like Haine, had little to say.

The army slid onwards and left behind a wide, dirt filled scar in the earth.

In front of the castle, which Spikepoint coveted so conspicuously, Captain Starling Dodd was making final defensive preparations. Numerous scouts and spies had been posted to neighbouring towns, and others were secreted in the wider countryside. Spikepoint could not bring any significant group of men within twenty miles of the castle without the alarm being raised. To Dodd's relief and delight his main force of three thousand men was not the only source of fighting men on whom he could rely. From further afield Gavelrigg had been busy in recruiting men, mostly by painting a very public and unpalatable picture of the life they could expect to live under King Spikepoint. Consequently, a variety of small brigades of gentlemen, some good, some bad, had come to the castle to offer themselves in its defence. This would allow him to treat the trained army as an independent force, not reliant on sticking close to the castle. He hoped this information was not generally known.

Frederick had returned that morning from his military exercises, what little good they had done him. With no fuss or favour it had been arranged for him to be anointed as his uncle, the King's, successor. In order to do that however it was necessary to at least have the King alert and reasonably lucid, something that had not been possible for a couple of days now. Gavelrigg was frustrated at this delay but Dodd was delighted, since it meant more time to make preparations and take decisions without the interference that would inevitably come his way within moments of a successful handover of power. He knew the Kingdom was in much safer hands with him. Still, the uncertainty in the air was as thick as the cloud that sat over them.

*

In his generously apportioned bedroom Baintha Brakk was roused from his night's rest by one of his assistants. As he lay there flapping his eyelids up and down, bringing his mind into action once more, he listened to a rather alarming story of a fire and a killing at one of his establishments. This was unpleasant news to say the least and he scrunched up his bedclothes as he listened to each new and more serious detail. The dead hobgoblin was a long term employee of his and a reliable one that he would have a deal of trouble replacing.

He leaned forward and upward, putting more strain on his stomach muscles than he was used to. With a great huff he was up and on the edge of the bed. He coughed and turned to face his assistant.

"Get the crew, all of them, now," he ordered.

His assistant scuttled off immediately to his task and Brakk stood and walked to a table, picking up his bits and pieces and getting himself dressed. He huffed and puffed and wondered at the meaning of it all. Who could be attacking his business? He had gone to great lengths to handicap his rivals and make sure he knew everything that might be being considered against him. This was a complete surprise.

He was soon ready and standing in the chilly morning air beyond his front door. In the minutes that followed. one by one, his henchmen, for want of a better word, began to arrive. Most of them running and panting through the quiet. Mala was the first to arrive. This hobgoblin had been his friend and partner for more than twenty years and was first by his side more from loyalty than proximity.

Marin followed soon after. She was unusual in hobgoblin circles, to be a female and successful at her particular line of work, normally associated with the male hobgoblins, that of tracking people and things down. In this she was well paid and her reputation well deserved.

Keeps came next. He was also a long term associate, though more partner than friend. His nickname came from his motto, which was that whatever he finds, he keeps.

Finally, Verm trudged into view. He was an oversized, enthusiastic hobgoblin, totally in awe of Baintha, his master and mentor.

The five of them went with Brakk's assistant and trusted him to direct them accurately to the scene of this inexplicable outrage. After half an hour of humourless travail they arrived at the blackened shell of what was once one of Brakk's stores. To be fair it was not all black and one part of the rear of the building seemed almost untouched by the heat of the fire. Verm pulled the clearly ruined door from its hinges and allowed them all entry. He threw it to one side and it fractured where it fell, blowing up grass and fragments of charcoal on impact. As they stepped inside the building gave a groan, increasing in volume along with the weight as each entered. It was still hot in places despite the water dripping from the walls that had been liberally applied the night before. There was little inside to rescue but Mala did his best to collect whatever items were still recognizable.

"Right," said Brakk suddenly, "where's his body?"

His assistant directed them outside and around the back of the building, at which point he crouched and pointed underneath. They all followed and with trepidation took a look. Keeps invited Mala to grab a leg each and they pulled this semi burned body from its hasty hiding place.

It was a grisly spectacle to behold, with the body on its back and almost all that part of him facing upwards burnt to a crisp. His lower half, which had obviously been touching the ground and partly protected from the heat seemed normal, except for an orange hue to the skin, which gave the impression that his backside, though not burnt, was most definitely cooked. The top side, all blackened crust, could tell them little except that his facial expression, what remained of it, seemed calm. Baintha looked on without his pulse being raised in the slightest. The scene, though unpleasant and certainly unwanted, was no harder to handle than a fall in monthly profits or the loss of a favoured waistcoat.

"Turn him over," ordered Brakk.

Keeps and Mala did so and it became clear at that moment what had happened to him. In the middle of his back a clean, vertical slit about two inches in length was obvious. Brakk's assistant had returned to the doorway of the building and noticed a scrubbing brush, or at least the remnants of it, over on the far side of the room beneath the window. He picked it up and leaned out of the window, shouting to the others his theory of the events of the previous evening.

"It was the goblin! He had a goblin with him, cleaning up. It must have sneaked up on him while he wasn't looking then stabbed him, dumped him underneath, set the fire, then ran off."

Brakk listened keenly but did not get carried away. He was right about there being a goblin at work here though.

"If that's true," piped up Marin, "why are there footprints for about another five or six goblins in these bushes and all around the store here?"

Brakk's eyes opened wide and he moved to Marin's position to see what she had seen. He stepped around the bushes and soon found that they had been disturbed and a little crowd had been there. He turned to look at Marin and then at the small tree near to where she was standing. He growled and threw his arms around the trunk, shaking it violently as though strangling it. His pulse rate increased rapidly and Marin made the most sensible observation of the day so far.

"Looks like the goblins want their goblins back."

*

Back on the far side of the hill overlooking Brown Root the Boiled Mice prepared to say farewell to Sigh Stratton and a further two members of their brigade, selected as his escort back to Milton Greens. This was by no means a simple or safe task and they had to move soon if they were not to be overtaken by whatever reprisal the forest was about to spit out at them. He had spent a sleepless night huddled amongst his rescuers as the evening had had a chill breeze. He was still fit and able to set off home to his family though. He had been questioned by the quartermaster closely during the evening but in exchange he had enjoyed some food and a mouthful or two of a liquid guaranteed to warm his heart.

The Lieutenant had also been a witness to this fellow's report and it was valuable intelligence. It seemed that he'd been out watering his vegetables at night, the best time so he claimed, when he heard quick footsteps behind him and then felt a thump to the side of his head. Events immediately after that were blurred but he remembered waking up wrapped up in a sack and on a boat. There were lots of other goblins about him and he was a prisoner amongst them. He heard many voices, those of men, and a child's voice too. He was probed instantly on this point and it was explained to him that a goblin child was taken too. This made sense to Sigh and he recalled the boss man saying he would keep one of them but he didn't know which. In his mind he connected the dots and realised that since he had not seen a goblin child amongst the other captives then that must be the one they had kept back.

The realisation that little Gurgle had been taken elsewhere was a blow to the brigade. He was the most innocent and vulnerable of them all and for him to have been segregated was a real setback on their ambitions for a single successful recapture. Most of the brigade knew that a child had been taken along with the others, and many had fantasised about being the one to rescue him and become the hero of the hour. Many also wondered for what special duty he had been diverted.

Sigh also recounted about how he was thrown from the boat, caught roughly and then bundled into a cart with the others. A few human men had been in charge of them from then on and they had had a very unpleasant journey, not only because of the uneven ground but also because of some dreadful whistling coming from one of the human men.

For a few days they had been kept confined in a town full of human men and women and they had been forcibly kept out of sight. The food had been scarce and meanly given out. They had at least all been kept together. The human man that had been looking after them was, so it seemed, very keen to get them off his hands. He'd kept telling them how much they were costing him in food and as the days went by he'd become increasingly irritable. He'd criticised Brakk terribly and kept insulting him for his lateness and unreliability. But when Brakk did eventually come to buy them the human man was much more polite, even afraid, and was just keen to make a good deal. Sigh wasn't sure how much of a profit had been made on them, if any. He was asked if he could remember the human man's name but he could not. Everyone had been careful to not mention names, except when it came to Brakk of course.

Another journey by cart had then taken place but that one was bigger and covered by a large cloth. They'd been kept inside a strong metal cage and they'd had no chance of getting through it. Brakk and a few of his ever present assistants had escorted them. Their first night in what he knew to be Brown Root forest was a miserable one, spent under Brakk's house, and where they'd been introduced to the larger cage that would be their home for who knew how long. Many of them were weakened considerably by this stage and everyone, including Brakk, though for very different reasons, had been keen to get them out.

Brakk had made it abundantly clear to them what he expected them to do and had been quite persuasive in his methods. He had distinguished the tough ones from the practical ones and had put them in different places so they couldn't communicate with each other in keeping a united front. Whenever he singled out one that he thought was emotionally weaker than the others he separated them and worked his charms on them alone. He was smooth tongued that Brakk when he wanted to be, and terrifying too, just when he seemed at his calmest.

Sigh it seems, had been one of the practical ones. He justified it by saying that he was just desperate to get out and felt it better to be working above ground than festering in a cage beneath it. He felt that his decision had been right at the time and in retrospect. Along with other like-minded goblins in the group he was soon found a position with some hobgoblin or other. What he'd particularly hated though, was that when he and the others had made their decision they were deliberately walked past the others still holding out and causing them all great unhappiness. When he left the underground he remembered that there were still four others that refused to go and remained in the cage.

They had introduced themselves to each other during the course of their ordeal and Sigh amended the Lieutenant's list, highlighting what he knew of their condition and location. He marked out one name in particular, Poppy Knittel, smiling with pride as he did so, and explained that she had been the one that had kept their spirits up and had comforted them all. When Brakk was around though, she had been as quiet as a mouse and rightly so. However, she had been totally implacable and would not leave the others. Sigh hadn't seen her after he gave in though, and that had been just a week before.

He hadn't seen any of the other goblins who'd given in before him. It was his opinion that they were all destined to be sold into the hands of hobgoblins in the forest and he was sure they would not be far away. The Lieutenant asked Sigh if he knew well the location of where they had been kept. He said he didn't know it accurately but that he knew it well enough. He had been taken around the forest quite a lot, for one form of work of another, and he had seen a lot of where things were. He drew a map and discussed Brakk's location with those that had some knowledge of Brown Root forest. Between them they got a good sniff of where to find him and more of the rest of their kin. Sigh sounded one important note of caution however. They needed to think of the forest not as a collection of trees but as a spider's web, with Brakk as the spider and his house as the sticky centre, from where all vibrations were felt.

Sigh's escort strapped and tied their belongings to themselves and after quiet instructions from the Lieutenant were despatched with their prize between them. In less than two days' time they hoped to see the gentle green fringes of Milton Greens once more. The Lieutenant also gave them a written report of events and discoveries made so far, for the benefit of the Council. He hoped that it would cause them to raise even more goblins for the effort but he very much doubted that they would. A thought popped into his head, in which he compared the danger he and his brigade were in compared to the goblins they served, and whether the chestnuts justified the difference.

Today was proving to be brighter and warmer than yesterday. There would be a response of some kind from Brown Root and he debated in his mind whether to sit and wait to see what it was or to continue with his own plans, trying to stay one step ahead of those wretched hobgobs. The latter most appealed but was also the riskier. But that was what they were here for, to take risks on behalf of their fellow goblins.

The quartermaster silently approached his Lieutenant as he lay just in front of the ridge on the hill, closely observing the dark forest beyond.

"Caught you, spy!" he said jokingly.

The Lieutenant rolled onto his back and looked up at him. He had nothing to say so just rolled back onto his front. The quartermaster was a little surprised but decided to lie down alongside him and try to see what he was seeing. He locked his fingers together and placed his chin upon them, then looked to his side at the Lieutenant, who then looked back.

"Today's going to be a big day," whispered the Lieutenant, without showing any sign of emotion.

"Do you feel it in your stomach?" asked Flap.

"Yes, I feel like this little hill is a huge mountain. I'm

stranded on top of it and I don't know how to get down, and a massive storm is soaking me to the skin."

"The escort's gone by the way. They'll get back safely, no problem. No one knows them."

"Thank you. Well done Flap. Well done for everything."

"Hmmm? It wasn't difficult," he replied, looking at his Lieutenant more closely.

"Not just that."

"You're right. It's going to be a big day. I feel it in my stomach too. It's vital to be in the right frame of mind. Are you in the right frame of mind Lieutenant?"

The Lieutenant looked at his elder friend.

"What's the right frame of mind?" he asked with a smile.

"That you don't give a damn what happens."

"What?"

"You heard. It doesn't matter a toss. Live, die, succeed, fail. It's all a joke. A bad joke played on us...and I've never found it funny."

"You serious?" asked the Lieutenant, slightly worried.

"Deadly. You've got to let go of them all."

"Let go of who?"

"All of them. Everybody. Everybody that you're responsible for, because you're not responsible for them, in the end. In the end we're all alone, in our own little five foot by two foot plot of earth."

"You're worrying me Flap. What's brought all this on?"

"I just want you to have the right attitude."

"Which is that I shouldn't care about anything, or any of us, the Mice?"

388

"That's it. That's it exactly."

"How does that help us?"

"When you stop caring, you're free."

"Free?"

"Free...and fearless...and totally objective. You'll be able to take the decisions you need to take. If we go into the forest again we'll lose people and you have to be prepared for it." The Lieutenant looked at his friend, who was staring into the forest, and felt he was looking a lot further into the distance than that. He decided to join him and have a good think.

*

Little Gurgle had spent a comfortable night despite the chill breeze that had been in the air. The greater profiles of the human men had obviously acted as a nice windbreak and his waterproof blanket had completed the experience. He was getting used to being woken by the sunrise and had begun to welcome its reassuring red warmth and the optimism of a new day. Tirgu had already beaten him to it and was sat by himself staring at the shimmering globe and wearing a gentle smile. He was listening intently it seemed, and without needing to turn his head he beckoned Gurgle over to sit with him. The human men continued to sleep, grumbling or dribbling, each to his preference.

"It's a good sunrise," said Tirgu calmly. "It's going to be a good day."

"What will we be doing?" asked Gurgle, an entirely

proper enquiry from a member of Tirgu's team.

"Going home," replied Tirgu, staring straight ahead. "Not your home I'm afraid, to mine."

"For Spikepoint?"

"Not exactly."

"Where are we going then?"

"Brown Root forest, where I'm from."

"How far is it?"

"We'll be there in five or six hours. I have some business to deal with. It won't take too long."

"Will you need me to do anything?"

"Just keep yourself safe and in the background...and keep those big ears of yours open. If you hear anything you must let me know."

"Sounds like there might be danger."

"Probably...but we'll look after that, don't worry."

"Why'd you leave the forest?" asked Gurgle all of a sudden, with a curious look in his eye. "Were you taken too?"

Tirgu looked down at his young companion and was pleased and surprised by the question. He decided to tell him as much truth as he felt appropriate, for such innocent ears.

"No, I wasn't taken. But I had good reason to leave. I was fierce in those days and made a point of not keeping quiet. I didn't care about anybody or anything and did as I pleased. I wasn't loyal to anyone either so I quickly made enemies."

Gurgle listened carefully and another question occurred to

him.

"What about your family?"

"My family? Well there's not too much of a story there. My poor old mother put up with a lot. A sister, married off somewhere. She was a bit simple so it was probably the best thing for her."

"Do you have children?"

"Children?" said Tirgu, his voice trailing off.

"You didn't have a big family? I had a big family."

Tirgu felt the conversation was getting into a sensitive area and tried to deflect things.

"No. There's not much to say about them. I was always independent, brought up that way. Listen, I didn't waste much time being young. I was keen to get on and get involved with everything. I had loads of energy and often went for days on end without sleep. I tagged along with some of the older ones and quickly matched them. There was always some business in the air and I had the nose for it you see, and the head to take care of it."

"What did you do?"

"Anything, everything...and for anybody. I always made that clear...no loyalties, no ties. A lot of people expected that from people they hired though, so I had to walk a thin line sometimes. Didn't always work. I took a few beatings."

Gurgle was shocked by this and found it hard to imagine.

"Who could do that?"

"Thank you Gurgle," replied Tirgu, laughing heartily. "But it did happen a few times. It was no problem...just

391

part of the job. I gave out far more than I received I promise you."

"You beat people?" he asked, not all that surprised by the idea to be truthful.

Tirgu looked closely at Gurgle and was wary about how far this frankness should go, for he had done far more than just give a beating in his time.

"Sometimes, yes," he said, tentatively, "when they deserved it."

"And when they didn't deserve it?"

"You're very inquisitive so early in the morning. Yes, then too."

"Why'd you do that? What did you think about it?"

Tirgu took a few moments to think under such withering questioning.

"Well, they may not have deserved it but it needed doing and they would have done something wrong...at some point...to justify it."

Gurgle just looked up at him without saying anything. Tirgu felt the look was a critical one.

"You're just young, you don't know anything. Life's a complicated business and bad things happen. There's no reason for it, it's just the way things are. No point trying to make sense of it. You could spend your whole lifetime thinking about it and be no closer to understanding it, never mind changing anything."

Gurgle looked away, disappointed at the route the conversation had gone down and by the negative tone in Tirgu's voice. A period of silence followed in which the sounds of slumbering human men mixed with the calling of birds. Eventually, the conversation restarted.

"Don't try to change the way life is and the way we all are," said Tirgu, almost pleading. "You just have to accept it for all its faults. Once you do that you'll be a lot happier."

"Are you happy?" asked Gurgle.

"I will be if we can get today's business done well."

"Will you be beating anyone up?"

Tirgu laughed at his straightforwardness.

"No, I'll leave that to you. Think you're up to it?"

"No. I've never been sure what you need me to do exactly."

"I've told you that Gurgle. Those ears of yours, very useful."

It seemed they suddenly came in handy, as something in Tirgu's voice didn't sound genuine. Gurgle was not convinced by this answer but didn't have anything else to say. At that point one of the human men came and said good morning to them and that signalled the end of their conversation together.

"When are we off?" the man asked.

"Get some food inside you first. After that," replied Tirgu.

"What's this about a detour to Brown Root?" asked the man.

Tirgu looked up at him, displeased to be questioned about it.

"There are too many loose tongues in this team. You'll find out soon enough," he said dismissively.

"But Spi...,"

"We're going to see Brakk if you must know," said Tirgu, cutting the man off mid word. "Off with you."

That signalled the end of all conversation.

*

After the quick and uneventful burial of his friend, Baintha Brakk turned his energies and intellect to finding a proper solution to this goblin problem. There was no way he was going to tolerate such an occurrence but there was also no way that he would give up on his trade in goblins. He was not the sort of person to fail to see something through. He had a reputation to uphold and it was on this that most of his success and security relied. The actions of these cheeky little interlopers could not go without the severest of punishments in reply. He knew they were about but had no idea of numbers. He expected that small team of goblins to be located soon. He had an inkling that more were hanging about somewhere. His plan for the moment was simply to send Marin and the others about until they got a sniff of them. Right now though he thought it wise to collect all the goblins that had been sold as slaves and keep them safe under his property. Better to have them all in one place under lock and key.

He paced up and down in the main room of his house with a hand to his chin, typical when Baintha was contemplating something. The trouble was how to get them back from their owners without causing them alarm or inconvenience so that they wouldn't think of making the arrangement permanent. The floorboards under his feet creaked at the strain made upon them by his bulk, and if his brain had had the ability to creak his would be doing so now under the strain of the questions he posed it.

He needed a convincing reason but not one that might frighten them as to the quality of the merchandise or any risk that might go along with keeping them. This whole business of the killing needed to be hushed up. If the forest got the idea that there were goblins on the loose, stealing their slaves away and stabbing them into the bargain then he would have them all back on his hands, along with demands for refunds. What would convince someone to hand their goblin back to me...but who would then still want them back in due course?

"Now...the first question...disease?" he whispered to himself. "They would certainly hand them back, but for good. Defective? No, easily refuted. Replacement by a better, stronger model? Possible...but contrived and suspicious."

His eyes burst wide and he clicked his fingers, then his head dropped again only a moment later.

"Ah balls to it. I'll just take them, say it's an emergency and I'll have them back next week. I'm Baintha Brakk, who the hell are they?"

He shouted down to one of his assistants and a hatch in the floor opened up, near to where he was stood. This eager young face looked up at him and enquired as to his needs.

"We need to get all the goblins back into the cage."

"But...they're still *in* the cage," came the uncertain reply.

"No, you dummy, the others!"

"The others? Why?"

"Because I want them where I can see them while these goblins are running about. You haven't breathed a word about there being goblins going round setting fires have you?"

"No Sir."

"Make sure you and the others don't say a word. Very important, pain of death, understand?"

"Yes Sir, not a word."

"Pain of death!"

"Yes Sir, pain of death."

"Right, on second thoughts I'll go get them myself. Gimme the straps."

"Yes Sir," replied his assistant and fished out what he needed. "Do you need me for anything else?"

"Back downstairs to your work."

"Yes Sir," he said, and closed the hatch on his head.

Baintha stepped out into the midday air. It was warm and getting warmer. This would at least mean that his customers would not need their goblins to set fires for a while. He noticed he was by himself and the area seemed deserted. He wondered at the progress of the others. For some reason he felt suddenly vulnerable. These goblins were clearly capable of killing hobgoblins and he would be their chief prize should they know where to look for him. He always had about himself his assortment of blades, though from looking at him you wouldn't know where they were kept. He was more than a match for any individual goblin but a bunch of them might be a tricky prospect. With a sinking feeling in his stomach he suddenly had the realisation that the goblin they had taken would have told them all about him and also might know how to retrace his steps to the house. He needed his bodyguard sharpish, Mala and Vrem. He went back inside and told another of his runners to fetch them, sharpish.

Once back outside he set off down the familiar pathways and made towards the nearest home that he knew to contain one of his goblins. Upon arrival he knocked at the door, straps in hand, and gave welcome to the face that appeared behind it.

"Good day. Baintha Brakk here. Just wondering how you're getting on with your new goblin."

"New is he? You wouldn't think so from how slow he works."

"Well now," chuckled Baintha, caught off guard, "I assure you he has potential for more."

"Hmmm, we'll see. Problem is there?"

"Problem? What makes you think that?"

"You stood on my doorstep."

"Yes, I need to take him back, just for a little while.'

"Oh? Why's that?"

"I hate to do this to you."

"You haven't done it yet. Why'd you need him back?"

"Well," said Baintha, wishing he'd spent more time

thinking of a good reason, "quality control."

"Quality control?" said his customer, laughing out loud.

"Yes, look, just leave him with me for a couple of days. I'll take good care of him and bring him back personally."

"Well, whatever the reason is, I need him to do some urgent cleaning up. I've got relatives coming over tomorrow and he's hard at work right now. If I don't have him I'll need to pay someone else to do it for me. Bad back you see."

"Right," said Baintha, growling under his breath.

He reached into many of his pockets and withdrew a few coins.

"This enough?" he asked, slapping them into his hand.

"I suppose. You need him now?"

"Yes, can I come in and get him?"

"Help yourself."

Baintha went inside and quickly spotted the goblin, on his knees and brushing away at an old blackened oven. Without any words he quickly bundled the goblin into the position he needed in order to strap him up. He objected at first naturally, though more from surprise than unfamiliarity. He had not the strength to struggle after his long morning's work and with a sigh went limp.

"Fancy seeing your old friends again?" whispered Baintha, in this goblins ear.

He didn't react to either the question or to being roughly picked from the ground and taken outdoors. Baintha was strong and held this considerable weight without any obvious discomfort. For a hobgoblin he was bigger than most and was able to swing him around his shoulder and onto his back. With a grunt and shuffle for comfort he made his way back home carrying this unusual load. As the next hour or two passed by Baintha was able to collect all the other goblins, though none of their owners would give him any objection and he wouldn't need to put his hand in his pocket again. The cage was full once more and they were pleased and surprised to see each other again. Mala and Vrem also came by sharpish, and held their place at Baintha's side.

*

The Lieutenant, the quartermaster, Crunch Tone, Slap Canopy and a few others were huddled together in the grass on the far side of the hill overlooking Brown Root forest. The brigade itself was hunkered down not too far away and was instructed to keep out of sight. It was the afternoon now and looking around from their position they could see a long way. Naturally the same was true for any hobgoblin observers that could well be sniffing about.

This group was pondering the impromptu map they were creating of the forest and the key places within it. Slap, using the information from Sigh Stratton and his own memory, had been the main artist and was confident that it could be relied upon. There was no one else with sufficient knowledge to dispute it and so it was going to be used.

The Lieutenant, and in fact everybody, knew that the forest would not stay quiet for long and they could not afford any delays as angry defences were undoubtedly being installed against them. It also seemed unwise to storm the forest for they would be outnumbered and highly vulnerable to every hobgoblin with a sword or frying pan. So, they had settled quite rightly on a plan for a raid on Baintha's property, though exactly where it was and what they would face when they got there was somewhat uncertain. In the Lieutenant's mind the issue was whether to go in mob handed or to try another sneak attack. The latter option was losing favour in all their minds since a strong resistance was expected. The conversation swirled around this issue and then moved on to the question of numbers.

"What kind of militia can they raise at short notice?" asked Crunch Tone.

"Not much," replied Slap, speaking from experience. "They've never been well organised like that. What they will do though is spread the word and every hobgoblin will be warned against us."

"Are you sure?" said the quartermaster. "That doesn't sound like something Baintha would do. He'd deal with things himself. I don't think the whole forest will have been warned against us."

"They will, they will," said Slap.

"No. Think about it," replied the quartermaster. "What do they know for certain? What?"

"That one of them was killed and a goblin missing,"

answered the Lieutenant.

"No, they'll also know we were there from the footprints and disturbances," said Slap.

"Maybe," replied the Lieutenant.

"Assume it," said the quartermaster.

"Fine," said the Lieutenant. "They know that a small group of goblins raided the forest and took one of ours back and killed one of theirs."

"But they won't think we'd send just half a dozen goblins to invade the forest," said Slap. "They'll assume there are more."

"Then why haven't they come looking to find out?" asked Crunch.

"Because only Baintha's handling it," reasoned the quartermaster. "That's why there's no big response. The forest hasn't been warned."

This logic of this last statement soon sank in, and agreement was reached on the point.

"How many should we send in though, and when?" asked Crunch.

"The lot, and as soon as possible," said Slap without hesitation. "Let's wipe out this Baintha Brakk."

"Let's be realistic," said the quartermaster. "That's a lot easier said than done. We have to consider only what's within our power."

"Why's that not within our power?" asked Slap.

"Because if we charge in there we'll definitely raise the whole forest against us. You don't get honey from a beehive by plunging your hands in, giving it a shake and pulling out great gobs of the stuff. You get a stick and poke it in, taking great care not to upset the bees."

"Poetic Flap, but not a good comparison," said the Lieutenant.

"Alright Lieutenant," replied Flap, mildly irked, "what do you think? Tell us the plan."

"We've come a long way and we're fit and ready. It's time to do something bold. We still have the element of surprise and with luck they won't have guessed our true potential. Why come this far and bring all these fighters if not to use them?"

The sense this made was like warm milk to those with a mind to receive it and there were many as such.

"True, fair enough," warned the quartermaster with his hand raised, "but...with respect...the more goblins we send into that forest the more will die."

This had the effect of cooling the thoughts of those warmed by the milk and there was silence for a while.

"If we must go in, then we must go in with the right frame of mind," said the Lieutenant, winking at his friend, "aware of the danger of death and not to be afraid of it."

"Is the brigade prepared for that? Are we?" asked the quartermaster.

"Well...let's ask them!" said the Lieutenant.

He got to his feet, and in plain view of the hillside and his Mice perched upon it he opened his mouth.

"Right! Stand up! Everybody!" he shouted, which they immediately did. "Did any of you sign up to this brigade lightly?"

402

They shook their heads.

"You all know there's a risk of death on this mission?"

This time they nodded their heads.

"Who wants some blood on the end of their blade!?"

The response was lukewarm.

"I said who wants some blood on the end of their blade!?"

Now there was more enthusiasm but not enough for the energised Lieutenant, who waved his sword in his hand.

"Listen! If you don't want some blood go back to Milton Greens right now. Get back there and help look after the babies and old folk. I'm here to do some work and earn my pay. Are you here to play or for pay?"

There was a chorus of "pay" thrown back at him.

"You want to earn your money right?"

"Yeah!" they shouted.

"Right!?"

"Yeah!!"

"How you gonna earn it?"

This was a more complex question, and had no uniform answer, so the Lieutenant provided it.

"You're gonna fight! You're gonna kill the hobgobs! How you gonna do it?" he said, poking his sword in front of himself to demonstrate. "Get your weapons out!"

This the brigade did, including the quartermaster and the others stood behind him.

"Right!" he continued. "Show me how!"

They each began to thrust with their swords and some yelled for the assistance and courage it brought.

"I'm not frightened. Show me how you'd kill 'em!" he

screamed.

They did their best to intensify their movements and he seemed satisfied.

"Right! I know where to get our goblins. You wanna go get 'em?"

"Yeah!"

"I said d'ya wanna go get 'em!?"

"Yeah!!"

"Then follow me!!"

With that he turned on his heels and charged over the top of the ridge. The brigade did not need further instruction and made after him. A great cheer was got up and if the residents of Brown Root forest needed confirmation of the forces arranged against them it was here.

CHAPTER 12

Tirgu, Gurgle and the human men had reached the forest that they were to visit. Tirgu had a purposeful air about him and he knew where to go. He had considered the idea of leaving Gurgle at the edge of the forest because of the danger ahead, but something compelled him to bring him along. This was a momentous day, he could feel it, and he wanted his young apprentice to see and hear all. He wasn't sure if it was his imagination or not but he felt Gurgle was having a growth spurt. Perhaps it was the time for him or the man sized diet he was on, but he didn't seem quite so little anymore.

They did not enter the forest via any of its main routes. They remained on horseback so had to take a pathway of some kind but Tirgu chose one that was quiet and scarcely used. He knew his destination well. At Baintha's place he had collected many a job in years past, and to where he returned invariably successful. He'd built his reputation as a tough, reliable and dangerous creature and where he'd extinguished his old reputation of bravado and unpredictability. He owed him a lot, both in practical and financial terms, and he was here to pay him a debt, though not in coin. Few creatures still held any trepidation for Tirgu or caused him to be nervous but Baintha was one. He'd built his business empire from nothing to the only thing in the forest in just ten years, and would have been a success with or without Tirgu's help. He was also well known beyond these borders and many a counterpart in the human community admired and did business with him.

There was no doubt about it. He was the King of the forest. Nobody called him that of course. One of his strengths was that he remained patient and approachable. Ordinary folk could talk to him whenever they wished and had no reason to worry for their safety. He had a reputation for many things but never for being a thief or bandit. Tirgu always admired his coolness under pressure. Even when things were going against him he kept a clear head and seemed to know the best course of action. Tirgu was eager to know how he would react to the problem he was about to give him. Baintha had an impossibly shrewd nature and could sniff bad feeling from someone from their posture alone. He also had a resourcefulness that had helped him escape from so many seemingly fatal encounters before.

He couldn't possibly know about what he had planned for him, unless Spikepoint had told him. That was unthinkable. Baintha might have tried to keep tabs on his old apprentice over the years but could only know of his successes and advancement in Spikepoint's employ. They had recently done business with each other over the goblins, though this was through intermediaries. No, Tirgu knew this visit would be a surprise and a nasty one at that. His approachability was usually a strength, but today he would show it to be his weakness. Just as in the human world a new King was needed and he would be the one.

There was no point waiting for Spikepoint's help. Tirgu could only rely on Tirgu to get his business done. Spikepoint would be busy for a long time to come and he did not share his confidence of a quick victory over the human King. Soon the whole world would be at war and as a hobgoblin of experience he knew that wartime was the right time to conduct dirty business.

Gurgle was still sat behind Tirgu on his horse as they gently meandered into Brown Root forest. It was a strange show for Gurgle and had a funny smell to it that he did not care for. He was surprised that as soon as they entered the forest all sunshine from outside seemed to weaken to nothing and be replaced by a sickly light, turned to brown after reflecting off so many trees. This place was dark and frightening and even the human men seemed unhappy at this diversion. Only Tirgu was calm.

"Right, I need you to keep your ears open Gurgle. You men need to be ready. As soon as Baintha knows I'm back we can expect trouble. Get your swords out and keep them at your sides."

The human men looked at Tirgu and then to each other. This didn't seem quite like what Spikepoint would want them to be doing. The more perceptive members of Tirgu's team knew this was out of order and that he was up to no good, but they were loyal to Tirgu first and would just wait to see what happened.

There were few locals about and those that did spot this band knew instantly to keep their distance. Their horses seemed to share in the emotion of the day and were a little less reliable than usual. Perhaps it was the stink of the forest and the sludge underfoot that perturbed them. Tirgu knew they were getting close and despite his best efforts his anxiety was beginning to build. This was a bad business and against the natural order of things but he was above all that and in charge of himself and his future. This would not be his first assassination but he expected it to be his toughest.

They approached a large crossroads, an inevitable step in their journey. It was fairly busy and keeping a low profile was no longer an option. They simply continued on and cared not who saw them. Many did, with swords held low by their horses' sides. The day's business was getting close.

As they made their slow way towards the centre of the forest they naturally spread out a little on their horses and let Tirgu control the pace from the front. When he suddenly stopped so did they. Tirgu was sniffing the air and dipping his head as though peering into the distance. With one of his arms he reached behind himself grabbing Gurgle and then lifting him down from the horse. He slowly did the same for himself moments later, then turned and signalled to his men to do the same. All this was achieved in complete silence.

Tirgu beckoned them all together and whispered quietly that the building in the middle distance was their goal. He instructed Gurgle to hold the horse's reins and keep them here and if possible to keep out of sight. That was what he fully intended to do. Tirgu and the men continued on, keeping their heads low and their sword points, for the moment, concealed. Gurgle wrapped the leather of each rein several times around his arm and tried to find a comfortable spot behind a tree from which to observe.

Gurgle watched them fan out and was surprised that even with his sensitive ears they made such little sound. Tirgu's brown and slightly shorter body stood out in the middle of the paler and taller human men, though he was only an inch shorter than the smallest of the men. The building they approached seemed quiet. Smoke rose from the chimney however and it was obviously a significant fire inside that was producing it. The building was large, made from wooden panels and had a lot of land cleared around it. The last twenty metres or so would have to be crossed in the open. He placed his hands on the wet tree trunk that kept him a secret and held it close. He could sense what was coming and couldn't take his eyes off the bobbing figures slinking through the undergrowth ahead of him.

Baintha Brakk and his bodyguards, Mala and Vrem were inside the building, but downstairs, attending to the goblins. The goblins had noticed that they were all back together, with the exception of Sigh Stratton. The ever perceptive Brakk gave an answer to their thoughts.

"Wondering about your friend?" he said to them, not expecting or allowing an answer. "Ran off didn't he? He escaped!"

Those assembled in the cage took this news at face value and all seemed to laugh and smile in defiance.

"Got him back of course. He didn't get very far...but

sadly, he didn't survive recapture. That's a real shame I must say."

The familiar hiss greeted Baintha's ear once more.

"If you caught him why bring us all back here then?" asked one of his more defiant captives.

Baintha, knowing the question to be a fair one treated it most unfairly. He snarled at this one in the cage and brought his face swiftly up to it, pushing his sharp brown fingers through the gaps in the wire.

"Don't want any of you running off till I've had the chance to *beat* some more sense in ta ya!"

Mala and Vrem both chuckled at this. They were stood someway behind him and below the hatch to the upstairs. The goblin in the cage had sense enough not to provoke them any further and kept quiet. There followed a few moments of silence and everyone's attention drifted to something new. There was dust coming down from the roof, something Baintha knew was only caused by people walking around above. Suddenly a great knock came at the hatch.

"Who's that?" shouted Baintha, expecting one of his assistants to call back.

No answer came and Baintha was immediately suspicious. The knocking came again but this time he did not answer and he waved at the others to keep quiet. He listened intently and the others quickly followed his example. He drew his sword and waved at the others to copy him. From the creaks he deduced the presence of at least three people up there and some heavy ones amongst them. Human men perhaps, or heavily laden hobgobs?

He crept up to the hatch and wondered whether they had gone, for after a few seconds there were no more sounds of creaking floorboards. Turning to his companions he pointed to a distant corner of the underground room they were in and explained, somehow by gesture alone, that they would find another exit there to the surface and see who was above them. They did so immediately and quietly.

Baintha was tempted closer to the hatch by the silence and turned his ear towards it. The goblins in the cage watched the scene and somehow felt that it was right to be quiet also. One of them imagined however that some rescue might be in the air and he suddenly let out a yell that broke the tension.

"Help! We're down here!"

The noise shattered the stalemate and the hatch swung open and natural light fell inside. Baintha's head was close to the hatch as it opened but his attention had been momentarily stolen by the goblin's shout. More than two arms reached down and grabbed Baintha by the body, forcibly dragging him upwards. On the floor of his house he found himself a second later with two human men he didn't know holding him down. His sword was kicked away from him and he looked up and around at everyone, marking their faces for the retribution he would give them. One face he could not have seen came around from behind these human men and looked down at this King of the forest, coming close to the end of his reign.

411

"Tirgu!? Tirgu! You're dead for this! Dead!" spat Brakk up at him, knowing his purpose in an instant.

"Is that anyway to speak to an old friend?" he replied smoothly.

Tirgu withdrew his weapon from its hiding place and pointed it at the prostrate figure on the floor in front of him. This was a new view of his old friend and one enjoyed by very few. Tirgu put the sword to his neck.

"Wait! Wait! What's this all about? Tirgu, old friend. Tell me! You owe me that courtesy."

Tirgu had always warned himself that in such moments he must not delay the job at hand with an indulgence, but now that he was here and felt in complete comfort he gave it.

"I've been away for a while but now I'm back...and you're in my place," he said after a few moments.

"As I thought. No one will support you," stated Brakk, playing for time.

"I don't need their support."

"Then get on with it."

Tirgu smiled and readied himself.

"One more thing," said Baintha, "a word of advice."

"...what?" asked Tirgu.

Tirgu paused a moment and then looked around as this verbal trick was designed to encourage him to do, but it was no trick. An arrow came from somewhere and struck one of the human men in the side of his neck and he fell to the ground with no sound from his mouth. Another came a fragment of time later and did as much for another of the men, this time in the centre of his back. The front door burst open and Mala and Vrem burst in. Tirgu had no choice but to move from Baintha and lunge at the doorway, as much from anger at his own weakness as at the intrusion. The point of his sword was swiftly aimed at Mala's throat but missed and using his weight Mala fell back pulling Tirgu with him into the open air. Vrem blundered into the house in a frenzy, dropping his crossbow, and barged two of the human men off their feet as they stood in shock at this sudden attack. The one human man remaining on his feet grabbed one of the feet of the rapidly fleeing Brakk and prevented him from crawling downstairs. Instead he was dragged into the daylight. This human man was in control and knew that their greater number and skill would do for them in the end. He held Brakk by the scruff of his neck, face down in the muck, with his knee in his back.

The other two men in the house quickly curbed Vrem's enthusiasm and they dragged him into the open air, flinging his lifeless body in front of Brakk's nose. Vrem's last breath fell clumsily from his throat, along with a good deal of cherry red blood. Brakk watched but managed to keep his cool. Now it was just Mala and Tirgu together. The human men panted heavily at such a shock after dragging their own comrades from the house into the light to see if there was anything to do. There was not.

Tirgu and Mala had by now broken free from their wrestle and faced each other. Both hobgobs snarled and were cut and bleeding.

The three human men still alive were too complacent at the scene in front of them as another arrow came flying in, hitting the man holding down Brakk in the shoulder. He moaned and fell on top of his captive but did not lose his grip. The other two turned and saw from where the arrow had come. Marin was in the undergrowth and had been helping as best she could. She reloaded her crossbow as quickly as her slim fingers allowed, for the two men were charging at her. It was done, she lifted and fired, hitting one of them cleanly through his chest and he fell at her feet. The other leapt over his friend and kicked the device from her grasp. She only had time to withdraw her knife before another was placed into her body. She screamed. Baintha understood the sound and Gurgle, still some distance away, would never forget it.

The man pulled her body through the grass into the open and her blood marked the journey. I don't know what it is about human men and dead bodies, but instinctively they feel the need to put them in a line, alongside each other and face up, perhaps so their souls would be able to seep into the sky, or so that their respective Gods might find it easier to pick and choose their adherents.

Mala and Tirgu circled slowly around each other. He knew Tirgu well, and his abilities, and after seeing and hearing how the struggle had gone his morale was low. He felt death was near. Tirgu also knew Mala well and he knew from their youthful encounters that he had always been the stronger fighter.

"What's it to be Mala?" goaded Tirgu. "Quick and

414

painless, or slow and cruel?"

"For me or for you?" came the defiant response.

Tirgu laughed and lunged at him but was easily sidestepped. Perhaps they were more evenly matched than Tirgu had hitherto believed. Gurgle watched these scenes unfold with a mixture of horror and fascination. His hands were stuck to that tree trunk with a power that exceeded the stickiest mulch ever made by his parents.

He began to notice a sound not related to the battle in front of him. A rumble made the hairs in his ears tingle. At first, the very finest and most sensitive hairs picked up the feeling. Then their less sensitive neighbours began to signal alongside them. It was a rumble at first, then came more subtle tones of shrieking and whooping. From his vantage point the contest between Tirgu and that unknown hobgoblin suddenly came to a stop and they both stepped away from each other and turned to look in a particular direction. They all seemed to be looking one way and Gurgle did the same. A swarm approached them! But of what? The trees obscured his view.

Tirgu backed away from Mala and looked in the direction of the rumbling. It was not an easy thing to astonish Tirgu but this was the only fair way to describe his reaction as about a hundred goblins, give or take a few, charged towards him with swords drawn. To be fair, their reaction was much the same upon greeting this scene and their charge slowed a little in confusion. Tirgu would normally laugh at the threat from a goblin fighter but did not do so in this unique situation. He turned on his heels and told his remaining men to do the same as the wave broke over them. Gurgle saw the goblins now and was equally astonished. He crawled from his hiding place and yelled to them but could not be heard.

The Lieutenant, his quartermaster, Slap and many others swarmed the place, capturing Mala and Brakk, though without knowing who they were.

Tirgu and his two remaining men, one of whom stumbled and winced from his arrow injury, came bounding from the scene and towards Gurgle and their horses. Their reigns were still tied around him and he stood as they approached. Tirgu roughly unfurled them from his arm and tried to help his men to their horses. The surplus steeds were abandoned. Out of the corner of his eye Tirgu noticed Gurgle drifting away.

"No you don't!" he shouted.

Tirgu grabbed at him and lifted him onto his horse, this time with Gurgle at the front and he behind. He held him tightly and refused to let him go. A few of the more inquisitive goblin warriors had followed the fleeing men and had seen Gurgle amongst them. They raised the alarm but the horses were faster than they. The quartermaster and many others held Mala and Baintha securely, whilst others tied and bound them. The area was somewhat alarmed but most of the hobgob locals kept their distance, particularly when these sword wielding creatures encouraged them so to do.

Tirgu and his shocked companions made their way swiftly from the forest. All except Gurgle dripped blood in varying quantities. Tirgu was wide eyed and had a thousand thoughts racing through his brain. What a thing to happen! Never would he have such a chance again and now he faced his Lord and the likely punishment for his disobedience.

The Lieutenant crept inside the house and heard voices from the hatch below. In he went and saw his glorious return to Milton Greens sitting there in front him. He snapped open the stubborn lock after a few attempts and brought them all out into the sunlight; a sight that overwhelmed those that had not seen day time for such a long time. Many preferred to collapse on the ground as their leg muscles could not sustain them after being kept inside the cage for so long.

Spontaneously, the Boiled Mice let out a cheer once the area was cooled and their prize lay at their feet. The quartermaster voraciously circled the perimeter and made sure that guards were quickly posted and that no force was being arranged against their band. The Lieutenant organised stretchers for the weaker captives; a wise precaution of the quartermaster. Those that needed them were bundled on board. The Lieutenant was anxious to leave as soon as possible. Once all the goblins and their two new captives had been readied they would be off. He did not intend to set fire to this building however, specifically warning Slap not to, as he felt that would take too long.

A goblin had a word in the Lieutenant's ear about the sighting of the young one, just yards away from where they had been. A wail of anger came from his chest. So close to getting everyone back! He couldn't split up their force to chase them, especially as they were on horses. That would have to come later. Instead he counted his blessings, all nine of them. The two hobgoblin prisoners would also make a useful gift to the Council. Let them decide what to do with them. They were both silent but the Lieutenant suspected one of them was Brakk.

Two members of the brigade suddenly appeared from the house dragging a young looking hobgoblin, who was clearly terrified, out into the light.

"He was hiding downstairs Sir!" yelled one of them to the Lieutenant as they threw him to the ground.

To the Lieutenant's horror the other drew his sword and put it to his throat as though to kill him.

"No!" shouted the Lieutenant and Baintha Brakk at the same time.

The Lieutenant kicked away this over enthusiastic goblin and reproached him forcefully. This was his own fault though since he had riled them up so effectively. The first word from this other hobgoblin's mouth was untimely however as it made the Lieutenant focus on him.

"Baintha Brakk?" he suggested to this one, lowering his face to speak quietly.

He did not answer and gave nothing away.

"That's him, that's Baintha," said one of the goblin captives suddenly, leaning up from her stretcher.

"Baintha Brakk?" said the Lieutenant again, but with more confidence this time.

"Aye," came the soft reply, "what of it?"

418

"You stole our brothers and sisters and for that you'll pay."

"I didn't steal them. That creature you let escape stole them, as you came running. He's the one. Tirgu!"

This was confirmation for the Lieutenant that the rumours had been right.

"But you bought them and sold them into slavery!"

"Aye," came the soft reply, "and what of it?"

One of the Mice holding him gave him a hefty thump on the back of his head for his frankness. The Lieutenant took this response as the end of the matter and knew he would get nothing further from him for the moment. They needed to be on their way.

The Lieutenant looked for his quartermaster amongst the throng and beckoned him over for a brief word. He slapped his nearest goblin on the back and came running towards his Lieutenant. His armour clattered as he ran and the Lieutenant noticed how quiet things had suddenly become.

"We need to move," said the Lieutenant.

"Yes Sir. What about the house?" asked the quartermaster.

"What about it? We're not going to torch it, I've said."

"We should search it."

"For what?"

"For whatever's there!" responded the quartermaster forcefully.

"Alright! You've got two minutes!"

With that the quartermaster took a few others nearby,

including Slap, and went into the house. It was no longer quiet as they conducted a clumsy and destructive search. Brakk was most displeased. He had a lot of money tucked away in various places and would be livid if the benefits of his hard work were stolen by these pointless little creatures. The sound of boxes being thrown, jars breaking and furniture being smashed spread through the air. Slap seemed the most enthusiastic of them all and anything of interest he threw through the doorway. Soon a small pile of objects was collected. The Lieutenant had not intended a quick search to become wholesale looting but that was what was happening. So be it, Baintha deserved it.

He looked at the three hobgoblin prisoners and wondered what kind of a journey it would be for them. Baintha was definitely coming but he suddenly realised that a group of prisoners might not be appreciated by the Council all that much. The younger one was clearly still terrified and the other, whom he did not know, seemed faint from loss of blood. He looked also at the bodies of the human men and the two hobgoblins, laid out in a row and face up. The human men seemed so big, like tree trunks, now felled. One of the hobgobs was a woman and he was surprised at the sight. They all lay there, still and pale, except where blood covered them. The wind flapped a little at their clothes and at the long hair of the hobgob woman. He breathed a big sigh of relief that none of his brigade was in the same way and he resolved not to push his luck any further. All except the woman had their eyes open.

It occurred to him that their troop would get the blame for

all these deaths and Baintha would have no incentive to correct them. This was another good reason to leave the other two behind. They would hopefully make it clear what happened and would not have the wit to blame their brigade for everything. He was not to recognise it yet but even bringing back one hobgoblin prisoner would be one too many for the Council.

Within the two minute window that they had been granted, the looters, for that was what they now were, emerged with their spoils. Baintha watched each closely as they walked one by one from his house, arms filled. To his relief he saw that they had taken only a few expendable trinkets. That was true however until Slap Canopy emerged with a smile and a jar full of coin. Despite the dust on the outside the glint of gold could be seen inside, mixed in with baser metals. His groan was audible to those close by. His hands were bound behind him and so he could do little to gesticulate.

The Lieutenant was not impressed by the scene and realised the limitations of command over others, in that it was possible only with consent, which sometimes had to be bought. He shouted to the brigade to ready themselves. No serious attack had been launched against them but many eyes were trained on them and would follow them all the way out of the forest and probably beyond. Keeps was amongst them but had not had the nerve to engage in the fighting, either before or after the goblin army's arrival. "I'm going to release the other two," said the Lieutenant to his quartermaster.

"What...now?" he replied incredulously, his arms laden with shiny goods.

"No, when we leave the forest. Let's go."

"Right."

The quartermaster yelled out the order, a perimeter of goblins was formed, the prisoners were shoved in the right direction, the stretchers were lifted and then the whole procession began the return journey to Milton Greens. The Lieutenant turned behind himself looking at the house and was shocked about how easy it had been. That was a fact he would not readily bring to the attention of the newsboy from the Milton Greens Pamphlet when he would inevitably pay him a visit. No sense worrying about that though whilst they were still in hostile territory. Because of the ease and success of their risky run in, many of the Mice were getting excited and a little out of control. The Lieutenant and his quartermaster gleefully took turns in reprimanding their excesses with voice and club as appropriate. They kept a steady pace, which was naturally limited by their special guests. Once the daylight of open ground lay ahead of them they cut loose Mala and Brakk's assistant. Mala nodded to Brakk with a look that conveyed more than just respect. Plans were made in that look, rough and unclear but certainly made. They rejoined their fellow hobgoblins, most of whom had heard the alarm and were heading their way. At the scene however there seemed no incentive on their part to attack.

The Mice made their way more swiftly, now that they were in open ground, and it was the Lieutenant's intention to keep going until they dropped from exhaustion. That would not prove possible of course and they made some ten miles before giving in and camping. That evening the watch was kept very effectively and there was not even a hint of fannying about.

*

A long wooden table accommodated many important figures from the King's existence. The old man himself was amongst them and he did his best to concentrate on proceedings but it was difficult for him. The encounter with Spikepoint had clearly, at least in Gavelrigg's mind, broken him for the last time. His nephew Frederick was newly arrived and sat downwind of his uncle. Various captains and ministers were also in attendance, as was Doctor Brand who did his best to make his King comfortable and aware of the things happening around him; a nearly impossible task.

"Sire," began Gavelrigg tentatively, "do you recognise your nephew and heir Frederick?"

The King looked for a few moments in the direction that Gavelrigg pointed but seemed not to understand the point of his question and turned back.

"Uncle! It is Frederick, your brother's eldest son."

The King again had his gaze drawn in that direction and slowly realised that all these words were being directed at him. He looked back and forth at them rapidly, the crown on his head being unable to keep up and seemed to hang in

423

space as his head rotated within it.

"I..." he began, "I do."

"Frederick," said Frederick.

"Frederick," replied the King, smiling.

He looked back at Gavelrigg.

"Do you know why we are here today Sire?" asked Gavelrigg, anticipating no sensible answer.

"A birthday...anniversary?" he replied.

"I'm afraid not Sire. I am afraid that today we must pass your legacy and crown onto Frederick."

The King took a few moments to absorb what was being said to him and his reaction was none too positive.

"Why must you do that? I am King," he said softly.

"I know Sire, but it is for the good of your Kingdom that we do this."

"Spikepoint."

"Yes Sire, Spikepoint is on his way to attack us."

"Can he not be brought back into the fold?" asked the King, making a hugging gesture with his arms.

"No," said more than one man.

"What is to become of me?"

"We will protect you and your Kingdom," replied Gavelrigg, smiling warmly and touching his arm.

At this reassurance the King lost his frightened look. Frederick was beckoned over by Gavelrigg and he knelt at the King's feet. Whereupon the King instinctively put his hand out and placed it on his head, as he had done so many times in the past and on so many noble heads. All those in the room were pleased at this reaction except perhaps

Captain Starling Dodd.

"Sire, will you recite the following words after me?" asked Gavelrigg.

The King nodded.

"I, King Hasdow the Second," began Gavelrigg.

"I, King Hasdow the Second," said the King.

"Freely and willingly..."

"Freely and willingly..."

"While I live..."

"While I live..."

"And in full sight of God..."

"And in full sight of God..."

"Pass on my worldly crown and kingdom..."

"Pass on my worldly crown and kingdom..."

"To my nephew and heir, Frederick."

"To my nephew and heir, Frederick."

Gavelrigg approached calmly and motioned with his hands towards the Kings head, so as to take the crown. The King's hands flew up to block him.

"No Sir, that is mine," he said defiantly.

"Sire!" said Gavelrigg suddenly, "You must hand it over."

"Have you lost your faith in me so easily Gavelrigg?" replied the King, shaking his head in sorrow.

The King picked up the crown from his head and carefully placed it on Frederick's head, as had been his intention all along. Gavelrigg was relieved and embarrassed simultaneously. Frederick kept his head bowed as he stood, and once upright opened his eyes and smiled. There was a smattering of applause and several of those present, including Gavelrigg but not including Dodd, came up to their new King and offered him their warmest congratulations.

The old King remained seated in his chair as even with the weight of his crown gone from his head he could not stand up. Gavelrigg interrupted the merrymaking.

"Gentlemen! There is no time for anything but the briefest of celebrations. Spikepoint is most likely on his way. He brings an army and intends to take over this castle and destroy everything we hold dear. If we fail to stop him we can expect destitution for our families and execution for ourselves. Frederick, Sire, a great burden has been placed upon your head. Will you bear it?"

"I will," said the new King.

"Will you all bear it?" he said, asking the others.

"We will!" was their general response.

"Good," he said, satisfied.

"I will bear it too," whispered the old King, but mainly to the audience in his own head.

*

Three horses held four riders. One was slumped over the side of his horse's neck and was doing his best to stay alert for the way ahead. His friend, the other human man, rode alongside and helped to prop him up and keep him well. Tirgu was frantically licking at his wounds in an attempt to disinfect them, even though he had applied the right unguents only an hour before. Gurgle was sat in front of him and could hear the swish of his arms and the slapping of tongue against flesh above him. It was not a pleasant experience and the tension in the group was palpable.

Gurgle was still stunned from his experience. It was a shock to see his own kind again. He closed his eyes in regret and frustration for not immediately throwing off the reins and charging to them. His mind's eye directed him back there time after time to teach him a lesson and chide him for his stupidity. He could have been on his way back to Milton Greens with them all and safe home. Another part of his mind tried to soothe him with thoughts of the danger he had been in and how unfair it was to put so much expectation on his young shoulders. It was simple, he eventually concluded. He was afraid of Tirgu and had been unable to get up from his spot. The scene was so frightening that it would have been unwise to charge into it in any case.

It was the first time that Gurgle had seen people killed. He had not witnessed it directly but the signs and sounds were clear enough. What's more he knew the killers, though some were now dead themselves. They were around him now and he was one of them, though he didn't blame himself for that naturally. The reality of what kind of people they were had been made plain for him and he could no longer delude himself that they were in any serious way good.

Tirgu's small band had been cut in half. Spikepoint would want to know why. He would also want to know what intelligence had been gathered or sabotage undertaken.

Clearly none, except the wisdom that sneak attacks often fail. Tirgu groaned at this blow across the head that fate had given him. As much as he tried to control his destiny the randomness of the world could not be fought off. Baintha was still alive and would divert his energies to destroying him. Now the threat he made on the floor of his house could well come true. He thought a little more about what happened. He hadn't had the time to observe the scene after he fled and it occurred to him that those goblins would have as much reason to hate Baintha as he, if not more. They would not be so vicious as to kill him there and then, unfortunately. That was not the typical goblin attitude. They would probably take him away though, back to Milton Greens with all the slaves too. All except Gurgle of course. He had time therefore, and correctly anticipated that no force from Brown Root would come after their small band any time soon, if ever.

Tirgu directed what remained of his men to where they had originally been ordered to go. They would be late of course and in poor shape. It occurred to Tirgu to invent a story to explain their losses and their absence. He began to share his thoughts with the others.

"What do we think of today's events?" he said, and after a few moments the uninjured man replied.

"Spike won't be pleased. You gunna cook something up?"

"Might do. Depends on how good you are at keeping secrets."

"If it keeps me out of the regular army I might be very good at it. If he knows the truth we'll be split up and that means front line duty for me and right now...that's not good."

"Very sensible...and you Gurgle? I know you're sore at me, but you wouldn't wanna go back with those useless goblins. You're far better off with me, though it may not seem that way to you. Can you keep a secret too?"

"It won't make any difference," said Gurgle disconsolately.

Tirgu looked down at the back of his head, smiled, and took this response to be broadly positive. The injured man also moaned his approval when prompted.

"Well then, what do you say to this...and tell me if it's not convincing? On the way to our meeting place, one of our horses pulled up lame...we had to stop early and camp in the open, not far from Brown Root. As we slept, hobgob bandits sneaked up and surprised us. We fought, lost a few men and then escaped as we are. What do you think?"

They swilled the concept around in their minds, as though pondering a fine wine, then gave their verdict.

"Pretty good," answered the uninjured man, "but...'

"What?" said Tirgu.

"Would Spikepoint believe that we could be sneaked up on so easily?"

"He doesn't rate me as highly as you imagine."

"Hah, don't underestimate someone's good opinion of you."

"It is a flaw and he would be suspicious, you're right. He might not accept it. Can we strengthen it?"

"I'm not sure how, but it feels too simple a tale."

"Yeah, I think we can get away with adding a little more to it. I could've gone into the forest and left you all in camp, maybe to meet old friends. He might find that more realistic."

"Then how did you get injured?"

"Right, I was there then, but drunk after my return from the forest and not in the best condition to fight. That could be how the bandits knew of us, by following me on my way back to camp."

"That's good, I would be convinced by that and he could forgive an evening spent in your own forest."

"Wouldn't he find out eventually?" interrupted Gurgle.

"When it comes to telling a lie Gurgle," said Tirgu, with a pat on his shoulder, "all you need is commitment."

"He's probably right," said the injured man, "he would discover the truth eventually."

"By then he'll be King and he won't care at all."

"Let's hope he is," replied the injured man, "and that he won't."

Tirgu laughed and suddenly didn't feel so bad about what had happened. They continued onwards and within a few hours caught the attention of one of Spikepoint's scouting parties and rejoined the fold.

*

Elsewhere in Spikepoint's camp preparations and plans were under construction. The Lord himself and his three trusted battalion chiefs were sat comfortably on furs around a makeshift but sturdy table inside the best protected tent in the camp. They each had access to food and drink, and warm fires illumined them. Haine was still coming to terms with his new position, but being a man of quality and composure he held his nerve well. Nevertheless he was in esteemed company and was clearly the most junior man there.

Spikepoint ruffled at the papers on the table that was between them. He was putting them in order so that his thoughts could also be in order. Tomorrow it was more than likely they would engage with the enemy. In recent days enemy was the only word used to describe their former friends and that, by inevitable force of psychology, was what they had become. Their destination was well known and the defences arranged against them could also be anticipated with some accuracy. Spikepoint knew what the King had at his disposal and what he had not. He would not have marched had he not been privy to much secret information from those within the King's ranks sympathetic to his cause. Many individuals, mostly at lower rank to be fair, had been disposed to accept his kindnesses in exchange for their insight into activities at the castle.

He had not heard much from the scouts he had sent about in recent days. In particular he had hoped to hear from Tirgu and his band. He looked down at one piece of paper, an elderly map of some kind, and then handed it to commander Haine.

"Do you remember our conversation Robert?" he was

asked.

"I do, my Lord," replied Haine.

"The plan is much as you anticipated. There is no better place to settle things. The ground is flat and open and though we have no surprise, we have greater numbers, and many on their side know what is coming and will quickly switch over to our side once we press our advantage."

"Yes my Lord."

"And you other Gentlemen?"

"Yes my Lord?" replied the other two battalion chiefs.

"Today has been a good day. We have made progress and are ready for the day ahead, which I expect to be even better."

"Sire," said Haine, "what will be your attitude to the prisoners we take, should we win?"

Spikepoint looked at him for a moment or two, not all that surprised by his concern.

"They will be well treated," he replied.

"Sire, that is easy to say in such gentle surroundings but not so easy after a vicious battle."

"Indeed, let us hope it is not so vicious then. Have you family amongst them?"

"No Sire."

"Friends then?"

"A few, but that won't interfere with my duty."

"Then why should you show concern for them?"

"For your future my Lord, and ours, so that we are not hated by those we defeat."

"If they are defeated they have no power," said Spikepoint

in response.

"If your reign is to be a success you must recognise the dignity of those you defeat, else your efforts will have been wasted."

Spikepoint was surprised by his eloquence and balanced his chin on his hand, after nodding for Haine to continue in the same vein.

"We should make efforts to incorporate them into our structures after we win, so keeping them busy helping us and not hindering us."

"Would that not just help them to hinder us? Aren't we better off getting rid of them?" asked one of the other battalion chiefs.

"Maybe," conceded Haine, "but the atmosphere must be allowed to change. Otherwise the cycle will repeat itself once the tide turns against us."

"You are too thoughtful Robert," said Spikepoint with a smile. "It's true that sometimes it is better to make friends with your enemy than to make war. But if you make war it must be finished, without compromise. History has no ear for those that have no voice."

"Yes Sire, I'm not trying to change your view. Instead I want you to spare those that could do us all good in the future."

"Ah, and how will we know these fine men when we see them?" said Spikepoint, raising his head.

"When they put down their arms."

"Any man that lays down his arms...I will attempt to spare, but I cannot guarantee it."

"May I instruct my men to do so?" asked Haine.

"May I instruct my men *not* to do so?" asked another.

Spikepoint laughed at this difference and Haine glared at the other man, not realising it had been said in jest.

"Gentlemen," said Spikepoint, "you are all leaders and fine men. I don't care whether one prisoner lives or another dies. It is not my concern. I leave such matters to you."

"All I know is, from experience," said Haine, "when you kill a man you make an enemy of his sons, his brothers, everyone. You make an entirely new enemy, and twice the size, with twice the motivation."

"True enough," said the third chief, who had hitherto been largely silent.

"I think we will manage, whatever our policy is. Let's get back to the plan of attack shall we?"

The three of them nodded at their Lord and he continued.

"Tomorrow, each battalion will assume readiness for battle. Scouts will go ahead and give word when we are near. Their forces will almost certainly be kept to protect the castle."

"Are you certain their forces will be there?" asked Haine.

"Of course. From where else could they find such a point of safety and defence, and from where they can be so easily reinforced?" replied Spikepoint. "They might throw a few men at us, just for sport, but that won't divert us from our goal."

"Most likely," said Haine, almost with a sigh.

"When the moment comes for battle I will decide the details and instruct you in the field."

He took his glass, recently filled with wine, and motioned that the others do the same with their glasses. They did so and held them close to each other.

"Tomorrow, we find our destiny," said Spikepoint gently, "and they find theirs."

With a clink their glasses came together and one of them shattered, staining one of the maps blood red.

*

The following day the Boiled Mice woke early, with the Lieutenant being among the first. The light on the horizon was still soft and he saw that dew still sat on the blades of grass. He made contact with the night watch and got his report. Things had been quiet and the prisoner had been quiet too. They had managed to make their way back to the river the previous evening and would be able to follow it back to Milton Greens and enter the forest in much the same place that they had left it. Sigh Stratton and his escort would almost certainly have made it back to the forest by now so there would be much anticipation and excitement about what was to come. It was a near triumph. All but one goblin found, no goblin soldiers lost and a key villain captured. But what about poor little Gurgle? He hadn't caught a glimpse of him but more than one Mouse had a clear sighting of a goblin boy in the grasp of that hobgob Tirgu. Who else could it be?

As he sat there eating what was left of a worm brick from the previous day he tried to imagine what the Council's reaction would be to the child still being held. They would be sorrowful no doubt, at least in public, but they would be unlikely to risk a further excursion to search for him. They would probably count their blessings as he had done. Another trip would meet with so much more hostility and unless they became skilled horsemen, which few goblins had ever become, they would have trouble tracking that band he was with. He would still feel that he had let down the poor Roundtops. The whole forest would celebrate but they would be the only ones with no cause to rejoice and would bear their grief alone.

Might the Council or others criticise him for failing to go after him, when he was so close? They might, and he considered for the first time whether his spilt second decision had been the right one. No, they were away before he had the chance to react. That would be an unfair criticism. The forest would think the mission a near complete success. The only question was whether or not to go after Gurgle. Oh, and what kind of response might there be against their whole forest? As he chewed and swallowed the last unpalatable piece he was approached by his quartermaster.

"Morning Sir."

"Morning," replied the Lieutenant.

"Do you want me to kick them all awake?"

"Yes, why not? No time to lose."

"Yes Sir."

He swivelled from his position and turned to face the majority of those still asleep, or pretending to be so. He looked down at the nearest creature still in dreamland and booted him up rather cruelly up the arse.

"Up! Up! Up! Get up you lazy Mice. Up!" he shouted. and like a flock of birds taking flight they did.

Baintha Brakk was sat among them and had already been awake for a while. The binding on his hands and feet had made it difficult to sleep. He looked about himself with barely disguised loathing. The quartermaster noticed this and approached him.

"Breakfast?" said Flap, and after some moments of silence, "Well, as you wish. I assume you don't mind if we have a bite. It is hungry work after all."

Baintha would not reply. Even if he had been offered food he would not take it. This was not such a good strategy in the longer term but he expected a rescue to come within days. Mala knew what to do. He would call upon many in Brown Root that owed him allegiance, and pay for the allegiance of many others both in the forest and beyond. These little fools would come to rue the day that they had had the nerve to invade his forest.

As many of the goblins got themselves organised they looked once more at the sitting figure of Baintha Brakk and gave him curses and sneers. More than one of them noticed the odour emanating from him and started to make comments.

"What a stink!" said one.

"That's not natural," said another.

"Are you diseased or something?" asked another.

He didn't respond to any of them. It was the result of a

437

skin disease in his youth and could not be cured. Despite his dignified silence they would not leave him alone.

"The river's nearby and I've got an idea," said one of them. "Let's give him a bath!"

This idea was received enthusiastically but Baintha recoiled from them. This only encouraged them further and they grabbed him bodily and pulled him towards the water's edge. The Lieutenant looked on and was tempted to stop them, just because of their indiscipline, but decided not to. It was little punishment for what he had done.

"Throw him in!" shouted one onlooker.

"Give him a good scrub!" shouted another.

He was put under the water but had to be clumsily pushed and rolled. None of the goblins seemed keen to follow him and do anything else so Baintha just emerged and scowled at them as the water dripped from his body.

"Get him out of there!" shouted the Lieutenant. "Come on, get some food into you and pack your things. We leave in three minutes!"

The brigade soon readied themselves and those assigned to looking after the rescued goblins made them ready also. In three minutes they were on their way and with a steady march hoped to be in their own beds that very night.

*

Tirgu made his way through various ramshackle encampments, with soldiers falling in and out of them, and approached the heart of Spikepoint's assembly. He had

438

been summoned once word of his return had reached his Lord.

There were many cauldrons boiling and small fires flickering beneath them. This was the kitchen area and he took the opportunity whilst travelling through to quickly tear off a handful of chicken breast from a poorly guarded roast. He munched the flesh and slurped the juice and within a couple of minutes the evidence was gone. He wiped his mouth and rubbed his greasy hand on the back of his dark trousers as he came to what was obviously his Lord's tent. He was noticed and beckoned inside by one of the guards.

There he found Spikepoint seated at a table that faced the entrance to the tent. It was a small table with room just for one and on it was arranged his breakfast. His helmet was off and was laid to one side, along with everything else metallic that would adorn him later. He stared out at Tirgu and did not greet him when he came in. This might have been because of his irritation with him for disappearing or because his mouth was filled with roast chicken, as Tirgu's had just been. Spikepoint enjoyed bread, mushrooms and fresh tomatoes in addition however. He had the decency to swallow before giving air to what he was clearly bursting to say.

"Where have you been?!" he spluttered.

"My Lord," began Tirgu tentatively, "we were attacked, and delayed."

"Yes, I'm told you lost three men and another wounded."

"Yes my Lord."

439

"Well, what happened?"

"We were attacked as we slept, near Brown Root forest."

"Why did you stray *that* way?"

"I'm sorry my Lord, but I wished to pay a brief visit to friends. I didn't think it would delay us too much."

"Well, who attacked you?"

"Bandits, my Lord."

"Bandits."

"Aye, my Lord."

"What kind of bandits?"

"Hobgoblin bandits. They must have followed me after I left the forest."

"How did they manage to surprise you all in your sleep? Didn't you post a watch?"

"No my Lord."

"That definitely doesn't sound like you."

"I was drunk my Lord, I'm sorry. I neglected to post a watch."

Spikepoint looked at him through narrowing eyes and bit into a tomato. The juice and seeds slipped down his chin and were then wiped away by a cloth.

"And that's how half your band were killed...as they slept? And how you got your cuts and bruises...whilst drunk?"

"Aye, my Lord, it was."

"Yes, I believe you. You see I had a word with the injured man in your band last night. He was eager to tell me something along the same lines. The thing was...I couldn't find a surgeon straight away to tend to his wound."

"No? He is still alive I hope."

"Oh yes, a surgeon came eventually, but this poor man interpreted the delay in only one way and he thought it best to tell me what really happened."

Tirgu shuffled his feet uncomfortably.

"My Lord..."

"What!? What will you say to me now? Let's have it!"

"Perhaps he was delirious?"

"Hah! I know the truth when I hear it. Delirious indeed. You thought you would just nip off and kill Brakk didn't you? Just a brief sidestep to attend to a little business, eh? You've cost me four good men!!"

"My Lord..." said Tirgu weakly.

"Your disloyalty after such good service comes as a great disappointment to me. All you had to do was wait, give me service one more time and I would have squashed Brakk like a beetle as a gift for you. But what can I do with you now?"

"I am still your servant."

"Indeed, and you will still serve me, though not in the capacity to which you've become accustomed. Your band is disbanded and what's left will serve me in the coming battle. You, you in particular," he said whilst pointing at him, "will lead from the front!"

"My Lord, I can of better service to you elsewhere," said Tirgu, almost pleading.

"No, no way! But don't worry, that little green pet of yours will stay with me. I'll return him to you if you survive and if you don't I'll look after him for you."

Tirgu looked up in disbelief and exasperation at fate's

continued assault upon him and he stood there in silence for a few moments. Spikepoint growled and reached with his fingers for a chunk of bread, of which there were many in a nearby bowl. He grasped it firmly, and with both menace and accuracy he threw it at Tirgu. It bounced off the top of his chest and startled him from his thoughts. He looked down at his Lord once more.

"What are you waiting for? Get yourself a uniform and get out of my sight!" bellowed Spikepoint.

As he watched Tirgu leave the tent his fingers gravitated back to their previous duties and fondled another tomato, which soon experienced its doom.

Tirgu closed the flap of the tent behind himself in something of a huff, quite understandably. What was he to do now? The camp would soon mobilise for battle and he was obliged to put himself at the front of it. Something he had always anticipated being able to avoid. He was not afraid of battle particularly. He just thought it a waste of his talents. He returned to where he'd made an impromptu camp with his band and found them sitting on the ground around the tent having breakfast. The injured man was nowhere to be found and was obviously keeping out of the way, either for treatment or to avoid Tirgu's wrath, both being good for his health. The other human man and Gurgle did their best to greet him.

"What did he say Tirgu?" asked the human man.

"We're done," replied Tirgu, as he sat down with a flump.

"Done? What'd you mean?" replied the man.

"Paul's told him everything."

"When'd he do that?"

"Last night, or this morning. He was kept waiting for a surgeon and he thought it was a trick to get him to say the truth."

"No! Damn him!"

"Yes. We're in the army now. I'm not your boss anymore. Go find a unit to fight with."

"But Tirgu...what about you?"

"I have to find a unit too, preferably one right at the front."

"What about me?" asked Gurgle suddenly, and both turned to look at him, eating a carrot. "Am I free?"

Both laughed well at the idea.

"No," said Tirgu, "I'm afraid not."

"Why not? You could let me go. I can't fight."

"I know. Spike's going to look after you for me."

"But why don't you let me go?"

"You think I'm gunna let those goblin fools have a total triumph over us? I went to a lot of trouble to get you. I'm not letting you go, so forget about it!"

Gurgle had suddenly had enough and summoned his anger, which was not particularly difficult considering all that he had been through. He lunged at Tirgu and bit him painfully but not deeply on his nearest arm. Tirgu did not respond well and threw him off and away.

"Aaaghh! What the hell are you doing you little sod!?" he shouted.

Gurgle was not the only one who could lose his cool.

"Let me go!" shouted Gurgle in response and many of the

443

men thereabouts had their attention drawn.

"Let you go? Let you go? Off the top of a cliff maybe or into a raging river I'll let you go. You think I'm gunna let you go after everything else has been taken away. You'll never get back to the forest to see your little goblin friends, never! You belong to me, I own you, understand? Do as I tell you."

"Never! I never will!" shouted Gurgle in defiance.

Tirgu was not pleased. He grabbed Gurgle by his shirt and began to drag him through the camp. The human man watched but didn't intervene. He began to pack up their tent, which still contained the little goblin's possessions. He had to find somewhere else to be.

Gurgle shouted and screamed and was not learning his lesson if he was being taught one. Tirgu had one destination in mind and despite the noise and painfulness of the journey they were soon close to Spikepoint's main tent. As they neared the flap Gurgle was picked up off the ground and carried inside. Their Lord was dressing more seriously for the day ahead. He looked up as the flap swung open suddenly and saw Tirgu flinging his little goblin inside and was clearly angry about it. Spikepoint could only laugh at the spectacle at first but took a much more serious view of it once he had listened to what Tirgu had to say.

"Have the little bastard," he shouted, "I'm off!"

He then stormed out as quickly as he had stormed in. Spikepoint nodded to one of his guards who went after him and most forcefully brought him back inside. He was put on the floor in much the same way as Gurgle had been. Now the two of them were lying on the carpet and Spikepoint moved closer to have a very important word.

"I see you're under some pressure Tirgu," he said softly, whilst kneeling, "so I'll make the choice a simple one. Either you calm yourself down, get into a uniform and report for duty, or I'll tell my guard over there to take you around to the back of the tent...and cut off your head."

Spikepoint gave him a few moments to absorb the proposal.

"What's it to be my hobgoblin friend?"

CHAPTER 13

Sam, John and Joseph sat with each other inside a largish tent, which was one of many belonging to Haine's battalion. They had heard a little commotion from somewhere nearby in the camp but had been unable to see what was going on. On such a day as this they expected some people to go a little crazy.

They had each been accepted as fully fledged members of Low Rise garrison after a somewhat accelerated training program, in view of their Lord's urgent need for fighting men. Before they had had time to enjoy their new standing they had been swept along to this place. Now they were in the field so to speak and there was no more talk of training. Their visit to Spikepoint's castle had been mercifully brief considering the bad food and poor living conditions they had enjoyed there, not that things here were much better. At least they had good weather.

They were much stronger now, both in their muscles and resolve. This was due to their daily diet of meat and exertion. Their former frailties had been diminished and there was little to tell between them in terms of fighting skill and strength. They had only a basic idea of what was to happen. Rumours flew about the camp as easily and as frequently as the flies. It seemed they were on the offensive against King Hasdow. As younger men they had not been exposed to anything from his Kingdom and had been interested only in local matters. This King was known to them by name but nothing else.

They were sat around with a number of others enjoying, if that was an appropriate word, some kind of stew that had been hastily prepared that morning. John peered into his bowl after it was suddenly refilled by a man in an apron. There were ingredients in it, he had to admit, but what they had once been was difficult to guess. The whole dish seemed to be covered in a film of grey grease that stubbornly refused to be shifted allowing John to access what was below. He tipped the dish slightly when the man had gone away and the grease was fooled into leaving. They had become used to this sort of food in their time away and whatever squeamishness they'd once had was mostly gone, for hunger always seems to win that battle in the end.

Joseph was the first to finish his food, partly from appetite and from a desire to probe the others for the latest information.

"Anyone know what's happening?" he asked to all the others present.

"I heard we're to march again today," began one of the others that Joseph did not know. "Might fight today too."

"Where'd you hear that?" asked John of this man.

"Overhead some others talking, from another battalion," replied the man.

"When?" asked John, whilst slurping stew into his mouth.

"Last night."

"We'll find out soon enough," said Sam. "When they need us to fight they'll tell us pretty clearly."

Many nodded at this sensible observation and the conversation floundered. They finished their food and dressed themselves properly. After a while a clang went off. This signalled that Spikepoint desired their immediate attendance outside their tents. They gathered as instructed and stood side by side in the open air. They were to be marshalled and brought together. Lower ranked officers ran about and organised the men they were responsible for, being very vocal, as some in their care were negligent of their duties. Their own officer paced up and down in front of them making sure their tunics were worn right and their weapons were in the proper place. He'd drilled them thoroughly and they knew what he expected of them. Only a few minor adjustments were needed.

"I hope you feel strong today boys," he began. "Big day ahead."

"What's happening?" asked Joseph, rather impertinently.

"You'll find out shortly, don't worry."

He looked around for guidance, once satisfied as to the condition of his men. The tents were all empty now and the full scale of the numbers of men in the camp was clear, if you were tall enough to see. A smaller army of non-combatants then got to work in folding down and packing away the tents. The centre of the camp was cleared first so as to make a large space. Once this was done all the soldiers were summoned to assemble there. Spikepoint's army was now arranged for his inspection. He slowly walked from his tent and found neat phalanx after neat phalanx on show. He smiled under his golden helmet. He was quite a sight, for not only was his helmet golden but a good portion of the rest of his armour shone with a similar brilliance. Many a man in front of him had cause to dislike him thoroughly for the impact he had had on their lives. Despite this, the sight of him brought home how serious an endeavour this was and all personal feelings were squashed under the weight of his purpose.

He moved forward with various attendants in his trail. Sam, John and Joseph were not too far from the front and had a good view of him, their first. He removed his helmet carefully and gave it to a curious little green creature to hold, who looked up at him nervously.

Spikepoint appeared to be a little over forty years of age and had considerable greying of his hair above his ears. His hair, where not grey, was generally light brown and he had brown coloured eyes to match. His shoulders were broad and his natural strength and fitness was plain to see, something not disguised by his armour. If they were to fight for this man it was good that at least he looked the part. He took the time to have a long look around, for this sight would not come again. He expected many of these men to be lost in the coming days, and he would not see them like this again. This eventuality would not form part of his speech, which began once he was satisfied at the scene.

"My men," he began softly but not without volume in the clear air, "look around you at this great sight!"

He encouraged them with his arms and they began to look around at each other, though their view was not as good as his. He continued once their eyes drifted back to him.

"Never have I seen such a force of men! What a sight you are! Together, we can conquer the world! Nothing is ever achieved except by force of arms and our enemy trembles at our power! Today is a fine day! A momentous day! For today we sweep away the old, stagnant order and put in its place something far stronger, far better. Today, the purpose of our lives is fulfilled! Great rewards are open to you now. Fine land...fine food...fine women! All for the taking. Today we become masters of the known world...and we will *all* become Kings!"

He paused a moment to allow his words to sink in and a cheer arose. He spoke again but used more of his body for emphasis.

"But," he continued, "there is someone in our way...an old man in charge of an old dynasty with old ideas. He lives off others, who themselves live off others, like ravenous insects! There is no dynamism, no decency, just decadence and laziness. They are creatures living off the labours of others! Today we wipe them away. Gone! As though they never existed! Our blood and sweat will *wash* them away...and in their place we will reign. We will decide our destinies once more."

He took a few more moments and allowed silence to do its work. He walked from side to side and showed on his face his admiration for those stood in front of him. He took a knife both long and sharp from the scabbard close to his chest and held it aloft.

"This is how we bring change! With this we make our

future! Do the same!" he shouted.

The whole army did so and the air was pricked with about five thousand, nine hundred and ninety nine cuts as Tirgu, now deep in this body of men, decided to keep his arms folded.

"Repeat after me! With this I make my future!" shouted Spikepoint, shaking his knife above his head.

"With this I make my future!" roared the crowd, doing similar with their own weapons.

"With this I make the world!" he shouted again.

"With this I make the world!" they roared again.

"No one can defeat us!" he shouted.

"No one can defeat us!" they shouted back.

"No one can even touch us!" he shouted.

"No one can even touch us!" they shouted.

"Good!" he shouted, though not so loud as before.

Many in the crowd still energised from this display repeated the word back to him and he laughed, lowering his knife. He took a few more moments to let things calm down a little, and to allow more time to think of something else to say, something good with which to finish. He looked out at them again and sniffed at the air. In the background he could see the camp staff quickly putting away the tents as he was speaking. Soon they would be underway he thought.

"Soon we shall be on our way...and your prize is just seven short miles away. When we get there we will see the enemy and he will see you! He will tremble! He will think himself a fool to be stood against us. We know...he is right!

His way of life is over...and *ours*...ours is about to begin! Do not let me down!"

With a flourish he turned and went back inside his tent and his retinue followed him, including the curious little green creature that carried his helmet. A great prolonged cheer followed them. Once they were all hidden the various officers gave their orders and the men were put into the proper battalion formations. For Sam, John and Joseph the immediate question about their fate had been answered. With a deep sinking feeling, that almost encouraged another look at their stew, they realised that today might be their last day alive. In truth this thought had occurred to them before today but after that speech it was now an expectation. Perhaps all that time ago they should not have been at home when those men on horses had come for them.

Tirgu had listened to the speech and found it no great surprise. Spike's tone had been pure theatre. None of his words made any sense under close analysis. He saw things very differently and he knew Spikepoint did also. It was not a surprise to him that his Lord was a hypocrite. He just wished that such hypocrisy might not have been directed towards him. It was his own fault though, for not succeeding in Brown Root.

There were few positives for Tirgu now. He was alone, despite being surrounded by thousands. He commanded no one. He was dressed in the tunic of an ordinary soldier. He, who had once the ear of the man in charge and been one of his key agents, was now a sword carrying slob and in with the rabble. If he had ever been tempted to rely on that man's favour before, he could certainly not do so any longer. Even if he was to perform well in battle he had too much pride to ask for his old position. No, their association, though Spike may not have realised it, was at an end. He would go his own way now and make something new for himself. The only problem was how to survive the day and get away.

He had been assigned to some meaningless grouping in Commander Haine's battalion. He knew of the man and had been surprised at his elevation to such a position. As one goes up another descends. He hoped not to be recognised. Sadly, he knew of only about ten other hobgoblins in the entire army so he would stand out wherever he was. With a groan he realised that word of his assault on Brown Root would filter back here soon enough. He would have to watch his back as well as his front. This was all the more reason to get away as soon as possible. He wondered whether the other side might be able to use his services, assuming there was still another side at the end of the day, and that he hadn't done them too much damage to be considered favourably.

As he held his flat sword in his hand he begged that time could be drawn backwards and that he could have the last day over again. Time goes forwards, why then can it not also go backwards. It would not be easy of course, like reversing a fast flowing river, but it was not inconceivable. He had no time to ponder a method, for an officer barked at him and those nearby to get themselves ready. He hadn't had to follow such orders for a while and needed to force himself to comply.

The camp was now little like a camp. Only Spikepoint's tents in the centre remained upstanding. The area was back to what it was when they had arrived yesterday, an ordinary field, though muddy and marked. Six thousand men or thereabouts were stood waiting to move. This number dwarfed anything that either forest could produce as a fighting force. Even in the human sphere this group would most likely break a few historical records.

They began their journey once Spikepoint, back in full battle dress, emerged from his tent and got on his horse. Many others enjoyed the same privilege of travelling and fighting whilst sat on such an animal, though it was not desired by everyone. Once his tent was empty it was quickly collapsed and his staff, thankfully not engaging in battle, took their time in finishing their work and made sure to keep a comfortable distance between themselves and the soldiers from fear of being dragged into a fight.

They were not too far from King Hasdow's castle. Their presence within his territory was neither a surprise nor unseen. Sharp eyed individuals, some within the King's pay and some not, had made the existence of this army known to the King in most forceful terms. Preparations and formations had therefore begun in earnest at the castle and a force of men somewhere between half and two thirds the size of Spikepoint's had been put out.

Within a few hours Spikepoint's army had made up much of the distance between their camp and the castle. They had encountered no resistance along the way, though there had been people around who made it their business to get as far away from them as quickly as they could. As they breached the last ridge Spikepoint saw his objective much as he had last seen it so recently. He also saw the defences laid out for his reception. His eyes did the counting. Both forces were impressive but it seemed Spikepoint had performed better in bringing bodies to the fight. Numerical superiority was his indeed but only if battles are fought by cold calculation alone would this ensure victory. A man may bring a larger sword to a duel than that brought by his opponent but it is in the wielding of it wherein the real power is to be found.

From below the sight of the opposition was unwelcome but accepted. Frederick's forces were fewer but had greater incentive. That would prove to be the true contest of the day, whether numbers could overwhelm the will to survive.

From the ridge the view was pleasing, as the well-kept grounds of the castle stretched into the distance. Grumbleweed would not be in the way of the battle but its inhabitants had not been confident of that and had mostly fled. Those who stubbornly stayed behind in hopes that the rumours were just stuff and nonsense now began to see the error in their thinking. The ridge was not large enough to accommodate all Spikepoint's men and most of them had no idea of the pretty view, if a military man, or the frightening view, if not, that lay below them. Spikepoint sat on his horse at the head of his men. His three battalion chiefs were sitting on their horses nearby and calmly watched the scene with him. Quietly, each of them scanned the ground between here and there for signs of obstacles or traps. In front of the ridge the ground sloped gently down into the low angled basin that held the castle and all its grounds. The defensive force was split into three groups, as was their army. Three square blocks of men, separated by channels about five metres wide, stood tightly packed in the short approaches to the castle. The main route in was therefore blocked by about four thousand men. Small groups of cavalry also trotted about and the men on these horses seemed to be in charge of things.

In front of the King's men, and at regular intervals, barriers had been assembled. From Spikepoint's perspective these looked like piles of branches and plants, freshly cut, and what lay on the far side was impossible to see. From the defender's perspective what lay on their side were deep cut ditches filled with water so as to make progress difficult and dangerous. There were a few gaps in between these structures but attempting to send many soldiers through them would create a bottleneck that could be easily exploited by defending bow men. Spikepoint had many bow men on whom to rely and Haine suspected that for the moment at least they would settle for a battle of arrows. This would only favour them he felt, since they had greater numbers and greater height from which to aim. Spikepoint also noticed this possibility but was wary of doing something that seemed so easy to anticipate. From his high position he could see how the far side of the castle was all but undefended. How he would enjoy transporting his forces there. Everyone knew this could not have happened however as a river and marshland conveniently blocked access. Crags and mountains swelled up on the other side of the castle and all these things forced Spikepoint to consider only a direct approach, a fact of geography made clear to all those that had never visited here before.

Now that Haine was here his confidence in ultimately being on the winning side took a blow. Starling Dodd had made extensive defences, much as he would have done, and there was no easy way through them. So, Spikepoint had to answer the first question of the day. What to do? The defences could not be outflanked. They appeared not easy to destroy or circumvent, at least without suffering casualties in the process. However, it was so often the duty of the side that brought the greater numbers that they should be put to use. This was what Spikepoint would most certainly do and on that Dodd had had no fear of relying.

As soon as Spikepoint's men had appeared on the ridge a bristle of excitement and trepidation ran through the defenders. Shouts and whispers spoke of the same truth that a great shining wall of men had appeared. If they were to survive they would have to knock it down or allow it to fall of its own accord. The word came from Frederick for the men to settle and the word rippled down the hierarchy swiftly and smoothly. These men were ready to defend and were not such fools to be there as Spikepoint had so confidently stated.

Frederick sat on his horse and tried to settle himself as well as his men. Starling Dodd was close by, as were a few other loyal and reliable captains. Each gave patient, sensible advice and did their best to show that everything that had happened had been predicted and that anything that would happen had been anticipated.

"Sire," began Dodd quietly, "he looks at us now and examines what he had not expected to see. Everything unusual makes him wary and there is much to confuse him."

"It won't be enough to put him off his attack," said the new King in reply.

"Indeed, the sooner he attacks the better, as that will show us how little patience and self-control he has."

"But he will attack, and reports put his numbers at nearly twice our own."

"Aye, but those are easily exaggerated. He sees us and if he felt so dominant he would come down and attack. He does not...so he doesn't feel dominant. Our defences make them wary. A battle begins with the eyes first of all, then it is a battle with the stomach to see if one has the nerve to begin. The battle with the arms comes last."

"Perhaps we should..."

"No!" interrupted Dodd quickly. "We do nothing until they do something. What we do depends on what they do. They are the aggressors and must make the first move. Then we make the right move in response."

The King did not appreciate such condescension but kept silent and absorbed the sense Dodd had made, however impertinently.

On the ridge Spikepoint remained silent and was happy to appear unmoved. His men had been ordered to spread out as much as they could on the ridge so as to steadily reveal their full strength and to give them all an idea of what was ahead. This was a display, like two frothing boars weighing each other's size and the likelihood of success in combat. Neither felt an overwhelming advantage.

Frederick looked behind himself and waved at a drummer. This was a prearranged signal to get some music in the air. This one drummer began a steady beat; one hefty hit of his drum every few seconds. This sound shook the still air and added a new dimension to events. All heard it and whatever conversation there had been before stopped at once. This seemed instinctively to be a presage for battle and many a man drew his weapon, expecting to be ordered forward. Another drummer came in at the right moment and the volume increased by the proper proportion. Soon others followed and a frightening pulse swept over the field. Thousands of hearts, many of whom were beating their last few thousand beats, had their rhythms attuned to it and the mechanisms of their bodies made ready.

The beat picked up and those on the ridge saw not just with their eyes but felt with their hearts and their entire bodies the physical reality of what was ahead. Spikepoint smiled at the sound and regarded it as a pleasing gesture. He bellowed from his horse and most in his army heard him, whether in front or behind.

"See how they welcome us with music!"

He looked around at his men and knew that now was his moment. He would not let the opportunity pass him by.

"Shall we offer them a gift in return? Arrows if you please!"

He signalled to his chiefs and they understood the wave. Bow men stepped from between the other soldiers and each found a spot at the front of the ridge. They would have to fly their arrows for about four hundred metres to clear the barriers and hit the enemy. From down in the basin the defenders saw this movement and knew what it meant. The hillside reacted like a startled porcupine as bows were drawn and arrows aimed.

The men below reacted instantly and readied their shields. Frederick and his staff, stood on horses between the men and the main gates, calmly retreated to a readymade shelter that would provide cover from such a weapon. Once safely ensconced, Dodd whispered something to his King.

"He is impatient and makes his first mistake."

Frederick smiled but was not entirely convinced. The men above were ready now and Spikepoint raised his hand. Muscles strained, eyes peered and sweat dripped from nearly one thousand bow men. He let his hand drop and with it any pretence that the day might end peacefully. A great streaky gob of wood was fired into the air, humiliating the corpses of trees by using them to bring more death.

The defenders shrunk their size, breathed in and swung their shields above themselves thus forming a further barrier to Spikepoint's ambition. They held their breath, expecting a thunk or two within moments. Their lungs had to wait and veins swelled in their heads. Then it came. First a thud here and there, then a rain. The men made sounds, but more from excitement at the ridiculousness of it than from injury. Soon enough though, genuine cries of pain could be distinguished from the boyish pleasure. From the ridge a successful hit was revealed each time a hole in the greater shield appeared. It was now pockmarked and there was no doubt that men were now dead.

Dodd and Frederick looked at the scene. In the roof of the shelter arrow heads poked through. Without the grass and straw woven in they would have continued on their deadly course.

Back on the ridge Spikepoint was relieved to get things underway. He ordered another volley and it was soon set free. A few more holes appeared but many fewer than before and he realised that this alone could not win the day for him. Each of his bow men had about twenty arrows so he had at most twenty volleys at his disposal. He allowed a few more from this precious resource and made the great shield in front of him ripple. It held and as the volleys became noticeably less successful they were stopped. The drum beats, which had naturally stopped on account of the arrows picked up again, and this time a roar of derision came with them, rolling up the hill to their foe.

461

"His arrows cannot win the battle for him," said Dodd calmly in Frederick's ear. "Soon he will come after us."

"You think he will come shortly?" said the King.

"Oh yes, he must. Pride expects it. When he gives in, as he certainly will, we'll use our arrows."

"He might even think better of the day and wait till tomorrow?"

"That's not him. I know his nature. He thinks he's in charge of events, but he's not even in charge of himself."

Back on the ridge Spikepoint withdrew his bow men and they took steps backward, revealing the sword wielding men behind them. Tirgu was ready and waiting within this mass of flesh. He was strangely unaffected by the imminent prospect of going into battle and felt no fear. Because fate had done him such a series of injuries it would be profoundly unlikely to work against him for a third time. He was in such a state of mind that the whole event was like a playground for him and he could act in it entirely as he wished, without risk to himself. Sam, John and Joseph were themselves in this mass and though they held their swords and adopted the stance they were far from ready for their first bitter taste of battle. They had each promised the other two that they would stick close by and protect each other. Quite how practical that would be was another matter, and if events were to overwhelm them they had also agreed there would be no dishonour if a rescue proved impossible.

As the thousands of men looked at each other and the likely conflagration soon to come their thoughts drifted back to home and life elsewhere. The faces of loved ones flashed over many a mind and a cherished experience came soon after. Quiet whispers of affection left trembling lips to those far away, and many a prayer for good fortune travelled on the gentle wind. God had been unkind enough to bring them all here and bind their fates together. The least he could do was to give each a sporting chance. Soon though, such warm feelings were replaced. They had to be, since the battlefield was a merciless place and one had to be merciless to survive in it.

Spikepoint's men heard an order. Those that had not already done so unsheathed their swords. Not everyone preferred the sword and some carried axes or clubs as suited them. Many a man put away his bow and withdrew a sword. The drum beats rolled on and it seemed to Spikepoint's men that as they came closer to moving the pace increased. As they stood on the ridge, a knot of sickness formed in their stomachs. Now it was happening and many a man turned his face away in anticipation of the terrible slide into danger. As much as their bodies could prepare them for the task they did so. Muscles became hot and feelings became hidden.

Haine, still sat on his horse, was directed to the head of his men. His orders had been simple. They would descend the hill and keep up a steady pace and they would have to get through, around or over the defences as best they could. There would be no point sending just one battalion at a time. The psychological effect of his entire army's simultaneous descent was what Spikepoint required. The three battalions would go together but his own reserve of around one thousand men and guards would stay on the ridge for the moment. They would stand still and give the impression that the same number of men could be sent a second time.

Haine and the other chiefs, named Anvers and Hugo, now stood at the front of each of their battalions. The men behind them did their best to stay in formation and give each other room to move. Many at the back had still not had the chance to glimpse what was happening below them. The staff and non-fighting men kept a clear distance from those ahead and their work was done for the moment. Medical staff had much work to do however and temporary places to treat wounded men were being prepared nearby.

Spikepoint was feeling excited but nervous. He was keen to ensure that nothing went wrong. He knew Hasdow would make defences and that he would be forced to contend with them. That was why he had made such a point of getting as many men as possible for the attack. No plan or prediction, however elaborate and well worked out, could exactly prepare a person for the reality. Something is always different and seemingly designed to confuse.

"All is well," whispered Spikepoint to himself. "See us on our way."

He raised his hand and all his chiefs saw the move. When it falls the battle will begin. He exhaled calmly and let it drop.

"Forward!" bellowed each of the battalion chiefs.

They prodded their horses and their snouts marked the very front of the formation. Down they went into the basin, slowly, trying not to bunch up. From below the signs of movement were picked up almost immediately.

Dodd and his fellow captains knew that they had to return to the head of their men. Frederick remained under cover and intended to spend most of his time there but he followed Dodd's advice, given more as a strong suggestion, that he should raise arrows at their descent. His more modest force of bow men made themselves ready. He and his horse moved into the open and he was now within shouting range of his men.

As the enemy made its slow way down the hill towards them the old King and Gavelrigg watched nervously through an open window in the castle. Gavelrigg made observations when it suited him but his companion was mostly silent. On occasion the old King mumbled something that seemed to be related to what was happening but his overall manner was nothing like it ought to have been when witness to such a scene. A number of ladies, attendants and servants were also in the room and each did their best to catch a glimpse, except when the stress of it became too much. Princess Ursula had secured herself a prominent spot and spent much of her time examining the new King's performance. Even though they had barely been introduced she felt it her duty to keep a watchful eye on the man she fully expected to make her husband. She seemed to have a confidence in victory that was so unshakeable that only ignorance could be the cause of it. More than once she had spoken rather rudely to those in the room that had predicted a sad end to the day. The new King gave the order when he felt that the enemy was in the right place. They had reached the first obstruction and were quickly squeezing through the gap and clambering over it. A few found themselves in the water on the far side, much to their chagrin, but it was nothing to worry about.

"Release!" shouted Frederick, and Dodd watched on approvingly.

A nameless man climbing from a wet pit raised his head above the level of the ground and tried to free himself. He saw the wooden welcome heading rapidly towards them and he let his grip slacken and he fell back into the water. His companion, also wet and nameless, had not seen this and poked his head above the level of the ground. He too let his grip slacken and he fell back into the water, but he had an arrow through his throat. His blood pumped free and his friend held him in that dark pit while he expired and nothingness called him back.

Haine was quickly getting angry. The progress through the barriers was slow and not enough of his men had the sense to keep their shields up. Anvers and Hugo were not making any more progress with their battalions than he was. Spikepoint looked on and was not surprised by the difficulties or the casualties. He was more patient than the men in harm's way. A few arrows hit into the hillside and his personal guard advised stepping back from danger. He was not going to do so and they were told not to suggest any such thing again.

Haine knew a charge was not practical with such obstructions in the way and he predicted that they would have to hold their position and take cover. He prayed that there were few forests nearby to supply the King with wood for arrows. He instructed his officers to keep their men in tight groups with their shields up and to crawl forward if necessary. Moments later another volley came in and with a guttural groan his horse reared up and threw him to the ground. He fell with a hard thud and saw his horse do the same. It had an arrow through one of its front legs and it stumbled painfully before dropping and writhing on the ground. He kept clear of it and raised his shield above his head, simultaneously moving forward to take cover behind the next green and brown barrier.

"Damn it!" he yelled. "Come on, come forward you men!"

Those through the first barrier, some wet some not, made their way towards cover at the next barrier. Soon, hundreds of men spread themselves out on either side of their chief. The arrows kept coming in with a surprising regularity. Haine looked behind himself and counted at least fifty men lying dead or injured. One of his hobgoblin fighters also appeared to be dead. He turned back and looked closely at the barrier in front of him. It was supported by a wooden lattice. He suddenly thought it possible to tip it over into the water beyond. That might prove to be the best way to make progress. He had the strength of arms available but would wait for the arrows to run out, if at all possible. As he pondered this, a man a metre or so behind him, who had been trying to huddle up to the group as best he could, cried out as an arrow struck him deeply in the thigh. This was not the spot to remain thought Haine.

"Listen to me," he shouted along the line of men at the base of this barrier, "we can tip this into the water beyond. We just have to push it and then clamber over and then run to the next one. Understand?"

Shouts both clear and muffled came back positive.

"Right, let's try!" he shouted.

Many men crawled upwards and found a convenient log against which to put their energy. Others came behind them and were ready to push those men themselves in order to give them extra power.

"Now!" yelled their chief.

Grunts and creaking sounds overtook the sounds of pain and distress. The weight and force of several hundred men is a surprisingly strong resource and the wooden poles that held the whole structure in place were buckling. Like a great tree cracking and splitting and collapsing the barrier turned and fell into the pit of water beyond. The men quickly stood and jumped over the pit as it was still sensible to avoid the tangle of water and wood that now lay in it.

Dodd was observing and was surprised by the success of this tactic. Those up in the castle moaned at the sight of such force and the feeling that their enemy was now that little bit closer. They feared mistreatment at their hands should the brave defenders not hold their ground and protect them.

The three battalions, with Haine leading the way, were making progress after some difficult minutes striving for cover. Spikepoint was most pleased at the innovation shown by his youngest chief. It was vindication of his faith in him and gave him added confidence in his own judgement at such a crucial time. If they could maintain that pace and get through all the obstructions raised against them then he would be delighted to add his remaining forces to be struggle, including himself, and give the crushing blow he was so eager to wield.

The arrows were coming less frequently now. Haine hoped it was because they were running low but it could just as easily have been because of their increasing skill at finding cover and the frustration this caused. They had pushed over one wooden barrier but the next was proving to be more steadfast. There were tempting gaps and he instructed his men (or rather he ran towards the gaps and they followed) to move through and take cover at the next barrier about thirty feet beyond. It was slow but they managed it with few casualties. Soon hundreds more men bunched up under the next barrier but a smell was apparent to them. They looked through the brush and saw not muddy water on the far side but a black and shiny liquid. It coated the branches and bracken and thanks to their enthusiastic approach many of their tunics also. It did not take long for them to recognise the difference and the meaning of it, particularly when arrows with their tips flaming came crackling through the air.

"Back! Back! Go back!" screamed Haine.

The barrier, which Haine and most of his men were rapidly running away from, burst into flame. The slower men also caught light and a few unfortunate souls became trapped at the base of it by other burning men blocking their path. They came running and stumbling back and were either thrown in the water or made their own way. This was a painful and humiliating trick and many men were now out of action, or at least preferred themselves to be.

Haine was not pleased and looked further down the line at the other battalions and their progress. In the middle, where Anvers' battalion had aimed, it was obvious that they were ahead. They had as many wounded and dead men in their trail as Haine but had no fire ahead of them. For some reason it had not caught or perhaps they had not enough oil for the whole length. Flaming arrows at the site suggested the latter explanation. Haine saw the opportunity and tried to spot his officers so as to redirect them. The wall of flame ahead gave them little choice as to the proper direction in which to go, so they would have to risk following the others.

Sam and John were on the ground and looking up at their commander. They had thought it best to follow the leader and so far, despite a little water and radiant heat, had not been affected much by the dangers of the day. Joseph had become separated and they did not know where he was.

They were frustrated and frightened and wished someone would lead them out of this unpleasant spot. Haine looked about himself and saw that general chaos was about to break. He shouted to as many as could hear him to move forward and follow him but with hundreds of men around, many screaming and shouting, it was nearly impossible to get their attention. Arrows still came down and every second of delay seemed to take another sword with it.

A weird screech filled his ears and he turned to see a hobgoblin racing up the line waving his arms and beckoning everyone to follow him. He had to take a second look, not only to believe that such a thing was happening but also to recognise an old acquaintance that he did not expect to see here. It was Tirgu, and somehow, even though they had not encountered the enemy, he had blood on his sword. Where it had come from was a question he had not time to ask, as Tirgu had a swathe of men already following him and he was whooping and jumping at the excitement of it. Haine saw that this was the movement he needed his battalion to make and he shouted at those near him to join in. So, the next barrier was passed by a fury of men. Where the gap narrowed and they bunched up the excitement was such that the edges of barriers were pushed and broken to make way, whether flaming or not.

Haine's battalion was now organised and moving in a purposeful way straight towards the enemy and Spikepoint shouted with glee at the sight. He noticed

Tirgu amongst the rabble and was pleased at his transformation. The other battalions were slower in reacting but soon they saw the way in which the momentum was flowing and they were pulled along with it.

Both Frederick and his horse sensed the danger and stepped back. Dodd was disappointed that they had not been able to keep them detained in the maze a little longer. He withdrew his sword and ordered every man in earshot to do the same. All the defenders were primed and ready. They were a little cramped however and not all of them could join the fight unless those at the front either died or made way.

The two armies were now less than a hundred metres apart and there was no further barrier between them. Fortunately, for Spikepoint's army at least, the enthusiasm of the charge subsided once they had gotten a clear look at the massed ranks between them and the castle gates. This allowed more men to filter through and strengthen those brave pioneers up front.

Haine ran through the gap in the last barrier and met many of his men forming a wall in front of him. Out of the corner of his eye he saw Anvers on his horse and ran towards him.

"Have you brought everyone up!?" shouted Haine.

"Aye! They're here or close by, but Hugo's men are still behind," replied Anvers.

Both men turned to look at the enemy. Haine saw that most were bent on their knees and then noticed why. Bow men were aiming straight at them and a volley came horizontally through the air.

"Shields up!" both men seemed to shout at once.

But, many men did not have their shields with them. Such things were not easy to carry through the chaos. Those that had them put them up and those that didn't fell to the ground. Some were not swift enough and fell by force.

"A battery! I want a battery! Shields together!" shouted Anvers.

The men of both battalions did their best to mix together and follow this instruction. Soon little clumps of men crouched with their fellows and held their shields in front of them.

"Forward!" shouted Anvers above the tumult.

Slowly these bodies crawled forward and a further volley of arrows thudded home, but this time with less success. The excitement was getting too much for many of those observing above and most of the ladies couldn't bear to watch any further. The dread of a bad outcome and fear for their loved ones below was clearly too much. At the window Gavelrigg and Princess Ursula were both transfixed and quiet.

Tirgu was getting impatient. He was not part of one of these advancing formations but knew not to run ahead of them. He stood with his sword at his side. If he had wanted time to go backwards he was some of the way there, since time seemed to be slow and crawling, like these sweaty humans moaning and groaning in front of him. His gaze was fixed ahead and he spied a small group of bow men who were clearly aiming in his direction. He saw their arrows set loose one by one and tracked their gentle path. He felt everything and was without fear. They loomed in his vision but he knew where they would go and where he was in relation. A man stood in front of him was in the path of one of them. He grabbed at this man's collar and pulled him to one side, just as the arrow darted past. The man broke free from his grasp and swore at Tirgu for distracting him. He did not understand how close to death he had come. Tirgu did not care in the least at his ingratitude and felt no reason to explain. He laughed instead and put his sword point dangerously close to his own eye as if to say that he should consider its use.

Sam and John were struggling together in one of the creeping groups and held their shields up. Their progress was painful and they considered that at any moment their lives might be taken. In their minds each new breath and moment of awareness was remarked at and treasured. They wondered how close they were to the enemy as it was too risky to stand up for a glimpse. Behind them they could see those without shields and those just arriving through the last barrier. It was a welcome sight to see so many on their side chasing up behind them.

Spikepoint could see that they were about to touch and he regarded this as his moment to commit the remainder of his forces. They would make the difference in the hand to hand battle.

"Let's lend a hand shall we?" he shouted.

They all understood and once he kicked his horse in the

ribs they followed in his wake. They moved swiftly down the hill with Spikepoint at the head of the chevron. As the slope flattened and he reached the first barrier he pulled out his axe and held it in his right hand. The other was occupied with keeping a tight hold on the reigns. He held his back upright and his head high. Dodd could not help but notice this golden warrior heading their way. He had waited patiently for this. It was just a shame it was coming right at the moment when their forces were about to clash. He gave the order anyway and his most skilful group of bow men stood and aimed specifically at this figure. They let loose half a dozen well aimed arrows. Only one managed to hit him but it bounced harmlessly from his armour. Dodd ordered another attempt. This time his horse was hit in the rump, stumbled a little, but was able to continue. At the front line the tension was unbearable and the shield wall was about to break open and a charge begin.

The battalion chiefs were not far behind and Haine saw his Lord coming towards them.

"Here he comes! Spikepoint! Get up and fight!" yelled Haine.

This was the moment that all had anticipated. Everyone could see what was about to happen and all were powerless to stop it. The shields were withdrawn and the men stood up. A growl shook the field as they stretched their backs and swung their arms, feeling tall once again. The defenders, also wishing to release their stores of tension, stood as well and within moments a great black hole of anger swallowed every man.

This soft patch of ground that had previously been the scene of so many comings and goings, markets, assemblies and so forth now had its soil defiled forever. Above, in the room, people wept openly at the horror and dreadfulness of it. The old King was not one of them as he had retired for some sleep. Gavelrigg looked down at the golden figure approaching his men and regretted not having the nerve and conviction to arrest him when he had him in his power. He'd known what was coming, they all had. Every man that died down there was now a stain on his conscience.

Sam and John charged into battle, as it had long been intended that they should. They met their nameless opponents and swung, stabbed and slashed at them, simultaneously trying to kill but not be killed. They soon learned what it took. They had been trained well. The defenders did not accept the charge well and came close to crumbling under the weight of it at first. Dodd and the other captains added their weight and held up against them. Frederick was becoming alarmed and felt he had little to say or to do. He hated himself for glancing to each side in hope of spying an escape route. His close Lieutenants looked to him for a response. They did not expect their forces to be commanded by anyone else. They could see the fear and helplessness in his expression.

"Your majesty! Our orders?" said one his Lieutenants and also a close friend.

"What can we do except defend?" he replied distractedly.

"Yes, but shouldn't we help?"

"How?" he shouted, angry at the repeated questioning.

There were no more arrows now. To have sent any away meant he would have been as likely to hit his own as any other. In the centre of the fighting the violence created great heat and energy, which in itself proved too much for those incapable of coping with its fury. Many wilted and collapsed under it. Tirgu was certainly not one of them. He was not a young hobgoblin but he was one of the few fighters there who had experienced this kind of intensity before. He also had a special feeling about the day and felt he was untouchable. He made his mark on them.

Sam and John each had more than one life under their belts and were simply glad to have avoided being added to anyone else's tally. They were soon exhausted and withdrew slightly from the very fiercest front line, keeping an eye out for each other. They were both knocked to the ground as a huge horse and rider came heedlessly through. It was Spikepoint, eager to get the taste of blood in his mouth. He held his axe low, ready to swing at any of the King's men foolish enough to challenge him or any that were loose from their fellows.

His men were making an impact and sweeping the old order away as he had told them to do. But there was a problem - the stubbornness of good fighting men unable to realise it. He eyed Starling Dodd, a young captain he admired and had tried to lure over to his cause but without success. Haine did not realise it, would never be told of it by Spikepoint and most likely would never believe it, but

Dodd had been first to be offered the command of his battalion. This happened in secret of course but the refusal was enthusiastic. Dodd was looking back at Spikepoint and longed to challenge him one to one. It would have been unwise to leave his men and risk himself though.

This forest of angry and broken men pulsed back and forth. From their protected promontory Gavelrigg and the ladies were starting to allow feelings of hope to swell in their hearts as it seemed their brave men were holding back the enemy. But, all three of Spikepoint's battalions were now engaged in the fight and it was truly just a matter of time before their greater number made the difference. He pulled his horse left and right behind the warring mass and either couldn't find a way to get directly involved in the fight or felt content just to let them know he was there.

The ground between them was now clogged with wounded, dying and dead men. Spikepoint directed some of his men not immediately at the front to pull some of them back and out of the way. The pits behind the last barrier were soon being filled with bodies, not all of them unaware of their situation. Sam and John were quietly happy to have withdrawn a little from the fighting and assisted in satisfying Spikepoint's request. They worked together and spent many minutes in this relatively safe duty with John typically under the arms and Sam holding the feet. This was actually less tiring than fighting.

Dodd realised that if this struggle of attrition continued they would lose. He had to turn the tide somehow or dampen their resolve. Frederick seemed impotent as he had anticipated, but this was a pretty brutal test for him so did not feel too surprised. It was time for him to get directly involved and see if he could be the spark that would ignite the whole army. He drifted from behind his reserves of men. He slapped a few trusted companions on the back and encouraged them to join him. Then they moved closer to the matter at hand. He withdrew his sword from its sheath and held it in his right hand. He then withdrew a dagger and held it in his other. He was hard to distinguish from the other defenders since he wore no marks of distinction. This would help him he thought, though many senior men on the other side would know him by his face. He wore a simple white tunic with a light chainmail over it. He wore no helmet but the yellow hair stuck to his head by sweat and dirt could serve as one.

Tirgu saw this man approach. He seemed to have his finger on the pulse of the battle and his eye picked out everything that was significant. Tirgu was not far from his Lord and looked up at him, still astride his huge horse. His personal guard of half a dozen unusually large men did their best to stay near to him despite his manoeuvres. They did not take their eyes off him. One had efficiently removed the arrow head that had been troubling his horse. Dodd now engaged the enemy with his small force of four men. He picked a vulnerable spot and attacked another group of four men but they seemed tired and distracted by their efforts and were quickly put down by Dodd and the others. A small gap appeared in the line and many other defenders that had not yet had the chance to fight noticed it. It was exploited and others began to follow him through. Soon the King's men were in amongst them, and it quickly led to uncertain feelings about who was an ally, who was not and where the front line really was. Each new moment diminished the clarity still further.

Tirgu saw this and suddenly felt the need not to fight anymore, preferring to stay where he was, as he anticipated that something interesting was about to happen. From nowhere, an arrow, perhaps shot by one of the more skilled bow men, hit one of Spikepoint's huge guards squarely in the chest, as he had been standing still for too long. He grunted and then fell forward, crushing against the ground the remains of the arrow that protruded from his chest. His companions naturally flocked to help him, momentarily leaving their Lord slightly less secure.

Tirgu smiled and looked about himself. A man lay at his feet. His arms were splayed out and his sword had fallen from his grasp. He was groaning but Tirgu didn't feel the need to help him. Instead he lifted him slightly from the ground and plucked away the man's bow. Then he took one arrow from his blood stained quiver. With his biggest smile of the day so far he turned and looked for a target for his arrow. There was only one and he couldn't take his eyes off him.

"I'm grateful to you," he whispered, "but I have to be off. What a strange day it's been."

He pulled his right arm back as far as he could and held the arrow's butt between his fingertips. He laughed gently, aiming at the golden point about five metres away, and then released. At that distance and in this frame of mind he was not in danger of missing. The arrow pierced the side of Spikepoint's helmet and poked out the other side. The man stayed on his horse bolt upright for a moment, but then his arm dropped and his axe fell from his grip. This was noticed only by a few at first and they were slow to react. Tirgu let his bow drop to the ground but it was clear who had fired the arrow. Burning eyes suddenly swung in his direction but Tirgu was not so distracted by his strange mood that he delayed. He turned and bolted towards the front line and tried to find a route through. Spikepoint's guard surged en masse after this dreadful traitor, determined to hack him limb from limb and burn what was left, but they were too slow.

Tirgu found a narrow path about a metre wide between two groups of men, each hacking viciously at each other. He darted through and where necessary dived over bodies and rolled under the swing of swords. He had no sword of his own as he had dropped it to pick up the bow. He held up his arms once he was through the worst of it and screamed at the King's men not to harm him.

"Spikepoint's dead!" he yelled, "I killed him! I killed him!" The confusion of this strange creature and the realisation that what he was saying might be true caused those men that he dived upon not to stab him at once.

Above, Gavelrigg and Princess Ursula stared at Spikepoint as they saw something amiss. The man slowly slid from his horse and fell to one side. His horse darted away. Both gripped the stone sill in shock. Spikepoint's guard were so angry and determined to get at Tirgu that they very nearly broke through the line, pushing men out of the way in their fury. But sufficient defenders came in the way and killed one or two of them for their zealousness. Their pursuit of Tirgu had failed and as he sat with a sword to his throat surrounded by the King's men he looked up at them and laughed such a laugh that they could not help but join in.

Once the reality of Spikepoint's death had reached enough minds, the will to fight evaporated and a coordinated flight soon began. The three battalion chiefs sounded the order to retreat but it was not necessary to give it. Anvers and Hugo, both on horseback, made quick progress but Haine, in the thick of the fighting and tired and wounded, was not so quick away. They had a head start though, in that the defenders had a pile of bodies and writhing wounded to overcome first of all.

The attackers were now turned away and facing back up the hill. This sight was enough to bring a cheer of relief from the defenders. Frederick ordered a general charge against them, his first unsolicited order of the day. He would make them all prisoners he hoped. Soon many were indeed captured and threw down their arms. Dodd ran along the lines and told the men to capture their enemy and not kill them. Sadly, his order came too late. Many of Spikepoint's men who had fought bravely found themselves run through.

Sam and John made themselves scarce. They had been

witness to Spikepoint's death but had been too tired and surprised to intervene. They bolted up the hill and managed to find reserves enough to keep ahead of their pursuers. As they charged past the last barrier they spotted poor Joseph, lying dead with one arrow through his chest and another in his stomach. They had no time to stop to grieve over him.

The chief of Spikepoint's staff, who was also his surgeon, saw the commotion coming over the brow of the hill. He knew at once that they were in general retreat and could only presume that Spikepoint was gone. He immediately ordered that everyone hold their positions. They would surrender as a group, respectfully, and he hoped they would not come to any great harm. This included little Gurgle, who was held fast by a couple of servants.

Few of Spikepoint's men not killed or captured remained below the ridge. Frederick led the charge and without much skill or grace managed to sweep a few of them into oblivion. He couldn't believe his luck and Gavelrigg up above couldn't believe it either. Nonetheless the scene below was grisly and they had suffered many casualties, but at least they were victorious. Nothing else mattered.

As the bulk of the fit and ready chased up the hill after Spikepoint's men the remainder started to examine the blood stained piles and did their best to segregate the dead from the living. Dodd and Frederick were now on the ridge. Dodd spied a man that he had known for many years and chased after him, shouting for him to give up and surrender himself and his men. Haine did not respond at first as his running and the sound of his own gasps prevented reception of Dodd's entreaties. In the end screaming muscles forced him to stop for a moment and he turned to hear these words, coming at him a second time. This short experiment as the chief of so many men had not gone well, but that was not his fault and in that moment he forgave himself for his losses and waved his arm at his old friend. Those within earshot he told to stop and surrender, most doing so without complaint. He assured them he knew Dodd and that he would treat them well. This seemed a better alternative to running.

Sam and John had only one clear objective in mind and it was not to surrender. Their youthful limbs kept them ahead of danger and they agreed that they would help each other get home to their families. If possible they would try to find Joseph's family and pass on the sad tidings. Their employ under Spikepoint was now at an end and they hadn't even been paid what little had been due to them. They had each gained considerable experience though and thankfully this held no weight to slow them down.

Within half an hour all those with a mind to surrender or without the energy to flee were under Frederick's control. A great pile of weapons was soon put together. The hands of the enemy were all tied and they were led to one side of the castle. Dodd and Gavelrigg had not been so confident as to prepare for this many prisoners and their fate would have to be considered carefully. They could look forward to a night under the stars and little sustenance to make up for all the energy they had expended whilst the sun had shielded them.

As for Tirgu, he was naturally segregated once it became clear that he was responsible for the turning of the tide and every happy feeling that ensued. He was still under lock and key in the castle but at least he could enjoy a roof over his head and some warm soup in his belly. His special frame of mind was wearing off at this stage and he found himself unable to laugh.

CHAPTER 14

The wonderful sight of the tips of Milton Green's mightiest trees could be spotted on the evening horizon. The Boiled Mice could sense an end to their exciting and perilous mission. Their only prisoner was behaving himself. He was even becoming friendly and cooperative in hopes that it would encourage them to treat him in the same way. His rescue would come when it would come and there was no point antagonising his goblin hosts in the meantime.

Throughout the journey Baintha had been relatively quiet. His formidable brain was pondering the various options open to him and calculating the risks contained in each. He was able to see fairly far and he soon settled quite naturally on the notion of an assisted escape. He had noticed that they were being shadowed along their journey by one or two hobgoblins, not that it was hard to imagine their destination. Nevertheless, Baintha could expect the spontaneous assistance of many hobgoblins, as they knew he would handsomely reward anyone that helped in his rescue.

The Boiled Mice had had a nerve wracking journey and it seemed that the closer they got to Milton Greens the more anxious they were that something would go wrong. The quartermaster had been good at scaring off their pursuers or at least keeping them at bay. Slap and a few other Mice had even crept out during the previous night and killed one over enthusiastic spy that had crept too close. They left his body were it would most certainly be found. This act had been neither sanctioned nor approved by the Lieutenant and he was once more annoyed with Slap's strong headed attitude. Despite this, the Lieutenant knew he owed much of the success of the mission to his fearlessness, local knowledge and quick thinking.

There were no more hobgoblins in sight now and they could only presume that they just wished to confirm that it was indeed Milton Greens to which they were returning. As each foot of ground between them and the trees suddenly became visible their excitement burst out into song.

"We say to you...all goblins, braaaave and truuuue...add us to your retinuuuue. We have done our duty...we have set ourselves free...give to us our bounty! Give to us our bounty! Give to us our bounty!"

The Lieutenant and the quartermaster walked happily whilst listening, and the latter smiled warmly at the former. Their task was done and they had been more successful than they could have hoped.

As they came within throwing distance of the nearest tree many of the Mice broke into a run, which the Lieutenant did nothing to stop. When they reached the edge they began to hug the trees and sing and shout with unbridled pleasure. Even those on stretchers, still weak and infirm, leaned upwards and sang the Mice's praises. When it was his turn even the Lieutenant was not above hugging a tree, though in his case it was quiet, tender and thankful.

They continued on and in, and were soon spotted by those

that lived thereabouts. Everyone was anxious to get home to their loved ones, none more so than those kidnapped. They were lucky, since it was too late to visit the Council and make a report. That would have to wait until the next day. They would have to find somewhere for Baintha to be kept however. Milton Greens has never had a prison. If ever a goblin got out of hand or committed a crime they tended to be punished then and there for it or were expelled from the forest. There were a number of secure buildings though, which could serve as a temporary jail, and first it was to one of these that the Lieutenant decided they needed to go. He could not rightly refuse the obvious request that the kidnapped goblins be reunited with their families as soon as possible. For this task he assigned the quartermaster and some twenty five of his Mice. Once they were all some good distance inside the forest and feeling secure they separated.

The quartermaster and his Mice carried and led the kidnapped goblins to their homes. One by one the quartermaster knocked on nine different doors and was met with moans of disbelief behind each. Every reunion was teary eyed and the Mice added much to the total stock of water.

It was an indescribably satisfying experience for Flap Phosphor. No mission he'd ever been on had avoided casualties or had such a pleasurable conclusion. For him he accepted in his heart that it could never be this good again and he resolved that he would not be a military man anymore. For the moment however he would proudly continue to call himself a Boiled Mouse and serve as needed. He was very conscious of the fact that there was one more door on which he still needed to knock but could not yet do so. Within an hour and a half the full round of reunions had taken place and the quartermaster realised that he hadn't been given any orders as to what to do after that. He knew that the Lieutenant would have headed back to the Hall of Goblins, despite there being no Councillors present at that time, since it had a rarely used cell, occasionally called upon for any petitioners held to be in contempt of the Council. Baintha would be ideally placed in there, as he could answer to the Councillors when they convened the next day. So, the quartermaster and his twenty five Mice went that way.

Word of the Mice's return was now spreading rapidly through the forest and the pathways were buzzing with excitement. The Lieutenant, as soon as he had got Baintha under lock and key, intended to pay a special visit to the Roundtops and explain to them what had happened and why he hadn't been able to rescue little Gurgle like the others. He wanted them to know what had happened before the forest broke out in jubilation, lest they form the impression that they might see their son.

The Lieutenant and the remainder of the Mice made their way to the Hall of Goblins to make a deposit of one hobgoblin. They found a few goblins wandering about but no coordinated activity. It was after the close of the day's business and this was to be expected. An official still manned the out of hours enquiries desk and the Lieutenant approached him.

The goblin sitting behind his desk eyed up this looming bunch of dirty and dishevelled looking goblins and didn't know what to make of it all. The Lieutenant walked up to the desk, pulling the taller and fatter Brakk on a rope behind him.

"Good evening," said the clerk.

"Good evening!" said the Lieutenant, loudly and excitedly. "I have a gift for the Council."

"A gift for the Council? I see. Who are you first of all?" replied the clerk.

"Who am I? I'm Lieutenant Chirp Rideau Tilestain, the leader of the Boiled Mice and these are the Mice," he said, pointing them out and feeling most indignant, "Is there no one senior about to welcome us?"

"Not that I know of I'm afraid. Can you tell me the nature of your enquiry please? This is the enquiries desk you know."

"You see this one here!" said the Lieutenant sharply, whilst tugging on the rope.

The goblin behind the desk nodded.

"This one kidnapped our goblins," said the Lieutenant.

"No I didn't," shouted Baintha, "I just bought them!"

"I'm sorry," said the Lieutenant laughing. "He just bought them."

"Is this true Sir?" asked the goblin behind the desk.

Baintha nodded, seeing no need to keep up any pretence.

"I see," said the goblin behind the desk.

He looked around his desk trying to find something that

might tell him what to do. Nothing leapt out at him

"Well Sir," he continued, "I wish that you had not."

The Mice laughed but to the Lieutenant the scene was quickly descending into farce. Where the hell was their welcome? For a moment he had a dreadful thought that Sigh Stratton and his escort had not gotten back safely. He slapped his hands on the desk and asked that question.

"Don't worry Lieutenant, they came back yesterday. The Council received them and all are well."

"Ah, thank god," said the Lieutenant, who allowed himself a sigh of relief. "Were you not expecting us?"

"I don't know. I am not the person to ask. I think it's best if you come back in the morning and address the Councillors in person."

"Come back tomorrow?"

"Yes Sir, tomorrow morning."

"Come back tomorrow!?" shouted the Lieutenant. "Don't you know what we've been through, the danger we've been in?"

"Well Sir..."

"No! I don't want to hear any more from you," yelled the Lieutenant, as one of his Mice patted him on the arm in an attempt to calm him down. "We've slept in the mud these past two weeks and eaten nothing but worm bricks..."

"And a couple of pies," interrupted Slap.

"Forget the sodding pies!" spat the Lieutenant. "This is serious. I'm sick of the bureaucracy and stupidity of this Council. We sweated our arses off, risked our lives and this is what you give us in return. Where's our welcome damn you?"

"Sir! I must ask you to calm yourself. I don't know if any preparations have been made. That's not my job."

"Not your job eh? There's a surprise. Don't you know anything?"

"Please Sir, if you don't calm down I'll be forced to call the guards."

"What?" said the Lieutenant, his blood beginning to boil over.

"I don't have to listen to abuse from anyone Sir. That's not in my job description. If you can't remain civil I'm entitled to close this desk and ignore your enquiry."

The Lieutenant was speechless and Baintha smiled at this unexpected turn of events.

"I don't believe this," said the Lieutenant after a few moments. He mouthed the words but had difficulty passing enough air to make them audible.

"Can you direct me to the nearest hotel please?" asked Baintha all of a sudden to the goblin behind his desk. "I have money."

At the comprehension of these words there began what can only be described as a fracas.

*

Tirgu was by himself and sleeping. It was quiet in the cold stone room in which he was being kept. There was light from a single candle and its flame drifted slowly back and forth as his clouds of breath made their way across the

492

room.

The latch on the door swung open suddenly and light from elsewhere came flooding in. His candle was extinguished. A well dressed human man came in followed by two large guards. Tirgu opened his eyes but had not the energy to do anything about it had they wished him harm. They brought furniture with them to enable them to sit. They put their chairs in a line of three, all facing Tirgu. He was relaxed and slowly moved upright as they settled themselves.

"Hello," said the well-dressed man, "I understand that your name is Tirgu. Is that right?"

"Yes, that's my name," he replied, half asleep.

"My name is Gavelrigg and I'm one of the King's ministers."

"It's a pleasure," said Tirgu, smiling one of his devilish smiles, but this time with his eyes shut after wincing in pain slightly.

"I want to ask you some questions about today. Is that alright?"

"Fire away."

"What was the nature of your relationship with the late Lord Spikepoint?"

"Oh him?" he said laughing. "I thought the conversation might go in his direction. We go way back."

Gavelrigg smiled and offered Tirgu a glass full of water. He accepted it and drank it at once.

"Here's to you...Spike my man," said Tirgu, raising the nearly empty vessel in salutation. "Wherever you are I'm sure you're up to no good and telling everyone what to do!"

Gavelrigg smiled but wondered if it was the best time for this interview. It seemed like Tirgu was drunk, even though that didn't seem possible.

"You want to know about the nature of our relationship you say. Well then, I'll tell you."

"Yes, I want..." began Gavelrigg.

"I'm speaking!" interrupted Tirgu sharply.

The two guards stood and took him by the arms, holding Tirgu down. Gavelrigg stopped them.

"You're only alive today because of me!" he shouted. "Get your hands off and give me some respect!"

"It's alright. Leave him be, let him up," said Gavelrigg in soothing tones.

There were a few recriminating looks between Tirgu and the guards but the mood was quickly calmed.

"Please continue Tirgu," said Gavelrigg. "I'm curious to listen to you."

"I want another bottle. I'm very thirsty. This castle is so dry. At least we had damp in Spike's castle."

"Go get some more will you?" said Gavelrigg to a guard, who reluctantly complied.

"You don't care a bit, you don't care a bit about me," said Tirgu after a few more moments.

"That's not true. I care about being alive and I think I have you to thank for that."

"It's about time someone did."

"We're all just tired and surprised at the way the day has

turned out."

"Me too."

"Now, as far as I know we've never had any dealings before."

"No."

"So then, what happened today was a spontaneous act."

"Spontaneous?" said Tirgu quietly, considering the reality of the word for a moment. "Aye, I suppose it was. That's a good word for it."

"Tell me more about yourself. How did you get involved with Spikepoint?"

"He hired me."

"Yes, but for what, and how?"

"Curious creature, aren't you?"

"Yes," replied Gavelrigg, laughing. "It's my business to know as much as I can know."

"Yeah? Mine too. You said you're a minister here."

"That's right."

"Well, I was sort of a minister for Spike."

"Really?"

"Oh yes. You don't believe me do you?"

"I'm prepared to believe anything."

"I doubt that."

"Come, tell me. Don't worry," said Gavelrigg, beckoning slowly with his fingers.

"I've known him for over ten years, well, knew him. A friend of a friend introduced us. I needed to be getting away from where I was and he told me this human Lord was offering some good work. I went to see him on my friend's recommendation and was soon given some. My reputation had got there before me it seemed."

"What sort of a reputation?"

"A reputation for getting things done, and done well. Things not everyone wants to do, or can do."

"What did you do for him?"

"Basic stuff at first. I did a lot of money collecting. I'm sure you know what that's like."

"Yes," he replied, with a smile.

"Well, I turned out to be good at that. Most of the farmers disliked a hobgoblin dealing with them but they soon learned to pay attention to me when I put a blade to their belly. Got a lot of money out of them that way. I was never a part of Spikepoint's main army. Some of them envied my freedom and tried to thwart me over this or that. Others liked the lifestyle I had and tried to get involved. Every now and again he would send me on a sensitive little errand. He had more enemies in those days you see and he often asked me to take care of them. Which I did. I remember one time he was wary of one of his Lieutenants. Ah...what was his name? Reboux, that was it. Lieutenant Reboux. He was a good soldier, decent enough, but he was plotting, so Spikepoint told me. He's plotting, get rid of him for me he said. He's to be sent with a message out of the castle. You go with him, but make sure you come back alone. Leave nothing behind. No traces of course. Reboux was surprised to have me along with him. Normally he delivered messages by himself. I told him it was to help train me. Train me in carrying a letter! He was suspicious but what could he do? Not go? We delivered the message of course, that was real. But on the way back, as we camped, that's when it happened."

"What happened?" asked Gavelrigg, relaxing on his chair and beginning to be drawn into this tale.

"I confronted him."

"Confronted him?"

"Yes, confronted him. I wasn't about to stab him in his sleep. That's not my style, not my style at all."

"What did you say to him?"

"Come on then, Reboux. What have you been up to? He looked at me pretty blankly and asked me what the hell I was on about. Plotting! Plotting? Aye, plotting against Spike. He laughed, then realised with a gulp why I had been sent along with him. Nonsense Tirgu, what've you been told? Plotting! Plotting what he replied? With who? I don't know I said, but you've been plotting. I haven't done a thing, this is stupid. This went on for a while, but he was convincing. After a while I explained and told him the truth of what had been said. He was thinking hard then and wondering what it could all be about. Then he twigged...it was for his wife. He wants Miranda he said. I didn't know who she was but again I believed him. Spikepoint might well have had his eye on her, married or not. He told me what she had told him. That he was sniffing around her more and more. Now we both saw. Spikepoint wanted me to get rid of him so he could get his hands on her."

"What did you do?" asked the guard suddenly, who got a

critical look from Gavelrigg for his pains.

"What did I do? Got on with the job of course."

"I knew it," replied the guard, unable to keep quiet. "You and your slimy sort couldn't do otherwise."

Tirgu laughed heartily. The guard did not respond well and needed to be controlled by Gavelrigg.

"What else was I to do?" said Tirgu, once his mirth subsided. "I wasn't about to go back to Spikepoint a failure with the whole issue wide open. So, I put him to sleep. It was almost dawn by the time I had finished digging his grave. The ground was ridiculously hard."

"Didn't he fight back?" asked Gavelrigg.

"Yes, he did, but the thought of his wife weighed on his mind. The more you have to lose the more it weighs on your mind, and makes it the more likely you will lose it. That's why I'm so good at my work. Nothing weighs me down you see. Can you gentlemen say the same? Probably not. He faced his end bravely, if you want to know. Does that make you feel better about your race?"

"Let's move on shall we?" said Gavelrigg, frustrated at Tirgu's condescension. "Remember that you're our prisoner here. Even though you killed Spikepoint that doesn't mean you're our friend. You probably killed some of our men yesterday and for that you can still be punished. Don't forget where you are."

"Fair enough," replied a more contrite Tirgu. "You're right, let's move on. I'll tell you that I stuck with Spikepoint because he was the strongest, but that was only because he was the toughest, the most ruthless. Few people are genuinely ruthless but he came close. There was no messing about when something needed doing and he had few vices...if you don't count ambition...and an eye for other men's wives."

"What caused you to fall out with him?" asked Gavelrigg.

"Ah, well. The last couple of days have been a bit stressful for me. I was on top of the world just two days ago. I had a plan, Spikepoint had a plan and everything seemed to be going right. Then it all went wrong," said Tirgu, chuckling to himself, but without finding it all that funny. "We didn't really fall out. He was angry with me because I lied to him. But he would have accepted me back into the fold if I'd performed well in battle, which I did...up to the point I put an arrow through his helmet."

"There must be more to it than that!" said Gavelrigg. "Why did you do it?"

Tirgu took his time and had a deep think about how to answer the question. He had been reminded by them that his freedom was not a certainty. He needed to be more careful about what came out of his mouth. Something that's true for all of us.

"Just frustration I suppose. Something was wrong about the whole adventure. It wasn't meant to be for him. I could smell it. So, I thought I'd save a few lives by taking his. I really didn't expect to escape or to get any favour from you. I just hoped to keep my life."

"Keep it you shall, don't worry," said Gavelrigg. "Although, you have about three thousand men on the other side of this wall that would very much enjoy taking it from you."

"Yes, I know. How long will you keep them for?"

"I can't tell you that."

"How long am I to be kept for?"

"Well, once I'm satisfied as to who you are and why you did what you did, I have no reason to keep you. Strictly you should be a prisoner like the others but because of the great favour you did us I think it would be unfair to deny you your freedom, as well as sensible to get you away from the others."

"I have a request."

"Oh?"

"I want to take one of them with me."

"One of who?"

"One of the prisoners."

"Out of the question."

"I think you wouldn't want to keep this one. He's obviously not a danger to you and he wasn't involved in the fighting."

"Who's this?"

"A little green fellow and much too young to be in such an unhappy situation."

"Who?"

"Only a little goblin. To you he's just another mouth to feed. He's no business being here and you have no business keeping him. I've been frank with you and helped you tonight. Let me take him when you release me...if you please."

"Does he know you?"

"Oh yes. We go way back," said Tirgu, smiling another devilish smile.

*

Croak Hebdo Uniross, the Leader of the Council of Milton Greens, banged his wooden mallet on the bench in front of him. The morning session of the Council was about to start and there was one issue of great import, which had pushed back everything else on the schedule. Whenever there was a prisoner in the cell from the previous day he or she was always seen first thing by the Council the next morning. Normally this wouldn't require the attendance of such an august person as the Leader of the Council but this was a special occasion.

He looked out over his junior Councillors sat below him, and towards a group of raggle taggle goblins, noticing that several had their hands tied. He also noticed a hobgoblin stood amongst them. Because of his failing eyesight, and the profound deterioration in his cleanliness, Croak was not able to recognise Lieutenant Chirp Rideau Tilestain, lately the brigade leader sent out of the forest.

All sorts of officials and guards were milling about. None seemed more eager to speak than the dishevelled looking goblin in the middle of the group but before he would get his chance the Leader of the Council beckoned an official towards a podium in order to get proceedings underway.

"The Council of Milton Greens is hereby welcomed into being once more this day! And none other Council may

speak in its stead! All others are but grass! Be upstanding!"
Everyone rose with the exception of the Councillors.
There was a lot of respectful nodding in their direction.
They then nodded back so that everyone could resume
their seats, assuming they had been given that privilege,
which the prisoners had not.

"My honourable Council, may I give you the first. Before
you are four goblins and one hobgoblin. They were taken
into custody yesterday evening, shortly after sundown, by
guards of the Great Hall."

"Were they indeed?" barked a rather fierce and unpleasant
Councillor. "Let's have their particulars."

"Yes Sir, with the exception of the hobgoblin they are all
members of the 'One Hundred and Seventh Milton
Greens Special Militia Brigade.'"

"What?" barked this same Councillor. "The same brigade
sent out to find the kidnapped goblins?"

"Yes Sir."

"Well what are they doing here and getting themselves
arrested outside the Great Hall?"

The Lieutenant raised his arm and was desperate to
explain and not to listen to any more nonsense from this
Councillor or any other. He began to speak was not
permitted.

"Quiet you lot!" grunted a guard nearby.

He then poked the Lieutenant in the back with his
ceremonial stick.

"When we need anything from you we will tell you to
speak. Until then keep quiet!" said this increasingly

irritable Councillor. "Carry on!"

"Thank you Sir. Reports suggest that they have recently returned to the forest, their mission complete."

"What?" said Croak from somewhere deep in his throat. "Who are they again?"

"Members of the 'One Hundred and Seventh Milton Greens Special Militia Brigade' Sir."

"Really?" said Croak. "What are they doing here, arrested?"

The irritable Councillor below had reason to be even more irritated because of the Council Leader's slowness at comprehension.

"Sir, they were arrested because they caused a disturbance outside the Great Hall yesterday evening, soon after their return from the outside."

"What kind of disturbance?" asked Croak, just about putting things together in his mind.

"Sir, we have a witness who will answer that question for you. He was the night desk attendant on duty yesterday evening. He has bravely consented to come and give evidence despite his injuries."

"Injuries?" asked more than one Councillor at the same time.

The Lieutenant rolled his eyes and threw his arms up in the air from frustration. He looked over to the public galleries and saw many a Boiled Mouse sitting in solidarity with him and the others that had been arrested. What a laugh this whole spectacle was. The Lieutenant tried to cool himself down. It occurred to him, not for the first time in the last fourteen hours, that no matter how angry he became it didn't help his cause.

The night desk attendant limped towards the witness stand, which was a little closer to the Councillors, so as to compensate for their poor hearing and the weak voices of some witnesses. He winced as he stepped up and took his place. A smooth talking Councillor smiled and spoke to him.

"Good morning. Thank you for coming and for being so courageous to attend despite your injuries. May we have your name?"

"Good morning Sirs. My name is Rumble Defoe. I was the night desk attendant on duty yesterday evening."

"Rumble? That's an unusual name."

"Yes Sir, it is. I was born during an earthquake."

At this a number of Councillors burst into laughter, as well as a few others within earshot. Rumble was not amongst them, but did not wish to waste energy by complaining.

"Oh, you're serious?" said this same Councillor. "I'm sorry. You just caught us by surprise I think. Now, please tell us what injuries you sustained."

"Well Sir, I have a badly bruised shoulder and have to wear this sling over my arm. I have extensive bruising all over my body and I also think I may have broken the little toe on my left foot."

"Oh dear, my poor Mr Defoe. Now...how did you sustain these injuries?"

"You mean *who* gave them to me?"

"Yes."

Rumble turned to look in the direction of the Lieutenant and the others, making an obvious implication.

"They gave them to me, Sirs," he said, and the Lieutenant very helpfully pointed to himself at this same moment.

"Yes, that one in particular. The Lieutenant."

The same guard that had poked the Lieutenant just before looked ready to repeat this kindness so he resisted the temptation to object. Croak grumbled into life once more.

"I find it quite objectionable that a straightforward public servant such as yourself should be subjected to abuse and assault, simply in the course of conducting his public duties. It is quite objectionable."

"Indeed Sir," said Rumble.

The other Councillors burbled their approval at this sentiment.

"Tell us what happened Mr Defoe," said Croak.

"Well, I was not long into my shift and had been sat at my desk for less than half an hour when a large group of goblins approached. This group was a part of the brigade. The one hundred and seventh. They had this hobgoblin as their prisoner. He was quiet. The Lieutenant, who seemed to be the leader of the group was quite impatient and soon became aggressive once he realised that things were not to his liking."

"Not to his liking?" asked Croak.

"He expected a parade or something, a pageant to welcome him home. I tried to explain to him that I was not privy to such goings on. That it was not my duty."

"Indeed," burped Croak.

"And so I suggested that he return in the morning when there would be others to assist him with his enquiry."

"I see, quite fair. What was his reaction to this?" asked Croak.

"He became aggressive and started to say things he shouldn't have."

"Such as?"

"He started talking about mud and worms. I wasn't sure of his meaning to be honest. Then he said a few more things that I wouldn't like to repeat, especially in this place."

"It is alright Mr Defoe, we are all grown goblins here," chuckled Croak.

"Well, he referred to the stupidity of the Council."

"Did he?" said Croak, no longer chuckling, and with his eyes wide. "Did he indeed?"

"He did Sir. I tried to warn him that he should behave himself, or else I would be forced to call the guards. But this didn't calm him. He just became more aggressive."

"Shame!" barked a junior Councillor, sensing an opportunity to put in his oar.

"Well, after that, I think nothing I could've said would've avoided what happened next."

"What was that?" said Croak.

"A fight broke out."

"A fight? He attacked you?"

"Well...not quite Sir, no."

The Lieutenant nodded that finally a little of the truth was

506

being said and he murmured as such. The guard made ready with his stick if anything further came out of his mouth.

"Not quite?" said Croak.

"They started fighting amongst themselves Sir, with the hobgoblin, to begin with."

"Ah yes, who is this hobgoblin creature?" asked Croak. "What's he doing here?"

This hobgoblin creature smiled but didn't seem anxious to address the Council just yet. He knew his turn would come. He was just allowing himself the pleasure of watching these creatures make such fools of themselves.

"The Lieutenant explained that he was their prisoner and that he was somehow involved in the kidnapping of those goblins they were after."

"I see. Perhaps he will submit to questioning later?" said Croak, looking for a reaction from Brakk, which did not come. "I said...perhaps he will submit to questioning later?"

Baintha Brakk smiled and then looked down at his fingernails. Croak was not pleased but he had his reaction. Rumble rumbled on.

"They were fighting amongst themselves Sirs and so I called the guards. While they were on their way I spoke to these...brawlers...in an attempt to calm the situation."

"Brawlers! That sounds right," interrupted the irritable Councillor.

"I shouted to them to calm themselves and see sense. I even came from behind my desk and tried to physically intervene. It was at this stage that I believe I sustained the injury to my toe, as the Lieutenant stepped on it."

"Deliberately?" asked Croak.

"I cannot say with certainty, but it is hard for me to consider it entirely accidental."

"Indeed," replied Croak. "What did you do then?"

"I found myself in the middle of the fight and was soon on the receiving end of blows from all quarters."

"Shame! Shame!" barked the now even more irritable Councillor, addressing his words to those in custody.

"This is how I sustained the various bruises on my body."

"And your injured shoulder?" asked Croak.

"I was knocked to the ground Sir, violently."

"Who did that to you Mr Defoe?"

Rumble looked back towards the Lieutenant but the implication was not that clear, as there was an uncertain look on his face.

"I cannot be certain Sir, I'm sorry."

"You cannot be certain...but you think it was caused by one of those in custody?" asked Croak.

"I think it very likely Sir, very likely."

"Then we shall have it out of them! Don't you worry about that," said Croak with considerable confidence. "What happened then?"

"The guards came shortly after and the main ones were arrested."

"The main *brawlers*?" said the irritable Councillor.

"Yes Sir. Then I went for treatment where it could best be found."

"Thank you Mr Defoe, please rest your weary body," said Croak, beckoning him back to his seat.

He turned his gaze back to the main brawlers and smiled at them, though this was not to inspire them with confidence for the process ahead.

"Now then! Which of you objectionable creatures is to be first?" he asked.

The Lieutenant raised his hand and was keen to put the record straight. He was annoyed for more reasons that he could remember. He should have been welcomed as a hero. Instead here he was, tied up and being talked down to by these pompous old fools, who were more of a problem for the forest than a benefit. To think how many chestnuts it was costing for them all to be here!

"Is that the Lieutenant waving his arm?" asked Croak. "If so, come to the podium and let's hear your explanation for this violence. It had better be good!"

The Lieutenant needed no further prompting. He stepped away from Baintha Brakk, Slap Canopy, Rustle Blacknose and another Mouse, who he didn't know all that well, and walked quickly to the podium. Once there he wanted immediately to speak but with a hand from a Councillor was instructed not to. The guard needed time to stand next to him once more. The Councillors even had the cheek to post further guards at the foot of their bench as though he was a danger to them. This hand was lowered once all was well.

"Is it my turn yet?" began the Lieutenant, with barely disguised contempt in his voice.

"Lieutenant," began Croak, gently but firmly, "it's clear something has gone quite wrong here. Please calm yourself and be civil. It's the best way to communicate."

The Lieutenant agreed but didn't want to give them the satisfaction just yet.

"Well Sirs, I've rarely heard such a one sided account of anything."

"Oh!?" barked the irritable Councillor.

"Oh!?" mimicked the Lieutenant, "Oh your bloody yourself!"

The Hall erupted in laughter but for his trouble the Lieutenant got the stick again, causing him quite a bit of pain. Rumble had not been the only one injured in the fracas.

"Order! Order in the Hall!" shouted an official.

"Lieutenant?" said Croak.

"Yes?" he replied, without the obligatory Sir in addition.

"Let's have some discipline if you please. It is to be expected from a soldier, especially a commander such as you and especially in this place."

The Lieutenant couldn't argue with this and he sighed a little and cooled his ardour.

"Yes Sir," he eventually replied. "Something has gone quite wrong here. My behaviour last night, and I think the reason for everyone's behaviour, is the great stress we've been through these past weeks. We've been in considerable danger and been through a lot...and we came out successful! It should be a triumph. That's why I am frustrated and upset. But what he said *was* one sided. I stand by that."

"Perhaps you can give us *your* one sided account then?" barked the irritable Councillor.

"With pleasure," said the Lieutenant, smiling directly at him. "I am Lieutenant Chirp Rideau Tilestain, the commander of the One Hundred and Seventh Milton Greens Special Militia Brigade, otherwise known as the Boiled Mice."

A few Councillors laughed at this name, as some had not heard that they were using it.

"Hey! If you laugh at the Boiled Mice one more time all these guards in front of you won't get in my way!"

A great cheer erupted from the gallery, since it was stuffed with Mice and was therefore decidedly partisan. The atmosphere was getting rather heated and the guards in question anticipated a charge but the Lieutenant held his ground.

"Lieutenant!" said Croak loudly. "That is no way to speak to this Council! If you wish we can hold you for another day? Perhaps after another night in the cell you will be more sensible?"

The Lieutenant was tempted to take him up on the offer and see who possessed the greater will, but he had a duty on his shoulders that could not be ignored.

"No Sir," he said quietly. "But I will not accept laughter at their expense for they did their duty and risked their lives and it was all for your benefit!"

"Yes, we understand that," said another junior Councillor, eager to ask a few questions.

"I don't think you do, otherwise we would have had a better reception than the one we enjoyed last night."

"Listen, you're the one under arrest and for violent conduct," said this same eager Councillor. "Yet here you are lecturing us on our failings. You called the Council stupid. Did you really say that?"

"Might have..." he offered, after a moment's reflection.

"Is that still your view? Do you take those words back?"

"That depends."

"On what?"

"How well you behave today."

"How well we behave?" he retorted, unable to believe his big green ears.

"I should be here being lauded, giving my report and receiving your thanks!"

"We would have been happy to do so had you not attacked Mr Defoe!"

"Oh, he's making half that up! I may have stepped on his toe but it was an accident. He just bumbled his way into an argument between friends and got himself in the way of blows meant for other people. Then he fell over awkwardly and did his shoulder in. What a clonk!"

This caused further laughter in the gallery, though again Mr Defoe was not amongst those partaking.

"But what caused this argument?" continued this same Councillor. "And why were you so abusive?"

"I wasn't abusive...really...much. The argument was caused by him telling me to come back the next morning...and because he didn't have the wit to work out

512

what was going on and to help me instead of worrying about his desk and his duties."

"He is an innocent party in all this Lieutenant."

"Aren't we all?" he replied. "Except Baintha."

"Baintha?" asked the Councillor, his ears poking upwards once more.

"Yes, we needed to put him in a cell. He's the only one who should have been arrested."

"Who is this Baintha? The hobgoblin?"

"Yes! Baintha Brakk. He's a criminal frankly. He took our goblins and he's the one we nabbed them from."

At this Baintha's brown ears pricked up, as he was keen not to have his name rubbished any further than it ought.

"Ah," said this Councillor. "Perhaps you should give us your report."

"I'd be delighted to. The main report I'll submit in writing if that's alright. A lot happened but I'll give you a summary now. Before I get started though...do you think?"

He lifted his hands in the air and motioned that it might be an idea to release him from his bindings. The Councillors chatted amongst themselves for a few moments. The guard that had been so enthusiastic in the use of his ceremonial stick tried to suggest with his eyes that to do so would be a mistake. He was to be disappointed.

"Alright," said Croak. "Release him."

"And the others? Not Brakk obviously," asked the Lieutenant.

"They can wait!" barked the irritable Councillor, still irritated over something or other.

The Lieutenant had his bindings removed and he flexed and rubbed his wrists.

"My report," he began after a few moments, "is simply that we did it! We got ten of the eleven goblins back, suffered no casualties at all and got one of those responsible for it as a prisoner."

"They're back! Why haven't we been told?" said Croak, looking about himself and at his officials.

"I would have told you yesterday but we came back too late last night and we couldn't deny them a chance to get home to their loved ones. So off they went."

"I see, of course," said Croak. "But you said ten of eleven. Who is missing?"

"Ah...little Gurgle Roundtop."

"The young one?"

"Yes Sir."

"He's still in the hands of the enemy?"

"I'm afraid so."

"Oh dear, oh dear, that is very sad. Have you any idea of his whereabouts?"

"Some. He was within our grasp when we found the others, just feet away, but he was taken off."

"Taken off? Where? By whom? We must get him back!"

The Lieutenant looked around and caught Baintha's eye, then pointed at him.

"I agree, and that creature over there may have an idea."

"What creature?" asked Croak, peering at what for him

514

was a considerable distance away.

"Our prisoner, Brakk!" said the Lieutenant. "He's been holding our goblins for the last few weeks in a cage under his house in Brown Root forest."

At this the Councillors and most of audience started to audibly hiss in Brakk's direction. He remained cool however, as was his way.

"He sold some of them as slaves as well," continued the Lieutenant.

"Slaves!?" said more than one Councillor at the same time.

"Aye Sirs, to his fellow hobgoblins."

"You did this to a child?" shouted Croak.

Brakk shook his head. He did not do that and he knew it was sensible not to let such ideas take hold in people's minds.

"Bring him forward!" he shouted again, doing his ancient throat no good at all.

Croak pointed at his officials to bring Brakk to a vacant podium opposite the Lieutenant. He was escorted by another guard but his bindings were not removed. The guard was considerably shorter than Brakk and they looked a strange pair side by side.

"Hobgoblin! What is your name?" spat Croak at this evil thing in front of him.

"I am Baintha Brakk."

"You were captured by the brigade?"

"I was, though they needed a lot of help and your little band of warriors murdered one of my employees!"

"Never mind that. Did you have goblins in your

possession?"

"I did."

"How many?"

"Ten."

"Not eleven?"

"No, just ten and only ten. I never had a goblin child at all. I don't know what that's all about."

"Where did you get these goblins?"

"From a human man. A trader. He sold them to me."

"You *bought* them?" said Croak, with the sound of disgust in his voice.

"He wasn't giving them away," replied Brakk smoothly.

"I hope they cost you a fortune. They'll cost you more yet!"

"They could be costly for you too."

"What do you mean by that?" said Croak.

"Well," began Brakk, "I think I ought to explain something to you all. I don't think you realise what you've got heading your way."

"What? Who? Some of your friends?" said another Councillor, getting a little aggressive. "We beat your lot away from the forest once before and we can do it again!"

Brakk smiled at this goblin and then gave him a wink that only served to make him even angrier. Croak realised the potential for trouble and sat back in his chair to think for a few moments. He then rose to his feet to give his voice greater reach.

"Clear the Great Hall! Take the public out!"

With a wail of disappointment various officials quickly

516

shuffled all those without a direct say in matters out of the hall. Rumble looked behind him and laughed at the Mice who had laughed at him as they were taken away. After a couple of minutes the hall was relatively clear and Croak adopted a more serious look. There was real business to be discussed now.

"Brakk. You bought our goblins. Where did you get them from?" asked Croak.

"Like I said, from a man trader," he replied.

"Where did he get them from?"

"That wasn't my business and I didn't ask."

"I think I can answer that question!" said the Lieutenant suddenly.

"Oh?" said Croak.

"It was as the first rumours suggested a hobgoblin named Tirgu. He was the one that did the kidnapping and he was there when we raided Brakk's place and got our goblins back. I wish I'd got my hands on him but he was away before we realised who they were?"

"Who they were?"

"Yes, he had a band of human men with him. His crew we believe. However, two of them were dead at the scene. Some members of the brigade spotted little Gurgle with him."

"He has the child?" blurted Croak.

"We believe so, yes Sir."

"What were they doing before you arrived?"

"They were fighting amongst themselves. We found two dead human men and two dead hobgoblins. They had

517

Brakk in their possession and would have killed him had we not intervened just at that moment."

"Really? So Brakk, you have the Boiled Mice to thank for your life!" said Croak, directing his comments in only one direction.

"You won't get any thanks from me you bloated old fool!" said Brakk harshly.

"What!? Get him downstairs! This instant!" demanded Croak.

"I think you'll want to hear me speak!" said Brakk quickly, as guards approached. "I know how to get Gurgle back for you."

Croak understood in a moment and told the guards to wait.

"Alright, you awful creature, let's have it. How can we get him back?"

"I know Tirgu, the one with your child. Your little band of goblins wouldn't stand a chance against him. It was only through blind luck that they managed to get the better of me. I have a proposal for you."

"I thought you might. You have that look in your eye," said Croak.

"To be honest, it's only a matter of time before all sorts of nasty creatures start to invade your little forest here and try to get me out. I'm worth a lot of money and I'll give a lot of it away for my freedom. Who knows? Maybe even one of your own will help me get out. I can make you wish they'd left me behind or cut my throat right then and there. But that didn't happen and now you've got a big problem, what to do with me. I know you don't want any hassle so I'll make things simple. I want Tirgu just as much as you want Gurgle. If I direct my hobgobs to go after them both and get Gurgle back I'll swap him for me. I think that'll save us all a great deal of bloodshed. What'd you think?"

Croak and the other Councillors absorbed this information in silence and once he had finished speaking all descended into a deep think. Croak was the only one with the real power and no decision would be taken that he didn't approve of. He looked out through his greying, milky eyes and saw the logic of it. This hobgoblin creature was a shrewd thing. Croak had a few more questions to ask though, before agreeing.

"Why are you so important that others would come after you?"

"I told you, because I'm rich and well known. They won't leave me here, pride wouldn't allow it."

"If we organised our fighters I think we could resist you...and them. What do you say to that?"

"You're not used to the outside world, you goblins. You don't know what awaits you out there. Trust me. You wouldn't want the world to turn its gaze upon you and I have the power to turn it."

"I don't believe that."

"Take care," he said, raising his hands to point. "You have a great responsibility on your shoulders for all those little goblins out there. Make the right decision, the safe decision, for their sakes."

"Why are we even listening to this dreadful thing, a slave master!?" said another Councillor.

"Don't be emotional," said Brakk menacingly. "Even though my hands are bound I'm the one with the real power. Don't force me to use it."

"What power?" said Croak dismissively.

Brakk reached into a discreet pocket with what reach he still retained and withdrew a golden coin. He handed it to the guard stood by. The Lieutenant was surprised and wondered where he'd hidden it, for they'd searched him thoroughly.

"Take a look," said Brakk expectantly.

Croak was handed the coin and he examined it carefully. It had writing on it that he found a little hard to distinguish. Fortunately, Brakk knew what it said and he helped the Councillors to understand.

"It reads 'Minted by Baintha Brakk...peerless...believe in me...the real Chieftain.'"

CHAPTER 15

Gurgle sat amongst a sea of strangers. He had never been part of such a huge group nor had he ever felt so alone. He'd spent a dreadful night, hungry and struggling to stay warm, despite the heat of those much bigger bodies close by. His immediate companions didn't seem to be soldiers. They looked like staff of some kind. They had kept him with them, at their insistence. That was preferable to sleeping alongside those smelly and unhappy beasts.

The day was warming up but nothing by way of food seemed to be on offer. The guards just concentrated on guarding. Gurgle's stomach, never a patient organ at the best of times, was giving him discomfort. He couldn't do anything he whispered to it. You'll just have to wait.

The sadness of defeat had taken its toll on them all. Few had the energy of yesterday and most now lay despondent in the dirt. During the night some had succumbed to their injuries and the morning flies enjoyed the quiet flesh.

There had been much talk of their collective fate but nothing definite had been said by their hosts. They would simply have to wait. Most of the intelligent conversation had taken place nearby, involving some of Spikepoint's senior staff members. They were anticipating a long stay but not a cruel one. They realised that their existence as a fighting force was at an end and they would only become a drain on the King's resources. Soon enough they would have to release them, though only a little at a time and not without a great warning ringing in their ears. Gurgle had nothing to say. He had no idea what had happened to Tirgu and for all he knew he was dead. He wasn't around so he hoped so. He hoped so much that it was true; then he could be on his way home, even if he had to walk by himself the whole way. Not that he even knew the way home. He just wanted to be free. It would be for the first time in weeks, ever since he sat by the river bank in Milton Greens and nibbled on his hunk of cheese. How he would love to be back there again, amongst his own kind and free from care. He had to admit that he was not the same goblin anymore and that the experience might not be as simple as he imagined.

He noticed a guard coming closer and looking eagerly around the camp. He was let through the hastily assembled fence. As he made his circuitous path inwards many dirty hands reached up for something but nothing came. Instead many received a kick for their insolence. The man seemed to be heading in their direction and when his eyes met Gurgles he stopped and opened them wide.

"You! Little one. Come here," he said.

Those around Gurgle, who had taken it upon themselves to protect him, objected to this request and held him close.

"I haven't time for this nonsense! Give him to me!" the man shouted.

These few human men and women continued to hold him in their grasp, forcing the man to take action. He charged up and literally ripped him from their arms and poor little Gurgle screamed at the pain of it. They cried out in horror at the man's meanness but there was little they could do.

"Why don't you listen?" he shouted, whilst grabbing Gurgle's shirt with both hands.

He dragged him away and they were quickly beyond the enclosure. Soon he allowed him to stand and they walked for a few minutes and came around the far side of the castle. This part of the castle had a large entrance and it was well guarded. Once inside, the man flung him into a corner and told him not to move. Another human man approached quickly whilst the other stormed off to his previous duties. The man knelt down and looked closely at this unhappy little thing.

"Gurgle?" he said, smiling. "Is that your name?"

Gurgle nodded meekly and the man smiled wider. He handed him a bottle of water and told him to take as much as he could drink but to do so slowly. He also stuffed some pieces of bread and ham into his pockets.

"He's right," said the man after a few moments. "You've no business being here. We're letting you go Gurgle, back to the forest."

Gurgle smiled instantly before allowing the man to finish his statement.

"Or wherever else Tirgu decides to take you."

His smile vanished.

"What?" he said breathlessly. "He's not dead?"

"Who? Tirgu?" said the man.

"No, he's very much alive," came a voice from the shadows. "It's good to see you again Gurgle. You ready to go?"

Gurgle was stunned and couldn't react. Tirgu knew not to

delay as he didn't want any scene to be created before they could leave. Tirgu quickly picked him up from the floor and lifted him onto the horse, which Gavelrigg had been so kind as to give him. Tirgu had surprised himself with his persuasiveness and things were looking up for him again. He too got on the horse and with a swift kick to its underbelly they were on their way. Gurgle's throat was still wet and he hadn't gotten his breath back from the shock. They trotted out. Gavelrigg was more than pleased to see this particular problem resolved and quickly going away.

As they made the castle smaller and there were no other souls around Tirgu turned his head back to his little companion and began to speak.

"Oh Gurgle, what a time we've had!? But at least we're still alive to tell the tale, eh?"

"He was going to let me go! I'm tired of all this! Tired of it!"

"Hey! I got you out of there. You should be thanking me! Why do you think they let you out?"

"I don't know," he replied, whilst eating a piece of ham.

"Because I asked them to. I really had to persuade them to let you go. They could easily have said no and you'd be still there now, fighting with hundreds of big human men over a handful of slop. Would you prefer that to this?"

"No," he said softly, about to put a piece of bread in his mouth.

"I thought not. You listen to me. Even though Spikepoint's gone we still have things to do. I'll get a new crew together with you and me as its leaders. What do you say to that Gurgle?"

"Why?"

"Why? Because there's still business to be done and there's always work for talented creatures like us, survivors!"

"But I don't want any of that!" he pleaded.

"You will," said Tirgu, trying to hide his anger, "just stick with me, you'll see."

This seemed to end the conversation for the moment. Tirgu was annoyed that despite everything he'd done for Gurgle he wasn't the least bit grateful.

"Where are you taking me?" asked Gurgle.

"You mean where are we going?" corrected Tirgu. "We're going home, to my home."

"The dark forest?"

"Yes."

"But isn't that dangerous?"

"Not if we keep a low profile. I need to check on mum."

"Mum?"

"My mother. I need to see that she's alright."

This caught Gurgle by surprise and he wasn't sure what to say. Then a thought occurred to him.

"Fine, just as long as we can go and see my mum straight after," he said.

Tirgu laughed and he needed a few moments to think of a suitable response.

"We'll see. Depends how I'm feeling and how well you're behaving. You still got your knife or anything with you?"

"I've got the little knife. They took the big one and

everything else they stripped."

"Oh Gurgle. That was good blade, a family heirloom. I'm disappointed."

"What could I do?"

"Not much I guess. Just make sure you never lose another of my blades again."

"You still got your blades?" asked Gurgle pointedly.

"No," chuckled Tirgu, "...but what could I do?"

"What happened in the battle yesterday? They all came running back over the ridge. I thought we had more men than they did."

Tirgu smiled and thought about the best way to explain what had happened. It took him a while to think of something sensible.

"You said Spikepoint's gone just then," said Gurgle, before Tirgu had a chance to speak. "What happened to him?"

"He's dead."

"How?"

"An arrow through the helmet. The same helmet you held so well for him just a few hours before. You held onto history there for a little while. That means you're special."

"My mother always said I was special."

"Every mother says that."

Gurgle was surprised just how quickly he was getting back into the routine of being with Tirgu. He fumbled in his pockets for what was left and found a piece of bread.

"Did he give you any food? I asked him to."

"Yesh," said Gurgle, whilst chewing the last of it.

"Excellent. Tonight though, we'll be enjoying my mother's home cooked specialities. I can't wait. What do you think of that?"

"What sort of food is it? I don't know your food."

"No? What did they give you in Milton Greens then?"

"Soup...stews...and pie."

"Not that different then, but I bet we have better grilled meat! Have you ever tried freshly grilled rat?"

"No."

"Then you're in for a treat...in about six hours from now. Unless we get killed on the way of course."

*

Mala and Keeps stood looking at the tall trees of Milton Greens and couldn't help but admire. Mala had recovered from his wounds, which were superficial, and had decided to follow Brakk, his master, wherever these goblins would take him. He was considering the best way to get a message to him. He guessed correctly that Baintha was already twisting them around his little finger and persuading them to do what he wanted.

They were crouching behind a small bump in the ground and keeping an eye out for everything that was to be seen. They hadn't the confidence to go into the forest just yet. For one thing they didn't know where to find Brakk and their reception would not be a welcome one at all. Back in Brown Root all kinds of upset had been caused. Those that had had their slaves stolen were most displeased. At first Brakk's assistants had tried to claim that they were still being kept under his house but couldn't be returned just yet. That story was quickly demolished by so many eye witnesses saying otherwise. The pride of the forest had been deeply injured, much as had happened to Milton Greens, though that incident was not widely known about in Brown Root.

For a range of reasons many in Brown Root now thought about what they could do to help. Mala and Keeps obviously had a personal interest in getting involved but whispers soon got around about possible rewards for anyone willing to lend a hand. There was no real organisation yet. That wouldn't come without a leader and Brakk was not available. Some hobgoblins had come straight to Brakk's house, not only to tidy up and guard it but also in hopes of being given some paid work in respect of his rescue.

For the moment Mala and Keeps had only a vague notion of what to do. Mala thought that he could be some kind of emissary or negotiator with someone in Milton Greens and be able to discuss options for Brakk's release. The problem for the moment was making it clear to any goblins they saw that that was what they wanted. It was obvious to them both that the mere sight of a hobgoblin near their forest would raise at best a storm of abuse and at worst a storm of blows. They also considered the possibility that they too would be captured, which would put an end to all their schemes. Facing Brakk as his fellow prisoner was not a pleasant prospect.

Neither of them knew much of the geography of Milton Greens but they did know about the Hall of Goblins and that the place was considered the centre of all things goblin. This was the place to go and they naturally guessed that it would be in the heart of the forest. They looked at each other and decided that there was no time to waste.

"Shall we go in?" asked Keeps, looking more for support than anything else.

"We shall," replied Mala, "...after you."

*

The brigade was now officially at ease and getting some much needed rest and recreation. They had been told to keep themselves ready for any trouble and to check in daily with the quartermaster. Not all of them were willing to meet him so frequently and some even thought their duty complete. The quartermaster would shortly have to report to his Lieutenant that the Mice were not even four fifths of their previous strength.

The Lieutenant was on his way to the Roundtop family's tree. He and the other Mice had been released, despite a lot of bluster and bureaucracy, as he knew full well they had no reason to keep them locked up. The Councillors also realised, thanks to Brakk's menacing attitude, that they needed fighting goblins at the ready in case of attack.

The Lieutenant's lumps and bumps were troubling him less now and he made good progress through the forest.

He was heading their way to try to be ahead of the news and rumour about the return of the kidnapped goblins. He felt a personal obligation to Thump and Screech Roundtop and wanted to tell them what had happened to Gurgle with his own lips.

He sucked in the forest air and detected the familiar humidity and leafy smell. The outside air was so much clearer but it could never smell like home. The area he trudged through was familiar to him but only because of the incident that occurred hereabouts. Despite this heavy duty ahead he couldn't help but think how things would develop for him. He hoped the Councillors would not dwell on all that silliness with Rumble Defoe, but knowing them if they wanted something to be held against a person they would have no fear of doing so. The fine welcome and very natural promotion he had expected was now seriously in doubt and he suspected that he would have to perform well a second time in order to gain their favour. To be fair, his duty could never be properly discharged until Gurgle was liberated and the threat to the forest from Baintha was cooled. It would never completely disappear and he knew there could be fresh trouble between the two forests now, whatever the outcome of this current problem.

The immediate area around the Roundtop's home was quiet and he was able to approach their door without being seen by anyone. He knocked gently and the door was opened by Thump.

"Good morning Mr Roundtop," he began.

"Well! Look who it is! Screech, come here, it's the Lieutenant! Come in," he replied enthusiastically.

He stepped inside and found them at their cleaning duties. He wondered where the rest of their children were. Thump left his mulching cauldron and Screech abandoned her washing to join the Lieutenant on the small sofa to which he had been directed. Before he had time to think the questioning began.

"What news?" asked Thump.

"Have you got him? Please say you've got him," said Screech.

"No, not yet, I'm sorry," he replied after a few moments and he saw their faces fall.

"Where is he then? Is he alright?" asked Thump.

"We came close to getting him back and we know he's still alive. We spotted him so we know he didn't drown in the river."

"Oh...thank God!" said Thump, clutching his garments.

"But where is he? Who's got him?" asked Screech.

"Let me explain," said the Lieutenant, raising his hand to get them to hold their horses. "Gurgle appears to be with the same hobgoblin that kidnapped him."

"What? Why haven't you gone after him?" asked Thump, to which Screech nodded.

"Please, let me explain...I didn't know where any of the goblins were to begin with. My brigade had to go out and look for them. It wasn't easy. We had to sneak into a human man town, looking for someone that might have known about them. After that we traced them to Brown

Root forest."

"Brown Root? I knew it, didn't I say so Thump?"

"Yes, you did, let him speak," replied Thump dismissively.

"Yes, back to Brown Root. We managed to infiltrate and get every other goblin back. Except for Gurgle I'm afraid."

"You got them all?" said Thump, surprised. "Except Gurgle."

"Yes, listen...has anyone said anything to you...have you heard any rumours about what's going on?"

"There was some commotion around the Great Hall we heard, and of course that one of the kidnapped goblins came back a few days ago. We had high hopes Lieutenant."

"Yes, I know."

"You're still gunna keep looking for him aren't you?" asked Screech.

"Yes, but not with the brigade," said the Lieutenant.

"What? By yourself?" she yelped at him.

"No, another solution has been suggested and the Council are going with that instead."

"What are they going to do about our son!?" said Thump, impatiently.

"Ah, it would take too long to explain. They're going to negotiate with a powerful hobgoblin that we've got as a prisoner and exchange him for Gurgle, assuming they can find him."

"What? What d'yu mean?" said the Roundtops, sharing a question each.

"Your son is now a very valuable little goblin and lots of

people are going to be after him. It might bring him back fairly soon, but it could be dangerous as they might fight over him."

"I don't believe this. Where is he now?" asked Thump.

"He's probably with the same hobgoblin that kidnapped him and he's public enemy number one in Brown Root right now. Something will happen soon I'm sure but I can't say how it'll turn out."

*

Tirgu and Gurgle were not too far from the edge of Brown Root forest and the late afternoon sun was losing the will to shine. Their journey had been a quiet affair and they had naturally avoided contact with every living thing. Again, Tirgu contemplated a subtle route into the forest. It was not his preference to keep sneaking into places but he was getting used to it. Fortunately for them his mother lived not too far from the edge and so he could get there without causing much if any disturbance.

He had also managed to persuade Gavelrigg to give him a couple of old blankets and he instructed Gurgle to wear one of them.

"Wrap it around your body," he said.

"Am I a secret?" asked Gurgle playfully.

"Yes, most definitely a secret, especially in Brown Root. When we get to mum's you can take it off but not before then."

"Don't you need to cover up too?" asked Gurgle.

"Glad to see you're thinking. I might do it in a bit but things seem quiet for the moment. From a distance I'm just another hobgob but you're a little green goblin and you stand out. I don't want anyone to notice you."

As the dark and low forest loomed ever closer Tirgu took more time about his movements and pulled his horse back to a slow pace. He was happy to wait for the evening to draw in and cover them both with its useful shroud. As they eventually came close to the edge they dismounted and walked alongside the horse into the forest. It was very quiet and Tirgu wondered whether they would see anyone at all on their quick walk in. Mum's was only five minutes away and they were soon approaching it. Tirgu tied up his horse on a nearby tree at the back of her property. He looked around carefully. One or two figures drifted through the shade but none seemed interested in them. This was just as it should be. He put a hand on Gurgle's shoulder and whispered for him to move forward. They crept around to her front door. Gurgle was disappointed at the state of her home as many planks of wood seemed loose and there was moss and mould aplenty. Tirgu also seemed upset by its condition. He obviously had not seen the place for a while. He quietly knocked at the door. No sound was heard so he knocked again, this time with a little more force. After a few more moments of silence they both heard a soft shuffling noise and the door then creaked open, but only by a few inches.

"Who's there?" said the person inside, with a weak but gravely tone.

"It's me, your son, let me inside."

"What? Tirgu?"

"Yes, keep your voice down and let us inside," he said again, insisting.

She was too shocked to do anything other than comply and the door opened fully. They slipped inside in a flash. Gurgle looked around but there was little light to see much by.

"Mum, why do you always wait till the middle of the night before lighting the candles? When it gets dark light them up, eh?"

"What're you doing 'ere son? Now?"

"Can't I come and see my old mum when the mood takes me?" he said, as he lit two or three candles and then closed the shutters to the windows. "How are you?"

"Not so good. I'm in a lot of pain son. I'm not too well."

"What's wrong?" he said, showing real concern.

"Just getting old, that's all," she replied. "What's this you've brought?"

"That's Gurgle, a friend of mine. He's with me now."

"He doesn't look too healthy either," she observed. "I'll heat something up for you both. It'll be the first meal I've made for you since last summer. I do wish you'd let me know if you're coming."

"I understand mum, I will."

"I don't like it when he just turns up on my doorstep," she said, directing her words to Gurgle. "He's not been much of a son to me lately."

"Mum, don't talk like that with guests."

535

"I'm used to saying what I like. I've got no one to tell me otherwise you see."

Tirgu kept quiet and so did Gurgle. She lit a match and started a fire in her small stove. Then she put a pot above it. The fragments of wood and kindling slowly crackled into life.

"I've not much food on the go at moment. Don't have anyone to feed but meself."

"No one else?" asked Tirgu. "Don't you share with your neighbours anymore?"

"Most o' them have gone off. It's quiet round here now."

"Have you seen any commotion in the forest lately?"

"Commotion? What'd you mean?" she said, turning to look at him.

"Anything unusual happening?"

"Not really, but they wouldn't come and tell me if there was."

"Has anyone come and spoken to you, about me?"

"No, don't be daft. You're mostly forgotten around these parts."

"Not for long mum."

"What you talking about?" she said, stirring the liquid more slowly because of her distraction.

"I've got a few people after me."

"Tell me something I don't know."

"This time it's serious. I need you to be careful and not let anyone know we're here. Understand?"

"Of course! I've not dropped you in it yet and I'm not about to start now. Your sister's been asking after you."

"Oh yeah, how is she?"

"Fine, until yesterday."

"What'd you mean?"

"She came round and seemed worried. She didn't say what about though. She just gave me some food and went back home."

"If you see her again don't tell her I came here. It might put her in danger."

"Meaning I'm in danger?" she theorized after a few moments.

"No mum, I'm here to protect you."

"From what exactly? What's all this about and why've you brought a goblin to my house?"

"Let's just have some food. I'll tell you later."

"No, you'll tell me now! You're my son and you'll do as you're told. Come on, out with it."

"I've fallen out with Brakk and sooner or later he's going to come after me."

"I've never liked him," she replied after a few moments. "What did you do to him this time?"

"We had a fight," he replied disingenuously.

"Liars don't get fed in this house!"

"No one's gunna get fed at this rate. Is that stove working or not?" he replied.

"If you want me to help you, you'll have to tell me everything."

Tirgu leaned back in his favourite chair, a possession of his younger days, and stared at his mother's back. Gurgle was unsure of what to think about this strange domestic disagreement. He just focussed on the empty bowl in front of him and wondered when it might be filled.

"It's serious this time, that's all," replied Tirgu eventually.

"Have you still got my old stuff?"

"Yeah, up on the shelf," she grumbled.

Tirgu stood and leaned up to grab a package from the shelf. He blew off the dust before placing it on the table. To Gurgle's eyes it looked like an old leather bag with no markings. To Tirgu's eyes this was a life saver. To Gurgle's surprise he pulled out a number of old but dangerous looking blades and other sharp things. He didn't put any on the table however. He just took a good look then placed them back inside.

"We'll clean these up tonight. They'll come in handy," he said whilst admiring them. "I'll give you a good one if you promise to protect me with it. What'd you say Gurgle?"

"Be your bodyguard you mean?" he replied.

"Exactly," he said with a smile. "You're the only one I trust, except mum of course, but she's not been handy with a blade for a long time...unless we're talking carrots."

"Behave yourself Tirgu. I haven't seen you for over a year so you can't treat the place as your own just like that."

Tirgu didn't like being rebuked but he knew he had no good reply. Being a less than dutiful son was a sore and emotional issue for him. He kept his attention on Gurgle.

"So what are you giving us mum? Gurgle here looks hungry."

"Just what's on the go...snail stew."

"Snail stew? It's our lucky night! Fancy some Gurgle?"

asked Tirgu, to which Gurgle nodded enthusiastically.

"That'll do nicely mum, thanks. Any mushrooms to go with it?"

"No," she said plainly.

"Ah, we should've had a look for some on the way in. Why didn't you say anything Gurgle?"

"How was I to know? I thought we were in a rush."

"That's no excuse!" he said with a fake frown. "I did teach you to look for them. You should've used your initiative."

"Tirgu, a little less initiative and a little more thought would've saved you a lot of trouble over the years."

"Listen to the voice of wisdom," said Tirgu, whilst looking at Gurgle but pointing at her. "What will she say next?"

Gurgle was amused and started to feel a part of the scene. The atmosphere of a home and family and food was an undeniable reminder of better times.

"It's ready, that's what I'll say next."

Gurgle's bowl was taken hold of and a brown, steaming volume replaced the air. A wooden spoon was placed next to it and he was invited to eat. Tirgu watched him closely as the distance between his little green nose and the shiny stew fell to nearly nothing. Even though he was hungry he was cautious about this concoction. He gave it a thorough sniffing but tried not to make noise as he did so. It seemed acceptable so he picked up the spoon, dipped it in and then enjoyed a slurp. This made Tirgu smile.

"What does this remind you of mum?" asked Tirgu gently.

She looked down at Gurgle and thought for a few moments about the question.

"I'm not sure I follow you Tirgu," she said.

"A long time back," he said as a clue.

"I remember you doing that as a child."

"No, not me, more recently."

"Oh son, let's not get into that."

"Get into what?" asked Gurgle, between slurps.

"Nothing for you to worry about," she said, trying to keep the matter unexplored.

"You think I could pop out tonight and see them?" asked Tirgu.

"See who?" his mother replied, her anxiety building.

"You know who," he said quietly.

"It's too late for that son and you said yourself you needed to keep a low profile. Stay and have some food."

"I will have the food but maybe later I'll just nip out and see how they are."

With a feeling of resignation she filled Tirgu's bowl and then sat down to watch them eat.

"If you must," she said after a while. "Do you want me to watch him while you're gone?"

"Where're you going?" asked Gurgle direct to Tirgu.

"To see my family," he said calmly.

"Your family!?" spluttered Gurgle, most surprised.

"Oh son, don't go at night, please."

"I can't go during the day can I?"

"Then don't go at all," she said forcefully. "I look after the plots with fresh flowers, don't worry."

"I need to go. Don't worry mum, I'll be fine."

"Can I see them as well?" asked Gurgle all of a sudden, perhaps not realising fully the situation.

They each looked at Gurgle with different expressions.

"Eat your food you!" she demanded of him.

"Don't stifle him," said Tirgu, seriously. "He's just got a healthy curiosity. Isn't that right?"

"Yes."

"He wouldn't have bumped into me if he hadn't been so curious," said Tirgu, followed up with another of his famous smiles.

At the understanding of this Gurgle quite naturally took umbrage. It was a reminder of their nasty introduction.

"Forget it!" he said angrily. "You don't need me here. I'm tired of all this."

He shoved his bowl away.

"What's this?" laughed Tirgu. "Hunger strike...a protest? Have we a little green martyr on our hands?"

"What's a marter?" he asked with his arms folded.

"I dunno, what's the marter with you?" said Tirgu, laughing.

"I want to go home! That's what's the matter! And I'm not eating another bite until you take me there!"

"What's all this about Tirgu? What's he doing here?" she asked.

Tirgu looked at his mother and she looked at him.

"I'm just looking after him for a while," he answered eventually.

She was dissatisfied with his answer and decided she

needed a second opinion.

"What're you doing here Gurgle?" she said softly.

"Don't ask him anything!" demanded Tirgu angrily.

"Don't raise your voice like that to me!" she demanded in return. "This is my house and if you want him fed I've a right to talk to him."

"Don't!"

"Shush! Now, Gurgle come on, tell me."

"He took me from my forest," said Gurgle, and it required considerable courage to do so, with Tirgu glaring at him all the while.

"I see," she replied and then turned back to her son. "What're you doing son? Why?"

Tirgu looked down at his own bowl of shiny stew and seemed unable to speak. Gurgle was amazed to see this creature, once so strong and fearless, reduced to quiet submission. Tirgu put his hands to his temples to support his head and probably to shield himself from all the eyes peering at him. He had nothing to say and in his mind he tried to blank out the world, preferring to concentrate on the dead snails bobbing around in his bowl. He watched them intensely, with the fascination of a child. His mother gave him time to come out with what he needed to say. She didn't have to wait for too long.

"It's all gone wrong for me mum."

"What has?" she said soothingly.

"I've made some bad decisions and they're gunna cost me."

"Is it Baintha?"

"It's everyone. They're all after me now. I'm probably the first person in history to have hobgobs, humans and goblins after him all at the same time. I'm not safe anywhere now."

"You're safe here son, always."

"That would be nice," he replied, putting his arm around her, "but it's not true no matter how much I want to be."

"Eat up you two. No sense wasting my nice food is there? It sounds like you'll need the energy soon anyway."

Gurgle unfolded his arms and began to eat again. Tirgu noticed this and was pleased for more reasons that he could possibly express. He picked up his spoon and began to eat as well. His mother was also pleased to see live bodies in her home once more. This bit of life helped to sustain her own.

"Even though I hardly ever get to see you, and I know you like getting into trouble that you're far better off avoiding, whatever happens Tirgu, I'll always be proud of you," she said.

"Don't be," he replied, as he slurped down a juicy snail. "Winter's on the way for me."

*

The decision of Mala and Keeps to walk into Milton Greens had been vindicated, in that they had not been stabbed on sight. A few brave goblins had come up to them and said a few choice words but they had soon departed once Mala had half withdrawn his sword. Their long noses had been pointing in the right direction it seemed as they gazed upon the only building that could possibly be the Great Hall. In a moment of levity Keeps made an observation about it to his friend.

"Great place to store dung!"

Mala laughed well and this made them unafraid to venture up to it and have words with one of the many souls that stood guard. It was late afternoon and they needed to make progress before the evening settled in. They walked up with confidence to what appeared to be the main entrance, only to be turned away by numerous goblin guards, and an unusually large sort at that. Some were about the same size as they were and this was not something they had seen too often before.

They stumbled quickly back from this spot and instead their attention was drawn to a lit side entrance where there seemed to be fewer guards and a greater possibility of a sensible reception. They approached cautiously and with their arms raised. The guards came from their posts and made a clear command that they should remove and lay down their weapons, which they were happy to do. One of them approached once this was done and then patted them both down. Keeps was inclined to make a further observation but thought better of it after catching a glimpse of his friend, and noticing his deadly serious demeanour.

"What're you two after?" said the goblin, once his intimate exploration was at an end.

"Were from Brown Root forest and we're here to

negotiate over Baintha Brakk's release," said Mala.

"Hah! You might find that a bit hard. What're your names?"

"Mala, and he's Keeps," he replied instantly.

"Alright, I'll have words with them indoors. Sit down there in the muck and don't expect a quick reply," he said firmly.

Another couple of guards had heard this exchange and walked over to keep an eye on them while the first went inside, looking for someone senior. He disappeared from Mala's view, but he was happy that something was being done. He didn't care about the demand that they sit on the ground. It wouldn't be the first time that he'd got dirt on his trousers. Meanwhile, the guard quickly found an official and explained about who had come to see them and why. The official was not pleased but he gave the impression that they had been anticipating something like this. He told the guard to let them wait for a while so that he had time to find someone even more senior. This process occurred a further three times until Croak himself received the news, just as he was about to go home at the end of a long day. He was the least pleased of those in the chain to receive the news but this was an issue that couldn't wait until the next day. He ordered that these two be brought up to his chambers, with a full guard of course, so that they could wag their chins at each other.

Croak sat in his chambers with a notary, who was there to make notes, as you might imagine. They both sipped leaf tea and waited impatiently for the two hobgobs to be brought up. After a few minutes and few more sips the doors creaked open and in walked two hobgoblins. For each of them there was a guard of four hefty goblins. Croak opened proceedings.

"Right then! You're here to negotiate with us over this Baintha Brakk character. Is that right?"

"That's right," said Mala.

"You're Mala?" asked Croak.

"I am."

"And you're doing the talking?"

"I am."

"What have you to tell me then?"

"We want him released."

"Hmmm, I guessed that. You haven't done this before have you?"

"We're prepared to pay."

"Are you? How much?"

"Whatever it takes. He's a rich hobgoblin."

"You haven't spoken to him have you?"

"No, not yet. We'd like to."

"Well, has it occurred to you he might not want you interfering. He's seems quite capable of negotiating for himself."

"Can we see him?"

"No," said Croak, without emotion.

"We demand to see him!"

Croak raised his hand slowly.

"Unless you want to end up spending the night in his company I suggest you keep your voice down. Is that understood?"

Mala and Keeps both nodded.

"Luckily for you," continued Croak, "he neither wants nor needs to see you. He expected you to make contact and he's already suggested a plan which is acceptable to the Council."

"Oh?" said Mala and Keeps in stereo.

"You're familiar with the name Tirgu?"

"Oh yes," said Mala, "we're familiar with him."

"If you can find the goblin child believed to be in his possession and bring him back to Milton Greens safe and well, then we'll release Brakk."

"What's his name?" asked Keeps excitedly.

"Gurgle Sycamore Roundtop."

"And if we find him you'll release Brakk...without any conditions?" asked Mala.

"That's it," said Croak, staring at him.

"Nothing else needed?"

"No. We just want Gurgle back safe."

"Right. We'll do that with pleasure."

"Safe mind! If he's killed the deals off and Brakk rots here. So be very careful."

"We understand," said Mala. "Come on Keeps. No time to waste."

"Good," said Croak as they darted out, "oh wait! Wait! Come back!"

The guards pulled them back before they got very far.

"There's something else," said Croak. "We'll send our brigade out after you. I want them there to keep an eye on things and to take Gurgle from you, when and if you find him."

"You want us to work with your lot?" asked Mala.

"That's right. They'll probably be useful to you as well."

"How do we know that if we give them Gurgle you'll give us Brakk?"

"We goblins can be trusted in such matters. If we did keep him it would just cause a huge fuss and that's the last thing I want. Come on, off with you. They'll follow as soon as they can be organised."

*

Now it was night. Tirgu and Gurgle had finished their food and were doing their best to relax. His mother was sleeping in one corner of the room on her small and simple bed. Tirgu watched as her chest slowly grew and fell with each breath. It had been a long time since he'd seen her and he realised that he couldn't recapture their former friendship so easily. Gurgle was getting tired too but he still had one more adventure to go on before he would be allowed to rest properly for the night.

Once Tirgu was satisfied that his mother was well asleep he turned his attention back to Gurgle and began to whisper to him.

"Hey, I bet you've never been out and about in Brown Root forest at night, have you?"

"No, but shouldn't we stay out of sight?" asked Gurgle sensibly.

"Of course, but its night. Who would expect us to be wandering around, and in Brown Root of all places?"

"If we're caught what'll happen to us?"

"Me? They'll have me. You," he replied, thinking for a few moments, "you I think they'll let go."

"Then let's go," said Gurgle, logically.

"Gurgle," said Tirgu smiling, "you wouldn't run off so soon...would you? I went to a lot of trouble to get you out. I've protected you and helped you all the time we've been together. I need you to stay with me for the moment."

"Till when?" asked Gurgle.

"Till the end," replied Tirgu softly.

"The end of what?"

"The end of me."

"Why're you so sure that'll happen?"

"Because I've burned so many bridges I'm surrounded by fire."

"What'd you think is gunna happen?" said Gurgle.

"They'll find us sooner or later. I'm not sure I can fight everyone off. Will you help me?"

"Fighting you mean? I'm too young."

"I've taught you a lot and you've seen a lot. Why couldn't you?"

"I don't think I could. It's not in me."

"You don't think you're tough enough?"

"No."

"Maybe you've not had many tough lessons in life as I have."

"Maybe."

"Then let me show you one. Come on, it should be dark enough outside now."

Tirgu stood quietly and reached into his special bag of blades on the floor. He withdrew a couple and gave one to Gurgle.

"Tuck that in your belt. We shouldn't need it but you never know."

Tirgu chose another for himself and they both left the house quietly. His mother's awareness was raised but not enough to lift her from her sleepy pit.

They crept slowly for their first few steps and gauged the atmosphere. It was a little misty but things could still be seen at some distance. Gurgle followed in Tirgu's trail and they walked for a while. No one seemed about at this hour but occasionally the sound of other hobgoblins in the distance was clear. Gurgle found the air cold and he was glad to have brought the blanket that Tirgu had given him earlier in the day. He wrapped it around himself and left space enough for his eyes, nose and mouth. Gurgle looked up into the trees and noticed the great difference in style to those in Milton Greens. They had the same habit of being black above a certain level though, when night came down. The ground was soft and slippery and not all that pleasant. Something of this evening was eerily reminiscent of his last walk through Milton Greens.

"Keep up," whispered Tirgu. "I don't want you to get lost."

"How much further?"

"Just a few minutes."

A few minutes later Tirgu diverted from the path they had been on and began to walk between the trees, beckoning Gurgle to follow. After a few moments Tirgu stopped in a small clearing, but apart from the space there seemed little else to distinguish it from the surroundings. He stopped and stared at the ground ahead of him but didn't say anything. Gurgle thought to ask what to look for but he was wise enough to stay quiet and just observe. This he did, and he looked at what Tirgu looked at. The ground here was generally uneven but Gurgle saw that he was looking at two mounds in the earth, both covered in thick moss. Then he looked again at the other uneven shapes in the earth and thought that they too might have been mounds but of an older sort.

"Where are we?" said Gurgle softly.

"The family plot," replied Tirgu, even more softly.

Gurgle realised what he meant but didn't want to ask any more questions. It was better to wait for Tirgu to explain everything when he felt like doing so. After what seemed like a very long minute of contemplation Tirgu turned to his companion and motioned for him to come closer. Gurgle stood beside him and Tirgu pointed downwards. There was a small stone at the head of one of the mounds. The stone was deeply greened by nature and he couldn't read what it said. Tirgu obliged and removed the mystery.

"My son's under there," he said. "Dry and cold."

"Your son?" whispered Gurgle, with his eyes wide.

"Yes, little Preda."

"How old was he?"

"Oh, quite young. He'd be about your age now though."

"Whose is the other one?"

Tirgu looked back in that direction at the longer but not higher mound.

"That's his mother."

"His mother?" asked Gurgle, genuinely shocked and saddened. "What happened to them?"

"Swept away," replied Tirgu after a few moments, and with a definite tremble in his voice.

Gurgle found the answer interesting but a bit unhelpful. He didn't press the point though. After a little while he could no longer resist the temptation to ask. Tirgu anticipated him.

"You're very curious aren't you? Don't worry, I like that about you. Even here."

"What happened Tirgu?" asked Gurgle, who rarely used his name.

"Swept away, like dirt...or useless old stuff."

"They're not dirt," said Gurgle, trying to bolster his mood.

"They might as well be. They're dirt and as useless as anything can be. What use are the dead?"

"They help the flowers grow!" pointed out Gurgle.

Tirgu laughed and put his hand down to pat him on the head. He did so and kept his hand there.

"It's more moss in this case but you're right. This is an early lesson for you Gurgle. We're all in a fast flowing river, though we don't realise it. At any moment we could be dragged under. The hands of others help keep us afloat.

Do you understand Gurgle?"

"I think so," he replied, but was far from confident.

"That's why I hang on to yours. I need you to help keep me afloat. I don't want to sink."

After a few more minutes of quiet Tirgu motioned to Gurgle for them to return. Their soft black journey was free from incident. Once back home they found Tirgu's mother only half asleep, laying awkwardly in her bed.

Tirgu and Gurgle sat around the table once more but Gurgle noticed that Tirgu was paying attention only to his mother. He looked alert and thoughtful. His mother's breathing seemed laboured and the expression on her face, though she was asleep, looked distressed.

"Is she alright?" whispered Gurgle.

"I don't know," he whispered back. "She doesn't look happy."

"She said she was unwell."

"Aye, but not from what," pointed out Tirgu.

"Do you think they know she's your mother?" asked Gurgle.

"Who?"

"The people who're after you."

"They know of my sister and from her they can find mum easily enough."

"What will you do? Will you stay here to protect her?"

"That's what I've been thinking about all evening," Tirgu replied softly.

"We'll watch her!" said Gurgle with an enthusiastic whisper.

"I will...you won't. It's bed time for you."

Tirgu stood and pulled back a curtain hiding another area of the house. He beckoned Gurgle forward and he was directed to a small pile of cushions with a blanket over them. Tirgu had asked his mother to prepare it in their absence. Gurgle did his best to settle himself. He had no idea where Tirgu was going to sleep, as there seemed no other place for anyone to sleep. That was not his concern however, and despite the loud, bubbling breaths of Tirgu's mother he soon fell to sleep.

CHAPTER 16

The Lieutenant was sat in a large chair in his family's tree trunk as his sister dusted all about him. She was happy to have him home but not so happy at the extra dust he had brought with him. His well-used boots were kicked off and lying lazily nearby. He was flicking through some newspapers that had been written about the brigade whilst they had been absent. He'd been out early that morning to collect them from the friends and neighbours he'd asked to keep them for him.

The commentary had been mostly speculative, with many interviews with family members of those kidnapped and with a number of Councillors without the wit to keep quiet. He had hoped for more profiles of himself but was disappointed at how little coverage he had received. Each time he did manage to identify a reference to himself his eyes poked out and his body lurched forwards only to sink back in disappointment once he gauged the shortness of it. He harrumphed his way through most of them, and his sister expressed her disapproval with accelerated dusting.

"Look at this stuff! Have you read any of it?" asked Chirp.

"No," his sister replied.

"Hardly a word about me!" he burped, hardly requiring an answer. "I mean, who writes this stuff? Didn't they know what I was doing?"

"Maybe because you weren't around they found it hard to interview you."

"Well, yes, that's what I thought, but even so. They've

managed to interview half the forest here. What about me?"

"They might be coming over to do an exclusive with the hero of the hour," she remarked sarcastically.

"You think so?" said Chirp, perhaps missing the point of her comment. "Maybe I should get tidied up."

"Maybe you should help me with the dusting."

"Err, no it's alright, you're doing a fine job. If any reporters do come I'll just take them for a walk. I can express myself better that way and act out a few of the more dangerous scenes, heh heh!"

A sudden knock came at the door and with a yelp the Lieutenant made the obvious connection in his mind.

"I wonder who that is?" he said, with a knowing smile on his face.

Before he opened the door he took a quick look at himself in the mirror, brushing and rearranging his clothes a little. The door banged again.

"Alright, alright. Hold your onions! You can have an exclusive, don't worry!" he shouted and then opened the door.

It was Flap Phosphor.

"Lieutenant, hello, how are you?" he said.

"Oh...Flap. I'm fine, what's happening?" he replied.

"Surprised to see me?"

"Yes, at least this early."

"I've got some news."

"Yeah? Me too, but it's all old and not very interesting."

"What do you mean?"

"Oh, nothing. What's happening with you?"

"It's the brigade Sir, we've been ordered to assemble."

"Assemble? So soon? For what?" asked Chirp, unable to hide his displeasure.

"A couple of hobgoblins came to negotiate with the Council yesterday, on behalf of Brakk."

"Yeah? So what? Let them!"

"Hang on, you know the Council want Gurgle back?"

"Mmmm."

"Well, they've sent these two straight off to find him and they want us to follow and keep an eye on things and to make sure that only we bring Gurgle back. If they can find him then we'll exchange him for Brakk."

"I see, makes sense I suppose. I was just hoping for a few more days to recover."

"And do interviews."

"And do...hey!" he said, laughing. "You know me too well. Where and when do we report?"

"The Great Hall, midday."

"Fine. Can I rely on you to get the rest of the brigade together before then?"

"I've already started, but a lot of them are gunna be hard to find if you know what I mean?"

"No, I don't think I do. How many are we talking here?"

"A couple of dozen at most."

"A couple of *dozen*?! Where the hell have they gone?"

"Come on Lieutenant, they've gone home...scarpered."

"Scarpered? Is that what you call dereliction of duty?"

"No, but..."

"But nothing! There's not much we can do about it this morning though. I just hope for their sakes they don't do any interviews whilst we're gone or I'll turn boiled mice into bloody roasted!"

This seemed to bring the exchange to its end. The Lieutenant went back inside and explained to his long suffering sister that shortly he would be off on his duties again. She was not altogether surprised and took life's twists and turns with grace and an even temper, unlike the majority of the goblin men in her life. He packed his bits and was soon back through the door.

*

Mala and Keeps had left Milton Greens as soon as they'd received their instructions. Their objective was clear but the method by which they might achieve it was not. Where was Tirgu? That was the question. If they found Tirgu they would find Gurgle, but he would probably have those human men with him and maybe by now a few more recruits to fill up the gaps after his cowardly attack. Plus, with those horses he could be over fifty miles distant. That gave them too much ground to consider searching, though what else was there to do but search? Baintha Brakk would have as much of an idea as Mala about where they might be, though Baintha would use his intellect to think of better ways to find them. Mala missed his confidence and power of direction.

They were both tired after their journey between the two

forests, with Mala in particular suffering a little more due to the bodily stress of his encounter with Tirgu. Keeps also suffered, but his fatigue was perhaps partly due to his guilt at not contributing to Brakk's defence when he should have done. Mala had not been aware that Keeps had been witness to the raid and would not be pleased to know it.

They were not interested in waiting for those goblins to follow them out of the forest. They would only be an annoyance. If they found Gurgle they could be trusted to bring him back considering the stakes. What was the point of having a whole army standing by, especially one that had raided their forest? Mala knew what anger that would provoke amongst his fellow hobgoblins. It was better to get ahead of them and do their own thing, even though their limbs ached for some peace, and if that was not possible then a little sympathy. They had no time however and they kept a quick pace. A goblin trader near the edge of the forest had been kind enough to do business with them the previous evening and so they were well fed and watered. They had slept in the open air over night between the forests, but this was not unusual for them so it was no great burden. Their anxiety had been such that they enjoyed little sleep and so had spent most of their time on the move, wearily making progress on the long route from there to home. It was possible to walk the whole way in less than one day but few were fit enough or burdened enough to do it. Even so, their return was much quicker than their approach since that big group of goblins had been fairly slow and cumbersome.

The business in hand was going to liven up Brown Root forest considerably. The parallel between the raid on Milton Greens and the goblin's subsequent excitement was an easy one to draw. Mala hoped that in their absence all sorts of hobgoblins would dust down their old weapons and armour and stand ready, or at the very least keep their eyes and ears open. He would put himself in charge, though frustratingly he hadn't been able to hear Baintha's word to that effect. In any case it was still a good opportunity to do right by his friend and employer. He would try to redeem some of the humiliation that the raid had inflicted.

As they trudged over hump and bump through the midday rain both hobgoblins thought in silence about how to find Tirgu and Gurgle. Both concluded in silence that they did not know how. A phenomenon not widely known much beyond their borders was that hobgoblins, as creatures, have a strong tendency in their characters towards the concept of fate. They didn't believe in gods or monsters but rather in the all-seeing providence that infects existence. From the tiniest raindrop to the mightiest King everything had a destiny according to its form, and each, despite its best efforts, could not escape it. This might be thought to be a universal idea but the hobgoblins took the notion to its extreme. Both of them felt confident that a creature such as Tirgu had no fate but the one he deserved. Tirgu himself would no doubt have agreed.

Keeps struggled to keep up with his slightly fitter companion. He was finding the journey most tiring, and this discovery he did not want to keep. On long walks he knew that after a while a certain mood drifts down. The mind is almost put to sleep while the legs are kept at work below. This allows perception of maybe only one moment in three and when one looks back on the whole journey little of it can be remembered. When it comes to tricks and spells, the mind puts even Zebulan McCranahan to shame.

Keeps felt it natural to defer to his older and probably wiser companion, who himself deferred to the even older and definitely wiser Baintha. He would follow his orders but desperately wanted a chance to redeem himself after his impotent performance. Many of us have dreams of battles and fights but the sudden reality of one can strike a blow heavier than any felt in the imagination and leave you prostrate and helpless before it. Keeps had had a taste of this and was determined to be better prepared next time. So, both of them succoured in their sleepy momentum continued on and soon saw Brown Root forest looming large once again. It seemed to be buzzing with activity and many eager young creatures welcomed them. They wanted news, orders and hopefully promises of payment. Though Baintha was very wealthy he was the exception in Brown Root and many a hungry creature was willing to put his scrawny arms to use.

Mala began the process of organising them. He ordered them into loose units, putting hobgobs he knew at the head of each. He was going to make the forest into fortress Brown Root, against enemies within and without, before going out after Tirgu, wherever he might be. The forest without Baintha in it was a vulnerable one. Baintha was skilled at dissuading his enemies but his absence was more tempting to them than free honey.

*

Gurgle woke up but was in no hurry to get up. His rest had been comprehensive and as is so often the case after a good night's sleep the mind and body need some time to emerge from this enjoyable state. The cushions and blanket had been surprisingly comfortable. As his mind slowly came together he listened and looked around only to hear and see nothing of anyone. He couldn't hear the breathing noises of Tirgu's mother.

He stretched a little and found the atmosphere very quiet considering the situation they were in. He wondered where Tirgu was and so stood from his pile to begin a search, using all the gentle politeness one would expect when in another's home. He pulled back the curtain and had an answer to all his thoughts immediately. Tirgu was sat quietly at the side of his mother's bed and she was still asleep. He looked up suddenly and saw little Gurgle awake at last.

"There you are...finally," said Tirgu. "You must have been catching up on a few days of lost sleep."

"I'm sorry," he whispered.

"It doesn't matter. Something's happened."

"What?"

"Come here."

Gurgle moved slowly over to them both and seemed unsure of what he had in mind.

"Gimme your hand," said Tirgu, whilst staring at him beneath half lids.

Gurgle raised his arm with his hand dangling at the end of it. He was anticipating a small smack or some other mean spirited little punishment for oversleeping. Such an occurrence had not been uncommon back in Milton Greens. Instead Tirgu simply took his hand and pulled it towards his mother, causing Gurgle some surprise. Before he had the chance to react his hand was placed against her skin. It was cool. Now he understood, but that didn't stop him retracting his hand an instant later from the shock of it.

"She's cold!"

"Yes," said Tirgu. "She died."

"What happened?" he asked, with all the innocence deserving of someone his age.

"She died, what'd you think happened?" responded Tirgu, tersely.

Gurgle looked at her more closely. Her mouth was open and seemed dry. Her pillow was to one side and it seemed wet in one patch. Her arms were by her side in an unnatural position compared to the rest of her body and Gurgle supposed that Tirgu had moved her for some reason. He wanted to ask more but Tirgu was clearly not in the mood. He couldn't control himself however.

"Were you with her?" he asked.

Tirgu looked up at him thinking whether his question had anything in it he ought to object to. Since it hadn't he couldn't refuse to reply.

"Yes. I was." he said, hoping that was enough.

"Was it her breathing?"

"I don't know."

"Was it her heart?" asked Gurgle again.

"I don't know!" he growled. "Check for yourself if you want."

"No, I don't want that."

"Then shut up."

Gurgle backed away from Tirgu. This level of tension was too much for him and he started to feel afraid. His mind was full of thoughts but now his tongue knew better than to bend the air.

Tirgu got to his feet and drew the blanket all the way over his mother's body. Now that she was covered he breathed a sigh of relief and turned his attention back to Gurgle.

"That's one less person I need to protect," he said softly, staring at the ground.

"Do we leave?" asked Gurgle.

"Leave?" he said, angry at his disrespect. "Leave my mother to rot in her bed? Is that what you think we should do?"

"No! No! I mean do we leave after burying her?"

"We can't go out and bury her now. It's day time. We have to stay put until dark."

This was not the answer that Gurgle wanted to hear. A full day in Tirgu and his dead mother's company did not appeal and he looked visibly distressed at the words. Tirgu detected this feeling but did not react well.

"You want to get away, don't you? I'm tired of your ingratitude! I've done so much for you! I rescued you from that forest of fools and your dead end family. I've shown you the outside world. I've shown you more in a month than you would've seen in your entire lifetime! I've shown you what you're capable of...and still! Still you want to get away from me. Well, you can forget it! Put it out of your mind!"

"My family are not fools," said Gurgle quietly.

"Yes, they are. They're just a bunch of little green idiots that don't know a thing about the world."

"No!" said Gurgle, as he started to cry. "Don't say that!"

"You're my son now, do you understand? Forget them!"

"No! I'm not your son and I never will be. I'm Gurgle Roundtop and I live in Milton Greens! You stole me from my family! I hate you!"

Tirgu growled at his son's disobedience, charged at him and picked him bodily from the floor in one swift move. With a hand on each arm Tirgu gripped him tightly and stared at him, much as he had done on the bank of the river that flowed through Milton Greens.

"Alright Gurgle! Now's your chance! I'm going to find out what you're really capable of. Take this!"

Tirgu put him down and turned to the table. There was a blade on it and he quickly swiped at it and put it in Gurgle's hand.

"I'm tired of your disloyalty! You'll never get a better

chance than this. Come on."

He opened his shirt and revealed the top of his dark and dirty chest. In the same moment Gurgle noticed one or two fresh scratches on it. Tirgu got on his knees and leaned forward, offering his vulnerability.

"Come on," he demanded. "Put the blade in! I'd rather it was you than one of the thousands of others that would love the chance."

Gurgle held the blade firmly but was crying full tears now.

"Come on!" he demanded again. "If you can't do it what good are you? You're not tough at all. I should have left you with all those fools in that forest of yours."

"I can't!" he wailed.

"Yes, you can! This is the only way you'll get back to the forest. If you can't do it you'll have to stay here and be my son. What's it gunna be?"

"I can't," he said more softly, and dropped the blade.

"Well," replied Tirgu, with relief. "I think you've answered my question. Are you with me now?"

"Yes," whispered Gurgle, looking at his feet.

"Will you fight with me...and help to protect me?"

"Yes," he whispered again.

"Are you *my* son now?"

"Yes," he whispered for a third time.

Tirgu felt it was time to end this suffering and he put his arms around him, embracing him, as he would like to do with little Preda, still so dry and so cold.

*

566

The Lieutenant, his quartermaster and the remnants of the One Hundred and Seventh Milton Greens Special Militia Brigade had assembled in the grounds of the Great Hall. There seemed something of an anti-climax to this gathering since it was not at all what they had expected to be doing. Most had anticipated a welcoming parade, general adulation and a well-earned rest. A few were already enjoying the last of those things despite the quartermaster's best efforts. Some seventy six Mice were present and accounted for.

There was a new task for them, but it was one without any sort of sensible thinking behind it. It made sense for them to collect Gurgle from whoever might find him, and then bring him home, but it was unclear whether they should be directly involved in searching for him or fighting with those that might have him. It was their duty to go where the Council directed them however and for those with a financial head on their shoulders it might mean many extra days pay.

This exit from the forest came without the fanfare of the moment or any kind words. A simple written command from Croak had been put into the Lieutenant's hand, which stated that the brigade should be reassembled and go from the forest to keep a close watch on those two hobgobs and to collect Gurgle should they find him. It allowed so much room for manoeuvre that he may as well not have written it at all. It felt to the Lieutenant like an afterthought. But, afterthought or no, it had the force of the Council, and they held all the nuts, figuratively speaking.

The Lieutenant was relieved to discover that none of the
Mice he had come to know well had failed to report for
duty. He was quite surprised by the sight of Slap Canopy
and his family. This goblin was prodigious to say the least,
as *two* wives came by to see him off. He also had many
children of different ages engaged in the same sad task, but
the Lieutenant couldn't be certain that some of the young
goblin women weren't in fact additional wives, as one or
two had babes in arms. The Lieutenant wasn't keen on
this practice of having more than one wife. In their history
it had sometimes been necessary to do it in order to
maintain the race, usually after war, and it made sense
under such conditions. It had not been necessary for a long
time however and only those with a keen interest in
reviving the practice for their own benefit still did it. He
noticed from listening to them all speaking that the wives
had the habit of calling each other 'sister'. The Lieutenant
reflected on the irony that his own sister, because of her
duties, often referred to herself as his 'wife'.

His attention was drawn away from this curious family
scene by his quartermaster. He whispered to him that
everyone seemed ready to go, subject to the emotional
goodbyes still in progress. So, shortly thereafter they went
on their way. The rest of the forest thereabouts was just
going about its normal daily business and few looked up
from their activities to wish them well. How disappointed
the Lieutenant felt, not just for himself but also for his
Mice, that the forest showed such little excitement at their

presence. Perhaps they would show more excitement because of their absence. In his heart the Lieutenant knew that their mission was not quite at an end, and perhaps the forest knew it too.

The day was cool and breezy and had not the buzz of that other day when Croak had sent them on their way with fine words and flags waving. The brigade's flag bearers were also still with them. Any damage to their morale from the obvious absenteeism was quickly countered by these goblins with their uplifted chins and unstinting loyalty.

Copper coloured leaves littered the ground and the wind ordered them into drifts that sometimes came as high as their waists. This was no obstacle though and they just swished on through. The quartermaster rustled his way up to the Lieutenant and had a word.

"Lieutenant!" he said.

"What is it?" he replied.

"What's the plan?"

"Plan? Follow the hobgobs and see what happens."

"Anything else?" said Flap, in good spirits.

"What do you mean?"

"Well, how much should we interfere?"

"I've been thinking that we should let them have a go and if they fail then see what we can do."

"Have we enough rations to wait that long?"

"Probably not, but maybe they'll feed us," said the Lieutenant, smiling broadly.

"We'll get nothing from them. We're not allies and we

never will be."

"Not with that attitude."

"Come on Lieutenant, don't get complacent. Even though the mission seems very hasty it doesn't mean we should be casual about it."

"Casual? Me? No, you're right. But until something happens, what can we do?"

"I don't know, but we shouldn't go out unprepared."

"Too late I'm afraid."

"We can't ride our luck a second time."

"No...but we can give it a damn good try!" he exclaimed, laughing at his own wit.

The quartermaster gave him a powerful slap on the back of his head, which everyone in the brigade either saw or heard. He hunched his body at the shock of it and then turned in Flap's direction with a flaming expression. The brigade came to an unrequested halt.

"What the hell are you doing?" he said angrily.

"Giving you a dose of the unexpected!"

"Do you wanna be sent back?" he said, even more angrily. "If you're not going to take this seriously then it's better that we all do!"

"What's wrong with you Flap?" he asked in all seriousness.

"No! What's wrong with you, you great clonk!?"

"Hey! Don't behave like this in front of the Mice!" he said angrily, through gritted teeth.

"It's better the whole thing falls apart than we go out into danger like this! You're not taking it seriously!"

"I am, calm down!"

"No! This isn't going to be easy and you need to buck your ideas up, right now!"

"What'd you mean?"

"I've seen commanders lead with their eyes closed and it always ends in disaster."

"Alright, you've opened them. Take it easy!"

"You need to act like a leader, right now!"

At this the Lieutenant laughed a little as he thought the request impossible to satisfy just like that, but because of this Flap's anger reignited. He grabbed his Lieutenant by the shoulder and began a further tirade.

"Lieutenant...Chirp! Don't take these brave soldiers out of the forest unless you're willing to die for them and willing to order *them* to die!"

"Eh?"

"Come here!"

The quartermaster pulled his Lieutenant from one side to the middle of the path and in front of the brigade, who were by now becoming increasingly bewildered by the scene. He swung him round to face them all.

"Right!" he began. "This is your leader. What are you prepared to do for him!?"

The Mice were fairly quiet as you can imagine but after a few moments one or two shouted out.

"To fight!" said one.

"To do our duty!" said another.

"To roast some hobgoblin's arse!" said a third, rather unadvisedly.

"There's something else!" said Flap. "Another thing you're willing to do!"

He waited for a few moments for an answer. Slap Canopy provided it.

"To die!" he said.

"To die! Thank you Slap...to die. Now, Lieutenant, I'm going to tell everyone what you're prepared to do for the brigade. Are you listening?"

The Lieutenant nodded more from nervousness than agreement.

"Right!" said Flap. "On your knees!"

"What?"

"Get on your knees!" demanded Flap, and the Lieutenant did so. "Number one! He's going to swear to protect each and every one of you with his life!"

He waited for a few moments for the Lieutenant to take the hint but he did not.

"Swear!" he demanded.

"I swear!" replied the Lieutenant, once he recognised the way things were going.

"Say it!"

"I'm going to protect each and every one of you with my life!"

"Two! He's going to think very carefully about every order he gives!"

"I'm...I'm going to think carefully about every order I give."

"*Very* carefully!"

"Very carefully!"

"Three! If I don't swear that I love the brigade more than life itself I'll cut my chestnuts off!"

At this the brigade laughed but the quartermaster raised a hand to stop them.

"Shut up! This is deadly serious! Shut up! Do you swear it Lieutenant?"

"I swear!"

"Swear what?"

"To cut my chestnuts off if I don't love the brigade!"

"Close enough," said Flap, smiling gently. "I'm not sure we've got a small enough sword anyway. Right! Goblin squeeze!"

From childhood play each of them understood this command and they swarmed together as a big group bumping and jumping into one another until they could no longer take it. The Lieutenant was thrown into the middle of it by Flap. The experience of the last few minutes had been so surreal that he had no option but to laugh like a child. The laughs of the other Mice all around him were so infectious you see.

*

Mala and two other hobgoblins sat in one of the back rooms of Baintha's house. They were together to discuss the strategy for finding Tirgu, getting Gurgle back and releasing Baintha. The objective was simple to understand but the means of achieving it was somewhat thornier. Keeps wasn't present as he had been sent off to marshal the volunteers, which was a nice word for them. Mala kept the business of what to do between himself and his key contacts within the forest.

The conversation was not really getting very far until the subject of Tirgu's family came up.

"I don't know anything about his family?" said Mala. "Anybody know anything?"

"I don't know of any," said one of them, a bloated fixer of problems called Murit.

"He's got family, course he has," said the third member of the gathering, another fixer called Bruach.

"Really? Who?" asked Mala, in between long sucks on his long tobacco pipe.

"A sister, just the one I think," replied Bruach.

"Where's she live?" asked Murit.

"I don't know...you'll have to ask around."

"No! You'll have to ask around, today!" said Mala. "Anyone else you know of?"

"He's got an old mum around somewhere. I could check for her too."

"Yeah, please do," said Mala sarcastically. "It just might help."

"He's not gunna come back to the forest to see them though, is he?" asked Bruach.

"No, probably not," said Mala.

"He could be worried about them," said Murit. "I'd be worried. Why wouldn't he come back?"

"Because the whole forest would turn him in the moment they saw him, that's why," observed Mala.

There was a little silence now as their minds got to work. One of Brakk's assistants came in with some leaf tea and put the doings down on the table between them.

"Well, what do we know of him? Wouldn't he come back to protect his family?" asked Murit.

"Nah...he's not like that. He's ruthless as hell," said Bruach.

"I don't think he'd be so foolish whatever his instincts were," said Mala.

"If he doesn't come back to the forest where will he go?" said Bruach. "He must come back eventually."

"Well, he was away for ten years, on and off. If he wants to stay away he won't find it hard. He's got a lot of friends amongst the human men," replied Mala.

"Ah, well I heard different on that," said Murit.

"Oh, what'd you hear?" asked Mala, whilst sipping some of the tea that had been put out for them.

"Plenty of human men been coming this way in the last day or two, getting away from some fight. A lot of them were injured. Big battle somewhere and a few of them stopped to talk about it you see, for a little water and what not. A friend of a friend of an enemy told me that they were swearing off at Tirgu something rotten. Didn't gather exactly why though, just that his name was blacker than mud. He's not welcome with the human men anymore."

"Then he's got nowhere else to go, right?" asked Bruach.

"He could live in the open," said Murit.

"Don't be daft," said Mala.

"How do we know he's even got Gurgle anymore?" asked Bruach.

"We don't, but it's likely," replied Mala. "We don't know anything yet, to be honest. That's why we need to get started straight away."

"What do you want us to do Mala?" asked Murit.

"Well, you can try to get more from the human men on why his name's mud. It could point us in the right direction. Bruach, you get after his family. Let's go!"

"Can I finish my tea first?" said Bruach.

"Yes," said Mala reluctantly. "You can finish your tea."

As Bruach sipped away, making the appropriate noises, Mala stood and walked to the front door of the house. He opened it and sucked in some fresh air to replace the dry and smoky variety indoors. He looked back at the two of them sat at the table and had something of a flashback. In his mind he visualised a time when Baintha was in charge and saw how he conducted himself and his business. When something needed doing it should simply be done, without prevarication. Mala grabbed this sentiment with both hands.

"Forget the tea!" he shouted. "Get out there this instant! Get to work!"

*

"I'm hungry," said Gurgle, all of a sudden.

This caused Tirgu to wake from his exhausted state and peer at him from across the room. He groaned and looked

576

about in hope of finding something quick and easy to give him. Nothing leapt in his eye except the barrenness of his mother's kitchen. She clearly hadn't been eating very much lately and that snail stew probably represented all the food she had.

"Have a look and see what you can find," said Tirgu, trying to give up on his provider role.

Gurgle got to his feet and began to sniff about amongst the pots and pans, jars and bottles. Where necessary he blew the dust off of things to get a better idea of what was underneath. Depressingly, what was inside most of the jars seemed very much like what was caked to the outside. He looked beneath the stove and found an old cloth bag. Carefully he peered inside and found lots of garlic bulbs. He pulled a few out and found them to be withered and decidedly past their best. He wasn't that desperate for food. He continued to rummage but little more was to be found. He soon passed his findings on to Tirgu.

"I can't find anything," he said.

Tirgu felt the need to come and check for himself. Gurgle was probably just being picky. He would find something to keep him busy so he could get back to his snoozing.

"I'm sure we can find you something," said Tirgu confidently.

After a few moments of more determined rummaging Tirgu also had to admit that there was nothing to eat. The two of them peered about whilst crouching uncomfortably. Tirgu had an idea but was not all that keen on doing it.

"Right, well, we need to get you some food," said Tirgu, thinking out loud. "I know!"

He got to his feet and turned back towards his mother, wrapped in her sheets on the bed, yet still with a noticeable presence. He moved back to her side but didn't pay much attention to her. Instead he peered around the edges of the little bed upon which she lay. Then he delved in with his fingers, prodding and exploring between the frame and the sheets. He didn't find anything at first so began to lift her up a little. He put his whole arm under her thin mattress and moved it about until making a small moan of discovery.

"Found it!" he said. "Let's see how much we have."

He withdrew his arm and at the end of it there hung a small pouch. Tirgu invited Gurgle over but he declined, preferring not to sit on the bed with him and his dead mother. Immediately Tirgu disgorged the loot and placed it in his free hand to examine his prize. He turned back to his mother, looking down at the shape of her face in the sheet.

"It's not much of a legacy mum," he said to her, "but it'll have to do."

"Is it enough?" asked Gurgle, fully aware of the potential of it.

"Enough?" responded Tirgu. "Enough for what?"

"Enough for what we need," he replied.

Tirgu stared at him for a few moments but not in anger. He pointed gently in his direction.

"I think I know your calling in life Gurgle. You shouldn't

be a fighter...you should be a thief."

Gurgle laughed at the silliness of the suggestion.

"I'm not a thief," he said after a few moments.

"No, but with an instinct for money like that, it wouldn't surprise me. Come on, we can use some of this to buy what we need. What food would you like from the market?"

"You're going out? In the daytime?" asked Gurgle, not quite approving.

"I don't like it but what can we do?"

"But it'll be busy at the market, won't it?"

"Yeah, but the busier it is the more anonymous it is too. That's helpful."

"What about me? I don't want to stay here."

"You can't come with me."

"I'm not staying here with a dead body."

"It's mum! What could possibly happen?" said Tirgu, laughing.

"I'm not doing it!" he replied forcefully.

"Then I guess you don't have a future as a grave robber," said Tirgu, sagely. "What are we going to do with you then?"

"Wrap me up!" he suggested.

"That won't work. They'll spot your green skin a mile off."

Both of them recognised the dead end they had talked themselves into and so they began to think. Tirgu looked at Gurgle and then his eyes were drawn to the scene beyond him. The kitchen was in a mess and was in need of a thorough cleaning. He looked at his green features and contrasted them with the brown and greasy backdrop. He then began to laugh as a particular idea came to him.

"Why are you laughing?" asked Gurgle.

"I've got an idea. Turn around."

Gurgle did so, and looked without purpose at the kitchen and the objects all about.

"Luckily for you, the older grease gets the less it smells," said Tirgu.

"What do you mean?"

"Snail grease for instance. It's good on toast. I wonder how it is on goblins."

"I don't understand."

"Grab a handful of grease from the cooking pot there and put it to use."

"Put it to use? How?"

"You're a bit slow aren't you Gurgle? Put it on your face!"

"No! It's horrible stuff."

"Well stay here with mum then."

Gurgle stopped talking for a few moments and pondered the choice. He looked a little closer at the dark goo and picked up a spoon. Tirgu smiled because he guessed correctly what Gurgle would prefer to do. Gurgle twisted the spoon through the grease and found it particularly thick and shiny.

"Can't we just stay here and eat it?" asked Gurgle, causing Tirgu to burst out laughing.

"No," he replied. "You're committed to it now. I'll need you to help me carry the food anyway so come on, get it on your face."

Gurgle turned back to the pot and the snail grease within. He played a little more with the spoon and extracted a gob of the stuff. He lifted it to his nose and tentatively allowed the odour inside. He couldn't smell anything.

"What did I tell you? No smell. It'll be fine, slap it on," said Tirgu, still much amused.

Gurgle took a finger and lightly touched the surface of the grease. It was surprisingly dry but still had a pull when he drew his finger away.

"Get it on! Come on, *I'm* getting hungry now. If you keep this up any longer mum'll start getting hungry too."

Tirgu looked down at his mother and quietly apologised for his cheek. Gurgle was still concentrating on the grease and slowly put a little on the end of his finger. Tirgu watched this scene intensely and felt eager to help, but he controlled himself to allow Gurgle to reveal more of his nature. A blob of long gone snail was put against his green forehead. The feeling was not as unpleasant as he had expected and so he began to spread it around.

"Well done. Keep going. I'm eager to see what you'll look like as a hobgoblin."

Gurgle was a bit more relaxed now and took a little more grease, spreading it on his face with greater speed and enthusiasm. Tirgu stood and walked over, eager for a better view of things. This show was surprisingly good entertainment. He recognised it as the first good laugh he'd had for quite a while. He watched as Gurgle did his best. They didn't have a mirror so Tirgu directed him to areas that he missed. His impatience got the better of him and he helped himself to some grease, doing his best to finish the job. They both smiled and began to laugh at the ridiculousness of it all. Tirgu thought to himself how much he enjoyed being with Gurgle and having a son again. It was a feeling he hadn't experienced for such a long time and some unfamiliar emotions were flowing through him. He looked down at Gurgle and saw that the greasification was almost complete. Gurgle looked up at Tirgu for a sign that he could stop.

"Almost done," said Tirgu. "You look like my old grandma."

"Is it good?" asked Gurgle, ignoring the comment.

"It's good. Let me get the cloak."

Tirgu was back almost before he had left. He wrapped Gurgle up in what was little more than a grey blanket and tucked him in. The effect was surprisingly convincing. He stepped back to admire his skill.

"Ah, hands too," he observed.

Gurgle dipped the backs of his hands directly in the pot and used what was left on his fingers for the various grooves and uneven places. Once Gurgle was satisfied so was Tirgu.

"What do you think mum?" asked Tirgu loudly, the volume being necessary of course.

"Don't say that," said Gurgle, frightened by his lack of respect.

"Oh cruel son, cruel son, don't make fun of me," said Tirgu to his mother, mimicking her voice.

"That's bad," said Gurgle, innocently. "You mustn't."

582

"Why not? She's dead. Once people are dead they can't do anything."

"But it's your mother!"

"No it isn't."

"What?"

"Mum's gone."

"No she isn't. She's over there!"

"That's just her body. It may as well be half a pig."

"But it isn't half a pig, it's your mother."

"I know that," said Tirgu gently. "What's your point exactly?"

"You shouldn't say those things about your mother!"

"Why not? What could possibly happen?"

"It's just bad luck, that's all."

"Bad luck?" laughed Tirgu. "I've had more than my fair share of bad luck in life and I didn't deserve even half of it. Bad luck gets dished out whether you like it or not. Did you deserve the bad luck of bumping into me?"

This was bringing up bad feeling and Tirgu thought it wiser not to press the point. He wished he could have taken back that last sentence. Gurgle also thought it wiser not to get into that kind of discussion.

"You shouldn't speak about dead people like that," he eventually pointed out.

"She can't hear me."

"Yes, but...if she *could* hear you, what would she think?"

Tirgu smiled and pondered the question.

"She'd probably just want to give me a slap on the head. I can live with that."

"Well, you shouldn't make fun of the dead."

"I'm not, really. I've done plenty of grieving in my time. Maybe I just can't do it anymore."

This seemed to pop the balloon of their conversation and they fell silent. Tirgu took a closer look at his little companion and made little touches here and there to improve his appearance. His features looked a little odd for a hobgoblin but he had seen many uglier creatures in the forest in his time and he felt confident they would not be detected.

"So," said Tirgu, once he was done. "What do you want to eat?"

"Anything but snail stew," replied Gurgle warmly.

*

The Boiled Mice, bruised but elated after their goblin squeeze, made good progress beyond the edge of Milton Greens. The Lieutenant was still a little shaken up and his thighs were feeling soft and nervous. He was worried about how the whole spectacle had affected the Mice's view of him and of the quartermaster. Flap himself had been silent since things had quietened down. The Lieutenant thought Flap had been right to correct him but didn't like the implications for his friend's state of mind. To be honest though, these concerns were insignificant compared to the weight of the duty on their shoulders. This had the effect of focussing even the most fickle of minds.

The day was running out but they were still making good progress across the open ground. The interesting delay caused by the quartermaster had not delayed them too much, and curiously it had been quite a spur to their mood and energy levels.

On the horizon all the Mice noticed the large clouds looming, broadly in the direction of Brown Root forest. A storm was clearly on its way. They had almost forgotten about the influence of the weather, as their previous trip out of Milton Greens had been so generously filled with fine, clear air. Back in the forest they often had little warning of bad weather and rain just seemed to fall from the trees as and when it chose. The canopy offered continuous shelter, so heavy rain rarely bothered the goblins except when it became slippery under foot. The idea of being stuck out in the open under a rain storm did not appeal in the least.

They couldn't hear any sound from this bank of cloud but it appeared more ominous each time they looked up at it. They wouldn't be able to take any shelter in Brown Root for obvious reasons and this led to the realisation of their first mistake, which was that they had brought no waterproof clothing with them, unlike on their first trip. The Lieutenant looked around and saw that this was not true for some of his Mice, and those that'd had the sense to pack such items were now wearing them in anticipation of rain. The Lieutenant walked over to his quartermaster and asked him about such gear.

"Waterproofs?" he said.

"I know, I know! I forgot to remind them to bring them," replied Flap, quite aware of the problem.

"Tents?" asked the Lieutenant.

"Yes, we've got tents! I'm not gunna forget those."

"I mean are they waterproof?"

"They're sort of waterproof."

"Sort of?"

"I guess we'll find out this evening."

"Anything else we forgot to bring?"

"Just some leadership! Ho ho..." joked Flap.

"It's your turn for a slap on the back of the head, I think," replied the Lieutenant, not much amused.

"Don't! I'll have to report you to the Council. Considering your record they'll lock you up for good!"

"Hmmm, I see your mood's improved!"

"Well, doing what I did seems to have lifted everyone's spirits and I think we're in the right frame of mind again."

"Let's hope so. It won't last if we all get soaked to the skin, I can tell you that."

"Maybe the storm will pass us by."

"No, I don't think so. It's got my name written all over it."

"Oh yeah, I see what you mean. What does it say? 'The biggest clonk in Milton Greens.'"

"Now you're *really* asking for it!" replied the Lieutenant with a smile. "This is the end for you!"

With that the Lieutenant felt it was his turn for some play and jumped on his quartermaster's back. The Mice all around smiled as it was obviously good natured.

"You're going to carry me all the way to Brown Root!" shouted the Lieutenant.

The quartermaster laughed and grabbed the Lieutenant's thighs and thought to give him a ride. This he managed for a few steps but the ground was a little lower than he assumed on one footstep and he stumbled forward. The Lieutenant was thrown and there was a yelp of pain, though not from him. The quartermaster crumpled to the ground and began to groan.

"My back!" he moaned. "Oh...my back!"

The Lieutenant rolled over to face his quartermaster and looked at him with grave concern.

"What happened?" he asked.

"You've done my back in! What does it look like?" he replied, whilst prostrate on the ground.

The Mice crowded around and looked down at their quartermaster. He was doing his best to keep his body motionless and waved away anyone that attempted to help him. He continued to groan, as much from feelings of foolishness as from pain. He lay on his side and stared straight ahead at a mass of feet. His helmet had rolled away. The Lieutenant came close and knelt in front of him.

"How bad is it?" he asked gently.

"Bad! I can't move," came the almost breathless reply.

"Well, what can we do to help?"

"I don't know," he whispered.

Beads of sweat started to drip down his forehead and his eyes darted about, reflecting the fact that ideas were doing the same thing in his mind. The Lieutenant looked down at his friend and companion and thought about what to do. The conclusion they both reached was inevitable but hard to admit. They looked in each other's eyes and knew what to do. The Lieutenant nodded to him.

"Stretcher!" shouted the Lieutenant.

A pathway was made through the group and a couple of strong armed goblins came in. They put it down beside him and they allowed him to a few moments to consider how he would climb aboard.

"Push it closer," whispered Flap, "till it's almost under me."

They slowly put their arms under his shoulders and legs and gently moved him onto to it. It was upsetting for them all to see him like this as he tried to stifle his agony. He closed his eyes then gasped as they set him down. Once he was still again he looked at his Lieutenant and tried to beckon him close for a word.

"I want to speak to you alone," he whispered.

"Alright," he whispered back.

The Lieutenant stood and directed his Mice some twenty metres distant and told them all to wait.

"I'm sorry about this," whispered Flap, once his Lieutenant was back kneeling in front of him.

"No, *I'm* sorry, it was my stupid fault," replied the Lieutenant.

"No, I've let you down."

"It's alright Flap, don't worry. We'll manage."

"Yeah, I think you will. Just take care...of *them*, of

yourself!"

"I will, of course I will. When we're done I'll come and tell you the whole story."

"Before you speak to any reporters?"

"Aye!" said the Lieutenant with a sad smile. "You first. I promise."

"Will you do me a favour?" asked Flap.

"Anything!"

"Put something waterproof over me."

"Sure," said the Lieutenant laughing, but only so that he would be less likely to cry.

"I think it's going to rain all the way back to Milton Greens."

In the distance their sensitive ears discerned what was clearly the first rumble.

CHAPTER 17

Tirgu opened one of the shuttered windows of his mother's house and took a long but surreptitious look out of it. There were one or two figures in the distance but no one close by. The weather also looked gloomy and grey. This was good thought Tirgu, since it meant the light levels would be reduced, thus helping them in their activities. He turned his head back inside and nodded to Gurgle.

"I think we can go out now," said Tirgu gently. "I want to take a look at the horse first. See if it's alright. It'll need feeding too."

Gurgle listened but did not reply. Tirgu opened the front door and took a furtive look around before beckoning for Gurgle to follow him. The daylight, though softened by the gloomy weather, was still unpleasant on Gurgle's eyes. He had clearly been cooped up for too long in that dark shack. Tirgu walked around to the back of the house and found the horse waiting calmly. It occurred to him that it could so easily have been taken by a thief and they were lucky to still have it. The horse looked unhappy however and clearly wanted a feed and a change of scenery. Tirgu rediscovered a pile of hay at the back of his mother's house. It was probably a relic of the last time that he was here, on horseback and in better times. It didn't look particularly nutritious but it would have to do. At least it was dry. Tirgu looked up at the sky and could sniff the moisture in the air. Some bad weather was on the way. Gurgle came around to join him. Tirgu looked at him and wondered whether the grease would survive a soaking. It probably would, but raindrops might bead a little on the grease and look strange.

"We can give this to the horse," said Tirgu softly. "Help me carry some of it."

Gurgle obliged and they quickly made a large pile of hay at the horse's feet. It dipped its head and reluctantly began to eat the only thing on offer.

"Get me that bucket of water," said Tirgu, pointing Gurgle in the right direction.

By the corner of the house there was a bucket. Gurgle peered inside and it was full of water but also full of leaves and didn't look too healthy.

"It's dirty," he said.

"Then empty it out."

Gurgle did as he was told and tipped it with his feet. It sloshed away, most of it disappearing under the house.

"See that barrel there?" said Tirgu, again pointing the way. "Take off the cover. There's more water inside."

Gurgle went over with the empty bucket. He put it down so he could use both hands to lift the heavy wooden lid. Tirgu could see that he was struggling so he came over to help him. He held the lid open and instructed Gurgle to fill the bucket. The water was cold and murky but was free from leaves at least.

"Put it next to the straw," said Tirgu.

Gurgle did so. The horse took a sniff of it but did not partake.

591

"When she's thirsty she'll drink it, don't worry. You ready?" asked Tirgu.

"Yeah," replied Gurgle quietly.

They left the horse and the house behind and made their way away. Gurgle tightened the cloak about his shoulders and made sure his ears were hidden away. Tirgu was also wrapped up so as to make himself less distinguishable from the typical hobgoblin. Whilst he remembered he fumbled under his cloak and quietly handed down a blade to his young companion, instructing him to put it in his belt and to be ready to use it. Gurgle could see from the way he adjusted his belt that Tirgu had a least one blade of his own secured there.

As grey ghouls they walked softly through the forest, gradually getting closer to their destination. They began to notice the build-up of people and beasts. Tirgu could tell this was a market day just like any other but to Gurgle everything seemed suspicious and out of place, himself most of all. He observed the clothing that the hobgoblins wore. It was practical but drab, which suited him down to the ground.

It was clear that at the market, most of the day's business had been done. A number of stallholders were in the process of packing up and indeed many had already finished for the day. Others still seemed keen to hang around for trade, as clearly they'd not had a good day. Tirgu considered that it would be better to buy something from one of these traders as their eagerness to sell ought to limit any curiosity they might have about their customers.

The market was still fairly busy but not as much as Tirgu would have liked. A few creatures seemed to be standing on the edge of things without any obvious interest in either buying or selling. As such Tirgu was suspicious of them. He remembered a number of things that Baintha had educated him about in the past, including how to assess what a person was doing just from a look at their appearance. He did so now and gave these hobgoblins a subtle look up and down for clues as to their identities. It occurred to him that if they were Baintha's agents they might have had a similar education. There wasn't a great deal to say about them on reflection. They were probably idlers or just waiting for someone. The reasons for a hobgoblin to hang around with nothing obvious to do are more numerous than you would believe, not that they really need a reason.

Gurgle had few hobgoblins at his eye level. This was a relief as he preferred not to look anyone in the eye. Occasionally a hobgoblin child wandered past the two of them and Gurgle did his best not to arouse their curiosity. Tirgu held out his hand and Gurgle knew instinctively to take it. If they were at the market as father and son then they should look the part. Gurgle noticed that Tirgu's hand was warm despite the cool and clammy weather.

Tirgu's eye was caught by many things. He remained composed and clear in his mind though. He was much tempted by the grilled meats on offer but he knew to expect too many questions from such a place. What flesh d'yu want? Well cooked or just right? Stick in or out?

Onion sauce? Garlic sauce? Mushroom sauce? As all these questions sizzled in his mind he found himself reconsidering his earlier caution. His life was in peril at the moment and he might not have many more chances to have this food that he loved. Being amongst humans for so long he hadn't had the chance. He was hungry and he had plenty of money in his pocket. Why the hell not?

He tugged on Gurgle's hand and moved over to what he hoped was the best stall from the many available. There were other stalls available, but Tirgu avoided these because he wanted to buy from someone too busy with other customers to pay much attention to him. A hobgob standing in front of him was after a big order. He pondered further purchases whilst wrapped packages sat in front of him. Tirgu looked beyond him towards the grill and eyed a rather juicy looking rat. Though the words could not be seen Tirgu hoped very much that it had his name written on it. He looked down at Gurgle and tried to catch his eye. He didn't want to draw any attention to him but naturally wanted to know what he might like from the grill. He tugged on his hand and Gurgle's gaze was drawn away from the stall and towards his father.

"Tell me what you want," said Tirgu quietly.

"Same as you, I don't mind," he replied.

"Good choice," said Tirgu, smiling.

When the hobgob in front had finally finished his order and paid for it he sauntered off, arms laden with all manner of greasy species. Tirgu stepped forward into his place and eyed the stallholder, who welcomed him quickly but warmly.

"Yes Sir," said the stallholder.

"Those two rats on the left there," answered Tirgu whilst pointing.

"These two?" asked the stallholder, once he had stepped closer to point them out.

"Yeah, those two."

"Right you are," said the stallholder. "What do you want on them?"

"Garlic sauce on both."

The stallholder nodded and set to work. He flicked them up from the hellfire and quickly pulled them off their skewers and into paper. He wore gloves naturally, as the work could be hot and dangerous. He began to wrap them up but almost immediately realised he had forgotten to put sauce on them. He reached behind himself and brought the pot around and in front. He took the spoon from the pot and gave each rat a thorough bathing in the white and creamy liquid. Tirgu observed the whole process with excitement and admiration. Gurgle was sadly unable to enjoy the same spectacle as he wasn't tall enough to see above the bench. Tirgu made ready to pay, hoping the process could be as smooth as possible. However, his mother had had some quite old coin in that pouch of hers and he was worried that the stallholder might find it way too little, way too much or just not acceptable at all. He hadn't spent money in Brown Root for quite a while and he knew how much the coinage kept changing thanks to Brakk and his schemes.

When the food was ready it was presented along with the demand for the sum in respect of it. Tirgu made a quick calculation and hoped that what he offered would be acceptable. The stallholder took a long look at the coins and then at Tirgu. For a moment Tirgu was worried, but with a grumble the money was accepted. They picked up their food and then quickly made their way away.

Tirgu and Gurgle retired to a quiet spot beyond the market and sat in the grass. Tirgu handed down a paper packet to Gurgle who received it warmly. They enjoyed a few minutes of carefree consumption. Gurgle had not tried this kind of food before but he liked it. The sauce was especially palatable. Tirgu warned him not to eat too quickly in case he smeared his makeup. They didn't have any more snail grease to make corrections and further supplies were unlikely to be found in the market.

As Tirgu slavered over his rat a thought occurred to him that gave him some pause. He needed to visit his sister to check that she was alright and find out what she knew of events. She was not a particularly shrewd creature. Instead she had a directness of thinking and speaking that Tirgu had always enjoyed. At the moment however that directness might put her in danger. As risky as the idea obviously was Tirgu was not the sort of hobgoblin that could easily abandon those he cared about. He could expect trouble from that husband of hers. He was decent enough as hobgoblins went and had always treated her well, but the same could not be said of his behaviour towards Tirgu. The only one who could be blamed for that was Tirgu, since he hadn't always been the friendliest of brothers-in-law. With the likely word of his value all about the forest not only would he have an interest in reporting his presence but might already have been visited by someone from Brakk's mob. As Tirgu weighed up the advantages and disadvantages of his idea his pace of eating slowed and he chewed his food a little better.

Gurgle looked up at Tirgu as he continued to eat. He noticed him deep in thought, as he was staring into space and looking about as cognizant of his surroundings as the rat that was steadily disappearing down his throat. He felt tempted to talk to him but thought it better to draw as little attention to themselves as possible.

Even though the tactic was obviously necessary Tirgu was not the sort of creature naturally suited to sneaking around in fear of his enemies. He knew this well and Baintha probably knew it too. Ultimately Tirgu's character would revert to type and he would be as he preferred to be and act as he preferred to act. His relationship with risk, like many creatures, was a curious one. People can quickly tire of a strategy that is not in accordance with their nature, regardless of its efficacy. He knew the risks of going to see his sister were great but his forceful curiosity held the levers of his heart. He decided to go and see her. He smiled and recalled a nugget of wisdom from Brakk, from days long ago. Before someone can convince another of a lie they must first convince themselves.

"How's the rat?" asked Tirgu softly.

"Pretty good," replied Gurgle, between bites.

"I think we should go a little further. There's someone I need to see."

"Who's that?"

"My sister," he said.

"Will she look after us?"

Tirgu smiled at Gurgle's innocence and his simple attitude to the world.

"Of course, why wouldn't she?" he replied, putting a hand on his shoulder. "There might be a bit of danger though. She's further into the forest and the more we're out and about the greater the chances of running into someone."

"Who's someone?"

"The people after us."

"Are they after me too?"

"Yes."

"But why? What did I do?"

"Oh Gurgle, that's too hard a question for me to answer, I'm sorry."

"But you said if they found us they'd let me go!"

"Well, yes I said that, but I can't even be sure of what *I'm* going to do, never mind what anybody else might do. How can I know what's going to happen? Listen, shush, keep things quiet. Remember where we are."

Gurgle looked away and down at the remnants of his rat. It's broken and twisted frame lay melted in the paper and Gurgle suddenly felt a deep sympathy for it.

"Listen we need to keep moving, are you ready?"

"Ready for what? To see your sister?"

"Yes, come on."

The two of them stood and looked around. There were fewer hobgoblins about it seemed and none that were idling suspiciously. Tirgu prodded him in the right direction and they continued on. Their two rats, or what was left of them, drifted on their paper carpets until thrown free and from thence into rodent history.

*

The fixer, Bruach, made his cautious way through Brown Root forest. He had asked a few friends to try to help him locate Tirgu's sister. He'd had a broad idea but needed advice from others to narrow his focus. It proved to be the case that her husband was reasonably well known in his own circle and within that circle his notorious brother-in-law had often been a topic of conversation. It is amazing sometimes just how far a simple and innocuous piece of information can be transmitted, especially when the subject is an interesting one. Tirgu had always had the knack of becoming the subject of a good conversation whether he wished to or not.

He and she were to be found somewhere amongst a group of homes in one of the tidier and more peaceful sections of the forest. Bruach didn't know exactly which house it was but with a little gentle surveillance he would be sure to discover it. The sound of soft thunder came from off in the distance somewhere and this had the effect of clearing the route of those that cared not for rain water.

He had chosen to come here by himself and had rejected

the advice of Mala that for the moment they should only go about the forest in groups. He'd been paranoid that Tirgu might be discovered somewhere in the forest and as such caution was well advised. Bruach knew better and was not from fearful hobgoblin stock. He would go where he pleased as he'd always done and if he should bump into Tirgu then all the better, as that was who they were after. Besides, he was just one and they were many.

The air was visible now as a sort of swift fog rolled through the forest. This was not helpful as his visibility of the area was much reduced. He came to the edge of a clearing and recognised it as the place described to him. There was a group of about eight good sized and half decent looking wooden houses and hers was somewhere amongst them. The residents, if present, kept themselves to themselves as there were no sounds of people.

He had never met Tirgu or his sister or her husband but their appearances had all been described to him. He felt confident that he would be able to spot them if a glimpse was offered. He began to wander down the main path that separated one group of four from the other. He gave the impression that he was just enjoying a stroll, which was not so convincing an activity considering the awful weather coming everyone's way. He had a strong waterproof coat on his back so was not worried about any rain.

He sniffed about from his position and was wary of just sticking his head through people's windows. He hoped that Tirgu's sister was home alone. Her husband was a working man you see and so could be expected to be out during the day. He reached in his pocket in order to have smoke and also to give the impression that he had a reason to be stood still. He spied a rough bit of bark on a tree that stood next to one of the houses. It would not be dry for much longer and so he needed to hurry before the first drops of rain fell. He put his pipe to his lips, walked over and then struck a dark match head against the dry wood. It took him a few attempts but with care he managed it and a puff of dirty grey smoke joined the fog on its journey. As he sucked in this soothing blend his attention was snagged by the sound of footsteps and the cracking of twigs. He suddenly saw a hobgoblin woman and she suddenly saw him.

"What are you doing back here?" she asked of Bruach.

"Just lighting up, sorry. This your house is it?" he replied.

"Yes, and I don't appreciate people skulking around behind it," she countered, rather directly.

Bruach looked her up and down and felt confident that he was speaking to Tirgu's sister. He kept his cool and gave no sign that he recognised her.

"I'm sorry for disturbing you. I'm just trying to enjoy my pipe before the rain comes. You heard that it's on its way I'm sure."

"I did, and I'll thank you to be on your way too."

Bruach smiled and nodded at her, noting her obvious nervousness. He finished his pipe with several long sucks and began to make the motions of leaving, allowing her to turn her back, but he had no intention of doing what she wanted. She returned to her front door and he softly followed her. As she reached her door he sped up and bundled her inside. He was quick and cared not for her safety, pushing her to the floor before she had the chance to make noise. He immediately knelt over her and put his hand to her mouth. With his heel he reached back and kicked the door, which slammed shut.

"Now then!" he said with excitement. "I've been looking for you!"

She attempted to speak under his sweaty hand and her meaning, though the words were unintelligible, was not hard to fathom.

"If I lift my hand," he said softly, "I don't want to hear any shouting or abuse. Do you understand me?"

She thought for a moment, then nodded slowly and deliberately. Bruach nodded back and felt satisfied enough to hear what she wanted to say.

"What're you doing? What'd you want?" she said breathlessly.

"I think you know why I'm here. I want him."

"Who? My husband?" she replied, still genuinely unsure of his meaning.

"No," said Bruach with a smile, "someone else."

"My brother?"

"That's him. Where is he? Where's Tirgu?"

"I'm not sure. I haven't seen him."

This was not the answer Bruach wanted to hear. His expression changed to one of obvious disapproval and simply by relaxing his muscles he allowed his full weight to push down on her body. He could feel her hip bones taking the full weight of his muscular frame. Her mouth fell open and a sound of deep pain emerged.

"Stop! Stop!" she begged, but he refused to oblige.

"Where is he?" he demanded again.

"I haven't seen him! I promise you!"

"Come on," he responded dismissively, "You're family, and family stick together."

"Please, get off me!"

Bruach changed his posture and allowed her a moment of relief. She gasped and took the opportunity to fill her lungs. Bruach felt that she was probably telling him the truth but that didn't mean he could simply take her word for it, without putting her to the test. He slipped out a knife that had been concealed in his belt and showed her the full measure of it. Her eyes focussed on the glistening point.

"You know where he is. Tell me and I'll be kind to that face of yours and just make a little cut here...or a little cut there," he offered, making the motions with his blade. "If you don't tell me I'll just have to be...unkind."

She withdrew her face the little distance it was possible to go.

"I don't know where he is!" she said, with her eyes firmly closed.

"Then guess! How can I find him?"

"I don't know!"

"What about your mother? Where does she live, eh? Where does she live?"

"In the old forest."

"Oh yes, whereabouts exactly? I'm all ears."

"Near the gala market," she whispered.

"How do I find it? Name, number!"

"It doesn't have any of that. I'd have to show you!"

He growled. Many a house in Brown Root was without a recognisable address and she seemed very plausible in her current position. He stood but kept her body on the ground by putting a foot firmly on her stomach. He looked around hoping to see something of use or interest but there was little beyond the usual domesticity. He looked back down at Tirgu's sister, lying nervously beneath him. He listened and could hear the sound of rain falling. It blocked out all sounds except those within the house.

"Near the gala market you say? How can I find it? What's it look like?"

"Go from the market towards the edge of the forest. It's a small shack about fifty metres from the main crossroads there. It's on its own, separated from a few other houses."

"That's not enough! I'd be looking for it all night. Give me more!" he shouted, this time with pressure from his boot.

"Some of the panels are painted blue! They're faded a lot!" Bruach smiled. He knew a little about the area and this information should be enough. He lifted his foot and she opened her lungs and her eyes.

"I think I'll go and see her now. If Tirgu comes by you'll let me know, won't you? Brakk's after him, but you probably knew that."

"He won't come here!" she said in defiant tones. "But if he does I'll be sure to tell him what you did."

"Please do," replied Bruach gently, without looking at her.

He turned and looked outside at the atmosphere. It was even foggier and the rain seemed only to be getting heavier. He walked away from her and towards the door. He opened it. Nothing seemed amiss and he stepped outside, his mind full of plans and expectations. The part of his brain concerned with perceiving a threat sparked into life but even with its great swiftness his body hadn't the time to react. A blade came slicing through the rain and lodged itself into his throat. He fell to the ground alongside the slaughtered rain drops and his lifeblood gurgled its disapproval.

*

For the Boiled Mice the journey towards Brown Root forest had become a thoroughly miserable one. Heavy rain pelted down from the creamy grey sky. Those that had waterproof covers used them but there was not the jealousy or complaint that the Lieutenant had predicted. The absence of their quartermaster had obviously focussed their minds on something more important than the trivialities of clothing. He had been despatched homeward and with a little luck would find himself in his own bed later that night. He would find no comfort in it though for obvious reasons.

The Lieutenant and his goblin warriors were getting close to their destination. They would not seek shelter within the forest but instead would camp some distance away from it. Even if they had managed to get into the forest the rain was so hard it wouldn't have made any difference whether they slept there or elsewhere. Through the mists the Lieutenant was confident he could see the same hill from which he and his Mice had charged down not very long ago. It had such a different aspect to it in this weather. Instead of the proud promontory it had seemed on their first visit it looked now like an evil hump, bleak and unfriendly.

Every few minutes deep claps of thunder shook the moisture from their ears and caused every eye to turn to the heavens. The relentlessness of the rain made them feel indeed like boiled mice, soggy and withered to the core.

When they eventually found themselves at the foot of the hill the Lieutenant wisely suggested they set up their tents and try to get out of the rain. It was near enough to evening now. They struggled with the conditions but thanks to the twin forces of experience and expediency they quickly made shelters for themselves. The possibility of any cooked food was remote and it would be worm bricks for them all. The quartermaster had been correct in his prediction. The tents were indeed waterproof, sort of. Each tent had room for about half a dozen goblins, depending on the size of the goblins. So, for the remainder of the evening and for some distance into the night each tent had a different conversation within it, along with

606

some very slowly drying clothes.

The Lieutenant was restless and spent much of the night on the move, either under his blanket or between the tents of his Mice. He didn't bother with posting a watch on such a night. No one would volunteer for such a duty and there was little to watch for in any case.

As the rain continued to fall the Lieutenant lay looking out through the flap of his tent whilst a few eager companions huddled for warmth behind him. Some were disturbed by the sound of rain and wind and it prevented them from falling asleep. Others loved such sounds as they blocked out the noise of the mind and took them away from the misery of the world.

*

Quick footsteps splattered through the sludge and the wet ground. They were going in only one direction, towards Mala and his centre of operations at Brakk's house. Evening had handed over control to the night and this young hobgoblin had some difficulty in keeping on the right path. Necessity fuelled him and he found Mala and the others soon enough.

He bounded through the front door and past the guards. Because of the heavy rain they didn't notice him until he was practically upon them. Whatever sleep or soft conversation there had been was quickly interrupted. Mala was amongst the hobgoblins inside and brought to life by this event. He looked at this junior thing and wondered what the fuss was. He expected Bruach back with news of Tirgu's sister.

"What's the matter?" said Mala.

"Bruach's dead!" said this junior thing.

Those about that had not so far seen fit to offer their attention suddenly did so.

"Dead? How? Where?" blurted Mala.

"His body's been left on the road, not far from here."

"You've seen him?"

"Yes! He's there! Come on."

Before there was a chance to ask any more questions he ran back outside, awaiting the others. Mala grabbed a few of them, including Keeps and Murit, and they made their way through the wretched storm, all with blades in hand. For the next ten minutes they retraced his route until they came to the spot described. They crowded around what was the unmistakeable shape of Bruach. He was lying on his back at the foot of a prominent tree. His body was tied to it and it looked as though he had been put there upright as his arms were in the air and there was a large mark in the ground where his feet seemed to have slid. The cause of his death was obvious, even in these conditions, for his head was tipped backwards and his throat was open to the air. It was overflowing with rainwater.

Mala let out a deep shout of anger, which for a moment overpowered the storm. He looked around for someone to blame but had only the dead shape of Bruach. He kicked him in the stomach.

"I told you!" he screamed through the rain drops. "I told

you!"

He was pulled away by Murit, and the others attempted to draw his attention back to something else. His anger was not sated and he gazed through the mists in search of the true culprit.

"Tirgu!" he shouted, believing that he was able to hear him. "Tirgu! Come out and face me! If you dare! Come on!"

There was no reply and as Mala stared into the dark the others began to release Bruach from his bindings.

Back at Brakk's house there was more activity than before. The two guards remained at the door and the hobgoblins inside sat or paced around with little to occupy themselves, except to speculate on what had happened and on what was to come. About fifty metres away Tirgu and Gurgle crouched and observed. The spot they had chosen was surprisingly reminiscent of the one Gurgle had occupied on his first visit but on this occasion it faced the side of the house rather than the front. He was cold, wet and frightened but feeling strangely excited. He was being swept along by Tirgu and had little say in matters.

"Stay here a minute," whispered Tirgu, looking deep into his eyes. "I'm just going to see to a little business."

Gurgle nodded, spellbound by his force of will. He'd had any number of opportunities to sneak off during the storm but was helplessly curious about what would happen and so could not do so. Tirgu sneaked slowly up to the side of the house, out of sight of the guards at the front. This weather was providing excellent cover for him and he hoped that the rain would carry on all night. He knew that the front door had a wooden bar on both the inside and the outside and that either could be easily knocked down to keep the doors shut. This was another useful little innovation of Brakk's, though not so useful to him on this occasion.

Gurgle could see which way Tirgu was heading and he slid through the wet grass in order to keep him in view. Tirgu crept along the wall, and when the opportunity offered itself he peeked in through little holes in the wall at those inside. He kept his blade close. Gurgle eyed it closely. It was the longest blade he had seen Tirgu use and it had a tough looking black handle that came over the top of his fingers to protect them. The top edge was straight all the way to the tip. The cutting edge was also straight for the first few inches but then jutted out at right angle before slowing curving around to a point at the tip. Some might have called it a small sword.

Tirgu almost managed to twist his eye around the corner of the house and spied the guards looking into the distance, obviously eager for Mala and the others to return. He could tell they were wet and inexperienced. That was their problem however, not his. He steadied himself and then began a swift movement. He ran at them and pushed one forcefully into the other. They both fell on the ground and Tirgu took this moment to slam down the wood, blocking the door.

"Help!" screamed one of them and the alarm was instantly raised. "It's him!"

Tirgu followed after them and as one lay on top of the other he grabbed the throat of the nearest of the two and plunged his blade into his body, making his eager words his last. The other wriggled free and managed to roll away and get to his feet. He frantically pulled at his weapon as Tirgu lifted his own out of his friend's stomach. The hobgoblins still inside naturally charged at the door but found it blocked. Tirgu noticed and was pleased. He turned his eyes back to the other guard who, not surprisingly, seemed reluctant to charge at him. Tirgu calmly walked in his direction. This was more than enough for the guard who dropped his blade and ran into the black.

Tirgu turned his attention back to the house and saw that they were trying to release the bar from inside. He knew this was a difficult thing to do. He guessed that others would try to climb out of a shuttered window at the back of the house. He quickly ran around and found that indeed a couple of them were trying this very thing. One was inside and helping to push his friend through. With ease Tirgu lashed out and sliced his neck open and then pushed him back inside with a hand against his face. Chaos was now in charge and inside the hobgoblins screamed and shouted at each other. Tirgu slammed the shutter down and laughed maniacally at them.

Gurgle saw everything and was stunned by how slow and deliberate Tirgu had been. He admitted to himself that he was no longer as frightened by the sights and sounds of death as he had once been. To be fair, little of it had been directed at him and it seemed to Gurgle that despite the violence so close at hand he felt somehow invulnerable to it.

Tirgu continued to circle the house, battering the wooden panels in different places and shouting at those inside. None of them seemed keen to come out though they were happy to offer abuse. Tirgu laughed at them but didn't seem to have much of a plan to invade. After a little while things calmed down and he seemed at a loss. He continued to prowl but it occurred to Gurgle that Tirgu was not thinking more than one or two steps ahead.

Mala and his group had released the body of Bruach and were dragging it unceremoniously through the mud back to Brakk's house. Mala was walking at the front of the group and he regularly checked behind himself at the efforts of the others. Nothing would satisfy him in this mood and despite their best efforts he was generous with his criticism.

He peered ahead into the shining gloom and saw a figure running away. He couldn't be sure but the figure resembled one of his guards. He didn't react immediately but after a few moments he suddenly felt uncomfortable and that he might be well behind the curve of events. He stopped in his tracks. He turned and expressed his alarm to the others.

"Something's wrong!" he shouted. "We need to get back, right now!"

He told the junior thing to abandon Bruach, which he was more than happy to do. By the time he had done this he looked up to see the others running away and almost out of sight. He took his time in following.

Tirgu continued to slowly circle Brakk's house and those few remaining hobgoblins inside continued to watch him circling. Gurgle was now thoroughly soaked to his skin and he'd abandoned his cloak since it was effectively one great big wet blanket. He believed his snail grease to be all but gone as well and his disguise gone with it. He was cold but managing, and felt lean and ready for action much like his father seemed to be.

Tirgu was wet through but felt hot and excited. The sight of that loathsome beast on top of his sister had naturally caused him to be angry and had brought out his impulsive side at the expense of his sensible side. This had put all other plans and thoughts away and left Tirgu with only a wild, pumping fury in his brain. He looked down at his blade and saw that not all the blood had been washed away from it. He took a finger and drew it along the edge. The tip of his index finger on his left hand was now dabbed in a deep crimson and he put it to his lips. It was diluted by the rainwater and lacked any richness. He'd had in his time the opportunity to taste blood from human men, hobgoblins and goblins; a member of a no doubt very select group. Human man blood was the best in his view and was far better than this flaccid and watery sample.

He looked back towards Gurgle but couldn't see him anymore. He was for a moment disturbed and circled the house again in search of him. Gurgle noticed this and stood from his new position. Tirgu smiled at him, lifted his blade in salutation then looked back towards the house.

Mala and the others made good progress and could see Brakk's house in the distance. At first glance there wasn't much to see but as they got nearer they could see a body on the ground. They all withdrew their swords and steeled their nerves. Tirgu was around the far side of the house but could hear their heavy breathing and sloshing steps. He was not about to hide so came out to greet them. They all slid to a halt about five metres from him and one or two fell over. Tirgu withdrew a small blade with his left hand and made a motion to throw it at anyone that got close. This kept the distance between them a generous one.

"There you are!" said Tirgu, doing his best to mimic surprise.

"Bastard!" shouted Mala. "You're dead this time!"

"Stay back!" laughed Tirgu. "I might take some of you with me!"

"Keep your distance," said Mala to those all about. "He's not going anywhere."

At that moment the front door finally burst open and several hobgoblins came out, emboldened by the return of the others. Mala told them to stay where they were. He was directing things now and relished, finally, the likelihood of Tirgu's death.

"Where's the goblin?" demanded Mala, not about to kill Tirgu without finding that out.

"Who?" said Tirgu.

"Don't muck about! Where is he?"

"Ohhh, he ran off ages ago! Keep up you worm!"

Now that the odds were reversed the group were all tempted to charge at him and take a piece. Tirgu knew this and they knew it but Mala needed him to talk. Tirgu was having none of it and was determined to make him boil over. The others crept closer.

"Wait!" shouted Mala through the rain. "Don't touch him!"

"What are you waiting for Mala?" shouted Tirgu. "Come and get me! I want to taste your blood!"

"Where is he!?" Mala demanded again.

Tirgu was silent for a moment and looked down at the tip of his blade. In the background Gurgle knew well enough to keep his head down.

"If I tell you where he is...will you let me go?" said Tirgu. Mala thought for a few moments, knowing that any positive answer would never be believed.

"No," he replied, "you know I won't do that."

"Then why should I tell you anything?"

"Because I'll make you a promise."

"What?"

"To bury you in your family plot."

"Don't make me angry," said Tirgu, upset by this sudden reminder of his most sensitive place.

"Come on," smiled Mala, "you know I'll do it for you. A warrior like you deserves nothing less."

"You won't put me there," said Tirgu, as softly as the rain allowed.

"I promise you, for the hobgoblin that rid the forest of Grim, you'll get full honours."

"No...I mean you won't put me there. I don't feel in the mood for death just yet."

"Oh, well, that I can't promise you I'm afraid," replied Mala, with a rain soaked smile.

The tension was now about to reach boiling point. Keeps was watching Tirgu's body intensely with particular focus on the little blade dangling from his left hand. He felt that his chance to redeem himself had finally come and the conversation that had just taken place seemed to be leading nowhere. They could find Gurgle easily enough he thought. He took a deep breath and then lost control. Tirgu's eye had drifted away from him and he suddenly bolted forward with his sword raised, intending to disarm Tirgu and put an end to this standoff. Like a bolt of lightning from the storm overhead Tirgu shifted his gaze, readjusted his body and let the blade fly free with an upward swing of his arm. His aim was good and Keeps clutched at his stomach, stumbled and fell to the ground. He was not fatally wounded but he might as well have been. For a second or two everyone stayed perfectly still, but the pretence was over and they all ran towards Tirgu. He was the first to move and gave a glancing blow to one of them as he darted into new space. Another fell to the ground and joined Keeps in his painful dance.

"Get him!" screamed Mala. "Kill him! I don't care anymore!"

Five now stood in opposition to Tirgu, though they lacked coordination and determination.

"Mala! I want you!" shouted Tirgu, his blade raised and

pointing. "Let's finish our fight!"

"Forget it!" screamed Mala. "Come on, kill him!"

They charged as a group at last, with all five blades swinging and slashing, but Tirgu jumped and rolled clear. They worked together now and pursued Tirgu to wherever he escaped. The rain kept up its relentless pace and the five of them finally seemed to corner him in front of a dense thicket of bushes. Tirgu stopped for a moment to catch his breath and so did they, for they saw no exit. He laughed and so did they, except Mala. Tirgu had an extra reason to laugh as one of the five soon discovered. Gurgle charged at the back of one of them and plunged his blade into him. He screamed and then swung an arm behind himself, belting Gurgle across the face, knocking him out and throwing him backwards into the sludge. His blade was lodged in the hobgoblin's back. He fell and began to crawl away, clearly wanting no further part in things.

"That's him, that's the goblin!" shouted Mala. "Grab him and take him inside!"

Two of the remaining four did so and dragged him inside the house, leaving Murit and Mala to face Tirgu. They came back for the other injured creatures moments later.

"I wondered where he'd got to," joked Tirgu, holding his blade erect. "What a slice of luck!"

"No more!" shouted Mala. "I've had enough now! Either you die or I die!"

"Fine...who's it to be?"

"I'm gunna rid the forest of Tirgu," said Mala, pointing a

617

blade at Tirgu's chest. "Don't stand in my way."

Mala pushed Murit away and beckoned Tirgu forward into the clearing, in much the same spot they had fought in before. He was tired of all this prevarication. The situation he'd feared so much seemed impossible to avoid, and it seemed better to face up to one's future rather than slink away from it. At least they had Gurgle now. Tirgu was indeed, at last, truly alone.

"You're alone now my friend," said Mala. "How does it feel?"

"I'm coping alright. How about you?"

"What do you mean?"

"These idiots can't protect you from me. You know I'm stronger than all of you."

"I think you'll see things differently when you're on the end of my blade."

Tirgu smiled and stood still for a moment. He hunched his shoulders and pointed his blade straight ahead.

"Then show me!"

Mala raised his nerve and concentrated on finding a way to kill. No more words. The rain showed no signs of mercy or good sense and continued to batter down. The wind was softer now however and if they had wanted to speak in whispers they could have done. Murit kept his distance and was ready to intervene for the right result, if the opportunity came by. The others in the house could not resist observing but kept themselves a safe distance away.

Mala made the first move and ran in close, offering a

swiping blow, which was deflected with a clang. Tirgu laughed at the tactic and offered one of his own. He charged around one side of Mala and tried to turn and disorient him. Mala was too quick and kept his front facing him. Tirgu slowed to a stop and then calmly walked towards him, always a frightening method he had found. Mala stood still for a moment and considered the right response. He backed away gently at first, without thinking. This encouraged Tirgu to move faster and catch him on his back foot. He raised his blade above his head ready to drag it down with merciless force but Mala's move had been a feint. He suddenly charged forward and stuck his boot into Tirgu's chest, knocking him over and winding him severely. Tirgu had not had the time to bring down his blade. He crumpled to the ground but managed to roll clear of Mala's sharp follow up.

Tirgu coughed heavily and looked shaken. The others who stood around smiled, and felt confident suddenly that all would turn out well. Gurgle had also been treated to a view of things, since his captors could not resist watching such a rare and high level contest. He was groggy but had quickly regained consciousness. He had an arm kept securely around his chest and neck.

"You missed that one, eh?" said Mala. "Sorry if I hurt you!"

Tirgu kept quiet, since he hadn't the breath to speak and would not waste it on Mala even if he had. Silence is often a better tactic than uttering even the finest words. He calmed his breathing and lifted his blade once more. His body was ready. He glanced for a second at Gurgle and saw his distress. This was no way to treat his son. He looked back at Mala, who had not taken his gaze from him.

Mala moved in to press his advantage. He swung his blade but kept a good distance between them so as not to be exposed to something similar from Tirgu. He summoned great force but kept his flexibility and gave Tirgu no signal. Tirgu tried to sidestep but was not quick enough and found his arm slashed. He yelped and rolled away once more. The crowd gasped with excitement.

Mala was growing in confidence and Tirgu found that his was sapping away. He looked at his wound. He would live he thought to himself, then laughed a moment later at the irony of it. He thought that silence was not such an effective tactic now.

"When did you get so good?" asked Tirgu, half in jest and half in deadly earnest.

Silence was now the right tactic for Mala to employ, but he made an error.

"When did you get so bad, I think you mean?" replied Mala, with considerable imagination for the circumstances.

"Overconfidence was what brought Grim down," replied Tirgu, "...be careful of it."

"I heard you stabbed him in the back!" said Mala, angrily.

"No...let me show you what I did."

Tirgu found that loose blood was running to the tips of the fingers on his left hand. He swung his hand upwards and flicked some of it in Mala's direction. It struck him with a gentle patter on his neck and face. He was annoyed and wiped it away with a growl.

"How does it taste?" said Tirgu, followed by a deep laugh that shook the rain drops.

Mala charged at him for a third time, determined to make it the last time. His course was true and direct and Tirgu did not move from his path. He held his blade low and Mala held his high. Mala swung his blade downwards and felt sure he would connect but his balance was gone all of a sudden and he fell. Tirgu had ducked and kicked him off his feet. Murit saw the danger and felt obliged to intervene as Tirgu stood over and looked down at this prostrate figure. Mala slithered backwards, allowing time for Murit to come forward, out of Tirgu's line of sight.

There was no time for anyone to think and all reacted together.

Tirgu looked down at Mala and recalled the last time he had held an enemy at his mercy. He would not delay this time. Each muscle fibre was ready to act and he thrust his blade into Mala. But it was not him! He had moved with not an inch to spare and Tirgu found his blade had merely ripped through his shirt and poked into the tree stump behind him. He gasped in anger and a fragment of time later felt a heavy hand on his shoulder and an indescribably painful sensation above his left hip. He lurched forward and felt as though he had been hit by lightning. He blinked and then saw the real source of the pain. A slim blade poked through his skin and was a moment later withdrawn. He knew what had happened and in an instant thrust a hand behind himself. He caught Murit's throat and swung his blade around, giving him his own bolt of lightning squarely through his belly button. Both hobgoblins stumbled away from each other, stunned by the pain and by the turn of events. Murit dropped to the ground and would be dead in less than a minute. Mala had gotten to his feet and was amazed that Tirgu could still walk. Tirgu held his feet and stayed upright. He looked around at the world, momentarily afraid that he was about to be taken away from it. Strangely, despite being in so many fights and battles this was the first time that he had been properly stabbed. He put his fingers through the hole in his shirt and felt the blood trickling out. He felt his wound. He tasted a little of the blood and smiled...a fine, strong vintage.

He would live he thought to himself, just as the ground suddenly lurched up at him.

*

By the following morning the storm had cleared and the rain had stopped. The Boiled Mice began to emerge from their sodden beds and stand in the early morning light. The gentility of the day ahead was plain for all to see as the sun sat on the horizon like the contents of a freshly cracked egg.

Many of the Mice were still wet and miserable and as such were slow in readying themselves. The lack of orders and clear direction in the mission also added to their sense of ennui. The wetness was an incentive to others though and a few eager souls were up and about, if only to try to dry themselves in the weak sunshine.

The Lieutenant was feeling the absence of Flap. He wanted his friend around so he could chat away the hours and share a little food. The breakfasts were always a good part of the day. He also missed the sense of reassurance that he gave, not only to himself but to the Mice as well. He would be back home now, being cared for by that wife of his and probably wondering what the Lieutenant and the others were up to.

The sky above Brown Root was still gloomy and would not brighten up for a while. The Mice were familiar with the same phenomenon above Milton Greens. From their spot on the far side of the hill they were difficult to see from the forest. It occurred to the Lieutenant that though this was a good idea in general it might not have been so appropriate at the moment. He looked around and thought that maybe they should make themselves known to the hobgoblins, or at least put themselves in a more prominent position. On the other hand, very few of them would understand why they were there and they might be exposed to attack. Flap would no doubt think caution to be the better option. He decided to keep the camp where it was but to have a little trip towards the forest to see if a line of communication might be opened up.

A Mouse that he knew by sight but not by name brought him a small plate of breakfast. Vegetable stew, herbs and bread was not a bad way to start the day. He sat for a little while and quietly shovelled it down. As he neared the end of it Slap Canopy sauntered over and seemed keen to speak to his Lieutenant. Chirp looked up at him and nodded for him to say whatever he wanted to say.

"I'm eager to see what's what," said Slap.

"What's what with what?" replied the Lieutenant, rather unhelpfully.

"With the hobgoblins! We should go and say hello."

"Do you think they'll want to speak to us?"

"Let's go and find out."

"You're very keen. Wet night was it?"

"Exceedingly, but I just want to see what's happening."

"I know. I was going to take a few of us and try to find someone to speak to."

"Count me in."

"I already have, now let me finish my breakfast."

Slap obliged and left the goblin to his private pleasure. When this was done and the Mice were all up and organised the Lieutenant selected a few goblins and they set off towards the forest. They didn't know what to expect of course and kept their wits about them. It seemed strange to just walk in but they had little choice as there was no welcoming reception. Like a gang of old friends they made their way towards the edge. They would not have the opportunity to see the forest again however as they noticed a strange gathering on the path ahead of them. There was a horse and cart and several burly looking hobgoblins stood about it. They were not moving.

"What's that?" asked the Lieutenant, intending it as a question for anyone with an answer.

"Looks like someone's going somewhere," pointed out Slap.

The Lieutenant frowned at this unhelpful comment. He decided to wave at these creatures rather than just approach unannounced. They did not wave back.

"They don't look happy to see us," observed Slap.

"No, but they'll have to see us," said the Lieutenant.

When the two groups came closer there was suddenly a burst of activity from within the cart and a large hobgoblin got to his feet. He had been out of sight before. Another few hobgoblins came from behind the cart, but to the surprise of the Lieutenant and his party they did not seem to have any aggressive intentions. On the contrary, they looked happy. As the Lieutenant and the others came within speaking range the speaking started.

"Your timing is good!" said one of the hobgoblins.

The Lieutenant didn't reply as he was a little confused. This same hobgoblin, who seemed to be the boss of things, carried on speaking.

"We were about to come and look for you goblins. Glad you saved us the trouble."

"What's happened?" asked the Lieutenant, his mind slowly moving in the right direction.

"We've got him! The little one," he replied.

At that same moment the hobgoblin withdrew a little of the cloth covering in the back of the cart and a tired and withered looking goblin child poked his head out and then stood up to see what was what. He spied this group of goblins but because of his lack of recent exposure to such creatures he took a while to absorb the meaning of it. The Lieutenant and his party stood in stunned silence before the moment was eventually broken by Gurgle.

"Are you going to take me home?" he asked of them.

"Yes, they will," said the hobgoblin, interjecting, "but not without us alongside you."

"You found him!" exclaimed the Lieutenant.

"Aye, we found him," replied the hobgoblin, as cool as could be.

"How? What happened?" asked the Lieutenant.

"We'll tell you on the way. Get your lot ready. We'll only swap him over once Brakk's in our hands. Only then. Understand?"

"Alright," replied the Lieutenant, after spending a few moments thinking about it.

"Right, come on then."

The cart and its occupants began their journey and splashed the Lieutenant and his party with wet, muddy sludge as they rolled past. This would prove to be the last hostile act of their present conflict.

The exchange took place in the evening of the following day. The Council kept its word and so did the hobgoblins. Brakk was released and he went back to doing what he did best. Brown Root forest was calmed and put back on a profitable path. The real chieftain was at work once more. The Lieutenant and his Boiled Mice were finally given the accolades and plaudits they deserved. A few weeks later they were formally disbanded and a banquet was held in their honour. This event was covered enthusiastically by the Milton Greens Pamphlet and Lieutenant Chirp Rideau Tilestain featured prominently. He had a bright future to look forward to. The quartermaster was also commended and given a generous pension, but he would fight no more.

Gurgle's family welcomed his return with wild excitement and relief, and enough tears were shed by his mother to soak the roots of their tree. His father found new vigour in his mulching duties and looked forward to one day sharing the secrets of his trade with his youngest son. For Gurgle Sycamore Roundtop the return to Milton Greens proved to be the end of a long and painful experience. It would take him some time to recover from all that had happened to him. His body was soon healed but his mind would take much longer to feel right again. For his first few nights back in his soft bed at home thoughts of Tirgu and their adventures together were never more than an inch from his mind. He struggled to sleep and only with a good cry did he seem to find any relief. After a while the mental pain subsided and a gentler, reflective attitude filled his head. The final moment of Tirgu and Mala's fight was still a very painful memory however and such he tried not to revisit it.

As for Tirgu, well, he got what he deserved.

*

As one thing ends another starts. As one door closes another opens. As one creature dies another is born. Events, like a colossal string of sausages, squelch on into the future, emerging from the meat grinder of fate, operated by the greasy hands of providence.

It is all done now. I have the privilege of seeing the future from the point of view of my past. I knew myself at the beginning of the book and I know myself at the end. I am relieved that things have turned out this way for Gurgle et al. At any moment the future can seem to stretch off in a trillion different directions, but in truth it follows only one path, *can* only follow one path, and I am so glad that you and I are on it together. That reminds me of another goblin saying, or rather, definition; a 'path', so the goblins say, is the accumulated wisdom of many feet.

I've written enough I think...and my dinner's almost ready.

I hope it's snail stew.

So that's that.

ON THE MATING HABITS
OF THE NORWEGIAN LEMMING

A romantic comedy novel

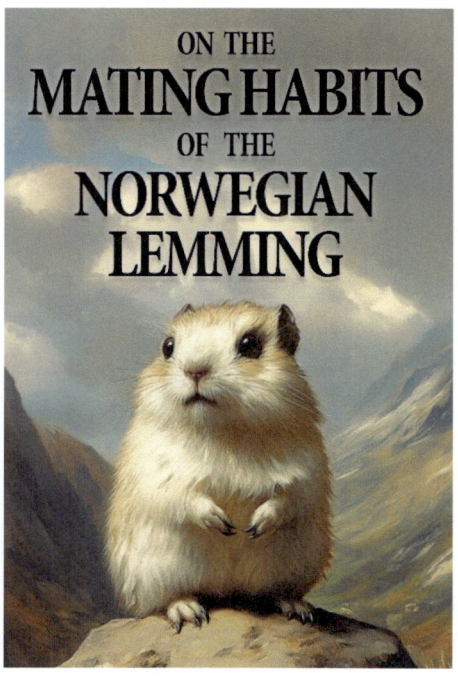

A University Professor travels to northern Norway
to study the Norwegian Lemming in their natural
habitat and this is his account of an exploration
into the souls of man and rodent

WORD FREQUENCY ANALYSIS

WORD	OCCURENCES	RATE
the	8553	5.31%
and	5478	3.40%
to	5097	3.16%
he	4176	2.59%
of	3823	2.37%
a	3366	2.09%
his	2765	1.72%
was	2668	1.66%
in	2101	1.30%
it	2008	1.25%
that	1929	1.20%
not	1847	1.15%
you	1774	1.10%
they	1583	0.98%
had	1582	0.98%
him	1319	0.82%
for	1250	0.78%
as	1224	0.76%
at	1175	0.73%
with	1112	0.69%
I	1078	0.67%
them	1076	0.67%
this	1052	0.65%
on	1023	0.64%
were	949	0.59%

but	930	0.58%
be	922	0.57%
their	895	0.56%
is	868	0.54%
from	818	0.51%
what	782	0.49%
would	747	0.46%
one	734	0.46%
all	710	0.44%
said	684	0.42%
do	668	0.41%
have	618	0.38%
Tirgu	591	0.37%
we	583	0.36%
did	558	0.35%
could	552	0.34%
by	543	0.34%
there	536	0.33%
up	534	0.33%
so	525	0.33%
Gurgle	507	0.31%
no	497	0.31%
back	492	0.31%
out	483	0.30%
are	463	0.29%
will	444	0.28%
about	438	0.27%
more	438	0.27%

been	425	0.26%
little	403	0.25%
or	400	0.25%
me	391	0.24%
then	390	0.24%
Lieutenant	381	0.24%
some	378	0.23%
looked	362	0.22%
an	358	0.22%
men	356	0.22%
into	353	0.22%
if	344	0.21%
see	333	0.21%
just	330	0.20%
now	325	0.20%
other	313	0.19%
your	312	0.19%
her	306	0.19%
around	298	0.18%
my	297	0.18%
she	295	0.18%
well	295	0.18%
get	294	0.18%
man	293	0.18%
way	292	0.18%
two	290	0.18%
which	288	0.18%
few	287	0.18%